The Flophouse Years

Moss Croft

Copyright © Moss Croft 2023

The moral right of Moss Croft to be identified as the author of this work has been asserted by him in accordance with the Copyright, Designs and Patents Act of 1988.

All rights reserved. No part of this publication may be reproduced, transmitted or stored in a retrieval system, in any form or by any means, without permission in writing from Moss Croft, nor be otherwise circulated in any form of binding or cover other than that in which it is published and without a similar condition being imposed on the subsequent purchaser.

ISBN: 9798389252424

The Novels of Moss Croft

The Flophouse Years

Rucksack Jumper

God Help the Connipians

Raspberry Jam

Boscombe

Stickerhand

Ghost in the Stables

Crack Up or Play It Cool

About the Author

Moss Croft is a pen name. Fiction writer, first to last.

Contents

Chapter One:
His Fourth Party — **Page** 7

Chapter Two:
Plaza Court — **Page** 37

Chapter Three:
Jimmy Crook Shows Up — **Page** 93

Chapter Four:
Antecedents — **Page** 119

Chapter Five:
Supper Shared — **Page** 199

Chapter Six:
Ravenscourt Park — **Page** 229

Chapter Seven:
Good to be Here — **Page** 287

Disclaimer

This is a work of fiction. Any resemblance found to real persons or events is the result of unforeseen coincidence.

A Note on Pronunciation.

The word Themagin is spoken with a soft Th, similar in sound to the manner in which the word think is said, or the place name Thanet. The g is said with a hard sound – the entire word comes close to saying the phrase 'them again' except for the softness of the initial consonant and antipodean accenting of the final vowel sound.

Chapter One

His Fourth Party

1.

Decent speakers for a house party. Dennis bought them two months ago and they make a difference. The first two parties were crap but now they're getting better and better. The first of each month. That's the plan and he's sticking to it. He put flyers on lampposts all over Charmouth and Lyme for this one. Anyone can come. He's free and easy. Says as much three or four times every day.

Laughing Llamas are singing Lost on the Freeway. Singing? It's the dreamy guitar solos that make this a great song. The words are not clear at all, the singer not even trying to compete with his band. Dennis has read them; they're on the record sleeve. Likes what they say. We all think we're going somewhere, none of us really are. That's what he makes of them, anyway. He thinks about hippy lyrics quite a bit, they're always pretty soothing. 'More like wailing than singing,' his father might have said. And as he thinks it, Dennis realises that Peter Harris—his father's recorded name—will not have said it about this song. Never heard it and that's a dead certainty. The record was only released last year, nineteen-seventy-one, Dennis already orphaned.

He won't be getting maudlin at his own party. These gatherings lift him out of all that, it's pretty much the point. He misses his mum and dad in certain ways, at certain times. And he likes Laughing Llamas more than he ever did the pair of them. Difficult parents, best not dwelt upon. He glances round the open-plan living room, stairs to the side, summer light seeping through the drawn curtains. Lots of revellers, high-heeled shoes left just inside the front door. Never any of those at number three except on party nights. Girls like to wear them but they don't look comfortable to Dennis. Might belong to the ones sitting on the stairs; there's a couple of girls halfway up. Mini-skirts which show their knickers. Good to see, that's his opinion. All the other lads here too, he expects. Major is in the room; he's been to every party so far. Dennis doesn't know his proper name. He first came across Major at someone else's party more than two years ago, back when the guy wore an eye patch and called himself Pretty. If anyone's brought dope it will be him. Drugs are for later; later or not at all. Dennis is as free and easy about that stuff as he is the rest of it.

The older girl sits next to him, next to Major. A woman actually, way older than anybody else in the room. In the house. But she's dressed like one of them: a proper hippy. A headscarf part-covers her hair. Dennis thinks it looks great. Swooshy colours like on the cover of Laughing Llamas second album, purple and blue and green. Not the same as the record sleeve, it just reminds him of it. Her long skirt might be made of the same stuff as the scarf. Very similar, nice and dreamy. Crinkly and not because she's forgotten to iron it. Ruffled up so you want to touch it, that's the way the skirt lives in the world. He thinks hippy clothes are actually better than mini-skirts. Likes looking at girls in both, but the psychedelic colours—worn long and loose—that's his tribe. Dippy hippies, just like Dennis. The woman is American, he has heard her accent. Thirty or even forty, he's shit at guessing ages. Quite a big arse. Dennis smiles to himself: he has taken to noticing the shape of every girl he meets. And they are all welcome at a Croft Road party. The fat ones and the thin ones, just so long as they join the vibe. There must be fifty people in here now. Maybe seventy. Some have gone upstairs—young people do that, it's where they get it on—some are out in the garden too. The start of August, warm out there right through the evening.

Mary has a glass of cider in her hand, so he goes up to her and chinks glasses, stoops to talk in her ear.

'Will you dance with me?'

'All night long,' she replies.

This could be really funny. Her older brother, Stephen, has a face on him like fun is a disease. Careful you don't catch it! Dennis and Stephen used to drink beer at sixteen—if they could get hold of it— but now his sister has reached that age, he acts like the stern father she never had. Disapproval on his face which is a poor look at a hippy party. Not that short-haired Stephen ever joined the club. He told Dennis earlier this evening that Mary should never have come—'It isn't suitable for a child'—but she's gobby now. That's Stephen's word for it; Dennis likes her, and if she voices a few opinions, it has to be a good thing. Everyone should stand up for themselves. Older brother, Stephen, can't stop Mary Bredbury from doing a darned thing. Dennis

His Fourth Party

thinks she looks grown up in the nicely shaped dress she wears. Starting to look sexy. He doesn't just think it, she really does.

Dennis just wafts himself about the floor hippy fashion, and then Mary clamps herself to him. A waltz that the music doesn't call for. He likes feeling her body pushing into his. Her breath smells of cider. Dennis thinks she might have drunk quite a few. Her dancing is uncoordinated, she had better rhythm when she was fourteen. Cider can do that to a girl; it'll figure itself out when she sobers up.

Away on the futon he sees the older woman—skirt and headscarf—cosying up to Major. Not a lovers' embrace, just leaning in. Talking together, everybody else excluded. The music is far too loud for easy conversation. Mouth to ear, they take turns, making sure each hears what the other has to say. Dennis doesn't know if Major is even into girls. Not that he's nervous or ill at ease in their company, not uptight like Stephen. No known girlfriends, never availed himself of the little upstairs room some couples disappear into at these parties. Dennis neither but he thinks about little else.

'You're the coolest person I know,' Mary calls into his ear, as they sway to the sound of the lead guitarist bending the high notes. Dennis hugs her more tightly; it's a lovely thing to be told. A fantastic lie. Dennis tries. He is cool in his daydreams if not his night terrors. There are few lads in Charmouth with longer hair, Major is the only one here tonight and he lives in Lyme. Nobody else hosts parties like these. The house and no one nagging him or waving a pair of scissors at his unkempt locks, they are the upside of being a nineteen-year-old orphan. Everything else is awkward; a world off kilter.

For more than a year he never thought of inviting the town in. He hated the way people looked at him on the street, in the grocery shop. All of it. Sympathy only makes you cry. He thinks he is coping better and better each month. Work has been his mainstay. Helping old people—that's his job—it takes you out of yourself. Mrs Bredbury has been nice to him over the months. Better than her son, his supposed best friend, Stephen. She invited him round for tea a few times, Stephen would leave the room if Dennis shed a tear. Called him a baby once or twice, called his parents lunatics. That one might be scientifically true but it's not something a grieving teenager needs to hear. And Dennis could do anger himself in spades. Smashed up his own bedroom one time, living by yourself is the place for it. No one found out, he cleared it up himself over the following days. Dustbin full to the brim two Tuesdays running.

The Flophouse Years

Mary—three years younger than Stephen—is a great kid. Dennis has known her since she was eight or nine, Stephen was the first friend he made when his family came to live in Charmouth. She was nice to him back when he was awkward for no good reason. Before all the rubbish happened. Stephen and Dennis were both misfits at school. Dennis's parents were always weird, no idea what Stephen's excuse was. Mary is the one who never changed. Didn't start treating him as half martyr, half leper on account of his parents' deaths. Everyone else did, even her big brother. He gives her—his dancing partner—a little kiss. Not actually on the lips but right next to them. Her cheek. She returns it. Her wet lips upon his own. Tongue straight in mouth. He feels a hand clasped firmly on his shoulder, looks around into Stephen Bredbury's eyes. The protector she doesn't need. Mary shouts at him, 'Kissing isn't sex!' Dennis bursts out laughing, can't help himself. He looks around the room while brother and sister debate what was nothing at all. If it was Mary's first snog, he's the right boy for it. Dennis would never harm her. His eyes meet those of the older woman, he senses that she has been watching him. He hopes she is not about to take Stephen's side. It would be the older person's perspective nine times out of ten. She looks like a hippy though, free love and everything.

Dennis resumes dancing and Mary leans straight back in, starts kissing him again. Stephen says, 'No, Mary.' Barks it at her like she's a dog. Dennis smiles into Mary's eyes. They don't have to do this now. He and she have never kissed before. His best friend's kid sister. Best friend through school, these days Stephen is too stiff by far. Dennis turned hippy when a different lad might have gone into the loony bin. Stephen has never really changed: an over-inhibited schoolkid turned university student. Too timid to smoke pot. They were both wimps in school but everybody is allowed to change. Dennis turns to the futon, most of the people in the room are staring at Stephen, want to see how he handles his sister. Or the lads might just be watching Mary because she looks a bit brilliant. Local stunner in a summer dress. Major has his tobacco pouch out, watching neither brother or sister, looking intently at his stash. Major is like Dennis: anything goes. Then his eyes meet those of the woman in the headscarf, the American. She gives Dennis a wink, a nice smile with it. Must be on his side. If it's a battle of wills, Mary will be the hands-down winner. He closes his eyes for a moment. Listens to the Llamas, the track with the saxophone playing all the high notes. Absolutely loving his fourth party.

His Fourth Party

* * *

Mary dances with her own friends, fifth form girls; Stephen has gone into the kitchen. Most of the guests are smoking and talking—digging the vibe—and then Dennis hears a shout from the kitchen. A girl's voice, very loud. 'He's got a gun!' He was about to talk to the American girl, the older lady whose name he has still to learn. He leaves her side, walks quickly to where the shout came from. There are no guns in his house. No guns in Charmouth, Dorset or on planet Earth if Dennis had his way. Peace man and all that. He's a believer. Not the wacky sort, it just sounds right.

The girl whose shout brought him out of the lounge points an accusing finger through the window into the back garden. Stephen is drawing water at the kitchen sink. 'That damned Gordon Stickland has brought his air rifle,' he tells Dennis. A gangly young man—their former school bully—stands in the centre of the small lawn, aiming his weapon at something on the fence. A tin can he must have picked out of the dustbin.

'Did you see him bring it?' asks Dennis.

'Yes. He boasted about taking it without his stepdad knowing. Showed it to everyone.'

'Why didn't you tell me?'

'Because you were busy doing unspeakable things to my sister.'

Dennis ignores the priggish comment. Necking never made a girl pregnant. And Mary started it, near enough. 'You should have got me. No guns: it's my only rule.'

'I thought your only rule was no fighting?'

'I reckon that covers guns.'

Dennis leaves Stephen and the others in the kitchen, goes through the backdoor into the garden. Nine o'clock, a little light lingers in the summer sky. Reddening to the west. 'Gordon,' Dennis calls to him levelly, 'you can't stay here with that. Take your gun home and they you can come back.'

There are two girls in the back garden, friends of Stickland's, Dennis presumes. The boy points his gun at Dennis. 'Bang,' he shouts in reply.

'Not funny, Gordon. Make love not war. No arguing about it. Take your gun home.'

'Bang,' he says again. Dennis just stares him down, and Gordon lets the thin nonsense of a gun slide to his side. 'I'll come in and leave the rifle outside. I can't walk home and back; it takes an hour.'

The Flophouse Years

'You can, Gordon. The party doesn't stop. A walk will do you good.'

'Fuck off. You're not my mum.'

'No. But you don't enter other people's houses bearing arms. Not the flophouse, Gordon.'

The two girls just watch. They don't seem to be taking sides although they were admiring the nob-head with the air rifle before Dennis came to put a stop to it.

The American woman has come to the kitchen door. 'Everything okay?' she asks. She could be their mum, not literally, wrong nationality and maybe only fifteen years older. A different generation though, it's a teenagers' party for the most part. Major and a couple of others have passed twenty. And then there's her.

'I think so,' says Dennis. 'This chap brought an air rifle to the party and I only accept beer, cider, that stuff.'

'I brought beer,' says Gordon.

'Harris house, Harris rules,' the lady tells the young man with the gun. She sounds authoritative although her voice is high pitched. She steps into the garden, goes closer to the rifleman than Dennis. Her head is free of the headscarf now—rich black hair upon her head—and a single long plait she has coiffed to curl across her left shoulder. He hasn't talked to her properly, so somebody must have told her his name. She said the Harris-house thing. The lady's neck looks nice. More tanned than most around here. Bronzed.

'Shit party,' says Gordon Stickland, heading around the side of the house, in the direction of the road.

'Is that your opinion also, girls?' the American asks his admirers.

They look at each other. 'It's all right,' says the one wearing jeans and a bright pink T-shirt.

'Take your gun home and come back,' shouts Dennis. He isn't for falling out with anybody. Peace and love.

The lady turns, puts her hand on his bare arm as she walks past. 'You handled him well, Dennis,' she says quietly as she goes back in to the kitchen. Re-joins the party.

'I told him he shouldn't have brought the gun,' says the girl in pink as she brushes past him, going back to the party.

* * *

Dennis puts another of his Laughing Llamas' records on the turntable. His favourite album, the one with Crazy Darkness on it. A couple of young ones have gone home but Mary is still here. He

His Fourth Party

wonders if this will get awkward; Major has his pouch out. Rolling up, as he likes to say. Sweet hashish. He sees the American woman looking at it intently. It might be her principal interest in Major, his funny smokes. Dennis has yet to speak meaningfully to the older woman, tell her how much he appreciates what she did when Gordon was waving his gun about. He wonders how she learnt about the party. Does she read local lampposts? Doesn't recall seeing her before, she's quite pretty—nice face—and definitely from his tribe. One of the hippies. She wears a black shirt; it could be a man's, judging by the cut, but her figure is feminine. The boobs. A man's shirt with nothing underneath, he has noticed that. Dennis likes it, the way her shirt hangs loose around her hippy skirt. A couple of buttons undone. He can see a fellow traveller a mile off. And she may have been on the road for years, Dennis only just getting started.

The doorbell rings and Dennis takes in the flashing red light visible through his thin curtain. A police car has parked at the gate.

'Shit, shit, shit,' says Major.

'Get it out of view,' says another voice.

The American woman stands at the same time as Dennis. Mary looks terrified. She might think they've come to round up underage drinkers. Never guzzled as many as she has tonight, Dennis is sure of it. Someone turns the music down. 'It'll be all right,' he says quietly to the two girls, the American whose name he still doesn't know and ashen-faced Mary. Then he turns to the room, speaks louder. 'Our friends from the local Constabulary have come a-calling. Always good pigging company.'

He goes to the front door, the older woman two paces behind. When he opens it, Dennis feels a small shock, it is as if he has been transported back in time. Two uniformed officers stand before them, one of whom—the policewoman—is known to him. Dennis has seen her only once before, it is enough. His recognition instant.

'Is everything all right here,' she asks, adding, 'It is Dennis, isn't it?' Seems to say it as an afterthought.

He steps out of his front door, no wish to be overheard by those inside. The American lady steps out of the house with him and she pulls the door to. 'Yes...Susan...Sergeant Ash.' Two and a half years have passed since Dennis last spoke to her; she attended this house on the most fateful day of his life. On sleepless nights he still recalls the welcome comfort she gave. Consolation for the distraught boy he became that dreadful afternoon. 'Just having a party. Is the music too loud?'

'No, Dennis. It is loud but that isn't our concern tonight. We have reports of a man with a gun on the premises, somebody carrying a gun. I recognised the address. I'm normally on the desk, wanted to see what was happening. What was going wrong here. Do you have a gun, Dennis?'

'No...' He's relieved it isn't Major's drugs she's heard about. If they found them and splashed the address across the local papers, the neighbours would be in uproar. '...I asked a boy to leave who had brought an air rifle. He was only mucking around. The lad's gone.'

'Guns are the most dangerous toys, Dennis. Are you sure it was only an air rifle?'

'I don't know much about guns, Sergeant Ash. Never touch them. Everyone said it was an air rifle. The lad went. Took it with him, I'm glad to say.'

'Can you tell me the boy's name, Dennis?'

'I didn't recognise him. Not local. A holiday maker, most probably. The party is advertised on...' Dennis lets his answer taper away.

'There was a boy showing off with a pellet rifle, ma'am,' says the American lady. 'I saw him in the yard, out there...' She gestures through the kitchen and out the back. '...and this young man, Mr Dennis Harris, politely asked him to leave and the boy with the gun did just that. He handled it very well, ma'am.'

The lady police sergeant nods at Dennis; she must have heard what the woman said, doesn't seem to pay it any mind. As if she can't understand American, doesn't speak hippy. 'We are aware of the adverts. Did you paste them to the lampposts, Dennis?'

'No ma'am...Sergeant Ash, I've no idea who made them. I told a lot of people about the party, so anyone could have done...'

The policeman who is standing back starts to laugh. 'Council work,' he says, while coughing into his hand.

Sergeant Ash nods. 'We're not here about bill sticking, Dennis. It's not priority. My advice to you, nevertheless, is that you don't do it. Very foolish and that's not just a fuddy-duddy opinion. It's only because you—or someone with your blessing—has been pasting signs all over town that a low-life with a gun has turned up at your party. If you invite only your true friends, then no-one will abuse your hospitality. Remember that in future. We do need to enter the premises, Dennis. Satisfy ourselves that there really is no weapon in there.'

His Fourth Party

Dennis looks around at the American woman. 'Can you do that?' she says. 'Are you really allowed to just come in and search people?'

'We're just ensuring the safety of everyone present,' says the policeman. 'We haven't said we are going to search anyone.' He steps forward, brushes his way past, dipping a shoulder to the hippy's chest. Grazing a loose arm across her breasts as he walks inside. Must have noticed them as Dennis did earlier. The free-range thing.

Dennis turns to follow, stops when Susan Ash takes a hold of his wrist. 'A word please, Dennis,' she says. The American woman turns to look at them both and the policewoman says, 'Alone.' Dennis nods at his party guest, has no fear of speaking alone with this particular policewoman. The American follows the policeman inside, slowly, not minded to catch him up.

'I haven't seen you since that awful business, Dennis. You were so young. I can't say I haven't thought about you. It must have been a terrible time you've been through. Are you sure you are all right?'

He thinks this is daft. He appreciated her concern back then, January, nineteen-seventy. Needed it. He has been through the mill but he's long out of it. Now she is reminding him of all he has never left behind. Nothing really leaves you, it's just the distance between then and now making it bearable. Same house, different life. 'I'm fine, Sergeant Ash. It took a while but, honestly, I'm fine.'

'Living like this?' she asks, gesturing the party, the crisp notes of Templeton Ca. now playing on the stereo. Somebody has changed the record for the benefit of the visiting police. Drug-fuelled Llama music in recess.

'This is the best,' he says. 'Come back when you're not on duty, let your hair down with us. Free as the wind, we are. You can stay over, it's a flophouse on party nights. People are welcome to stop, those who don't fancy the walk home. Stay anytime if you need a bit of floorspace, it's somewhere to throw down a sleeping bag.' He bears a face-wide grin and—fair play to her—Sergeant Ash is slowly mimicking it. Doesn't take offence.

'I can't say I like pop music, Dennis. I'm very pleased to hear you're bearing up. You've been through a lot.'

* * *

He finally learns that her name is Annabel. He and she are sitting beside each other on the floor of the lounge. Both futons are full, an amorous couple keeping the one by the window to themselves.

The Flophouse Years

Annabel takes a long draw and then hands the spliff to Dennis. Major's expertly rolled joint. He mimics her drag, even lets the smoke out of his nose as she did. Mary is sitting to his right and he tries to hand the silly-ciggy over her head to the lad beyond. Not that he is any older, Dennis doesn't feel protective of the youth of Charmouth in general, just this one. And it's not disapproval, young Mary isn't quite ready for drugs. More cidered up, to his reckoning, than she has ever been before.

'Hey,' she says, reaching up to his outstretched hand, taking the joint from him regardless. Her mouth grins but her eyelids draw close together. Trepidation in the triumph. She puts it to her lips. Dennis glances around. He feels a caution he has never previously experienced at this time in the evening, his friend's sister normally long gone by the midnight hour.

'Where's Stephen?' he asks. He thinks Mary looks a little dazed by her pull on the doobie. Must be psychosomatic, nothing can have ruffled the brainwaves that quickly.

'Home. He's gone back home.'

'He went home without you?' says Dennis, speaking over the sound of the Laughing Llamas. They've been on the deck most of the evening.

'He took me home. I sneaked back without him knowing.'

She seems to have regained her composure. Dennis laughs to himself. 'How did a stiff like him wind up with a sister like you?' says Dennis, and she takes his cheeks within both her hands. Begins to kiss him once more with a passion he doubts he deserves. Loves her like a sister. He has to ease her off. Quickly coughs into his hands and she starts to do likewise. Neither he nor she smoke cigarettes. Not in normal time. The hash is a monthly treat, surely a first for Mary. 'You're great,' he says into her ear, then turns away. Looks to his left, into Annabel's face. She has narrowed her eyes, not unkindly. He thinks she might be appraising him.

Blended in well all evening—this American woman—however old she is. Guys several years older than Dennis have dropped in before, it is not meant to be a kids' party. Annabel is a first, both her age and her nationality. Dennis likes breaking new ground. He thought she was getting close to Major—heads locked together for an age—but now he has taken himself to the kitchen. Rolled it, lit it, retired to a safe distance. She looks outdoorsy. Her face is more than tanned, it's a tiny bit weathered. Her top is a button looser than it was; as she

His Fourth Party

brushes up a little ash on the carpet, leaning forward, Dennis can see the tops of her breasts. They're as free and easy as he's feeling. He looks up into her face, worried lest his perusal is obvious. Annabel smiles right back at him. Maybe she has engineered him that small peek, a gratuity for throwing a decent party.

'Are you a real San Francisco hippy?' he asks. She continues to smile, does not look minded to answer the question. It might be the hash. It slows a lot of people down. 'It would be a first,' he adds. 'Half the hippies around here are only playing at it.'

While he is rambling, Mary, sitting to his other side, is just rolling her head with the music. She's the prettiest girl in the room but it looks a bit daft. Not caught the vibe properly. He remembers when she used to dance to Danny Clare and all the other romantic mush aimed at young girls. No more than six months ago. She's most likely only heard the Llamas at his parties. If Mary Bredbury is learning to dig proper music, she has him to thank.

'I've been there,' Annabel finally offers. 'Haight-Ashbury, it was pretty wild. My home town is Providence, Rhode Island. I'm east coast, not west.'

'You're an islander? I don't know where it is on a map.'

'It's not an island. It's a state.'

'Rhode Island is not an island?'

'You got that in one.'

Dennis tries to think how come this lady is here at all. He has taken back the spliff, has a second pull. Wants to laugh out loud. He doesn't think it's the hash yet, just the situation. He saw the lady's breasts wobble. Haight-Ashbury. All are welcome to his monthly parties; there are no fly posters about it in Rhode Island. He is pretty sure about that, ninety-nine percent certain. Ninety-nine-point-nine. 'Do you live around here now?' he asks.

'I heard I can stay the night.' She gives him a smile sweeter than any expression he has seen her pull so far. Coy, eyelids a-flutter. 'You throw my kind of party.'

'You're welcome to stay. I'm the home-owner and I like to share.'

'I know you're the home-owner, Dennis Harris, and I like sharing with you.'

'How come you know? This is only my fourth ever party.'

'Oh, you know? Three can make a lot of noise.'

Dennis laughs a lot at that. It might be the dope after all. Everything is funny. His first party was a flop. He can wangle his days

The Flophouse Years

off work around his parties. He thinks by holding them on the first day of every month it will become a fixture. Spread the love with Harris. He wrote that on the first draft of the poster, then got cold feet. ***Party! Party! Party!*** was all the redraft said. Date and address, a silhouette of a hippy smoking a cigarette. ***Sleep in the flophouse, go home when you've sobered up.*** That was in his smallest writing along the bottom. His first party was the Mayday bank holiday. About twenty people came, most of them working the following day. Not enough to shake a peace sign at and still he ran out of beer. It was crap but he drank a skinful, and four girls from Lyme slept in the house with him. Not with-him with him. They were in the lounge and Dennis up in his bedroom. It's nice to host. Annabel laughs along with him. Hard to read what her laughter means. She's welcome to stay the night. He hasn't said it, only thought it, but she runs her hand up and down his bare arm. She must be telepathic. This party has been the best. A great evening. Gordon and his gun were a blot; the police lady a surprise. More pleasant than unpleasant once he figured they weren't on a hash hunt.

Someone has put Templeton Ca. back on the turntable. It's decent music but not his favourite. Crisp and clean where the Llamas are messy. Chaos is Dennis's friend. Mary has put an arm around his back and he feels the American lady do the same. Best party by a mile.

2.

She arrived around six o'clock. Very, very early. There were no more than six or seven in the flophouse at the time. Dennis has had plenty of opportunities to talk with her. Never really tried until now, once he's got stoned. He can be like that with proper adults. Stephen's mum always tries to chat but he doesn't like to. He can see it now: Annabel couldn't be a more approachable person. No need for his reticence. The majority of the partygoers are from his old school. Some are very young, kids like Mary, a few older guys who dig the music. Something put him off talking to her and it wasn't her clothing. He likes that a lot. He thinks there is a woman wearing one on Laughing Llama's first album cover. The same sort of headscarf, although it no longer adorns Annabel's head. Talking to her is the easiest thing now he's a bit doped up. He wants to trust older people, the adults. Trust is a good thing, just not so easy come by. People who are incredibly old—the type he looks after at Plaza Court, in their eighties and nineties—are no

His Fourth Party

trouble. The struggle is with those his parents' age; the hippy-woman—Annabel—must be younger than them. Surely. He was a bit of a rebellious kid at the time of their deaths. Kept clear of most people their age ever since. Shrugged off an interfering uncle. His manager—Lorraine Chadwick, at Plaza Court—can be a busybody. He used to like her but he's gotten wary over time. Emma Bredbury is all right—Mary's mum, Stephen's mum—he just doesn't think she gets on his wavelength. Churchy where he is free and easy. Means well, he can see that; she worries about him living alone and being young, more so after what went on with his parents. Just her and Lorraine, Dennis doesn't mix with any other adults. Ever.

When Annabel came into the house—and he had no idea of her name at that point—she said, 'The big hippy party happens here, right?' Said it to everyone in the room. Two of those people were playing guitar, inexpertly strumming Crazy Darkness on their acoustics. He and Stephen were sorting out paper cups. Dennis is trying to avoid breakages; only two proper glasses remain in the house since the last party. He's bought three different sizes of throwaway beakers; paper plates too. Someone or other always seems to bring food. Loaves and fishes at a Croft Road party.

'It sure is,' Major told her.

He's an oddball. Long, long hair, the makings of a beard. Drawls when he talks, dropping Americanisms in with his West Country burr. Pot to the parties. Major is learning how to be a thatcher—there's a call for it down here, thatched cottages dotted all over the place when you get out of Charmouth and onto the country lanes—dresses hippy all day, every day. Why he chose the military name is a mystery. It's a better name than Pretty which is what Major called himself when Dennis first came across him. That was at someone else's New Year's party back when Dennis still had parents in the house. This one, number three Croft Road.

'Good to hear I've found the right place,' she said. Then she sat down near Major, just along the futon, not cosying up. Focussing her attention on the two young guitarists. Watched them respectfully as a person might if the playing was any good. After the first song—a poor rendition if ever Dennis heard one—Neil started to sing another which he's written himself. He has put some good licks into it but it's a hopeless song. And he can't sing very well. Jason helped out, tried to harmonise the chorus, then he couldn't remember the words. Dennis heard the new girl—old girl too, which is stating the obvious—

whispering to Major. Next thing, Major was pointing to the stairs, describing something internal in the house. Major has stayed over many times although he and Dennis seem more like colleagues than friends. One has a house, the other an endless supply of head-spinning loco weed. That's the recipe for a worthwhile party. They don't talk to each other a lot. Major can be quite standoffish but Dennis doesn't mind that. We're all freaks one way or another.

'I need to wash,' said Annabel, taking to the stairs. Dennis figured then that she's American. The accent. She carried a small rucksack, really small. It has a tumult of different colours patterned over it, not like any rucksack Dennis has seen for sale in Lyme or Bridport. Not even in Exeter. She took herself upstairs. Major had directed her to the bathroom, he presumed. As soon as she reached the top of the stairs, he heard her talking to the two girls—Mary and her friend Barbara—who were already up there. Preening themselves for the party; young girls do that. Mary might stop if she becomes a proper hippy. Starts letting her hair hang loose.

'Do you know who that is?' Dennis asked Major.

'A girl who likes a party.'

Dennis smiled at the typical Major answer. 'She's not your mum, is she?' he tried again.

'If she applies, I'll give her the job.'

The flippant answer reminded him how little he knows about Major. He lives in Uplyme and rides a bike. Dennis assumes he lives with his parents, doesn't know it for a fact. A couple of years his senior, maybe more. He has a decent rucksack of his own which he uses to bring records to the parties. Brought some round once or twice when there was no party. Introduced Dennis to the jazz-infused guitar playing of Dario Renzo.

'She's American,' said Dennis. 'That's a first.'

'First of many, Harris my friend. The legend of your parties has drawn her from that place.'

Turning to Neil and Jason, the guitar players, Dennis made a cut-throat gesture. 'Okay if we put some proper music on now?' And he started pulling The Horse's Mouth out of the album sleeve. The two guitarists acceded, no delusions about their talent. Those boys aren't close to any good.

* * *

Stephen was in a buoyant mood when they were preparing the house

His Fourth Party

for the gathering. Before seeing his sister snog Dennis. 'Now we've got a Yank here, we can turn Charmouth into our own San Francisco.'

Funny comment and Dennis couldn't work out if Stephen Bredbury was impressed by the older woman's arrival or simply making a joke at his expense. Dennis is the hippy. Stephen's record collection begins and ends with the plaintive Monk Elba. Gloom and self-pity on an acoustic guitar. He likes studying biology more than partying as far as Dennis can tell. Stephen spends term times in Southampton, at the university there. He missed the first two parties—could have missed a lecture or two instead but chose not to—always invited, him being Dennis's oldest friend but times are changing. Ducks and swans: Mary is Dennis's favourite Bredbury these days.

Major turned the record up loud although it wasn't even seven o'clock. Didn't want the girls upstairs to miss out, Dennis supposed. The Horse's Mouth is his album, Dennis hadn't heard it before. The sound of drum solos and a squealing lead guitar carried all over the small semi-detached, no words at all on track after track. And people were starting to arrive—the party starting to feel like the happening he always envisaged—tins and bottles building up on the kitchen side. The fridge crammed full with white wine and lager. The American woman was still somewhere above him, bedroom or bathroom, changing or making up her face. A girl from the next road—another one Dennis remembers from school, from the year below—brought in a plastic box full of egg and cress sandwiches. 'How hippy is that!' declared Dennis. He wasn't being sarcastic, doesn't think that way. If there is food, someone will scoff it; it's all good from his vantage point. He recalled meeting the girl's mother when he was walking to work a few days back. She asked him, as they spoke on the road, if he was eating all right. Dennis gets a lot of that.

This one is the first of August party and school is out. Midweek, so it suits school kids and students better than those in work. Nothing keeps Major away, of course. Dennis thinks he thatches hungover. Straw is straw: it could be the job for it. Some of the arrivals commented on the décor in the house. Dennis has jettisoned all his parents' belongings. Slowly accrued alternatives that suit his taste. The seating in the lounge is low, two futons face each other. He has a television, as his parents never did, he and Major shifted it into the understairs cupboard for the night. Taking no chances. The room's centrepiece is a fancy coffee table which he picked up in a second-hand shop. Literally. He had to bring it home on the bus. Carry it from the top of the high street, the bus-stop. The table has engravings of elephants carved into it. Towards the end of his first party, he told the sleepover girls it was from India. That he fetched it back after visiting a guru. It was a lie—a joke and a boast—which he couldn't maintain for even a minute. Quickly admitted that he bought it in a Bridport junk shop. 'Not bad for Dorset,' his honest refrain.

While Major's funny drum music was playing, Dennis's friend Sharon arrived. Paul Kelly, her fiancé, accompanying her. She will be twenty-one and married in the autumn. Mental, he thinks, but he is always pleased to see her. Sharon's not a hippy but he doesn't hold it against her. She is to marry a moron, that is her misfortune.

'You can put your wine down in the kitchen,' he told them.

'The cost of this. No way,' said Kelly. He helped himself to some crisps he didn't bring, an egg and cress sandwich too. Shielded his wine from the hippie-hoards because a pea-brain doesn't understand reciprocity, karma. Sharing.

The room was teeming with people by the time—name still to be learnt—Annabel came back down the stairs. Dennis watched her. Liked what he saw. An older girl who blended in with the young ones. She struck up conversations with girls of all ages, one or two with boys. 'Lovely party,' she said in passing. She knew who he was, that it was his house. That was apparent in her singling him out for the remark. As it sunk in, Dennis told her he liked her skirt, its swirling colours. 'Thank you,' she said. It's not like him to compliment girls on their clothing; older and from another country, he wanted her to feel welcome. That was it though, she went back to talking with Major after the quick exchange. And Mary was downstairs by this time. She hung around him quite a lot. He felt flattered and a tiny bit encumbered. It is nice to annoy Stephen, and Mary looks terrific. She's just a kid, three years his junior. The American is a woman in every sense. She might be older than one or two of his teachers were back in school. And later, in the evening, when the two police came and she stood next to him while Sergeant Ash was lecturing him about one thing or another—being nice with it, Susan Ash is probably the only officer in the entire police force who has a proper nose, not a snout and a little curly tail—he thought that the hippy was the older of the two. When she last came to this house, Susan Ash felt like the older sister he never had. January the twenty-first, nineteen-seventy. A hell of a day. Pure hell. A much older sister, and this American woman could be a few years beyond her. Older than the policewoman. His memory of that time—Sergeant Ash and all the other police in the house—is sketchy, unreliable. Parents taking their leave the way his did can bugger up a youngster for a time. Even the police-lady could see that. Dennis likes having an older person at his party, one who joins in without judging. Sergeant Ash said she doesn't like pop music which is plain stupid. There's something for everyone. Now this older hippy is helping make his parties feel authentic. Tuning in, she really looks the part.

Why not sleep in the day?

It's a line in his favourite Llamas song which is blaring out of the stereo. And they all think it, everyone in the room, he is sure of it. It's more than just the hash. Stephen once accused him of pretending to be a hippy. That old square has gone to bed. His kid sister is a thousand times cooler. Gone to bed although Dennis has mystically summoned a bona fide hippy from Rhode Island into number three Croft Road, Charmouth. Dorset is the new California. This is Dennis's doing. His hand over the top of the beaker, shaking and shaking— sticking the posters on the lampposts—rolling the dice.

* * *

Dennis puts on Coast to Coast. It's the first album he ever owned, Laughing Llamas, of course, but not their latest. He has that one too. Owns the lot. Senses that Annabel is watching him, observing how he behaves. He wonders what she's been drinking. It's hard to tell when they are all holding paper cups. He guesses it's Bacardi, cannot come up with a reason why. Earlier, he talked to everyone except her, smiled her way a couple of times. Looking back, it's crazy. She helped out with the gun, the police. He thinks maybe the American was kind of dancing with him, when he was holding on to Mary. Thinks the young girl was a prop. Or it could be the hash. Major's shit can fuck with his mind. He kind of likes it and he's kind of scared. Like going on the big dipper at the fairground.

'Rhode Island is not an island and there is not a single croft on Croft Road.' He giggles when he has said it. She smiles back at him. It probably isn't funny; he's got a racy mind from the dope. Speeding up and slowing down. Lost track of what makes a joke. Giggly Dennis, it happens every party. He sees that her eyes are green, thinks it is an unusual combination with jet-black hair. But maybe it isn't. He only looks into girl's eyes when he's drunk too much. Pulled on a spliff.

While he stares into the face of the American, young Mary is tugging on his sleeve.

'Is she your girlfriend?' asks Annabel.

Dennis gives the quickest, subtlest, shake of the head. Not wanting to offend Mary but she really isn't. Stephen's kid sister is in some weird mood. The earlier kissing was pretty outrageous. He's kissed girls before but not much.

'Are you with anybody?' he asks. Tries to sound chatty—might have failed—it would be a bit rich if she thinks he is propositioning her. A woman in her thirties. Forty? He hopes she's not that old. He thinks she looks sexy, so if she is forty it would make him a weirdo.

Whether she heard him or not, Mary says only the single word, 'Toilet,' and rises unsteadily to her feet. Leaves the room. Dennis turns his attention exclusively to Annabel. Listens best he can.

'No. It's just me in England. All alone but for the welcome company your party brings.'

'Were you in Charmouth last night? No, let me guess. Lyme Regis?'

'No. I came here from London. Caught the train this morning...'

'That's amazing. How did you know where to come?'

'I think I might be a homing pigeon, Dennis.'

He laughs like he is watching Tonight at the London Palladium. Belly laugh that could be for the funniest punchline he's ever heard. Manages to arrest it when he sees she doesn't laugh at all. Might have meant it. Can't recall anything about homing pigeons in the Laughing Llamas lyrics. She holds his gaze and Dennis leans into Annabel, puts his forehead against hers. She allows him this intimacy.

'Homing pigeon,' he whispers into her ear. Crazy image, she's from Rhode Island wherever that is. His whisper sounded serious. No giggling at all now. 'Welcome home,' he whispers, and she turns her head. Their lips brush together, not that he planned it. A kiss that fate willed.

3.

Dennis puts a hand on Mary's arm, leads her into the now empty garden. 'A bit late,' he tells her. 'Is it time you were heading home?'

Quarter past one and she only turned sixteen last month, he wouldn't want to cop the blame from her mother if she discovers Mary went back to the party after Stephen had already taken her home. Not that Dennis is the sort to throw a guest out—not unless they bring a gun—it's just that Mary's been looking a bit lost for the last hour.

His Fourth Party

'Dennis,' she says, 'you know how I feel about you.'

She throws an arm around his neck, tries to kiss him one more time. He likes it but doesn't really know what she feels for him. She's drunk on her feet, that'll be what has brought on her funny mood. He allows her tongue back into his mouth while worrying that she'll be cross with him in the morning. Taking advantage. Before he has thought how to get her home, Mary has put her hand on his crotch. It feels wild but they don't have that sort of relationship. He places a hand on her breast, outside of her clothing. Thinks about her mother who would expect better. A change of mind, he removes her hand from his trousers.

'Dennis,' she says again.

'Wait here.' Dennis steps back into the kitchen. There are still a few kids knocking around, the music only on low. A select group by this time of night: those with nowhere else to be. The American woman must have taken herself upstairs. It's a flophouse, says so on the flyers. He doesn't think she got off with anybody. There were none in her age bracket, she can't be too fussy if she has. He thought she might be into him for a moment or two, all the homing-pigeon stuff. Could have been the dope playing with his mind. 'Major.' He says it quite sharply, attracts the attention of his fellow longhair.

'Yep.'

'Can you kind of keep an eye on shit while I take little Mary home?'

'You take her home good and proper, man.'

He goes straight back to the garden, no smile for the double entendre. If Major thinks he's the sort to take advantage, then he doesn't know Dennis Harris at all. Hippies have hearts!

Back in the garden, Mary is crying. He puts a caring arm around her shoulder. 'Whoa. What's the matter, kiddo?'

'I thought you'd left me,' says the young girl. Once more she takes his face and tries to kiss him with a passion that she barely has the energy for. The taste of sweet cider passes from tongue to tongue.

'Mary, Mary, you need to be in bed.'

'Let me sleep in yours. In bed with you.'

'No...no. Sorry, Mary. I'm taking you home.'

'To my bed. You can climb in with me, Dennis.'

He cannot help his comforting arm from slipping down to her hips, feeling the curve of her bottom through her thin summer dress. Blue, floral: not a hippy dress but half way there. She's quite a kid sneaking back to the party after big-brother Stephen has walked her home once. Priceless. Looks pretty brilliant too. He even thinks Charmouth cannot contain her. She's bound for greater things is young Mary.

'I love you, Denny.' She pushes her hands under his T-shirt. Gently holds him, leans herself right into him.

He really likes Mary but her abridgement of his name is presumptuous. Dennis likes his proper name and no other. 'You're drunk. We mustn't do what we might regret.'

'You don't love me, do you?' she blurts out. Shaking with tears, Mary pushes her face into his chest, pummelling him and then wrapping both arms around him like a limpet. She's in an odd state, might be the way of all first-time drunks. Dennis likes feeling her close but her mother will play merry hell if she stays the night in the flophouse. It cannot happen.

'I'm getting you home, Mary. Come on.'

She wilts into him, as pretend a swoon as there could be. He holds her up, prevents the fall that couldn't hurt her. Dennis—far the taller—raises her off the ground, one arm firmly around her back, the other at the crook of her knees. She is featherlight. Dennis has lifted one or two old ladies and gents at work, into and out of wheelchairs. Picking up Mary Bredbury is a doddle.

'Hey, lovely girl...' He tries to charm away her tears, the odd distress. '...I can carry you home and feel your heart beating next to mine.'

'All the way. Carry me all the way.'

He senses joy in the way she says it, a half-smile crooking the left side of the lips he has kissed.

It is a half mile of mostly main road. No traffic at all, not another soul. Four times he has to put her temporarily on her feet, adjust himself. Not that she is heavy at all but a body is not a rucksack. Four or five years ago, this girl rode on his shoulders. Playing games in the back garden of the Bredburys' small bungalow, and down on Charmouth beach too. She has only been to his house for these four parties. If she even was at the first; Dennis can't recall either way. She is the girl he has put his hands upon more than any other, only in the play of years past. None of the sexy stuff she's started on tonight. A protective mother in the family home. And his friend, Stephen—the only male in the Bredbury household—would remind him of his sister's age, even during those innocent beach games. The pair rest beside the post office and drunken Mary again begins to kiss him. He wonders what she'll think when she's sober. Dennis has scarcely had a proper girlfriend. Thought about Mary a time or two, mostly that

His Fourth Party

she was too young, too pretty. Wouldn't be interested in him.

'Got to get you home,' he says, again trying to lift her off the ground. Mary pushes her hands under his sweatshirt and Dennis imagines Sergeant Ash showing up in her police car. Charging him with indecency when Mary is the guiltier. He feels her legs with his hands but that's because she won't walk it. Carrying her: burden and pleasure, one sweet girl. And the policewoman is behind the desk at the station, only on his mind on account of seeing her again after two and a half years.

'Come into my bed,' she slurs into his ear, their heads close together as he walks with the drunk girl in his arms.

When they reach Morgan Crescent, arrive at the gate of the Bredburys' bungalow, he again puts Mary feet first on the ground. Gets her vertical. 'Got a key?' he asks.

She clasps his hand and draws him beside her, stepping into the garden. Dennis lets her lead him around the side of the house. They move in silence, the girl putting an upright index finger to her lips. Moving so freely he wonders why he has carried her, what he has proved. In this house reside a brother, mother and younger sister— hopefully all sleeping—who should not hear her re-entry. Don't know she is not already abed. At the side of the house, she tinkers with a window. Dennis thought it looked closed but now sees she has left the interior latch unclasped. She pulls it slowly upwards, the lower sash window juddering up the cord. Then Mary turns and kisses him on the lips once more. 'Come to bed,' she says again as she hoists up her dress revealing dark knickers, the slender legs he felt in his arms. Scrambles through the open window into her bedroom.

Dennis stays put. Only stares into the gloomy room into which she has climbed. He would like to go in, to lie beside Mary. Enjoy the pleasures others take in his flophouse. He thinks she is drunk, sure to hate him for doing anything of the sort once she's sobered up. As he watches from the garden, Mary pulls her dress over her head. Shadowy inside the darkened bedroom, the white of her bra illuminated by moonlight. She beckons him with a crooked forefinger and his mouth opens, mesmerised by the display. He realises as he watches, that in one of the twin beds she stands between another girl sleeps. Her younger sister, Monica, is oblivious to the raunchy show. Mary begins to remove her bra, Dennis watches without attempting to climb in. It is absurd; he cannot join her in the room with a sleeping sister. The young stripper is drunk beyond reason. Then a call comes

The Flophouse Years

from inside the house. An adult voice. 'Are you still up, Mary?' The voyeur has only the briefest glimpse of the topless girl. Immediately he ducks into the shadows, runs on the balls of his feet. From the garden, from Morgan Crescent. Faster than he has run in weeks, doesn't stop until he reaches the main road.

* * *

Back at the flophouse he finds only four partygoers still in the lounge, they are just sitting around. Looking pretty stoned. Major and the two guitar boys, plus a girl called Hannah. He knows her name only, no idea where she fits in. No music plays and they have his television out from the understairs cupboard. Extraordinary, no programmes are broadcast at this hour. The whacked-out revellers are watching a small white dot in the centre of the screen, the set is emitting a low whistle. It is faint but unpleasant. He always thought it was there to prompt the turning off of the set, not entertainment. Dennis has missed the last forty minutes of dope puffing.

The girl is holding the joint they share. 'Major says that there are a bunch of Cyborgs from far, far away in deep space beaming their message to us every night on the BBC. That's funny, yeah?'

'Then Major is full of shit, isn't he?' says Dennis, turning off the TV. 'Time for the lights to go out. You can sleep down here or there's a spare room upstairs. A few have crashed there already, I expect. Hope you've brought sleeping bags.'

'Sorry, man,' says Major. 'You weren't here. I didn't mean anything...'

Dennis cuts him off. 'Sure. There are no Cyborgs and I'm sick of that bullshit.' The guitar boys giggle to each other. That comes with smoking pot. Dennis doesn't say it but being a pair of pricks exacerbates the problem.

Hannah looks from Major to Dennis and back. 'Can I use your phone? Get my mother to come and collect me.'

'Your mother will collect you at this time?'

'Sure. She always waits up for me.'

'The phone's in the hallway,' says the bemused Dennis. 'If she doesn't pick up, I'm not carrying you home.'

Hannah shrugs, the comment lost on her. She must be twenty-one years old, a school year or two above Dennis. He's sure it was two. Making her mother drive here at this time is stupid. Sleepover, for God's sake, no one will touch you unless you want them to. He says none of it. Live and let live. Cyborgs out in deep space: that stuff is complete bollocks.

* * *

When he climbs the stairs, he can see into the room in which his parents once slept. A dim table lamp is still on in there, the door left ajar. Snoring. Sleeping bags angle across the floor in every direction. He has long since disposed of the double bed in which his parents went to sleep. Dennis is proud of his flophouse. He pokes a proprietorial head around the door, looks at tonight's crop of floppers. He cannot make out who is who but it's been a hell of a party. The horseplay with Mary was a bit unexpected, he enjoyed the feel of her in his arms, his hands on bare legs as he carried her across Charmouth. Wonders if she'll look him in the eye tomorrow. Can't imagine she'll want him when she's sober, still a boy can dream.

There is a keep-out sign on his own door. He thinks it a little abrupt but it serves a purpose. Opens the door and steps inside, flicks the light switch on as he closes the door. He is momentarily startled, someone in his bed. Not the first time and at least it isn't a couple humping. That happened at his second party; a sign is not a sentry.

4.

Dennis is in bed with the American woman, with Annabel, and neither are clothed. The passage from door to bed felt complicated, his free and easy disposition taking a five-minute breather. The mood has changed now that a little of his flesh touches hers. Getting into his own bed was a negotiation. Something akin to Kissinger figuring how Nixon could cosy up to Chairman Mao. Felt that unlikely to Dennis. The prevarication was his, she clearly chose his bed with some purpose.

'Do you know this is my room?' he asked, trying not to sound accusative.

'Couldn't be sure. It was my hunch.'

'I've a sleeping bag in the cupboard. I can sleep on the rug, I guess.'

'I don't wish to deprive you of your own bed, Dennis.'

'It's not that big...and you're kind of in it.'

'Is that a problem? Is it the young girl?'

Dennis was standing in the dark, moonlight through thin curtains allowing them to see each other's outlines. Annabel's no-longer plaited hair fell onto her shoulders as she raised herself up from the bed in which she lay. 'Mary. No, Mary's not my girlfriend...'

'Quite a lot of kissing for a casual acquaintance.'

'Summer, she's bored. I'm her brother's friend really.'

'The guy with the glasses?'

'Uh-uh.'

'He's a friend of yours?'

'Yeah. An old friend.' Dennis looked keenly at Annabel, swaddled in the sheets and blankets of his bed. Liking her clipped American accent. An unclothed shoulder peeking out.

'I never would have thought that.'

'Me neither, really. He doesn't get me these days.'

'But I think his sister does. I think she gets you quite a lot, Dennis Harris.'

'Annabel...' He whispered her name; it felt intimate to be using it although he was standing to attention like an army private awaiting permission to fall out. She pulled herself upright to talk, knees making a tent, sheet clutched to the bare bosom he was certain lay beneath. '...Mary is great.' He nodded as he said it; sixteen and drunk, even toked on the doobie tonight but she's got a lot going for her. 'I can't hear a bad word said about her; it's just she isn't my girlfriend. Not quite ready for boys yet. She'll go far. She's clever, too. I think the cider messed with that tonight. Got really blotto. And she tried to smoke the shit. The last thing Mary needs is a hippy holding her back.'

'Oh, Dennis, we hippies don't hold anyone back. The gate is open to the world. You treat her well. A lot of men would just take advantage. Treat free love as an open buffet.'

'I'm for free love...' He's a hippy; it's part of the creed. '...but not for ignoring feelings.'

'How does that work, Dennis?'

They were both talking in low voices, a raft of people asleep in the next room, some downstairs too. The flophouse had flipped from party to boarding school dormitory, from fun to exhaustion. Dennis felt excited and scared. He didn't dare go in to Mary's bungalow, clamber through the window into her bedroom. Inviting as the prospect—the near-naked teenager—appeared. He got that right, a mother up and waiting, and when she sobers up Mary might regret so much as kissing him. They never have before. As he was walking back, a slow saunter after his initial sprint from Morgan Crescent, he wondered quite what got into her tonight. Remembered again the feel of her hips in his hands as she pressed herself against him. Throwing

His Fourth Party

herself at him—it probably was the cider—she looks sexy but never acted that way. Not before. They have shared a few pretty personal conversations in recent weeks, Mary more attuned to him than Stephen. Never come on to him before, not to anybody as he has heard about. And Dennis is worried about her wider family. Keeping on the right side; they are all good to him. Free love is not a marriage contract, that is pretty much the point. Her mother goes to church. A big fan of all the strict rules her daughter seemed on the verge of breaking. Mary and cider.

The lady in his bed, hair undone, fluffed up across a propped-up pillow, let the sheet slip from her fingers. He saw his second pair of breasts of the evening. Stared. Annabel smiled calmly, moved slightly aside in the narrow bed and patted the space beside herself. Veteran of a thousand nights like this if she has been a hippy since she was his age. Then he realised that notion was quite impossible: it is only six or seven years since the first hippies emerged. Walked upright out of the Californian forests.

'Dennis,' she whispered, 'you said this was your fourth party...'

'I did.'

'...and it has been terrific. Putting yourself on the hippy trail, my sweet friend.' He liked hearing this, it fulfilled a dream. 'Now it is time to come to bed.'

'Your kind of in it. You're not happy sleeping in the room with others?'

'Not happy at all, Mr Harris. I only ever sleep with the master of the house.'

That started him giggling, not a hashish giggle, this time. He didn't join in with the dumb-bells downstairs at the end. The hash he smoked is long out of his system. Her phrase was a funny way to tell him what was what. He took off socks and jeans, left on his underpants and T-shirt, slid himself under the covers. Earlier Dennis had put his forehead against Annabel's when they were smoking dope. She probably gave him a sign then; he is pretty sure she did, he was wary of overinterpreting what it meant. Inexperienced. And he got kind of excited about Mary. Dick like a telegraph pole when he was running from the bungalow. And Annabel inviting him into his own bed, to lie with her. Top night of his life. Dennis is unsure exactly how this will unfold. Not a juncture he has reached before. Mary looked terrific but a little sister in the twin bed and her mother shouting from the next room called the shots. And Dennis likes her too much to have taken advantage of anyway. Young kid, wasted at the fag-end of a party. This woman is older, knows what she's doing. Looks that way.

Annabel pulls him into an embrace. With her hands she discards his remaining clothing. Underpants. She rolls him on top of her and he feels the gorgeous compress of her bosoms beneath his chest. Her lips upon his, with a delicacy that tells him he is in safe hands. High time this hippy got shot of his virginity.

5.

He left the bed to open the curtains, to let sunlight into the room. Saw it shine upon her black hair which splays across the pillow. The sounds in the bathroom, others down in the kitchen, have stirred him from a fitful sleep. Now, back under the covers with Annabel, he once more places a hand on those parts of her which she has allowed him, as no other girl has before.

'Will they go?' she asks.

'Some will, some won't. It's a flophouse. I let everyone do as they please. It's hardly the Ritz, nobody takes advantage.'

'You're a good guy, Dennis. I saw the jar in the kitchen. Does everybody put in, do you think?' She refers to a pint glass half-full of coins, a pound note or two. Nothing is Free: Everything is Ours, his handwriting, a sticky label on the side of the glass. People who flop contribute. Most do, he draws on it for stuff he shares around. And it pays for breakages.

'There aren't many hippies around here, really, but they have to try it if they want to stay.'

'And you want to be here not down in London or over in the US. Where there are more of us.'

'I've a job here in Charmouth, Annabel, can't be going to San Francisco. If I did though, I'd be the sixth Laughing Llama, wouldn't I?'

Annabel laughs, puts her hand on the back of his head. Pulls him towards her own so their two clusters of long and sleep-dishevelled hair meld into one. A kiss upon his lips. 'You're a special one. Not quite a Llama, I heard you trying to sing to the record last night, remember? Special though. Where do you work, Dennis?'

'Flats,' he says. 'There are some flats nearby for old people. Round-the-clock support. I help them. See they're all right.'

His Fourth Party

'You do care work?'

'Deputy warden. It's care work. Yes.'

'The hippies are branching out. I'm proud of you, Dennis.'

He grins at the lady who has been to Haight-Ashbury, who comes from an island that is not an island. Hasn't the first idea what she's doing in Charmouth. He puts a hand upon her naked hip beneath the blanket.

'Are you working today, Dennis?'

'Tomorrow. Today is for free love, don't you think?'

'Oh, that might be overrated. If you're happy with little ol' me, we can take a little pleasure beneath the covers.'

She is smiling levelly at him. He launches his body upon hers. He must have drunk forty beers before he could honestly say he enjoyed the taste. Sex is something else, fulfilled his expectations first go.

* * *

It took a lot of hinting and prompting. Dennis wondered if a couple of the lads were sticking around on the off-chance Annabel would spread the love more thinly. Finally, at four in the afternoon, the pair alone remain in the house.

'Dennis,' she asks, 'is it okay if I stay here for a few days?'

'With me?' He cannot read English girls, hasn't a chance with Annabel from Rhode Island.

'Me with you and you with me, Dennis. Unless you want me to go, try your luck with that other girl.'

Dennis looks down at the frayed rug. 'Don't make fun of Mary,' he says. Repeats his mantra once more that she's a great kid, one who will find better than him for a boyfriend. 'When she's ready,' he adds. He's thought about her a bit and really thinks she is too young for all of it. Shouldn't even be trying sex yet. More than three calendar years his junior.

'I'm sorry, Dennis. You're so kind to everyone. I just meant I'd like to stay so long as I'm not stepping on toes.'

He smiled, likes to be told he's a good guy. 'Stay as long as you like. Mi casa is yours and all that.'

Now it's just the two of them, they start to tidy up the house. Dennis taking the old carpet sweeper from the understairs cupboard, rolling it over the crumbs across the lounge floor.

'Let me do that, Den. You know which cupboards to put everything into.'

The Flophouse Years

'You've no need to clean,' says Dennis.

'It's my mess too. If I stay, I help out.'

While they work in close proximity, he puts an occasional hand upon her person. Indecently once or twice and she seems okay with it. You with me and me with you.

'Have you seen the sea?' he asks.

'Here at Charmouth? Not yet.'

'Let's go.'

Dennis points at her sandals, discarded to the side of the kitchen. He pulls on a pair of plimsols.

'Are we going bathing?'

'We can. I was just going to show you the lay of the land. I like the sea. The cliffs and the river. Famous rocks here. They're really old and shit. Dinosaur footprints or something but I'm not really one for history.'

'Or even palaeontology, I gather. I'd like to swim.'

'It'll cool soon,' he says, but she takes his hand, leads him back up the stairs. In the bedroom she strips. Dennis again looks at her naked body as she roots in a small bag, withdraws a light-blue swimsuit, steps into it and quickly encloses her ample breasts. Dennis turns his back as he pulls on his trunks, then his jeans back over them. Hopes the traipse through town might dull his ardour. The sight before her swimsuit enclosed her, the memory of last night's love-making—this morning's too—are new and exciting experiences. A proper hippy now.

They leave the house, Annabel in the same purplish skirt, a different blouse covering her swimsuit. They take the shortest path to the beach. Many swimmers are trudging back the other way, late afternoon. They walk side by side, he occasionally swinging an arm across her shoulders. At other times he leans back and views Annabel's once-more plaited hair, the deep tan of her exposed skin. He feels like a different boy; walked this way so many times, never before with a girl to whom he has made love. The only other girls he has knocked around Charmouth with are Mary and Monica, and that on account of his friendship with their brother. When Annabel was a nameless older woman inexplicably at his party, he thought her odd. Out of place. Now he sees that she is beautiful, wonders why it took him so long to notice. Maybe not the beauty of any prevailing orthodoxy. Something rarer. Eyes that look upon him kindly, skin electric to the touch. A warmer embrace than he has ever known.

His Fourth Party

A couple of people greet him, Dennis well known in Charmouth. It's a titchy town and his family tragedy made the national news. Part of the shocking wider story.

'Is this your Auntie?' asks a lady with small children.

Dennis has misplaced her name, she lives on the same road as Stephen, just a door or two from the Bredbury family. 'She's a friend,' he says. Reddens a little, expects Annabel might say a lover—being a fully-fledged authentic hippy—but she doesn't. 'A friend from America.'

The lady nods sagely. One of her children shouts, 'She's a yank.'

'Yes,' says Annabel, 'the Yankee doodle dandy,' and the little boy laughs.

At the beach there are still plenty of people in the water. Beachgoers, holiday makers, all enjoying the August sunshine. He points to a wooden bridge that connects the two beaches. They cross over it and look down on children wading in the water. Dipping their nets in and out, not that there are any river crabs. They fish for nothing, for the purpose that trying brings.

On the beach the pair put down two towels. Annabel unclasps her long skirt; removes the white blouse she wears. Dennis looks across the beach, looks up at the cliff face. Not at the girl he has slept with, the limbs he hopes to mingle with again tonight. 'Let's swim,' he says lowering his jeans.

They skip-run into the waves. Annabel braces herself at the cold of the sea, then laughs. 'As bad as Rhode Island,' she shouts.

At the earliest opportunity, Dennis has dived, head under, comes up crawling. It is not deep, just deep enough. She is far behind him, water over her knees and no more, proceeding slowly. He looks back, likes what he sees: Annabel in her costume. He shouts to her, encourages her, she is simply taking in the scene, looking to left and right at the arc of the shoreline. Dorset hills behind. Inching forward until the water starts to lap at her thighs, makes its way to the bottom of her swimsuit and she pushes off. Joins Dennis, fully immersed.

'You live in a great spot,' she shouts.

He cuts the water, angling his hands as he long ago learnt to do. 'I can't leave it,' he shouts. It's a funny thing to say. Not something he admits much. He hasn't even been to Southampton to see Stephen yet. A full year at university and the offer always open. He buses to Bridport regularly. No reason, just that he went to secondary school there. It's way bigger than Charmouth. His Aunt and Uncle ferry him to Taunton occasionally, where they live, but he is throwing off the shackles of family. They are no damned good: that's been the lesson of his life. Hippies are family now.

'And you really don't mind if I stay?'

'As long as you like, Annabel. I'm always here; the flophouse is always open.'

* * *

Back at number three Croft Road, Annabel prepares a simple pasta meal. A packet of spaghetti from the cupboard, onion and tinned tomato. Nothing fancy but she has done better than he would have managed with the same ingredients. They eat it from cereal bowls in front of the television. Like an old married couple, he thinks.

'You're not a big talker,' she observed when Dennis turned the set on. 'I like that.' Nicely put but he worries that she doesn't. That he ought to find more to say. The programme is a police drama, set up north. All the actors talk with Lancashire accents. Annabel makes a good fist of impersonating them. 'What you want, copper?' she giggles.

He wants to ask her what she sees in him; where she is going next. Have all her boyfriends been fifteen years her junior? But nor does he wish to ask anything that might knock out the stuffing, make their bed less comfy. Deny him access to her most intimate places. He likes her being here, the miracle of her wish to stay. The party was terrific—best by a country mile—the month in between can be a bit fallow. This feels like a step change. Like he's finally living.

'Have you been in England long?' he says.

'A month. I stayed with people I know in London, Americans. Everyone wanted to show me the sights but I'm not bothered by all that. The busby hats. Then I came here to find you. We are both survivors, Dennis.'

Chapter Two

Plaza Court

1.

In the Co-operative stores, Dennis holds six separate shopping lists in his hand. Picking out groceries for occupants of the flats, the extra care housing scheme situated just a street away from here. It's complicated, each resident pays for his or her own, Dennis the conduit. Pen and paper accompany every shopping trip; he must give them each the exact change when he gets back to Plaza Court, when he distributes their fare. No room for mistakes on this job: the old folk count their pennies.

As he browses the narrow aisle, searching the shelves for the particular tins of choice, a voice says, 'Wild Man Harris.'

He glances around but it comes from another aisle.

'That was some party up at Wild Man Harris's flophouse.'

Dennis steps away from his task and rounds the corner. Neil Sullivan, one of the guitar players from Tuesday last, is putting on a deeper voice than he really owns.

'Wild Man Harris,' he repeats, a little grin sitting on his face.

'Hi Neil,' says Dennis, glancing over his friend's shoulder. There are only a few in the shop and one of them is his mother. 'What are you doing?'

'I just carry it for her. Helping out at home until I get a job.'

He doesn't intend to but Dennis lets out a short snigger. Neil isn't much of a hippy. Hair an inch over the collar, that's the lot. He sings a couple of Llamas' songs but his voice is never quite on it. A mummy's boy this afternoon.

Neil steps forward, out of his mother's hearing he says, 'At least I don't get it on with my old lady. I hear that's your thing now, Wild Man.'

Dennis laughs aloud at that. He doesn't have a nickname and the one Neil is trying to foist upon him misses the mark. He's sure of it.

The Flophouse Years

Perhaps he should feel insulted: Neil is comparing his first proper girlfriend with his mother, and there is not a hint of similarity between them. And the two guitar boys were trying to cosy up to Annabel themselves early evening on party night. 'Give over. She's one of us. I've made a connection.'

Neil stares him down. 'Old woman lover. You should at least get her to shop for you.'

This one really rankles. He and Annabel don't order each other around. Hippies don't. Before Dennis can put Neil straight, Mrs Sullivan has come back to her son. He wonders if she knows he has a woman back in the flophouse, a lover who he suspects to be about twice as old as his own nineteen years. They've talked but it's been quite limited on the personal front. He hasn't asked her age for fear of sounding rude. And hearing Neil's barbed comments makes him think he might, once again, become the gossip of the town. It was truly dreadful two years ago. At least living with a woman—a good-looking woman, however many years older she happens to be—will make him the envy of the boys. Something the death of his parents could never do. Pity was the mainstay of that one, the heart and lungs and whispered aside of it.

'I'm working, Neil. I come here to fetch all the stuff the old folk need.'

'Oh, that's nice of you, Dennis,' says Mrs Sullivan. 'And nice you've got company at home. You're far too young to live alone, so I wish you both well.'

Dennis nods a thank you to her comment, it's a pleasant sentiment. He imagines she knows very few details about his houseguest—his sleeping arrangements—her son might have said something but not the whole hog.

'Neil, why don't you do what Dennis does? Volunteer with the old ladies while you're at a loose end.'

'I'm paid by the council, Mrs Sullivan. They wouldn't trust volunteers with money or all the care tasks I have to do.'

'I'm not doing that, Mum. I grow my hair because I'm going to be a rock star, not a girl.'

Dennis raises his eyes to the ceiling. Mrs Sullivan sees the expression and copies it. 'Good for you, helping the old ladies. If your mum was here, she would be ever so proud of you.'

Dennis glances down, never enjoys hearing either parent spoken of. Fears where the conversation may turn. Coughs a sound that could be taken for a thank you, doesn't say the words at all.

'And my lad's a flipping layabout. Aren't you, Neil?'

Her son protests, not with a convincing line of argument. 'Waiting for the right job to come along. No point in doing the wrong one.'

Dennis excuses himself, must press on, gather up every item on the six lists. Take them back to Plaza Court. When Mrs Sullivan has collected all the goods she wishes to purchase, he hears Neil begging his mother for a chocolate bar. The lad must be eighteen by now, plays a few chords but his singing is atrocious. Helping old people isn't girls' work, it's good karma.

* * *

He arrives back at the flats, sees Lorraine Chadwick through the open office door. She drinks tea and eats biscuits, slouched down in her swivel chair, grey skirt riding up her bare legs. The warden, his manager. He coughs and she stands and sits again in a single motion which enables her to cover the white slabs of her thighs. Dennis enters the office to sort the shopping; always finds it an easier task when she is not in here. He needs to concentrate on the sums, and Lorraine's mouth doesn't have an off switch.

'Are you all right, honey,' she says.

Dennis grunts. She has taken liberties with his name many times, never does it in company. Strange manager indeed.

'Everything all right at home?'

Shit, he thinks. She's heard too, and Lorraine Chadwick doesn't even live in Charmouth. 'Home is good,' he tells her. 'Always someone crashing at my place. Don't worry over what you hear about me, Lorraine.'

'Crashing, you call it?'

'Yeah. Dossing in the flophouse. Taking time out from their obligations. It's our way.' Dennis pulls on his long hair with his right hand. An affectation. I'm a hippy, it says. Not with words but it is in the gesture.

'So, if I get a bit tired of…I don't know…my cat, I can come by and stay for a few days.'

The correct answer is no, correct for this old stick-in-the-mud, but nor would it be true to his philosophy. 'Everyone is welcome, Lorraine. You're one of everyone.' Truth is she's a silly old spinster but he prefers not to entertain unkind thoughts. Too much of that in this world. He has yet to learn how old his new girlfriend is, knows his manager turned forty last year—they had white wine in this very office—must be forty-one now. Five or six years older than Annabel, that's his hope.

He lays the shopping out on top of the second desk. Goes through the long receipt, making a tick against each item, putting it aside. Then he does the adding up. Sorts out the correct change for each of the six residents. Mrs Chadwick occupies herself, perusing the notes which Tracy made during last night's shift. Making a periodic humph noise as she does it. Wants to talk about what she reads but Dennis isn't biting. Shopping to distribute, can't be delayed by motormouth.

'Have you noticed any change in Mrs Carmichael?'

He waits before answering, completes an addition and writes down the total. 'She's always been frail; I'm worried she's taken a turn. Very tearful yesterday afternoon which is unusual for her. A bit better when I saw her earlier today. She's not back to her usual self. Not yet.'

'Crying about what? What's upset her?'

'Her son.'

'Oh, that's ridiculous. He died in nineteen-twenty-four.'

Dennis doesn't reply immediately. He has never thought Zoe Carmichael to be ridiculous. It's not that she hasn't come to terms with the loss, just that reminders bring back the sadness of all she has missed. He has worried that he is one of them: a reminder. Another lad of the age all memories of her late son must centre around. 'I don't imagine she ever wants to forget him,' says Dennis.

'Thinking about him is hardly going to make her happy, is it?'

'That wasn't my point, Lorraine. She doesn't want him out of mind, never wants to lose the memory.'

'But it won't make her happy. Don't muddle your own feelings up with those of the residents, Dennis. And a little bird tells me you've a lady staying in your house now.'

Which of his nosy neighbours has Lorraine Chadwick's telephone number? Can't see where else she would have learned this. 'Hippies don't have all those old hang ups. Not like monks and nuns...' Dennis is answering in the affirmative while losing the thread of precisely what he should say. Can't be shouting, mind your own business, at his manager, tempting as the prospect is.

Lorraine is laughing now. Doing so like she's smoked some of the dope the dull old stop-at-home would never dare to touch. 'Monks and nuns! Not in your house from what I've heard.'

'I need to give the ladies their shopping.' He leaves her to ruminate over his private life, whatever truth, half-truth or downright lie she

Plaza Court

has learnt. Dennis goes up to the flats. Groceries to give out. Not gassing and gossiping, sticking to the job he's paid for.

* * *

'Thank you so much, Dennis,' says Mrs Johnstone. Thak-chew show mu Dence, are the sounds her mouth makes.

He nods sagely, doesn't laugh about the oddity of her speech, false teeth falling forward with every jaw movement. Mrs Johnstone has been wheelchair-bound since suffering a stroke eighteen months ago. It has impeded control of her tongue and her ability to weight bear for more than a few seconds at a time. Dennis must push her down the corridor in a wheelchair if she is to leave her flat whilst he's on duty. Wheeled her to lunch club and back earlier today.

'Shall I put it in the cupboard?' He has laid out her shopping on the work surface of the small alcove kitchen.

'No. Leave it now, Dennis. I like to decide what order to eat my goodies in.' She gives a little laugh, clasps the loose false teeth with peeled back lips as she does so. 'Can you stay and talk?'

Ker shtay and tor, are the sounds which Dennis hears. He understands her slurry speech well. Concentrates hard on everything she has to say. 'For a little while. Lorraine might have something for me to do; at least all the shopping is in the right hands now.'

'I heard, Mr Dark-Horse Harris, that you have become very modern. Taken a lady into your house.'

He is still standing in the little kitchen, Mrs Johnstone looking up at him from her glide-about chair. It is a small-wheeled chair, she has not the strength to propel one with her arms. She can shuffle her feet to take herself the short distances within this small flat. That Mrs Johnstone has learnt Annabel is living on Croft Road—she has not left Plaza Court in months, the dining hall down the corridor her only outing—is a low-voltage shock. What she says or thinks about his lifestyle cannot hurt him. There was glee in her comment, as if she is enjoying the scandal. No condemnation detected in her tone. None so far. It is embarrassing if he has become the talk of luncheon club, done so for the second time in his employment here. Quite a few in Charmouth know about the flophouse, the way people come and go. Neighbours have complained. It only started properly this summer, it's as plain to see as his garden gate. The old folk never mention it whether they know or not. Lorraine Chadwick, alone, has been funny about it. How Mrs Johnstone knows the significance of the latest visitor is a mystery to Dennis. Six days Annabel has been in Charmouth. That is the length of this boy's first serious relationship. The sporadic houseguests of recent months have included a character or two. None quite stopped him from feeling alone. Not until Annabel. Six days and counting. He fears it may not last—female company, a shared bed—hopes with his hippy heart that it will. These six days have been good ones. And it is all a private matter in his mind. Doesn't affect how he does the job. Always on his game at Plaza Court.

'I was so pleased to hear about her, Dennis, that you have found a suitable young lady…'

Maybe Mrs Johnstone hasn't heard the finer details. Or maybe she's old enough to consider Annabel young. Dennis has called Annabel beautiful, glamorous and sexy, whispered these terms into her ear in the bedroom. Never young, never thought to try that one for size. And she laughed when he used the others. 'I've a good dose of Italian blood in me,' she said, 'it doesn't make me Sophia Loren.'

'Frankly, dearie,' continues Mrs Johnstone, 'I was worried that you were of the other sort. You know, a whoopsie.' She tries to make the flop-handed gesture, imitate the way one or two TV comedians imply that a man is queer. Smiles apologetically as she does it. 'It must be the long hair which made me think that. It would better suit a girl. Well done finding a young lady who likes it that way.'

He looks directly into her eyes. She is beaming back at him, false teeth still falling forward, trying to escape her mouth with every expulsion of breath. There is no malice in her eyes; she is pleased for him. The old and the young don't share a radio frequency. She must mean well but every word is an insult: happy he is not the homosexual she assumed him to be. 'Thank you,' says Dennis, begrudgingly.

He never laughs at the old people, tries to work out why they see the world the way they do. A few comments about his long hair have had him biting his tongue. Not this one. He will share the exchange with Annabel tonight. She will see the funny side, bound to. And Dennis is paid good money to tolerate the prejudices of old people. Simple as that.

* * *

He calls into Mrs Carmichael's flat. The small staff team at Plaza Court worries that their wittiest resident is losing her sparkle. She is ninety-one, that her best years are in the past should surprise no one. She has told him she has no wish to go on forever but Dennis cannot imagine

Plaza Court

the place without her. Zoe Carmichael has lived here far longer than the three years he has been in the job.

'I'll just turn off the wireless.'

She thrives on company, always keen to hear from him. In cautious terms, he has even described a party or two. She told him that they sounded 'a hoot'.

He asks how she is feeling to day. She talks arthritis—which has long bent her double—and the struggle to remove herself from bed in the morning. He knows all about this; on the early shift, one of his tasks is to assist her in swinging her legs around, getting into a position from which she can rise up to her walking frame. It is only her tenacity and the value she still places upon her privacy, which enable her, once out of bed, to dress alone. Lorraine has always said that—unlike the old people's home on the main road—the set-up at Plaza Court helps residents keep their independence. This frail lady is the living proof.

'How about you, young sir?' she enquires.

'Same old everything from me, Mrs C. All quiet on the western front...'

'Liar, liar, pants on fire.'

It is unusual for Mrs Carmichael to be so direct and already he fears she is about to pass an unfavourable judgement on his newly changed living arrangement. How she knows, he can only speculate. And Dennis has no idea if Annabel is a transient guest who has allowed him pleasures no other ventured to, or a life partner. Somewhere in the middle is his guess; an American is unlikely to live in Charmouth forever. He knows of no others. 'What have you heard? he asks.

'Heard? I'm expecting our mutual friend to sack you if you don't marry her in place of whatever snapdragon you've found for yourself.'

She has heard a lot and her phrasing amuses him. Heartens him for being so far removed from her tears of yesterday evening. 'I'm not the marrying sort, and Lorraine would be last on the list. But she's gone and told you something about me, hasn't she?'

'She has told me everything about you, young Dennis. Does so whenever she comes in here, and in all the other flats too, I imagine. Complains about you mostly but that is the way with unrequited love, isn't it?'

'And I've told you my opinion before. She's daft but not quite daft enough to be in love with me. And old enough to be my mother.'

'Yes. And you've gone and upset the applecart now, Dennis. I hear you are living with a woman who is older than our mutual friend.'

He shakes his head. 'It's not true at all. She's never been to my house. Knows nothing about my private life. About who I choose to live with.'

Mrs Carmichael's eyes dance across his face. She has unpicked the local gossip with him before, this is Dennis's first turn in the hot seat. 'Don't get defensive with me, Mr Harris. If I'd thought twenty years ago that I would be talking to a long-haired boy about living with a woman he is not married to, I would have guessed it would be to…I don't know…threaten him with a shotgun. Times have changed. I've changed. I'm all in favour of it. If I could have lived with Duncan for six months before we were married, I would have called the wedding off. And that's the truth as I can only now see it. Young people are learning to live more thoughtfully than we ever did back in my day. Smart…'

'You're not ticking me off for it?'

Her neck is always at ninety degrees, face to the floor, bent with age, she swivels her head as best she can. Takes his eye. 'I'm not, Dennis. I'm certainly not doing that. Tell me about her.'

'I have someone in my life, Zoe. Someone I care about. She's not older than Mrs Chadwick. Who has never met her, by the way. The boss just makes up half of what she tells you. And Annabel is as young at heart as I am. It's like we're the same age deep down.'

Mrs Carmichael doesn't reply immediately, keeps her wrinkled face locked on the young care assistant from the awkward angle arthritis grants her. 'You have had the most difficult start in life, Dennis. Be careful. I wish you only happiness. And my "be careful" is a caution not a criticism. If I was small-minded once, I am no longer. I'm sorry if I teased you about Lorraine. I think she would share your bed tomorrow but you'd be a fool to let her. Annabel is your lady-friend's name, is it? I would love to meet her. Bring her here, I can make a pot of tea and you could fetch us all some scones on your shopping trip.'

Dennis smiles. Has no idea if Annabel would be amenable to so twee a social engagement. It is an offer appreciated on his part.

* * *

As he writes in the medicine book, signing off which residents he has given which tablets—final task before shift's end—Lorraine Chadwick starts on at him again. 'I'm not sure if everyone in the council is happy with a deputy warden opening up his home as a flophouse.'

When he finally lifts his eyes from the book in which he writes, she is staring at him, a look of indignation on her face. And it is daft talk: never seen the mayor on Croft Road; nobody will know unless she tells them. 'I do what I'm paid for, Lorraine.'

'Yes, you do, Dennis. I've been telling you for three years that you've got what it takes for this work. I got you made up to deputy warden. Tracy didn't like that one bit but I backed you. Young and long haired and still I backed you over her. Don't squander your career by chasing pork crackling, Dennis. If you weren't so mixed-up you could probably find yourself a proper girlfriend.'

A year or two back, he listened to her advice; time has proven Chadwick to be a hopeless case. Blinkers like a dray horse. Annabel is what he needs right now. Might be all he will need for as long as he's got. The finer details will work themselves out.

Last night, when only he and Annabel were home—no one flopping since party night—the doorbell rang. He went to answer it but the step was empty. Ring and run. 'Hello,' he called out, and then a projectile came over the front hedge. A bag of flour burst at his feet. Not an assault, a fool's caper. He heard feet scurrying away. Whoever threw it must have ducked behind the hedge; Dennis never saw the prankster.

A girl's voice shouted, 'Fuck off, Harris. Harris the mother-fucker.' He knew exactly who it was although he has seldom heard her shout. Never sworn at him before, he is certain.

When he went back inside Annabel gave him a searching look. 'Nobody there,' he said, stooping to brush flour off his carpet slippers.

'I heard a girl's voice.'

'It's a bit shit,' he confessed to Annabel. 'I don't owe her anything but she can't handle it, can she? Just a kid.'

'Talk to her. You do mean the girl you were kissing at the party, don't you?'

'She was the one kissing me.'

Annabel laughed at that. And Dennis had enjoyed kissing Mary at the time. So drunk she showed him her tits after he'd walked her home, Dennis never told that Annabel the finer details. Mary is regretting it would explain the flour.

'And you know we are not out to hurt anyone. I'm even meant to be committed to free love. If she wants to join in...'

Her words tapered away when Dennis dropped eye contact. He

believes in it because he is a hippy, just not so keenly if he dwells upon either of these two, Annabel or Mary. Free love would cheapen them: he didn't say it last night, keeps these thoughts to himself. Still trying to figure the outer limits of his hippieism.

'I can manage my own life, thank you,' he tells Lorraine. There are some struggles in it but none that this old sourpuss can help him with. 'And I never eat the crackling.'

He rises from the desk as she laughs at his sign off. Four o'clock has arrived, shift over. It is a vicious cackle he hears; it might be the jealousy which Zoe Carmichael referred to. Lorraine Chadwick is one weird warden. Dennis leaves Plaza Court, sets off for the flophouse.

* * *

He feels a little agitated as he takes in the outdoor air. Shouldn't worry if Charmouth is talking about his choice of housemate. Of lover. Needs to rise above it. The afternoon sun is strong, within a few yards he can feel sweat trickle from his scalp, his long thick hair. He turns around and looks back at Plaza Court: a big concrete box, sitting between the fire station and the primary school. One road back from the main road. They might be the three ugliest buildings in this pretty seaside town. Head back, keeps going; crosses the main road and then he takes the lane down to the sea. No longer making his way home. A sea breeze might clear his head.

He wants to talk to Annabel about the shift; needs to think it through before he tries. Tell her that he and she are public property. She won't understand it: this is not Rhode Island. He has figured from their conversations thus far that Providence, Annabel's home town, is even bigger than Bridport. She says it's a city. He wonders if she's wrong. Dennis knows about Chicago and Los Angeles, Philadelphia and Atlanta too. Thought he knew all the cities in America and Providence was never on the list. Either way, he doubts if Annabel knows what it's like to become the subject of relentless gossip. She has experienced a tragedy like his own, lost family in the public eye. She has told him very little: bereaved of a husband she had separated from a few months before it happened. January twentieth, nineteen-seventy. Whatever people spill about the personal lives of others in Providence, Rhode Island, it won't be half as bad as Dorset tittle-tattle. And Annabel might have been in California by the time it all happened. He hasn't worked out the time line. She prefers talking about the Laughing Llamas and Dennis does too. This—the rubbish

Plaza Court

which the likes of Lorraine Chadwick prattle on about down here in Charmouth and the surrounding villages—is the world's most annoying form of gossip. Bar none. Dennis is dead certain about that.

The beach heaves with people, holiday makers by the hundred. Some locals too, no doubt. Towels and a good quota of sun umbrellas are dotted across the sand in both directions. Dennis doesn't recognise anyone, not from where he stands. Heads bob up and down in the water, kids splash in the shallows. He walks onto the sand, saunters in the direction of Lyme. Not to go there, just to keep moving. Thinking as he walks, it has long been a habit of his. The shift just passed and his changing life. Never imagined himself living with a woman so effortlessly, nor did he give a second's thought to how others would see him if he did. It simply wasn't on the cards.

As he passes the last of the beach huts the sunbathers thin out. A young girl jumps up from her beach towel. 'Dennis, Dennis, come and swim with us,' she shouts. Not so young, thirteen, a scrawny little thing. It's Monica—Monica Bredbury—Stephen and Mary's younger sister.

'Who's with you?' he calls back. The girl lying on the towel adjacent to the one Monica leapt from, now turning around in her red swimsuit, is well known to him. Flour power. Not yet a week since he cradled her in his arms.

'If he's staying, I'm going,' Mary tells Monica.

'But you like him.' Monica wears a look of surprise, narrowing her eyes as she stares down big sister.

'I do not.'

'Mary, try not to be angry with me. I only came out for a walk. Didn't know you were going to be here.'

She sits upright on her towel now, legs, arms, even a plunging neckline are a show of skin, a contrast from Dennis in his jeans, his white work-shirt still buttoned at the cuffs. She picks up her jeans which lie beside her, puts them across the tops of her legs. Dennis tries not to stare. An eye-catching girl in swimwear.

'I'm sorry about the party, Mary.' His voice tapers away as he tries to look at her directly. Plastic-rimmed sunglasses cover her eyes. She could be studying him, could be scowling with hatred. In a quieter voice, he says, 'You were a little drunk.'

'She was sick on Wednesday, Dennis,' shrieks the little sister. 'Sick, sick, sick!' Then Monica turns to Mary. 'You told me Dennis is nice; you said he has eyes like Danny Clare. What's he done? You must still

The Flophouse Years

fancy him? His nice eyes haven't gone blank or anything. Look!'

'You wouldn't understand, Mon? Actually, he's a turd-head.' With a turn of her shoulder, Mary excludes Dennis from the conversation. 'Another Dorset thicky.' Then she whispers to her sister, does it loud enough for him to hear it. 'Drugs, Monica, he takes them like we drink water. He's as stupid a boy as you could ever meet.'

Dennis shakes his head without being sure which part he wants to deny. He thinks Mary unwise to be telling any of this to her sister. Monica looks wide-eyed; young enough to think a funny smoke can turn a man into a monster. If she tells her mother, it might scupper Stephen's and Mary's attendance at his parties. Emma Bredbury is very anti-drugs. All parents are, and churchgoers the worst of them. First of the month, Mary will always be welcome whatever silly names she calls him now. He doesn't think he's a stupid boy; wouldn't argue that she's about five O-levels cleverer. Not smarter than him at all when she's put away half a dozen tins of cider. 'It's not like that.' Dennis is stuck for words. Mary puffed on the joint she is accusing him of enjoying. He won't say it. Not dropping her in the shit. What he feels towards her will never change.

'It's always like that for stupid turd-heads, Dennis. I don't know what you're even doing here.'

Monica giggles. 'Sorry, Dennis. You can't swim with us after all. My sister knows her turd-heads and you're a big one. That's right, isn't it, Mary?'

As the skinny sister giggles away, Dennis notices how dejected his recent admirer appears. She has the liveliest face but—sunglasses held in her left hand—it has not come with her to the beach today.

'Mary, I didn't mean you any harm.' He drops onto his knees, down into the sand beside her.' You'll find someone better than...'

She strikes him across the cheek with the flat of her palm. Sounds like a pistol-shot.

'Fat chance,' she hisses at him. 'You didn't like the look of me when I showed you. Then you ran to the next woman you could find. Plain nasty!'

Dennis rolls backwards on the sand as he sees her raising her arm again. 'You're not listening to me,' he says. 'I thought you would regret....'

'You don't think at all, Dennis. Get out of my sight.'

Dennis rises, spreads both hands and then gives her a peace sign and a smile. Mary gives him the reverse. Face screwed up in a scowl

Plaza Court

and her righthand thrusting out two-fingered fuck-off.

As he turns, walks on, he thinks it crazy. Mary looks gorgeous, of course he liked it. It wasn't the only consideration. He cares about her; thought she might have hated him the following day if he had done what she was drunkenly asking him to do. Didn't know at the time that Annabel was waiting in his bed. Annabel whose mother doesn't impede any carnal thoughts he has about her.

'Come back when you've stopped being a turd-head,' shouts Monica. It makes a few sunbathers sit up, look round. Dennis walks on, further from the town. He knows a path back through the woods, will return to Croft Road without bothering Mary again. Always nice to see her, really wishes he hadn't caused her this upset.

* * *

'Dennis,' calls Annabel as he steps inside the front door, 'come and meet Herbie.'

He walks through to the kitchen, the room from which his lover's voice came. Annabel sits on a chair at the small table beside a long-haired man who Dennis has never seen before. A thick black moustache, matching long hair, leather waistcoat. He wears no shirt beneath it. Dennis wants to kiss his girl, his woman. Feels inhibited by the visitor. 'Hello,' he directs at the stranger.

'Hey, man. Nice drop-in you've got here.' Herbie's accent is as American as Annabel's. Or more so. Dennis thinks he talks with exaggerated emphasis. Long flat vowels, a cowboy's drawl.

'You're welcome, fella. Enjoy your stay.' Dennis can't help himself from copying it ever so slightly. 'D'ya plan to be here long?'

'Just getting the feel of things,' says Herbie. 'I'm the kind-a fella who likes to keep on moving on.'

Dennis looks him up and down. The man has a deep tan, his uncovered arms look strong, although his face is comical. He has a feather in the headband that keeps his hair out of his face. Not a special one, from a gull by the look of it. Dennis would find similar lying on the local beach. Herbie is older than Dennis, five or ten years. He can see that, calculates the guest is still well short of Annabel's age. Not that she has disclosed what that is.

'I've peeled a few potatoes. Fodder for the working man. Are you hungry yet, Den?'

'I can always eat. You've figured that out by now, Annie.'

He sees Herbie look intently at him. Annabel is always Annabel; he thinks the abridgment is for his use alone. And she may call him Den, he likes no other to mess with his name.

* * *

The three hippies eat a modest meal. Corned beef from a tin with boiled potatoes and green beans. Sit together around the tiny Formica table in the cramped kitchen.

Herbie speaks about himself. Born in upstate New York, a long way from the city. When he says it, Dennis thinks it sounds unlikely: born in New York, a long way from New York. Like a drug-fuelled riddle, not that Herbie looks to be in the grip of them. Not currently. He tells Dennis a little about the circuitous route his life has taken. 'I haven't been to San Francisco,' he confirms when Dennis asks. He's not the authentic hippy he makes himself out to be, in this untravelled lad's opinion. 'Spent time on the west coast of Canada, not the US.'

Dennis continues to ask him questions and he names three different places in Canada where he has lived, glancing at Annabel each time.

'He's cool, he really is,' she says to Herbie.

Dennis infers that Herbie doubts his hippiedom, quite an insult if he is to stay in the flophouse. And what does Herbie want to do that he might not be cool about? If he wants to smoke a joint, Dennis can imagine no young person in their right mind calling the police. Not even Stephen. It isn't hurting anyone. Free and easy: everybody's inching there way towards it, Dennis at the front. If Herbie plans on sleeping with Annabel—the free-love stuff—she should discuss it with him first. Or better still, she could say no. That'd be simplest.

Herbie looks intently at his potatoes and beans. He turned down the meat, made out it was some kind of principle, or it might be the appearance. The gelatinous mush looks weird, the white and the transparent fat around the side of the dull red cuboid that Annabel extracted from the tin. Dennis smothered his slice in ketchup, has eaten it this way once or twice a week since his parents passed away.

'The truth is, friend...' Herbie holds his host's gaze as he speaks slowly. '...I'm a draft dodger.'

'First in the flophouse,' says Dennis. Straight back at him, quickly seeing why he was reluctant to explain himself. 'Croft Road has to be a better place to hangout than Vietnam. Not so much as an air rifle allowed here. That's right isn't it, Annie?'

She nods but does not speak.

Plaza Court

'It's a principle to a lot of people,' says Herbie, 'me included. But more important than that, I'm a coward. The great get-your-balls-shot-off adventure in the jungle, it doesn't do it for me, man. I kind of hate the very thought. When I was a kid, my daddy took me hunting. Drove us to Allegheny, not so far from Buffalo where we lived. Good shootin' down there....' Herbie drawls the word shooting like he's squaring off at the OK Corral. '...that can be fun, man. But I have to tell you, the fun is predicated on the certain knowledge that the moose which we go after do not possess or deploy guns, grenades or napalm. I think it's critically important that they have none of that shit. Hell, if a moose had so much as a hunting rifle, I'd let them keep Allegheny. Nothing there but trees and grass anyway, you can get that stuff anywhere. Antlers, they have antlers, might try and charge you with their funny antlers. But frankly, if the Viet Cong only had antlers I'd have hopped on the plane. Guns generally beat antlers, Dennis. If you've a gun and you can't beat a guy with antlers, that's a very poor show. If the Viet Cong only had antlers to try and butt me with, and I'd a hunting rifle, hell, I would have given it a try. If good ol' Uncle Sam said it was for the best, why would I argue. The odds would be on my side, you see. But those guys—the Vietcong, Dennis—they have guns. That's the big flaw in Nixon's plan. And the other fella before him was no better. The yellow peril has lots of guns, that has been in the news. Muchas Pistolas down Hanoi way. Not my scene, I'm afraid, man. Very, very afraid.'

'So, you don't like communists?'

'I don't know if I like them, I've never met them. If they're going to be coming at me with their antlers, I shoot them on account of that. The rough horny bits coming out of their foreheads. Not their communism, Dennis. Politics is other folk's shit; that has always been my philosophy. If they just stay home and be communist, I wouldn't shoot them. I don't shoot republicans but I can't say I'm partial to them. Won't shoot them unless they rush me with their nasty little antlers. Nixon? I'm not even shooting him, I'm dodging him. Getting myself in a different country from our psycho-crazy swivel-eyed president. The killing of the first born, that seems to be his thing with this draft and the stupid guns-versus-guns war, when guns versus antlers would provide far greater chance of success. Dodging is both a principle and a calculation, you see.'

Dennis gives him a nod. 'Good for you. I'm with you.'

'And I am principally a great big coward. A world full of cowards

The Flophouse Years

might be a better world than this one, my friend.'

'Possibly,' says Dennis, confused where this man's point ends and his joking begins. 'A lot of things take courage; I'm not entirely against it. Using it to kill, that's an abuse of courage, don't you think?'

Herbie turns aside. 'We have a deep thinker amongst us, Annabel, darling.' Then he reaches across the small table and shakes Dennis by the hand. The boy thinks only of the term of affection he used. Still wishes to talk to Annabel alone, find out where Herbie fits in. 'Now, I hear tell that you work in an old people's facility. Looking after the ageing folk.'

'I do, Herbie. Independence flats. They're pretty neat: each one is self-contained, kitchenette, bathroom, all that. We encourage the residents to look after themselves as best they can. Put in a lot of help to keep them going if they struggle. It's a good scheme.'

'Who do you work for, Dennis?'

'Dorset. For the county council.'

Herbie the hippy stares at him as if he cannot understand the simple words.

'It's a local authority scheme.'

'The government, Dennis? Do you work for the government?'

'Not exactly...sort of. The local government. It's nothing to do with Ted Heath or any of that. It's just the best employer for looking after old people. Better pay than the private care homes.'

'I see. I think that's great, Dennis. Helping people is a good thing for the most part. Do you ever think these old people...' Herbie opens out the palms of his hands, gestures as if sharing something he draws from the air around them. '...could be part of the problem? A big old part of everything that's gotten fucked up in these troublin' times.'

Dennis cracks a smile. 'Bigoted as hell, some of them,' he concedes. 'What to do about that...' As he talks, the conversation with Mrs Carmichael drops into his mind. '...some learn late. A lady today—very old, in her nineties—she learnt that Annabel is living with me. Not being married can be a big deal for old people.' Dennis feels his cheeks colour, discussing his own sleeping arrangements with a near total stranger. 'I expected disapproval but she was really cool about it. She said living together unmarried would have improved her life. A trial run with her husband would have knocked their mismatch on the head before it began. Something to that effect.'

'An old lady said that?' queries Herbie. 'Bring her down the hippy house. Never too late to take up free love.'

Plaza Court

Annabel is looking at Dennis with a furrowed brow. With concern he thinks. He wonders if she has inferred he's been bragging about bedding her, and he really hasn't. 'This is one small town,' he says. 'Everyone learns everything about everybody else. If Charmouth is becoming more broad-minded, it must be a good thing.'

Herbie has a forefinger to his lips. 'Don't tell them about the draft dodger in their midst. Their enlightenment will have its limits. That generation loved their wars. Half of my generation love this war, I'm still to convert them to my wiser cowardice.'

Dennis laughs. 'I'll not tell them about that. Or about the toking we do down here on party nights.'

Herbie nods at him, glances again at Annabel. 'And it's okay if I stay here a few days?'

'Sure, Herbie. A draft dodger will always be welcome. Every flophouse should have one.' Dennis puts a finger to his lips. Knows how to keep a secret.

* * *

A record plays—Herbie as pleased to hear Laughing Llamas as Dennis—at a volume which allows them to talk, concentrate. The three of them play Rummy, Dennis scoring. The same arithmetical skills he uses for the old people's shopping. Annabel isn't much of a card player, knows the rules but she throws away good cards, keeps ones of little value.

'I'm not a competitive person,' she says.

The other two hippies are locked in combat. While they play, Dennis and Herbie discuss other card games they enjoy, the nuances of divergent rules, the strategies required for each formulation. Dennis used to play a lot at the Bredburys' house; Mary and Stephen are both good players, Monica not bad. He has tried poker, canasta, old maid and all stops between them. Then the talk moves on to more esoteric games: shove ha'penny, craps, bagatelle. Annabel washes the pots and the guys fall into playing Klaberjass, a two-hander they both know. When she comes back into the lounge, she watches the boys. Stands and stares at their faces as they study their cards. They must remember what has been thrown down, calculate what their opponent may hold before choosing what to do on their respective turns. Concentrating like their lives depend upon it.

It is after eleven when Dennis says he is tired, work to go to tomorrow, he will go to bed. He looks searchingly at his girlfriend.

The Flophouse Years

'Herbie and I need to talk,' says Annabel.

Dennis feels leaden as he takes himself up the stairs. He is nearing six-foot tall but weighs nothing. The lead is all in his mind. The draft dodger has muscles like a boxer. Little need for the cowardice he professes. Dennis has no wish to fight him, enjoyed playing cards, and it isn't losing that has given him this angsty feeling. He fears Annabel has a connection with the man which trumps his own. The bedroom in which Dennis sleeps is not large at all. The second bedroom—to the rear of his semi-detached house—but since he cleared out half the furniture, the stuff he did not need, he finds the place more spacious than he ever did when his parents were alive. He still uses his old single bed. Annabel jokes about it, his wish to cling to her through the night, but she has stayed. Laughed, not objected. Dennis doesn't really make plans, didn't expect to share a bed. Hoped it might happen, hoped it a few times squared. Thought about doing it with quite a few girls before Annabel. Mary Bredbury in the mix, kept that one to himself. Stephen's kid sister; didn't turn sixteen until the time of his third party. A thought can feel like a real thing but it isn't quite that. He shouldn't think about Annabel downstairs with Herbie. She'll be up when the talking is done. What happens will, the secret is to roll with it.

His parents' double bed had to go. No question about that one. It left the house within a few weeks of their demise. The very first thing he arranged when he was back here after staying at his uncle's. Dennis in charge. Their bed needed to be gone from his sight forever more.

As he slips under the covers, underpants still on tonight, fearing it will be his first night alone in a week, he tries to listen to the talking downstairs. Cannot hear a word. Annabel is a noisy lover and he hears no sounds which suggest she and Herbie are up to that. And they are hippies—free love—he's supposed to grant her the option. He hopes she doesn't go for it. Dennis leaves the bed to open the door a crack. There are low voices, talking. They might be whispering in each other's arms or she might be dealing out motherly advice. She does that, although hers is contrary to anything the deceased Mrs Harris would have counselled. Eighty percent hippy, he would say. The other twenty comes from being a survivor. He and she have a lot in common: both the eighty and the twenty.

A forlorn Dennis falls asleep when his ruminations have completed their umpteenth circle, nods off an hour after curling up alone in his bed.

Plaza Court

* * *

In the dead of the night, the naked flesh which he pined for rouses him from that fitful sleep. He wraps his arms around her, hugs Annabel, feels her naked breasts squash themselves into his chest. Kisses her mouth.

'Baby, baby,' says Annabel, 'Dennis, my love, we were just talking down there. Herbie hasn't seen his family since sixty-nine.'

Annabel consoling the misplaced draft dodger, fellow American and like-minded peace-monger. It's how it should be. And everybody needs to talk, Dennis knows that. He can struggle with it a bit; Annie too, he thinks. They talk plenty but not about what they miss. Parents, a husband. He isn't sure if she misses him at all but she might. She said that she lost him, same day, same way. He told her a bit more about his loss than she did him. Or maybe he was just as vague. He has long since learnt that no amount of talking can bring about a better ending. In the early days he talked to his Auntie Jean, his Uncle Stan: completely useless, mostly just made him feel worse. It's different for Herbie, he can talk about the people waiting for him when the war is over. With Dennis, he mostly talked antlers; the rules of craps were interesting, his political spiel utterly nuts. Maybe that is what draft dodging—being on the run—does to you. From good intentions to self-absorption; Herbie's become the champion of his own crazy thoughts. Said it like he was being shot at in a foxhole, and this is only Charmouth. Annabel might have told him how safe it is here, straightened out his thinking. Dennis doesn't ask. She returns his kiss, puts a hand behind his head as they lie together, entwined once more in his childhood bed. 'You can trust me, baby,' she says.

'It's all right,' whispers Dennis. His hand rummages under the covers, pushes down his underpants. Feels where he wants to join her most intimately.

'Oh, my hungry boy,' says Annabel, as he rolls on to her hips, hugs her tightly. 'Come to Annie,' she whispers, and he thrusts himself inside her once more.

2.

He makes toast in the kitchen. Wears jeans and a T-shirt, acceptable clothing in sheltered housing, unadorned by the badges and bangles of his other code. The early shift today. He arose quietly, didn't wake

The Flophouse Years

Annabel. Her compatriot is the lighter sleeper. He was lying on the futon when Dennis passed through the open-plan lounge, looked to be sleeping. Now he walks into the kitchen where Dennis eats a quick bite. Herbie has not a stitch of clothing on him.

'Are you always up at the genius hour?' he drawls.

Dennis keeps his eyes away from the man's cock. 'Early shift, I'm afraid. Did I wake you?'

'I have an ear out all the time, man. Ready to flee at a whenever. You know how it is?'

'You're okay here, Herbert. Hippies are always flopping, so no one around here will know you're any different. That you're lying low.'

'Any of that spare?' The guest points at the toast in Dennis's hand.

'Plenty of bread,' he says pulling another slice from the open packet, putting it in the toaster. 'I have to go in five minutes.'

Herbie starts to talk about sunrise on Vancouver Island. A racoon eating from his hand when he was sleeping rough. Herbie and the animal foraged in the same dustbin. He paints a quaint picture of the creature, its masklike face, almost human in its skill at wangling food. They were both scavenging. It all sounds a bit disgusting, eating out of waste bins.

'You don't fancy putting some clothes on, do you?'

'Just the two of us, man. I'll be back under the sleeping bag once you've gone to tend the old folk.'

'Annabel might come down.'

'Like she's not seen this before,' says Herbie.

The younger man looks away. Feels another wave of the insecurity that hobbled him when first he went to bed last night. He allows Herbie time to complete the tale of Vancouver Island—sleeping in a tent in December; rain and sleet and shitting in the woods with the bears—then Dennis takes his leave. Heads for Plaza Court.

'Hang loose,' Herbie shouts from the open front door.

Dennis hopes that his neighbours are still in bed, not looking at the naked man. He hears the rattle and buzz of an electric milk-float. 'Shut the damned door,' he mutters to himself.

* * *

This is a strange working day. First off, the sleeper-in did not come down for handover. It's happened before—the no show—but almost never. He knows that a stand-in covered last night's shift, she must still be up in the sleeping-in room. Alison, who usually does Tuesdays, is on holiday. Dennis sets to work regardless; nothing much has changed is the usual handover fare.

A most private man lives in flat number eleven. Mr Dawson, an eighty-four-year-old former architect. Dennis knows the details of every occupant of these flats, has read through a lever arch file on each of them. They include social work assessments; it's all part of securing their place in so scarce a resource. He finds them interesting, insightful. Mr Dawson is one of the more independent in Plaza Court. His arrival one year ago was a puzzle to Dennis, although his social worker, Jane Taylor from the Bridport office, was insistent that the man needed this sheltered housing scheme. Mental illness—a torment that seems to be behind him—is John Dawson's Achilles heel. He can walk to the shops by himself, manage his money and cook a decent meal. Bathe himself too; looks after his own medication. They are keeping an eye out at Plaza Court, a watching brief. Jane believes his demons might return.

Mr Dawson is always courteous with Dennis. Their very first meeting felt to be at cross purposes, the new resident asking why Dennis had entered his flat. He seemed not to have understood the arrangements, primarily because he couldn't see the need. Plaza Court is a warden-plus scheme. Sheltered housing with an arm around the shoulder, is Lorraine Chadwick's neat summary. When Dennis tried to explain it to him, Mr Dawson interrupted. 'Are you a boy or a girl?' Dennis did not let the little dig rile him. Many elderly people have yet to come to terms with all that is modern. Young people doing things their way. He introduced himself more fully. 'Dennis Harris?' said the old man. 'Have you always lived in Charmouth?'

'Yes. Since I was eleven.'

'Then you must be *that* Dennis Harris. I read about you in the local paper. The national papers too, I think. Well, I don't imagine you can do anything for me.'

That was a year ago, and after the conversation Dennis talked it over with Lorraine, kept his initial drop-ins to Mr Dawson brief. When the gentleman settled—the former architect proving himself to be a talented artist, painting water colours of great skill, landscapes of a richness and variety that evidence a remarkable eye for detail—they began to relax in each other's company. And Mr Dawson was not the first resident to pronounce a negative view of Dennis based on his association with tragedy. And the boy could not be more blameless.

The Flophouse Years

At Plaza Court, Dennis has become well appreciated; he is a concerned and sensitive young man. Conscientious too. Just today he has helped nine residents for whom rising and dressing requires verbal prompts or a helping hand. Bathed Harold Marsden; successfully threaded a needle for Mrs Johnstone, whose failing eyesight prevents her from fulfilling such tasks unaided. Potatoes peeled in advance of luncheon club.

He calls in on Mr Dawson just after eleven, later than usual but the man has no pressing needs. Today Mr Dawson is still lying in his bed—pyjamaed—it is unprecedented.

'I thought you'd left me, like the others,' says the former architect.

'Who's left who?' asks Dennis.

'Every last one of them. These flats are all empty, you know?'

'No, Mr Dawson. We're all here. I've called in on pretty much everyone this morning.'

There is a total flatness to John Dawson's tone of voice while speaking rapidly. 'Very funny. You would say that, wouldn't you, long-hair. You're in on it like the rest of them. Nobody is here really. I'm not as stupid as I look, you know?'

'Now, what's the matter?' Dennis feels quite perplexed; he has always thought Mr Dawson the easiest resident to look after in Plaza Court. The man's caustic comments when Dennis first introduced himself quickly gave way to civility. Dennis complimented his watercolours, asked questions. How he does it. Mr Dawson was pleased to talk about his art, explain techniques, brushstrokes, the mixing of certain colours. Looking around the flat, Dennis sees a canvas prone on the floor. It looks as though the distressed man has stomped his foot right through it, trashed a well-captured landscape. 'You can see everybody if you want to, Mr Dawson. Come to luncheon club in an hour. I'll arrange a place for you.' Mr Dawson is one of only four out of the twenty-six occupants of Plaza Court who makes his own midday meals, doesn't come down for lunch.

'Gone to those lengths, have you? Actors in, pretend the place is running normally. You're a sneaky one, you are. Where's the petrol?'

'I'm sorry, Mr Dawson, I don't know what you're referring to.'

'Get everyone out, burn the place down. That's what they said, wasn't it?'

'Mr Dawson, no one can burn this place down. Our alarm rings in the fire station next door. It's perfect.'

'Stop being so smug. Stop acting. I know what you're up to. And I know it's all that I deserve. I'll be getting my just dessert, not that it makes it any easier to bear.'

'Mr Dawson, no one is trying to harm you.'

'They don't have to try, do they? It's been coming to me for a long time. I'm condemned and you know it.'

'Mr Dawson...' The gravity of the situation is dawning on Dennis. No point in appealing to reason; John Dawson doesn't hear it. '...I think I should call a doctor...'

'There's a phone down the corridor. I would have done that already if I thought it would do any good. This isn't a sickness. It's a bloody persecution.'

'...or Jane. I could ask Jane Taylor to come and see you.'

'She's not dead?'

Dennis feels himself go cold. What a shocking assertion. Jane is a young social worker, younger than his own girlfriend, if Annabel is still that now Herbie is on the scene. He doesn't know Jane Taylor very well but he likes her. Wears jeans to work, flowery blouses; smokes and smiles. Could be one of his tribe—a bit of a hippy—in her free time, not that he knows it for a fact. 'I'll phone her. She'll come down to see you, I'm sure she will.'

'Not if she's dead, she won't,' says Mr Dawson.

Dennis leaves the flat. Closes the door carefully, gently. Mr Dawson is not at all well. This is a first for Dennis. One or two of the ladies get confused about dates and times, call him by the name of a son faraway. They can be more than muddled up, a bit senile on occasions. Mr Dawson is sharp as a knife. His strange assertions—Dennis has petrol with which to burn down the flats—form part of a disturbing delusion. Dennis feels frightened on his behalf.

When he gets to the office it is predictably empty. Tracy is on leave and Lorraine will be coming in later, covering the evening shift. As he dials the number for Jane Taylor, the door opens and another lady walks in, not one known to Dennis although he can guess who it is. The only one who'd come in here without knocking.

'Hello, chuck,' says the woman.

She's ginger haired, a little plump. Mid-forties, his best guess. 'Diane?' says Dennis. He assumes it is the night-cover. Lorraine told him that a lady from a similar project in Weymouth had agreed to take on the extra shift. She has slept about four hours more on the premises than she's being paid for but sleep is sleep.

'Well, I'm no burglar, Dennis. Not in broad daylight.' Everybody knows Dennis Harris; he has never set eyes on Diane before.

'I'm just making a call, no worries if you need to be off.'

'I wanted to talk to you. One of the men here was funny in the night.'

'Flat eleven?'

'That's the one.'

'I'm just calling his social worker. If you'd written it in the book, I would have gone to see him first thing.'

'He's just a bit crazy, that's all. I don't see what good a social worker can do. He kept me up talking though. Gone doolally, quite funny all the stuff he kept saying. That's why I needed to sleep all morning.'

'But Diane, John Dawson is normally bright as ninepence. Cleverer than me or you. Used to be an architect.'

'You, maybe, not cleverer than me. I've never gone off my rocker.'

'Did you read his file? He's had mental illness before, looks like it's here again.'

'That explains something, I suppose. Anyhow, I don't think they can cure them when they get to his age. Nice to meet you, Dennis. I'd best leave you to it. My kids are home alone.'

Diane walks out to her car; Dennis thinks he might tell Lorraine that having her work the night has been a mistake. She's incompetent. He's wasted hours because she didn't inform him that Mr Dawson was in a state; not so much as a note on the desk. 'She has bucketloads of experience,' Lorraine had said about Diane. Yeah, yeah, yeah. Doing the wrong thing time after time adds up to nothing. Can't knock a nail in a bowl of custard.

The phone connects with the Bridport office, a receptionist tells him that Jane Taylor is not at her desk. He asks why and she says the single word, 'Visits.'

Not dead. Dennis doesn't ask but infers it from the receptionist's breezy reply.

'When will she be back in the office?'

'An hour or two. Lunchtime is what she's written in the book.'

He is pleased to hear it, leaves a message for her to telephone Plaza Court. Dennis confirms it is important. Poor Mr Dawson is in torment, he is sure Jane would wish to know. She's a professional, nothing like Diane whatever-she's-called. Custard Brains.

* * *

Dennis calls into the kitchen to see if cook needs a hand, finds she has

Plaza Court

everything under control, a hot meal in the offing.

'Thank you,' she says, it's for the potatoes he peeled before her arrival.

Back in the office, he puts up the lunchtime medication. Some residents manage their own, some do not. He puzzles over Mr Dawson. He has always been in the manage-their-own camp and now Dennis wonders if he has swallowed a tablet in weeks. The poor guy was out of his mind. Most scarily of all, he said that Jane is dead. The thought of it makes Dennis shudder; could his crazy assertion prove prophetic? The receptionist wouldn't have known if she'd been in a car wreck in the last hour or so. Not if it only happened around the time Mr Dawson suggested it. Predicted? The young man is worrying about Jane Taylor now. Then he thinks the doing of it might make him as mad as John Dawson.

Dennis walks the corridors in a stupor. Trying to think how he might alleviate John Dawson's harrowing mood. He remembers mention of an attempted suicide on his admission notes: that stuff upsets Dennis no end. He doesn't think about it from one month to the next, the thought that so talented an artist might wish to call it a day. Jane called it 'most serious attempt' in the note on his file.

He visits Mrs Carmichael's flat, knows it is her company he needs and not the other way around today. 'You here again,' she says, but it is good humoured. They talk only about the tennis; Zoe Carmichael is an avid fan. She glued herself to Wimbledon—delighting in the clarity of picture on her colour television—just a few weeks back. Dennis knows little about the sport but feigns an interest for her sake. He's a good listener. Good at it most days of the week. He doesn't want to tell her about Mr Dawson. It might alarm other residents knowing that one of their number has gone insane. It's upsetting Dennis quite a bit and he's staff.

Back in the office he looks hard at the telephone, an activity that seldom prompts it to ring. Today is an exception, he snatches the handpiece off the cradle. Quickly disappointed, it is not social worker Jane, only Lorraine Chadwick on the other end. Can he hold the fort for an extra hour? She has to take her cat to the vet and the only available appointment will make her late for work. Dennis agrees. He has no objections to speak of. He doesn't mention Mr Dawson; the deputy warden shouldn't call upon the warden's counsel while she's off duty. He hopes to have resolved things before she gets here. Not cured him of course; Dennis isn't so naïve. They should have a plan in

The Flophouse Years

place; Jane Taylor will know what's for the best. He doesn't like conceding to Lorraine's authority. Not since she's turned funny with him—or he rejected her mothering—whichever of the two has actually happened. A bit of both.

A shuffle of old people makes its way to the dining hall. He leaves the desk and goes to bring Mrs Johnstone down. He will do the same for Mr Marsden straight after. The two in wheelchairs. Tries not to rush them while fearing he may miss the phone call.

Cook is serving out a meat pie. There are two volunteer ladies in today. Quite old, retired ladies, they can carry plates. Lorraine says they are acclimatising themselves to Plaza Court in readiness for the inevitable. Said as a joke but Dennis has come to think her humour heartless.

'Thank you so much, ladies. I've office work to do today, I'm afraid,' says Dennis. Takes his plate of food down the corridor with him. It is cook's complaint about Lorraine, that she will not eat with the residents. She cannot level such a gripe at him. Dennis likes their company, always eats with the old folk. He hopes they recognise that today is an emergency not a snub. He doesn't disclose the nature of it. Don't alarm the masses. Insanity would do that, unsettle everybody. He's sure of it.

He has not been in the room two minutes when the phone rings once more. Answers with his mouth full of pie. 'Jane,' he says, 'thank God you are there.'

She stops him, slows him down. When she has understood why his speech is indistinct, the social worker advises the deputy warden to swallow his food and then speak.

He does as she asks and doing it makes him cough. He drinks some water and then talks again into the phone. Quite clearly this time. 'Mr Dawson has gone off again. We've never seen him like this before. He accused me. Thought I was going to spread petrol about and burn the flats down. But I'm not.'

'Dennis, you're worried, I can hear it in your voice. I've been through this with him before, remember. I can drop by later, and I'm going to call his consultant first. Fill him in. Will you be there all afternoon?'

Relief surges through Dennis. He has feared finding Mr Dawson swinging on a noose or on his bathroom floor, wrists cut to ribbons. Everything he hates to contemplate. She says it will be towards four o' clock before she can arrive, Dennis lets out a long sigh before saying a soft thank you.

Then Jane Taylor changes tack. 'I'll rearrange,' she says.

'How do you mean?'

'I'll put back my other appointment. Only a home help assessment, nothing that can't wait. You're right to be worried, Dennis. Poor Mr Dawson. I'll make the call straight away. See you within the hour.'

* * *

He has called in on John Dawson once more, felt a wave of trepidation before doing it. The man was sitting in his armchair, dressed in his best. Staring at the walls with an intensity that might have seen right through them.

'Not started yet?' said Mr Dawson.

He didn't check what he was referring to but Dennis thought he meant the fire. The one he won't be starting. Not ever. He asked about dinner instead, checking if Mr Dawson had eaten. The answers weren't entirely rational.

'You know a bit about poison, I expect?'

That phrase got to Dennis, made him feel upset, accused, and he was only trying to help. The man was as weird as he had been in the morning; Dennis isn't sure how to tell if he's getting better or worse. Mad is mad. Mr Dawson's tone of voice was as flat as Plaza Court's corridors and then the content went right off the scale. Nothing Dennis could say was going to bring him back. The prim and proper John Dawson of old.

'We all get what we deserve, Harris. I've got away with it long enough.'

Why he has taken this dark turn is beyond Dennis. The landscapes which John Dawson paints—even the one he destroyed at some point during the last twenty-four hours—look beautiful; he is a man of art not of murderous secrets. It's like he's misplaced who he really is.

* * *

When Jane pulls into the car park, Dennis is watching from the office window. Runs out to greet her.

'Are you all right, Dennis?'

'Yes. Just worried for Mr Dawson.'

'Shall we see him together?'

'Only if you think it best.'

The social worker wears summer clothing, a short denim skirt and a thin orange blouse. Her legs are as white as a bedsheet; the first time

The Flophouse Years

he has seen them not enclosed in jeans. Her fair hair is loose, unkempt.

As they walk up to flat number eleven, Jane tells Dennis that Mr Dawson can go to hospital if needed. 'Dr Ghosh remembers him well, still sees him at outpatients. He thought it might recur. It's often the way with this type of condition.' She pauses, Dennis's face has fallen, doesn't look reassured by the help at hand. 'He has psychotic depression. I don't think you can care for him at Plaza Court. Not until he's better.' Dennis winces, nods his head.

In the flat, Jane does most of the talking, and then she listens to Mr Dawson's description of his fears. A pessimistic prospect he seems to believe with certainty.

'Are you burning the place down, or aren't you?' he directs at Dennis.

'This young man is only looking after you, John. Not burning anything. Nothing at all.'

'Ha! That's what you would say, Jane. All on the same side, you lot.'

Mr Dawson tells them that Charmouth is deserted, Bridport too. Everybody has left, gone to the moon or thereabouts. Jane laughs but only briefly. 'I can prove it's not so,' she says. 'If you'll come with me in the car, we can drive to those places. Swan along to Dorchester while we're at it. See that they're okay up there too.'

'You can't do that. It's all deserted. And why would you help me anyway? After everything I've done? No. I've got your measure.'

Dennis wonders again what crimes Mr Dawson has committed which have brought him to this point of despair. Or do we all harbour disproportionate feelings of guilt? Might be the root of all madness. Jane Taylor doesn't pick up the theme and he thinks her wise for not doing. A Pandora's box of horrors; lid down, nail it shut. That would be Dennis's coping mechanism.

'I can and will,' says Jane. It takes a little negotiating but Mr Dawson relents. 'Do you mind if young Dennis comes along for the ride?'

'Oh, the more the merrier,' says John Dawson. Misery lives in his tone of voice, fear his all-encompassing facial expression. 'The more the merrier.'

* * *

Back on the corridor—Mr Dawson inside preparing an overnight bag, 'just in case we're caught out late,' as Jane put it to him—the social worker asks Dennis if he is able to come along, as she proposed. 'I

Plaza Court

don't want to be alone in the car with him. He really is in the weirdest state. I'm so glad you phoned me, Dennis. You take your job more seriously than many. I appreciate that.'

'I'd like to come but it'll be an hour before Lorraine gets in. I can't leave the flats unattended. It's a strict rule.'

'I'll wait,' says Jane. 'You mustn't leave them alone, of course. We'll go when Mrs Chadwick arrives. Can I use the phone, please? Cancel my other appointment. Getting him to hospital is the more important by far.'

* * *

When Lorraine comes into the office, she gives Dennis the funniest look. Head back, peering down her nose, eyes widened at the unexpected occupants of their small room. Mr Dawson is sitting on a dining chair, shirt and tie, a small suitcase beside him. He has his legs tucked under the seat on which he sits: a schoolboy sweating it out in headteachers office. Dennis is at the desk, writing up his shift in the daybook. Jane is sitting on the same desk. Her short skirt has ridden up, thigh in touching distance of his moving pen. She and Mr Dawson are talking about the architecture of St Mary's Church in Axminster. It distracts the patient sufficiently.

'Here again?' Lorraine directs at the social worker. It is not fair comment, Jane an infrequent visitor to Plaza Court.

Jane Taylor starts to fill the warden in about the situation. She words everything carefully in her client's presence. Fulsome praise for Dennis. His foresight in phoning her, for seeing the need to sort this out quickly. 'We're just taking Mr Dawson for a drive,' she confirms, giving Lorraine a knowing wink, unseen by the old man. With her hands she makes a figure aitch: hospital. Dennis gets it, he's unsure if Lorraine latches on.

'Must you sit on the desk?' says the warden.

The reprimand is a bit rich. Earlier, Dennis advised Jane that she oughtn't use Lorraine's seat or desk. 'She goes a bit mental if anyone else sits at it,' he said. Then he placed a hand over his mouth.

Mr Dawson raised his eyes at the indiscreet wording. 'She won't be in, you know. Not while I'm here. Mrs Chadwick hates me. She can't forgive me, you see.'

It brought them back to their real purpose. Jane used the phone extension on Dennis's desk to tell reception in Bridport to cancel her other visit. She left Lorraine's side of the office untouched as Dennis advised. And now that she's here, the warden seems concerned only about the proximity of the social worker to her deputy. Mr Dawson has a bag packed—waits patiently—Lorraine hasn't exchanged a word with him.

'We can't talk about it, everything is in the notes,' Dennis tells her. She is yet to learn how unwell he is, may or may not have picked up that he is hospital bound.

'You need better clothing if you're going to sit like that on desks,' Lorraine tells Jane. 'Keep yourself decent.'

The social worker shrugs.

When they go out to the car, Dennis climbs in the back beside Mr Dawson. Lorraine Chadwick has come out to see them off. 'I bet you feel like a gooseberry,' she says to him.

He laughs heartily. Seldom one to do so and this is definitely his first time today. 'Gooseberry!' he repeats. 'Feel like a gooseberry.'

'Is she always like that?' asks Jane as they are driving away.

'Like what?'

'So possessive,' she whispers, Mr Dawson still staring back at the receding flats. 'Thinks she owns you and we really weren't up to anything.' She leans her head back, releases a short laugh. 'We barely know each other.' Her voice is back to its normal pitch.

Dennis reddens at the thought which made Jane laugh. Lorraine disapproves of Annabel, reacted to Jane sitting on the desk beside him. Mrs Carmichael jokes that the warden is his jealous suitor. Forty-plus and she might be as immature as Mary Bredbury.

Mr Dawson starts laughing as if mimicking Jane. It is unclear what has prompted his amusement. Who can guess what he's made of the odd talk? Lorraine's gooseberry nonsense or Jane's analysis. He might think it integral to his own persecution, the darkest of gallows humour. Incredible that he has agreed to come on the ride, even packed a case for it. Dennis knows nothing about mental illness.

* * *

At the hospital, Dr Ghosh's secretary had everything in hand. She directed them to the Sir Walter Raleigh Ward and a junior doctor took over from there.

'Tricked me, young Jane,' said Mr Dawson, and yet there was no displeasure in his voice. He had conceded that the streets of Charmouth and Bridport were reasonably populated. 'I think they're all actors,' he said once or twice. Jane didn't get into a debate. Said they'd hurry along to Dorchester. Dennis and Jane spent a while at hospital, waited with him until the junior doctor had clerked him in. Jane and Dennis answering any questions that stumped the patient.

As she drives him back to Charmouth, Dennis asks the social worker what will happen to Mr Dawson now.

'ECT, I expect. It's the only thing that works with him.'

'I think that stuff is barbaric.' Dennis has read about it, electro-convulsive therapy. It sounds truly awful: the electric shocks scramble the patient's brain. He tries to bring to mind the nub of the article. 'It can cause memory loss,' he says.

'Better than suffering, Den.'

In her reply he hears the use of Annabel's pet name for him. Can't quite decide what he thinks of its wider application by the mini-skirted social worker. He thinks Jane has prevented a suicide—he has never heard a vision bleaker than the desolation Mr Dawson believed to have befallen Charmouth and Bridport—hates the thought of the shock treatment but doesn't argue the point.

'How old are you now, Den?' He tells her that he is nineteen and she queries if he intends working at Plaza Court forever.

'I expect so.'

'You've no loftier ambitions then?' laughs the social worker.

'I think I could do Lorraine's job in a few years.'

'You could do it now, I reckon. Why not aim higher, sunshine?'

Another nice lady is being over-familiar with him. Dennis often feels that his recent past makes half of Dorset think they are his friend, and he is genuinely close to no-one. The glances and kindly greetings which he receives with every social worker's visit to Plaza Court have led him to assume his orphaned state has been discussed up in Bridport, at the social work offices. Jane is one of the better ones. She's being more than pleasant; it's like career counselling although Dennis has no need of it. Jane is qualified and rates all that. Education and the stripe on the shoulder. Dennis just wants to help people. Been doing this job since leaving school; why change what suits him? The money is enough; hippies eschew material things. Not everything, not long-playing records or lava lamps, just all of the superfluous stuff. He concedes he may not do it forever, simply has no alternative plan. 'So long as I enjoy it, why not?'

A few miles outside Dorchester, already after six o'clock, they come to a small diner. A misplaced motorway service station marooned on the A35. Jane pulls her car into the carpark.

The Flophouse Years

'Will you get a meal with me?' she asks.

He feels a little awkward. Annabel may have cooked for him, may be seeing more of Herbie than he would have wished. Far too much if the man remained unclothed. He doesn't raise it, Jane likely unaware of his living arrangements. Beyond the fact that he has no parents waiting expectantly for him, of course. He murmurs agreement with her request.

The prices on the menu are a shock to Dennis. A newspaper of fish and chips is the only luxury his weekly wages run to: twenty-three pence, gets them from Sea Shells Fish Bar, peas included, a couple of times each month.

'I can pay for yours, Den. You're doing me a favour.'

He wonders briefly if she actually knows he's living with an older woman, wants in on the action. It seems unlikely. 'Where do you live, Jane?'

She has driven in all directions today, bringing him back to Charmouth when her office is in Bridport. She tells him that her home is up in Chard. Miles away, another county.

'Do you live on your own?'

'I share with another girl, Claire. She's a social worker too, works up in Yeovil. Somerset Social Services. How do you find living alone? You're still so young, Den.'

He would like his proper name back. Prevaricates before answering. 'I'm only on my own a bit. Run it as a flophouse. Any hippy can drop in.'

Jane laughs and he wishes she hadn't. He is deadly serious about keeping an open house. It's his only religion.

'It's true. I've got a draft dodger there now.' He's pleased with himself on saying it, quite a coup and it avoids mention of Annabel. The last thing he wants is this social worker going all Lorraine Chadwick on him. Pouring scorn on his first relationship.

'Really?'

'Yes...' As he speaks, he remembers Herbie's plea to keep his fugitive status a secret. Dennis shouldn't be boasting about it. '...well, he's gone now but he was here.' Jane looks across the table. Scrutinising him. Dennis fears being disbelieved. 'You're not with Nixon, are you? Won't be alerting the authorities.'

Jane shakes her head, her long fair hair. 'They've got it right about not fighting that stupid war. Just surprised you know a draft dodger. There's no draft on this side of the Atlantic.'

'I know some Americans. Hippies don't bother about countries or any of that. We're all people of planet Earth. Everything is shared.'

'Sure. I hope you know what you're getting yourself into?'

'What do you mean?'

'I get all the not fighting wars—agree with it—but hippies are all a bit into drugs and everything...' For a few seconds she looks into his face as if trying to gauge how to pitch whatever objection is inside her mind. '...druggies can really fall to pieces. Do themselves in with their pills and smokes, Den. I've seen it with my own eyes.'

'Jane, I've thought...' Dennis has no idea where she stands on all he believes. '...about this stuff a lot. All these drugs, they don't solve anything, and I know what you mean, they can do harm. But opening up the doors of perception—that's not my line, all the hippies say it—that's real learning. I do a job, keep myself clear of everything most of the time, but I'm not against it. Drugs are enlightening: not in themselves, they do it by giving you access to parts of your brain that you wouldn't know existed without a bit of a smoke.'

'Could be. The thing is, I've a horrible feeling our friend, John Dawson, uncovered the passageway to one of those parts of the brain. Absolute hell for him, Den. I doubt any of us are immune. That's the downside of drugs. A reason to avoid them, the chance of facing all that.'

He looks into her electric blue eyes as she faces him over the white-topped dining table. He's growing comfortable with her calling him Den, her concern. He's right and she's wrong though. He's smoked marijuana and he's okay.

'Do you believe in the free-love stuff, as well,' she asks. 'No long-term relationships, just go with who you like?'

She seemed to say it quite casually. Dennis is unsure if she is cautioning or offering. His cheeks have coloured again but he nods, mumbles out a 'Yes'. So far, he's only tried Annabel and the thought of sharing her with Herbie is freaking him out. He gets it in principle. Being possessive is bourgeoise, every hippy knows that. Dennis is hazy about exactly what bourgeoise means. Another word for possessive, most likely.

* * *

When she is dropping him off at Croft Road, on an impulse, Dennis invites Jane inside.

'Sorry, Den,' she says. 'I've agreed to go to a do at Claire's tennis club later tonight.'

'Okay,' he says with a shrug. 'I throw parties here on the first of every month. Next one is the first of September. Come when you like, stay as long as you like. Crash. Bring Claire. Or bring a boyfriend if you get lucky before the first.' He has already asked her about that and she doesn't have one. 'Everyone is a hippy at heart, Jane.' He has climbed out of the passenger seat, walked around to the driver's side. Talking through her open side window. 'It's a serious invitation,' he says, looks at her appraisingly. 'I would love you to come. You're my favourite social worker and I've come across a few.'

Jane makes a thumbs up. 'I really might,' she says. 'Love the Laughing Llamas.' He has told her his musical tastes.

Dennis leans in and kisses her momentarily on the lips. 'Free love,' he says, turns and walks into number three. He thinks what he has just done might be the coolest thing ever. If Annabel was watching, it will make her think twice about Herbert and his chest hair. Touché.

3.

Just two days before the September party—his fifth—Herbie is preparing to leave the flophouse. He has a ticket to travel on the night train to Edinburgh; a different hippy house awaits his arrival there. He expects to spend a month in Scotland.

'Gotta keep on lying low,' he says, and 'Thanks for the refuge, Harris, my friend.'

Dennis is unsure if the next house is a contact of Annabel's or someone Herbie knows in his own right. He is cooking Herbie's final meal, with a little help from Jason who will be staying tonight. Dennis feels relieved that he will finally have Annabel to himself, no old friends muddying the waters. She has been true to him, he thinks. Slept every night in his bed. Plenty of time alone with Herbie while Dennis was at Plaza Court although she was out at her own job many days. Annabel works on the nearby polytunnel farm; picking and clipping, cutting and planting. It's all cash in hand; Dennis thinks she is without permit, shouldn't really be working in Dorset, being an American.

'Farmers never bother about all that,' she told him. Said they are the same here as in California, Rhode Island or any place he cared to name. It's a law of nature: farmers do as they please.

Dennis got on okay with Herbie—on balance—he's a mean

Plaza Court

Klaberjass player. Could use some pyjamas but Dennis never raised it.

Jason has brought sausages and beans, stolen from his mother's kitchen. They have potatoes and tomatoes in the house, the latter provided gratis, courtesy of Annabel's employer. Jason is Neil's guitar buddy, although he has not brought his instrument with him this time. He has brought Helen, a girl in sixth form. The flophouse has become the number one place in Charmouth for youngsters to have sex. Nothing official but the third bedroom is pretty much designated for the purpose. Jason has used it before, two weeks earlier. A girl called Jill.

Annabel and Herbie talk intently about what he will do next. Herbie has no money to get back to Canada while thinking it a safer refuge than Britain. Trudeau can be trusted: if all the world leaders had hippy wives, it would put paid to war. It's a consensus they arrive at every time the conversation gets political. Annabel suggests Herbie should head into Europe, go south. Easier to live on little money where the sun shines longer. Winter is months away but she says England maybe as cold as Rhode Island, Scotland colder still.

In the kitchen Dennis doesn't talk to Jason. He listens closely to the conversation in the other room. Thinks Annabel is implying that she will stay here a while. He hears her tell Herbie that her job helps her to give, not just take. 'Contribute to Dennis's flophouse.'

Finally, he asks Jason where Helen has taken herself.

'Getting the room ready. A blow-up mattress to go under the sleeping bag. And she's brought candles, says they will help her get into the mood.' The girl will not lose her cherry without a few bells and whistles.

'Watch the candles, Jason. You don't want the fire brigade coming before you do.'

Jason grins. Stealing food from home is the least he can do for Dennis. 'I'll keep an eye out. It's just Helen who needs that stuff. First time and everything.'

Young people treat Dennis with a certain dignity. Never patronising and that would pretty much sum up their parents. The youngsters relish his parties, the opportunity to get drunk in a village where publicans—quite literally—know their age. The Americans are the strangers in the flophouse, the almost-hippy house that he has established. Dorset hippies are a very particular strain. And he thought himself a fraud for a time, pretending to be into free love when he was mostly only desperate to lay naked next to a woman.

The Flophouse Years

Desperate for any except Mary Bredbury, for the confusing reason that he thinks her too young, deserving of better. She was in the frame of mind for it at his last party. Mary can do better than him, not that his defect merits a warning sign. She's about twice as clever as Stephen and he got better marks in school than Dennis ever managed. Mary can do better than Dennis Harris, begat by Peter and Sally Harris. Two dumb-fucks who quit this life long before their number was up. Shoved off for Valhalla when he might have used their support a little longer. His barely finished childhood. Annabel will probably leave for Rhode Island when she's had enough of him. She liked having Herbie around, he could see that. Dennis fears he is of only limited interest. What they have in common—January the twentieth, nineteen-seventy—is the very thing they never get around to talking about. He tries to push these maudlin thoughts from his mind. She's staying for a while, that's what he's heard.

In their first days together, Annabel told Dennis how she came to know his address, learnt that he kept a hippy house. A girl advised her of the details. Another mystery girl to Dennis, somebody called Daisy who lives in London. He's never been. So many people know about him and his past. The thinnest little sliver of it: a day in January. 'She might come by,' Annabel told him. It has not happened in August.

Annabel is a survivor. Once an adherent of the same religion—clique of off-the-scale crazies—that his parents belonged to. The teenage Dennis Harris felt allegiance to it before distinctly changing his mind. Seeing the ordinary light of day. That Annabel changed her mind is obvious. She's a hippy now. Never shared the precise arc of her conversion. 'It's painful to talk about,' she said when, on their third night together he was telling her his story. Tears in his eyes, so agonising it may be unhelpful to dredge it up, although he briefly shared the memories she cannot.

'We're ready to serve out,' says Jason.

'Food's up,' shouts Dennis.

The two Americans come into the kitchen. Herbie will not eat sausage, takes his vegetarianism all the way to his stomach. 'I'll have one of his,' says Annabel.

Jason has nipped upstairs to fetch Helen. She comes to the table but seems uncomfortable eating with the others, head down looking only at her plate.

'A shame you're going to miss the party,' says Dennis to Herbie.

'I hope you get a great turn out, man. I worry about that stuff, you know. Can't stick around if the world and his wife are dropping in. Always a few fascists in that combo.'

'I wrote to Daisy, Dennis. Asked her to come this weekend. In time for the party.' He looks at his girlfriend, still no clearer about who Daisy is, however much the girl knows about him, his past and current lifestyle. 'She's not written back but she has the address. Might just show.'

4.

Dennis has agreed to work the early shift on the Friday. Friday the first of September. He usually takes party day off but Lorraine Chadwick is in hospital, an operation to be performed upon her. A lady's complaint and so he has been spared the details. Dennis will finish at four; Tracy will relieve him at that time and Annabel has promised to do all the preparation for the evening's party. Mostly just putting breakable things into secure cupboards. Clearing the floorspace in his parents' old room. That's where floppers sleep.

The shift is all going to plan when the ambulance pulls up. He knew that it would be coming and still Dennis feels a tightening in his stomach. Mr Dawson is back. The ward sister in Dorchester advised Dennis that he has recovered. He took the telephone call at the start of his shift—eight in the morning—only nurses and care assistants at work. His return to Plaza Court has come around far sooner than Jane Taylor predicted, and she told him that she's a born optimist.

'Is he back to his old self?' asked Dennis of the ward sister.

She couldn't answer that, never acquainted with the Mr Dawson of old. 'He doesn't wish to stay and we've no right to keep him. The treatment has worked.'

Dennis swallowed hard before replying to that. Treatment he would not have prescribed but if Mr Dawson is better, then he is grateful for the outcome. 'Can he care for himself?'

'Not too bad,' said the nurse, 'and you're paid to look after him anyhow.'

That stung. Dennis wants to look after people, likes to. He has no psychiatric training, worries that Mr Dawson may once more accuse him, unfairly imply he is of ill intent. Petrol.

As soon as it reached nine o'clock, he phoned Jane. 'Is it about your party?' she asked on picking up the call. He explained that it was not, that Mr Dawson is returning. She promised to call in and see him later today, told him that she has a full diary but will pop into Plaza Court at the beginning of the evening. She'll head on down to his party afterwards. Dennis was pleased to hear that. His impromptu kiss might have been a misjudgement, at least it hasn't caused any ructions. And if Jane brings a boyfriend, he'll give the guy a wide berth.

Mr Dawson steps down from the ambulance and laughs. 'Lovely Charmouth weather,' he declares as Dennis takes his arm to guide him to the door through pelting rain. Once inside, Dennis helps him out of his coat. 'So good to see you,' says the returnee. 'What was your name again?'

He looks well but he isn't right. Closely shaven, thin hair combed neatly into place, shirt and tie. His old smart self but there are changes. When Mr Dawson talks it is slower, a slight stammer evident. Dennis spends time with him, settling him. He has forgotten his own flat number. The poor old guy seems flustered, talks about Plaza Court like it is his old house. 'I'll go upstairs later.' His cheerful mood never dips and that's good to note. 'I've always lived alone,' he tells Dennis. 'The nurses mean well, it's just that hospital wards and I don't suit each other.'

'Soon get you painting again,' says Dennis.

'Oh, I did all those when I was younger. I don't think I have the patience for it these days.' He says it breezily enough. The electric shocks seem to have flushed away the depression. The collateral damage worries Dennis: what are we if half our thoughts are culled? Even if it's the most despairing of thoughts, they are still a part of who we are. He gets a few miserable notions running around his own head, won't be trying on the ten-thousand-volt hat.

In Mrs Carmichael's flat, she too seems unusually tired. 'Summer is over,' she tells him. He thinks not. He is to host his last party of summer this evening with or without the blustery rain. He chats to her a little but she is down in the dumps. When he sees that she has failed to prepare any lunch, Dennis asks her if she would like to come into the luncheon club. 'They don't want me there,' she says. Momentarily he worries that she is suffering the same delusions that Mr Dawson has just put behind him. Had blown from his brain at some cost. 'Many in the dining room think me stuck-up, Dennis. Think it because I used to be. I don't expect you would have liked me back when I was that way. That's the problem with being known for so long, staying in the same small town. One isn't allowed to change.'

Plaza Court

'I can just bring a dinner up to your flat, Zoe. No need to mingle if you don't wish to. You will still have to pay for it though, I'm afraid.'

She confirms that money is not a problem. 'You are a sweet boy,' she adds. He should take that as a good sign, a normal comment. Tries not to let show his dislike of the term. Cool and sweet are poles apart in his mind.

When he returns a little later bearing fish and mashed potatoes, she seems confused, may have forgotten what she had agreed to. He returns at two-thirty to collect the plate. Zoe Carmichael has eaten nothing. Dennis doesn't mention the money. Cannot charge her for food uneaten. Records in the handover book only that she is not herself.

* * *

When he arrives back at the flophouse several older hippies who he has never met before have already arrived. They are in the lounge talking about Herbie although they all sound English to his ear. A few Americanisms dropped in but that's just hippy-speak. Nine or ten authentic longhairs, headbands and beads: it's a good haul. Annabel is the well-connected one; her phone calls—not his flyers—have drawn the high-class hippies to Charmouth.

He seeks out Annabel who is in the kitchen, then re-enters the lounge with her. One of the hippies plays acoustic guitar. He had seen her when he arrived. Thought her clothing odd when he first saw it without looking closely. Now that he stops to listen to her playing, he can see that she wears a see-through waterproof although she is seated in the lounge, a thin kagoule that could double as a shower curtain. The translucent material shows what is beneath: skin, breasts, nothing that comes from a clothes shop. Beneath the odd rainwear, her legs are bare. No shoes upon her feet. The guitar covers a little but it is only a well-crafted plank of wood. When she leans back, so ridden up is the waterproof, he thinks he sees the hair between her legs. Dennis wonders if she intends to stay like this when all the revellers have arrived. Half tend to be school age, sixth formers. They will be impressed but might blab to their mothers. A snatch of snatch, it's another first for the flophouse. He wants to laugh—all are welcome to his parties—hadn't reckoned on nudists before today. The girl fingerpicks a quiet rendition of the snappy song Ronson Johnson currently has riding up the charts. Getting a lot of air play. She sings it well, a voice which holds the long notes.

All the days we had together
Will never add up to forever
A year, a week, or just an hour
Time plucked like a pretty flower
For me and you, you and me
Another day has dawned

Dennis mouths the words without thinking about them; the girl's breasts sit upon the body of the guitar, wrapped in nothing that hides them. It could be cellophane, so thin is her funny choice of clothing. He looks nowhere else for a few seconds, then consciously turns away. He can't say he was well brought up but even Dennis knows staring at titties is bad form.

As she finishes, he leads the applause then stops as the room joins in, takes a hold of Annabel's hand. 'I need to change clothes. You too, right?' He pulls her up from the floor she sits cross-legged upon. She is shaking her head but lets him lead her up to the bedroom they share. 'Who is that?' he asks as he is pushing the door closed.

'Not comfortable with Daisy's natural guitar style?' A little grin spreads across Annabel's face.

'That's her?'

'My friend, Daisy. Yes, that's her.'

'I don't know her. I thought she told you where I lived?'

'You don't know her, Dennis. She just followed the news story. Knows a bit about a quite a few survivors. Would you like me to have a word, suggest she put on more clothes?'

'No!' He says it more sharply than intended. 'It's cool. People hang however they choose in the flophouse.' Dennis prefers her nudity to Herbies, keeps quiet about that. 'The survivor thing…God, none of that talk tonight. It's party night—first of the month—I've had a tough day at work…'

Dennis has been stroking Annabel's arms as they speak, a hand to her waist. Now he pushes her gently to the wall, hips to hips, hands under the back of her skirt.

'Feeling this way, are you?'

He replies by clamping his mouth upon hers, forefinger and thumb tugging at her knickers. The door is closed, the keep-out sign already sellotaped to it. He and she couple, Annabel standing with her back to the wall. Quickly, not roughly. Dennis is never that.

'I hope that was me, not Daisy,' she says as he clings to her, spent.

Plaza Court

'You, Annabel, only you,' he whispers. 'I used to dream I would get lucky on party night. One month ago, you came to my bed. I love you.'

'And there's little old me thinking you got horny because one of my young friends is hanging free and easy in your living room.'

* * *

The house pulsates to the dreamy sound, Laughing Llamas of course. Speakers up at nine, he can almost taste the bass. The youth of Charmouth drink beer from paper cups. There are more full-blown hippies in the flophouse than have ever before descended upon this seaside resort. Neil and Jason try to talk guitar to Daisy. Talk about which chords she likes; does she think it important to include the G base when holding down the C chord. They talk nonsense which enables them to look at her breasts. Jason's girl, Helen, is moochjng around the kitchen. Dennis has noticed that the girls have only limited interest in Daisy. And a boyfriend who deserts her for the first near-naked hippy he stumbles across must be a poor catch. Dennis wanders from lounge to kitchen and back again, seeking out Annabel. Trying to be less obvious in his perusal of the nude.

The snare drum ensnares. Dennis hopes to be the most laid back of hosts. He prepared nothing, Annabel and the hippies did that. He had sex before opening a beer. An order of play he resolves to adopt for all future parties. Sex is actually better than pot, more natural. The doorbell rings. Never locked on party night, probably even left ajar. Everyone is welcome, especially now Lorraine Chadwick is tucked away in hospital. Whoever rung the bell could just as easily have walked in.

Dennis goes to answer, Annabel following behind. A young woman in a black skirt and white blouse stands in front of them. Short black hair neatly in place, a boy's style framing the most girlish of faces. He thinks she looks like a pretty secretary, or an attendee at bible study. Could be a girl from a couple of decades ago but for time travel being only make-believe. Might stand out more than Daisy at this bohemian gathering. He glances at Annabel, she shrugs. 'Hello,' he says, 'have you come to the party?'

Why wouldn't she, the flyers don't specify a dress code. Long hair, short hair. Anything goes, a hippy in the buff has set the pace.

'If I may,' says the girl. 'I think I'm expected.' Then she stretches out a hand, indicates a wish to shake his with hers as squares do the world over. 'I'm Claire.'

The Flophouse Years

Not a Claire who Dennis can bring to mind, the expression on his face might reveal it to her. He takes the hand, pulls her in. 'Raining out there,' he says, although it is only sea mist. Before letting go of her hand, he leans in and kisses her on the cheek. 'We're a friendly lot. There are beers and cider in the kitchen.' He likes her clothing, the contrast. 'Do you know anyone here?'

'No. My friend was invited; she'll be here in a little while.'

As they go across the open-plan lounge, Daisy is standing, guitar against the sidewall. She crosses their path on the way to the kitchen. Nothing covering her that isn't translucent. Her thick head of dark hair looks zany falling upon her funny plastic sheet. Boobs bobbling as she walks, a small forest between her legs. Every boy's head has turned her way.

'Just fixing myself a drink,' she says.

'We don't all have your tasteful dress sense,' Annabel tells the new arrival.

'She looks lovely,' says Claire. 'Am I to strip similarly later?'

Dennis laughs, pot-free, her comment truly unexpected. He is unsure if the girl is taking a rise or embracing their ways. 'Everything is free and easy,' he tells her. 'No one has to do anything and no one will stop you from doing what you please.'

As they talk, Stephen comes into the party from the street. 'Have you seen my sister? There is annoyance, even desperation, in his voice.

'I've not but she could be here, mate.' Dennis has no idea what Mary has told Stephen about the party one month ago. She told Monica too much when they met on the beach. 'We don't announce them coming in, Stephen. It's a rave-up, not a debutantes' ball.'

His erstwhile friend glares at him.

'Have a drink, Stephen,' says Annabel, gesturing the kitchen.

As they look through the door into that room, they see the smartly dressed newcomer, Claire, talking to the girl whose bottom now beams at them from within her rainwear. Dennis thinks this is his best party yet. And he got first-time laid at the last one. If he can make up with Mary, life will be perfect.

* * *

The rain is coming down heavily outside, nobody drinking beer or mucking about in the garden at this party. Indoors, it's all going mental. Party mental, some good, some less so. Mary was upstairs all along—in the bedroom Jason and Helen used two nights ago—Mary

Plaza Court

doing something or other with Gordon Stickland. It's preying on Dennis's mind that air-rifle boy might have done to her what he had the decency not to. If she was too young just one month ago, then by his reckoning, she still is. Surely, he thinks, Mary would not let that big moron be her first. He's thought about Mary, how she looks—the bedroom window strip show—quite a bit more than he really should have. Might be his only secret from Annabel. She's too young and too precious. Dennis tells himself he did the right thing by going with an older hippy. Mary is too good for him. And she must be about a million times too good for Stickland. He even worries she is doing it to pay him back. Going into his boxroom with that boy at this party. Mary must know he and Stephen both hated Gordon at school. He was a bully—the pair of them easy fodder—days long gone. Gordon works for the council, same employer as Dennis, but he's on the bin rounds. Hasn't the aptitude to work with old people; pointing an air rifle and shouting bang isn't care. Gordon doesn't help anyone, just humps bins from kerbside up to the rear of a lorry. Perhaps they were only talking up in the little bedroom—no bed in there, Jason and Helen used a blow-up—but Gordon is crap at that. At conversation.

* * *

Dennis sits cross-legged on the floor of the lounge, next to Daisy. He was there first, she came and sat next to him, attracted most likely by the bong pipe they are passing round. Bubble-bong, Major has been upstaged. These hippies have all the accruements. Before she sat, Daisy took her plastic rainwear off. 'Too hot in this,' she said, must have turned the temperature up for all the fellas in the room. Dennis feels his face burning up sitting next to her. Trying not to look. The pipe arrives at Daisy first and she holds it so that hands and bong cover her crotch. Draws deeply from the tube, a plastic curly pipe covered in a thin film of green and red fur. 'Top shisha,' she says, smoke escaping her mouth with the words. Dennis reaches across to take the pipe, then pulls his hands away realising how near to her private parts they are. 'Don't be shy,' she says, moving her cupped hands a couple of inches nearer.

'Thanks.' His hands graze naked flesh, a bare inner thigh, as he lifts the pipe off her, once more uncovering what Daisy seems happier to show the world than most girls. Annabel is not in the room but he feels Mary's eyes upon him like a hawk. She is sitting on the floor beneath the front window, Gordon's arm across her shoulders. Dennis tries not to look at her or at Daisy. He is mostly observing Jane Taylor. Jane is on the other futon with her friend, Claire Rawlings. They live together; Jane wears jeans and a T-shirt which contrast with her friend's secretary look. Arms around each other. Kissing. He has told each of them that anything goes, and tonight it certainly does. Dennis is reappraising Jane. Wonders why she invited him to share a meal a couple of weeks back but that was probably the motherly concern he's always getting. Little orphan Dennis. He hasn't spoken to her yet, not at length. Chatted a bit with Claire before Jane turned up, before he learnt who her expected friend was. Claire told him that she didn't generally go to hippy parties. Loved the music, very happy to give it a try. He should have put two and two together when she said there was a tennis club dinner which she was glad to be missing. 'Some of the younger ladies wear short skirts but your friend takes it further and that is a delight to see.' At the time, he thought it sarcasm, now he has surmised that she likes looking at ladies' muffs as much as Neil and Jason do. And Dennis Harris. He tries to be discreet. Tries and fails if Mary's glare means anything.

When Jane gives the necking a break, Dennis catches her eye. With a vague hand gesture, he indicates that he would like to talk. Hopes that is what he has indicated, the pot is snaking into his brain. Everything can get hazy at this time of a party.

Jane takes herself off the futon, kneels down on the rug beside him, between Dennis and Daisy, and he is strangely glad to be separated from the other girl's naked flesh. 'You came,' he observes, although it scarcely needs his verbal confirmation.

'I called on Mr Dawson early evening, that's why Claire was here alone for so long.'

'I like her. You've got a nice girlfriend.'

Jane puts a finger to her lips. 'No-one knows at work. It's between you, me and the hippies, please. I think he's okay.'

'He?'

'Mr Dawson.'

'He's a shell of who he was.'

'It wears off. The effect of the ECT will wear off in time. He'll find himself again. He was just like this when it happened before. They only discharged him because he lives in extra-care housing. Beds in psychiatry are a pretty scarce resource.'

'I like Claire,' the intoxicated boy tells the social worker again, looking into her face quite intently before adding, 'and not ECT.' It might be the dope he has had. He wants to make it clear. He approves of Claire; completely cool about girls loving girls. The shock treatment won't be getting his vote.

'It is only like the stuff you're smoking, Dennis. Wears off. Best not overdone.'

He puts a hand on Jane's thigh, upon her jeans as she sits in the cross-legged posture adopted by all these hippies. His thoughts are racing. 'Free and easy,' he says, nuzzling up against her, hand on jaw turning her into him and kissing her lips as Claire was doing just a couple of minutes earlier.

She barely stops him but withdraws at the first opportunity. 'You're sweet but that's really not my thing,' says Jane.

'Just testing,' says Dennis, and he giggles.

'Oh, me too,' says Daisy, the freest and easiest in the room, in Charmouth. Dorset-wide would be a safe bet. She leans across Jane, a hand on her other knee and proceeds to kiss her upon the mouth.

Jane slides herself backwards, pulls away. 'Sorry honey,' she says and rises from the floor, takes to the futon to sit with Claire once more.

'That didn't go to plan,' says giggling Dennis to the naked girl.

Daisy seems as high as he is, pushes him gently backwards and rolls on top of him. Then she kneels upright, Dennis beneath her. 'This is for throwing the best party,' she says.

Dennis tries to look around the half-lit room from his prone position. He wonders if he has embarrassed himself in front of Jane Taylor. It seems likely. Then he sees Mary, away by the record player, cross-legged too, Gordon Stickland by her side. He glances at Daisy's smiling face, hair and boobs, then back at Mary. She is looking deathly daggers at him. The harsh judgement of a bright kid who recently fancied him, that's what he guesses. Poor mixed-up Mary threw a bag of flour at him in the bargain. Maybe this free and easy malarkey gets everyone knotted up some of the time. Dennis never warmed to Herbie. He glances at Jane. Her brow is furrowed as if querying him, none of the hatred that he saw in Mary's eyes. Perhaps he went too far, wouldn't have kissed her if it was a boyfriend away on the sofa.

When the music stops, he excuses himself from beneath the nude girl, goes to the record player. A mound of vinyl beside it, very few still in their sleeves. From the centre label alone Dennis can pick out his favourite Llamas' album. Puts it on the turntable. Side two.

Drive in crazy darkness, gotta get away from this town

Where no one's to be trusted, where there's no love to be found
These feelings running through me, they will never let me rest
Drive in crazy darkness, from the east coast to the west

He slides down next to Mary. 'Hey,' he says.

She turns from him to Gordon. Her bin-man beau has fallen asleep leaning against the wall.

'Hey, Mary,' he tries again.

She leans into him, speaks close to his ear so only Dennis can hear. 'Disgusting. Your parties are disgusting with girls showing their fannies.'

'We're free and easy. It's just our way.'

'Disgusting. That's why Stephen has gone home. I should have gone too but Gordon wanted to stay.'

'Is he your boyfriend then?'

'He's a normal boyfriend. Not a disgusting one.'

He senses that Mary is not as drunk as she was one month ago, cannot decide if that's good or bad. 'Hey,' he tries, 'I'm not one for stripping off but we never stop anyone from doing whatever they think is funky.'

'You rolled around with her...'

'She was being playful...'

'...being disgusting...'

'...well, what did you do upstairs with him?' Dennis gestures the snoring ape beside her.

'Just shut up,' says Mary, hanging her head, letting her fair hair cover her eyes. He can see tears tracking down her cheeks.

Dennis puts a hand on hers. 'I'm sorry Mary. Come and see me alone. We'll talk. I am sorry.'

She glares at him through tears. 'You've an old-lady lover now. Sleeping with your mummy. You can't just change your mind and decide you want me.'

Annabel is in the room, glancing at her young lover talking quietly to Mary. The bass guitar hums a hell of a riff as the Laughing Llamas tell everybody how it is.

Drive in crazy darkness, got my foot down on the gas
Fast as the tin can rattle along, I'm out of here at last

Plaza Court

While all my friends and family drink and dance and feast
I'll drive in crazy darkness, from the west coast to the east

Annabel comes up to them, puts a hand on sleeping Gordon, gently shaking his shoulder. The boy looks up. 'I think you need to take Mary home, fella,' she tells him.

Mary hears and narrows her eyes at Dennis, a flash of anger for this woman's interference. Each knows who the other is, Dennis has never seen Mary and Annabel speak a word to each other.

'Come on then, Mary,' says Gordon. Stupid, obedient Gordon.

They stand up, he takes her hand in his. 'Thanks for having us round, Dennis,' he says, then points at Daisy, catches her eye. 'You're a tinker. Really, really wild. I like it.'

As the couple leave there is pain in the young girl's body-language, each step placed upon the floor as if tramping out a fire. Her upset seems to have passed the thick lad by; not so much as a comforting arm. Gordon drank beer, ogled Daisy, had his first pull on a bong pipe. And a little time alone with Mary in the upstairs room, that's the one Dennis can't stop thinking about.

* * *

'What's happening downstairs? asks Dennis as they enter his bedroom together. Since Mary left, he had three or four more pulls on the bong pipe. All the locals went home except Jason and Helen who are back in the neighbouring box room. Jason seems to have staked a claim to it. The hippies, the bong and the spinning records remain in the lounge.

'Having an orgy if I know that lot,' says Annabel.

'And we're not joining in?'

'Having our own. Just the two of us. More select I would say, Denny.' She pushes him down on the bed, begins to unbuckle his belt for him, then pulls at his jeans. He laughs hysterically, lifts her blouse to put hands upon her naked flesh. Pot is coursing through his system, this willing lady plenty for young Dennis.

5.

Two weeks after the party, Dennis chances to be on duty when Jane Taylor comes down to Plaza Court, another visit to John Dawson.

Monitoring how he is progressing outside the psychiatric hospital.

'You again,' says Lorraine Chadwick. Her odd greeting prompts Jane to look enquiringly at Dennis.

'Hi, Jane,' he says. 'You were right.'

'I was? Right about what?'

'He's much better now. I don't like the sound of the shock treatment but Mr Dawson says it's done him the world of good.'

'I don't like the sound of the shock treatment,' parrots Lorraine. 'Our Dennis is a bit soft in the head, Jane. Wants the cure without the medicine. Does most of his living shy of the real world. What he says is right enough. Mr Dawson is as good as new.'

'It sounds horrible, I know,' says Jane, directing her comments towards Dennis alone. 'They get an anaesthetic so they don't feel the shock when it's happening. Whatever it does to the brain, it seems to work, and I'm grateful for that. Has his memory come back?'

'Pretty much. Come and meet him.'

Dennis stands, walks from office to corridor, Jane Taylor follows him.

'Honestly Dennis,' says Lorraine, 'she can find number eleven on her own. She's a qualified social worker for Christ's sake.'

When they have walked up the corridor far enough that his manager cannot hear, he says quietly, 'Sorry if I was out of order the other week, Jane. Really sorry.'

She turns her face to his and smiles. 'You were fine. I enjoyed the party. We're discreet with each other, yeah? You're a cool kid.'

They hear a cough and both look around. Lorraine is peering from her office doorway, looking at the two talking quietly, heads leaning into each other as they walk.

'I don't know how you put up with her,' whispers Jane. 'Think about doing a few night classes or something, Dennis. Do whatever it takes to get yourself qualified. You should aspire to my job, not hers. Wardens turn slowly into witches, it's strange but true. Aim higher, my friend.'

He grins to himself. He had a tiny little crush on Lorraine Chadwick when he was sixteen, Plaza Court his first ever job and a brilliant refuge from his displeasing home life. And Lorraine was so good about the tragedy. Kept his job open for eleven weeks while he wasn't working. In no fit state to do so. Smoothed his return. Tried to counsel him about what had gone on but Dennis was having none of that. A hug a shift; he liked those back when he was too feeble to seek out better. He knows the old bat must feel rejected by him, and he is no longer the kid he was back then. Growing into the world, finding a place. Keeper of a rock-and-roll flophouse, a hippy lover. Jane's social work idea is interesting. He's not sure that he's bright enough and there is no social work office in Charmouth. The future can't be pinned down. If it's going to happen it probably will. Most hippies are butterflies, flit from one thing to another. Dennis can't picture leaving Plaza Court, it gave his life certainty when all else was slipping away. He only gets off his head on party night; it's work that pays the bills, keeps the flophouse ticking over. He should think about what Jane says anyway. She criticises hippies, then sort of is one. Smoking grass is not obligatory.

* * *

In the evening, Jane long gone and Lorraine too, with only an hour to go before the sleeper-in comes to relieve him, on an impulse Dennis calls on Mrs Carmichael. He knocks on the door, awaits her reply. She can still put herself to bed, although she was not in good spirits when he did his earlier round. Tears. There is no reply. He listens and listens without opening the door, sometimes he can hear the snoring or even the breathing of his charges in that other realm. No sound comes from this flat tonight, none that reaches Dennis.

Tentatively he turns his key in the front door, enters the bedsitting room. The bed is empty, the room in gloom although the curtains are open. They let in moonlight. By the door of the alcove kitchen, Mrs Carmichael is slumped on the ground, dressed in her finest skirt suit, not the dressing gown she was already in when he called just two hours earlier.

'Zoe,' he says, concern flooding him. He goes to her, bends down, touches her shoulder lightly. Cannot really understand what has happened to her. She is warm but not responding to his words. He leans in trying to look at her blank eyes, believes that he can feel her breath upon his cheek. 'Zoe,' he says, 'let me get you on the bed. Fetch the doctor.'

She makes a noise, not words but a deliberate exhalation; mouth twisting the sound without managing a clear meaning. With an arm behind her back and another under her legs, Dennis lifts Zoe Carmichael's fragile body from the floor. Very cautiously, he steps to the bed and lowers the frail old lady down upon it. As he does it, he can see her face in the light of the full moon. Her lower lip droops horribly. He knows this symptom. At the weekly night classes which he attended for his first two years in the job, they went over it time and again. Mostly during tea break. The auxiliary nurses in the cottage hospital comparing all the strokes that they had been witness to. Pulling their own mouths out of shape in imitation. Plaza Court has had stroke victims; Dennis feels the deepest despair that Zoe Carmichael should be the first felled by one while he is on shift. 'I need to call the doctor, the ambulance,' he says, looking into her wise face. The light in her eyes no longer shining back at him. They are open—a flicker of activity—but the zest has left. 'I need to get you some help, Zoe.'

'Thank you, David,' she says. 'I love you.' The clarity of her diction surprises him. His name is Dennis but Zoe Carmichael has spoken frequently of her long-deceased son.

In the office he makes the call. Tells the operator the exact flat number to come to, says he must go back to her. There will be no one with Zoe Carmichael if he does not. As he puts the phone down, he finds himself crying, not his typical state. The phrase, no one with Zoe Carmichael, upset him. A greater disturbance than he can explain.

Back in the flat she is lying on the bed, curled up like a question mark, her bent spine long making this the pose she holds upon a mattress. Mrs Carmichael's eyes are not open but he fears it is not sleep which draws her down. Dennis talks: he tells her that Nastase should have won Wimbledon. He knows nothing about tennis but it was her contention those few short weeks ago. He wants her attention, hopes to keep her in the room. When he puts his head close to the frail lady's mouth, he can still feel her breath. She does not acknowledge him. He keeps talking, tennis mostly. Says there is always next year but he does not believe it himself.

While he is trying to feel her breath, putting his cheek close to her mouth, she moves an arm, fingers grasp his long hair. At that moment, the door which he had left unlocked opens, two ambulance men walk in just as he is trying to extract himself from her tangled fingers. It must be an odd sight.

'This the patient?' says one.

'She's had a stroke,' he says, finally able to bring his head up.

'Are you her son...grandson?'

'Deputy Warden of Plaza Court,' he says.

'Really?'

He has had this reaction before. He isn't the only long-haired

Plaza Court

council worker but they are a persecuted minority.

'And what were you doing with your head on her chest, young man?'

'Listening to her breathing. She took hold of my hair; not spoken for nearly thirty minutes.'

The ambulance crew draw close to the bed. 'Stand back,' says the taller of the pair, and Dennis obeys.

They examine her quickly, then one of the crew puts a firm hand on her forehead, pulls back the skin with his thumb so that her eye opens, does the same one eye along.

'Dead. Passed away, I'm afraid.'

'She took hold of my hair...'

'Maybe. She's warm, only just gone.'

Dennis puts a hand to his mouth. Poor Mrs Carmichael. Released. Back with her son for the first time in fifty years. He is not turning sentimental, only sinking under the weight of our certain mortality. We are none of us here long enough.

* * *

When he arrives back at Croft Road, almost midnight—a doctor certifying the death and an undertaker removing the body before he left; a phone call to a niece who never visits—he finds Annabel sitting in the lounge with another lady. Not somebody he knows.

'Teri will be crashing here,' she says. He nods assent and only then does Annabel seem to register his haunted appearance. 'You look done for. What's the matter, Den?'

He explains that someone died. He has spoken to her of Mrs Carmichael but she does not seem to register the difference between the many old ladies whose tales and foibles he relays. When he says, 'Ninety-one, that was her age,' she laughs nervously.

'What do you guys say? A good innings.'

'I don't know if it was good or not. It was an innings. I think she deserved better than whatever was served up. A lifetime grieving a lost son.' Annabel shakes her head; it looks like sympathy to Dennis. Must see that Zoe had a hard life.

Shortly after this exchange they go up to bed. In their room Annabel tells him Teri also works on the polytunnel farm, explains her situation. 'Man trouble. Teri's husband is a violent bastard. Beats her. I think she needs to get away from Charmouth altogether. Out of his reach. I'll work on that tomorrow.'

The Flophouse Years

He can see the sense in Annabel's plan. Teri's innings sounds like a crock of shit so far. In the narrow single mattress, he finds himself turning his back, trying to sleep as alone as he is able. Annabel means well but she isn't concerned about the elderly ladies and gents who occupy his day, a larger portion of his thoughts than he lets the world see. Perhaps it is death she wants to avoid. He thinks Annabel is as troubled by it as he. She once had a husband, another life in Providence, Rhode Island. She has told him only a little. Her husband is as dead as his parents. Not shared much beyond the similarity in the manner of their passing. The twentieth of January, nineteen-seventy. A day worth not thinking about.

6.

The October party has been and gone. A good one, although he got nervous when Annabel dropped acid. Everybody kept their clothes on. Teri was there with a man. Dennis asked Annabel if he was the roughhouse, the bastard, but she said not. 'This one put the other one in hospital.' He puzzled over that: didn't come out of the hippy playbook but the bastard had it coming. Then Annabel was out of it, lying on the bed talking to herself, putting a hand in front of her face and laughing. Drugs are mostly cool but she looked demented when she was tripping.

Now, the Saturday after, Mary has called round out of the blue. Stephen is back in Southampton, back at university where he studies biology day and night, and she never came to the most recent party. With or without Gordon the binman.

'Come in,' he says.

'Nuh. Come and walk on the beach with me.'

Annabel is hovering and he looks to her, she nods assent. Annabel sometimes says he would be better off with Mary. With a girl his own age. Sometimes—and only those times when he is thinking of Mary Bredbury—he wonders if she's right.

Dennis puts on shoes and the pair head out, walk in silence until they have crossed the main road.

'I think I'm finally over you,' she says.

Dennis is not sure what he feels about that. A bit of everything. 'You look terrific, by the way.'

She ignores his ill-timed comment. Mary is in a summer dress, although the weather is distinctly autumnal. She has a short denim

Plaza Court

jacket to keep herself warm. The floral red below shows her narrow waistline.

'I don't know what I ever saw in you. Always thought you were cooler than Stephen but that's nothing really. That Jack Russell on a lead is actually cooler than him.' She points ahead, dog straining at a leash.

'It probably is. I'm glad you're not mad at me, Mary.'

'I never said I wasn't mad at you. I said I'm over you. I understand that after everything that's happened...after your mother...you might need a relationship with someone like you've picked. You hung around my mum a lot after it happened. Why you start having sex with your mother...well...that's why I'm taking psychology in school—probably—but it's mad. You're mad, Dennis.'

He hangs his head down, long hair falling forward. 'I don't see it like that. I might have been a fool to let you down. I was scared, Mary. Taking advantage of a drunk teenager isn't my thing. And I do care about you. Surely you know that much.'

'Then you go straight to the mummy you've lined yourself up. If I'd known she was waiting, I would never have come to your stupid party.'

'Mary, try not to get cross. I want to be your friend. What's...' He pauses, tries to gather his thoughts before speaking. '... what's going on between you and Gordon.'

For a moment she doesn't answer, simply looks aside, eyes turned away from him. 'I think he's worse than you, that one. Pretend you never saw us together, Dennis. Swear to me you won't mention him and I in the same breath ever again.'

'Sorry I asked.' Dennis sees that Mary's face has gone red in the course of this exchange. Fears Gordon took advantage in the way he would not.

'Is that it, for you? Married to your mummy now?'

'Mary, this hurts me. You know I don't believe in marriage. Never will, it's a hippy thing. Don't tie me down with paper and promises. Live for the now. But, Mary, my mum was the oddest person. Most days I think that I didn't even like her, and then again, I do think about her every single day. Annabel is older than me, she's not my mother. We're just free and easy. You saw her, cool with me coming out here with you...'

'Cool because she knows I hate you.'

'Do you, Mary? I feel only good things for you. I'm so, so sorry that I hurt you. Did I tell you...' They are walking on the sand now, trudging alongside the sea. The ripple of each incoming wave coming to rest two or three feet from the line they walk. '...about an old lady called Mrs Carmichael? Zoe Carmichael.'

'Yeah. You mentioned the name loads. I remember when you came to tea at ours after you'd come back to Charmouth. When you were first on your own in that house. I remember the name, Zoe. It's a much nicer name than Mary. I worked out that you liked her even though she was dead old. You've not started doing all the frisky sex stuff with her, have you?' He cannot stop himself from laughing and Mary does the same. She mutters, 'Granny love,' as he puts a hand on her back. A flat palm and they stop in their tracks.

'Your funny, Mary, but this is serious. Mrs Carmichael passed away. I was on shift. I couldn't stand it, another precious person leaving the shore. The thing is...' He lowers himself onto the sand, sits down in his jeans. Pats the ground next to him.

'I'm not getting this dress sandy, Dennis.'

She looks into his eyes from above, Dennis thinks she must see the sombre intent he emits. He is so pleased she called around, if only to spit a bit of venom at him. 'Sit on me,' he says. 'I'll keep my hands to myself.'

She crouches down and then turns, puts her bottom on his thigh, perches like a ventriloquist's doll. Necessity not intimacy. Both stare forwards, facing the sea, taking in the turn of the coastline running off to Weymouth, the Isle of Portland. He has a hand on her shoulder, keeping her tort posture steady.

'Zoe Carmichael had a son. Over the years she told me quite a lot about him. I can remember it all, so important to her that it's stuck with me. Born in nineteen-oh-five. Too young to be called up for the war, the first war. When he was nineteen years old—the same age I am now—the poor lad died in a motorcycle accident. Just him and the bike, nobody wore helmets back then. It wasn't done. The only time I ever saw Zoe get angry was when she told me that she never wanted him to have the stupid bike. Said her husband thought it fine. "Make a man of him," was a term she recalled him saying. And Zoe thought that was nonsense. Men never rode motorbikes at all until about twenty years before this tragic accident. It deprived her poor lad of ever being a man. Nineteen-twenty-four that happened, Mary. And when poor Mrs Carmichael had a stroke three weeks back, dying in my arms, on my shift, in my flats up there...' He gestures away behind him. '...she called me David. Not by mistake, she was never confused,

Plaza Court

not Zoe. It was hope or faith or the memory that never leaves. She liked me well enough—we got on like a house on fire actually—but I was never him. She lost who she most needed in nineteen-twenty-four and the rawness of it was still there when she passed away, September the eighteenth. This year. Close on fifty years since she lost her son. Mary, you owe me nothing, I ask for nothing. You will be in my heart for that long. And all I ever did was feel close to you. Want more for you than a boyfriend as pitiful as me.' She turns and buries her face in his shoulder. He holds her and strokes her hair, a flat palm on her fair locks. 'I'm so sorry,' he repeats. The pair of them shedding tears like coastal mist, and Dennis has no idea for whom they weep.

The Flophouse Years

Chapter Three

Jimmy Crook Shows Up

1.

He arrives by taxi, nine o'clock on the dot.

In the morning Annabel told Dennis that she had a surprise guest lined up. He thought it would be Daisy or Herbie—the second not a surprise that would quicken his pulse, and Daisy's near nude stunt was amazing but he can't remember what her face looks like, nothing about her quite as special as her sheer nerve—and then it turns out to be this guy. Astonishing. Jimmy Crook and he's wearing his trademark top hat. Pretty implausible in Dennis's book, yet here he is. The dazzling presence emerges from the back of a black cab; Crooky is on Croft Road; the coolest hippy ever to set foot in sleepy Charmouth. By an ocean's width.

The pair of them saw him only the Sunday before but that was when Jimmy Crook was on stage at the Alexandra Palace. Performing. Dennis and Annabel in the audience, just a part of the crowd. They went up to London with Thompson and his girl, Georgie. Thompson is the name that Major has started calling himself by. Thompson, once known as Pretty before becoming Major. Dennis knows of no reason for his ever-changing name. Thompson might be closer to the real thing. He and Annabel both agreed about that. The four shared a hotel room and did so for the economic prudence of it, nothing orgiastic intended or occurring on the night. In fact, there was no sex at all in the hotel room. Cost a lot for abstinence but having another couple in a neighbouring bed is the most off-putting thing. Dennis was pleased to note that Thompson and Georgie were equally chaste. Hadn't wanted to listen to them going at it all night and they have been a couple for no more than four weeks, don't live together as he and Annabel do. One year. Exactly one year in a shared bed for Dennis. Twelve months of him and Annabel.

They saw the man in the top hat—the man who has arrived at his

The Flophouse Years

party by taxi—only from the back of the auditorium. It was heaving. The London Music Festival: more than a week of the best rock music money can buy. It's not finished but they had tickets for one night only. Other nights, other bands. Which is how come this guy can be here. Join the first of August party on Croft Road. Utterly astonishing that he's here. He is out of the car but exchanging a word with the taxi driver through the open car window. The top hat looks an encumbrance for this task, bumping the top of the cab's window frame as he leans in. Then he turns and walks up the path of number three Croft Road. Jimmy Crook, bass player on every Laughing Llamas record, nineteen-sixty-seven to the present day, has come to enjoy Dennis's sixteenth party. The young hippy doesn't think life could get any better than this. Cannot. How his girlfriend has pulled off this coup is beyond him. She works on a polytunnel farm, he can imagine no strings that could tug a Llama in from there. Fancy him coming down to Charmouth. California to Dorset. Even seeing him in London seemed a bit of a dream, San Francisco being the natural habitat of all hippy bands. They rocked the Alexandra Palace. Opened with Lost on the Freeway. Dennis mouthed the words of every song. Three of them toked but Georgie doesn't like to. Jimmy Crook coming to his sixteenth party: exactly what the term mind-blowing was coined for.

Dennis keeps staring out of the front window, he doesn't go to answer the door. Plenty of other hippies do that. 'Hi, man,' and 'Crazy Darkness,' and 'We've got Moroccan shit,' they call out. Jimmy Crook flashes a peace sign, the tiniest hint of a grin invading the corners of his well-tanned face. Grainy Californian features.

Annabel is looking at Dennis looking at Jimmy.

'What's he doing here?' he whispers.

'I know some people who know some people.' She smiles, lips held together.

Dennis thought his parties were getting a toehold on the hippy trail. This is the great leap forward. When the bass player enters the lounge a troop of revellers congregate around him. A couple of excited hippies, several youngsters from Charmouth. Mary Bredbury is one, standing between Neil Sullivan and Jason Hardcastle. Neil says, 'Wow. This is really wow.' He can barely look the famous man in the face. Jason is equally awestruck, beaming like a nine-year-old given his first bike. Mary is wearing shorts—cut-off jeans, cut near the top of the thigh—and a T-shirt without bra. A summery hippy: wears it well. Dennis thinks she's just giving it a try. Never seen her dress like it

Jimmy Crook Shows Up

before.

The Llama wears sunglasses, briefly he takes them off. Gives angelic young Mary a stare. 'Nice to see you,' he drawls. Mary smiles. Cannot say a word back, tongue-tied in the lee of a rock god. The two boys, Neil and Jason, try to talk to him. It crosses Dennis's mind that Jason should tell the new arrival that Mary is off-limits. He is the boy dating her at present. Instead, these two lads mostly just repeat how amazing Crook and the Llamas are, how much they love his music. 'Far out,' says Jimmy Crook. Jason echoes the phrase back and Crook repeats it once more. 'Far out.' That seems to be the size of it. The two Charmouth boys point at the turntable and then at the air around them. The music playing when he entered the room—throughout the two minutes he has so far spent in the flophouse—is awash with bass notes played by the surprise guest.

> *She said if you talk to loud, you'll only wake the baby*
> *He said, 'Do you love me?' and she said*
> *'Maybe you're more disturbed than I am*
> *Trying to find your love in this...'*

It's a cracking song, Dennis loves it. Edgy, about prostitution if his interpretation of the lyrics is on the mark. Laughing Llamas have been the backing track for every one of Dennis's first-of-the-month parties. Perhaps that simple truth has willed this visitation. Other music makes its way onto the turntable, none close to the frequency of the band with Jimmy Crook's fingers dancing up and down the frets of the bass guitar. The Llamas are the mode, one might say, figuratively or statistically.

Jason has been dating Mary since early summer. She's been through a string of them. Sixth formers and a couple of dunces. Gordon Stickland was the worst; Dennis tries to imagine that Mary hasn't allowed any of them to do what she offered him and he chose not to—thought it wrong—one year back. She talks to him these days but not about that stuff. And whether he is kidding himself or not, with Jason there can be no pretending. Dennis knows he has been in her bedroom when her mother was at an evening prayer group. Little sister Monica spilled the beans. 'Mary is a silly free love hippy now, Dennis, it's terrible. She sneaked Jason Hardcastle into our bedroom, told me to watch TV in the lounge. Did the gubbins with him, I expect. No, I'm sure. Hardcastle grunted like a pig, you know?' Embarrassingly, Dennis actually does know, can recall swinish sounds coming through the bedroom wall when he did something similar to Helen in the flophouse. To Jill who came before Helen; to Ruthie who came after. He wishes Monica hadn't told him. Dennis has Jason down as a bit of a nob, it's a disappointing match.

'This is my girlfriend,' says Jason, pulling on Mary's hand, bringing her within inches of the top-hatted one.

'Far out,' he says. This man may have been smoking some of what his band often sing about during his long taxi journey. London to Charmouth. He takes his glasses off once more—they are an affectation in the gloom of the open-plan lounge—looks Mary Bredbury up and down. If hippies were the judges at Crufts Dog Show, this is what it would look like. 'Your girlfriend, you say?' A little questioning intonation upon the first word, as if Crook cannot believe that so ravishing a creature could possibly be satisfied with Jason Hardcastle for a lover.

Dennis is still standing back, Annabel beside him. Like everyone else, his eyes and ears are on the celebrity. He's a bit fixated on Mary too, she is the easier on the eye. Shorts and the loose top which she wears make her difficult not to watch. She is a crooked-arm's length from one of the five most famous hippies in the world. The top five are all Llamas. Neil Sullivan gives the star guest a glass of cider. Farm stuff, local. A large quaff makes him cough, laugh. Mary looks around at Dennis, meets his eye for the very first time this evening. He thinks she looks uncomfortable standing before God. And the deity loses a little sheen with every lecherous leer he makes at the young girl. Jimmy Crook has put his left hand—his glass-free hand—upon Mary's upper arm. It might not mean anything but most hippies don't grab hold of girls until the party has turned freaky. Dennis finds it daunting when his start turning that way, some of the late evening stuff. In any case, Mary usually leaves long before then.

* * *

There was an incident on New Year's Day—Dennis's ninth party—when the post-midnight fare was getting steamy. He and Annabel often drift off around this point—they share a bed up the stairs—couples getting frisky in the lounge just seems to be nature's way. The happenings at the flophouse could be the talk of Charmouth, Dennis hopes sixth formers have the sense to keep their mouths shut. At the ninth, he stayed downstairs specifically because Mary was still in the lounge. He would have liked her to leave but didn't want to ask. Has no control over her, no claim greater than that she seems to have stopped hating him. A friendship resumed with a light coating of frost remaining upon it. She is civil with him, and he loves her like Stephen would if he was a better older brother.

He felt embarrassed seeing Mary watch the partial unclothing taking place. Strictly not participating. She might have stayed behind only to confirm her disgust at what hippies do; Mary blows hot and cold on the subject. He thinks of her as a conflicted and sensual girl. It all started when she began kissing him at his fourth. He wonders if he misinterpreted that one. Perhaps she wasn't drunk at all when first they danced together.

Late night at the ninth, a guy from Birmingham grabbed hold of Mary, pulled her into a bear-like embrace. One or two unattached hippies have been turning up at his parties, Dennis never learnt the guy's name. 'We've no one else, babe,' Dennis heard him say as he rough-handled her. Dennis stepped right in, saw no sign of consent from Mary when the man dragged her across a short length of carpet. He isn't law enforcement but it's his house. The coarse man—traitor to the cause in Dennis's view—had already put his hand up her dress. And Mary—Dennis was as certain as any doped-up host could be—had paid the filthy looking drifter no attention at all. None. Across the room, a half-naked man lying atop a woman, her skirt riding up as she returned his kisses, may have aroused the hippy beyond his capacity for self-control. That time of the evening and that sort of a party, Mary really shouldn't have been there. Not that her foolhardy presence excused the groping hippy, not to Dennis's mind. If it's not consensual, it counts as fighting. Banned!

'Leave her be,' snapped Dennis. The laidback guitar playing of Dario Renzo was radiating from the speakers, his sharp rebuke contrasting with its mellow notes. No vocals accompany Renzo's jazz guitar, Dennis's barked words stirred a few from close to sleep. Even the copulating couple—or close to copulating, the lighting seriously low at that time of night—looked around. Twisting their necks and peering as if to understand the fracas. Dennis took Mary's hand; helped raise her out of the hippy's loosened embrace.

'Keep your spleen in place, man. Free love...or is she your girl?'

'I'm not his or yours. Twat!' said Mary, removing her hand from Dennis's and skimming her open palms down the front of her dress, as if to brush away the man's invasive touch.

'You have to leave.' Dennis pointed an accusatory finger at the man from Birmingham. He hadn't played bouncer since Stickland and the air-rifle.

'Come on, pretty,' said the drifter to Mary. 'You aren't his, so this little Nazi's frigging authority kick is nothing to do with us.'

'Twat!' she shouted more forcibly, and turned her face from him. Dennis gathered his arms around Mary to comfort her. She was visibly upset. Without a word for him, she pushed Dennis away too.

'It's my house, leave!' said Dennis to the hippy.

Mary took herself to the front door and the man followed her.

'Stay, Mary,' whispered Dennis. He feared, if she didn't, the randy no-good would be trying his luck in the front garden.

'Calm it, prissy,' the hippy told Dennis. And he is never prissy at his parties. Anything goes, he always says it. Anything except what that guy was trying to do.

Without a plan all three were on the short front drive. 'You want me?' asked the hippy, stretching a hand out for Mary. She kept her own folded in front of her chest. Ignored him entirely.

Dennis took hold of Mary's arm. 'Just wait,' he hissed in her ear. 'Let him get gone before you go anywhere.'

Mary didn't struggle, quietly she mouthed the word, 'Twat,' at Dennis. He hoped she meant the guy he was seeing off the premises, that she saw some merit in how he was keeping them apart.

The hippy walked up Croft Road, never looked back in their direction. 'Another time, sweet doll,' he shouted loudly from the corner of the main road.

'Never, Mary,' Dennis said, finally releasing her arm. 'This shit isn't for a girl like you. Some of these guys can't help themselves. I don't want them taking advantage...'

'So, you've got a house. Mr Monthly Party. If there was somewhere else to go in Charmouth, I'd be there, Dennis. You don't own me. And I can smack a hippy in the chops if that's what it takes.'

'Mary, Mary, I don't think you necessarily could. He looked a pretty rough sort. Let me protect you.'

'You've got fatty Annabel. What I do has nothing to do with you. You've got your own hippy who's just as randy as that one.'

'She really isn't like him at all, Mary.' Something in his words drew a slew of tears from her. 'Let me walk you home. He might be hanging around.'

Mary held her head bowed down, fair hair falling forward. The air was crisp; January the first's party, this was already the post-midnight

Jimmy Crook Shows Up

second. A sharp frost across Dorset. Mary wore a long black dress made of paper-thin material; she must have been freezing cold. Dennis put an arm across her shoulder, keeping the girl warm. After a moment's wriggling she fell into him, an embrace.

'I remember the last time you did that. I hated it,' she said through tears.

'Let me get a coat,' he said. An arm more loosely on her shoulder now. He pushed the front door back open, would not let her leave his careful touch.

Annabel was in the hallway. 'There was trouble?'

'He's gone now, I'm just walking Mary home.' The older woman nodded, a faint smile. He feared that she believed there to be a greater connection between them than Dennis knew to be true. Since his fourth party Dennis has had a girlfriend of his own. Not Mary Bredbury and she is no one's understudy.

He picked his trench-coat off the hook. 'Do you have one?' Mary shook her head. He stepped back onto the drive with her. Pulled the door closed and then put his own coat over the shivering girl.

'It's heavy,' she said.

'Everything is heavy between us, Mary.'

And it still seems to be so. They are like shadow lovers, no physical intimacy since the missteps at that fourth party; he living with his older hippy every day of the year past, Mary trying to find a replacement. Going through them like a proverbial butterknife. The world turns and they do not.

Now she is Jason Hardcastle's girlfriend. It won't last, Dennis is sure of it. Mary told him she will be applying for university in the autumn term, all her teachers say she must. Whatever that lad has to offer the girls, it isn't between his ears.

* * *

Someone has turned the music off; Jason's acoustic guitar is in the hands of the living legend. Top hat and shades are off now, resting on the arm of the futon. There is no sound at all in the lounge. From the kitchen, giggling and the sounds of drinks poured into paper cups are audible. Then a group of girls come through to watch. Jimmy gives the instrument a downward strum, a major chord ringing around the room as he looks inquisitively at the air. The tuning is close to what it should be. His hand mutes the frets and he adjusts a couple of strings, quickly turns a couple of pegs on the headstock. Picks two strings and they resonate together. Strums and nods, guitar tuned more precisely than Jason can manage.

Jimmy Crook can play guitar better than the local boys but it isn't exceptional. His bass guitar is in London; drummer, lead, rhythm and keyboard players are all there too. Or back in San Francisco, their London gig over. A soloist he is not, not on any recordings owned by Dennis Harris. He has a growly voice, up and down in the right places, the right amount for the most part. He's never sung the lead on a recorded track. Dennis has all the albums; Crook is credited with backing vocals like all the Llamas except lead singer, Carl Carlsen. He is picking out a rendition of Charmed Life. It's from a stage musical, not hippy music at all, pre-war stuff. Jimmy's version is a bit roughed-up. Sounds better for it. He sings about love falling into his lap, a girl on his arm wherever he goes. Looks at Mary while he sings. Unwavering in his stare. 'Making eyes,' says a line in the song, and he raises both his eyebrows focussing intently upon her watching face.

Annabel is still whispering to him that it is wonderful to have Crook here. Whimpering about it. Might feel that she has done Dennis the best turn of his life. Done it just by knowing who she knows. Strings pulled, people who know people. One or two Haight Ashbury hippies have turned up at Dennis's parties since Annabel has been a fixture in his life. At least, they said they lived there off and on. American, smoked a lot of marijuana. Stronger stuff than he is used to. He never verified the stories but they looked and smelt like they were Haight Ashbury hippies. Jimmy Crook is of a different order: his face on seven different album covers that Dennis owns. Mostly back of the pack but he is a Llama. Original line up too, not like the drummer or rhythm guitar. The second-half substitutes. Right now, peace-loving Dennis Harris feels like thumping his hero. Crook is ogling Mary—at seventeen, she must be under half his age—without a hint of embarrassment. And Mary isn't Daisy, she has a reasonable amount of clothing on; summer in a seaside town. Jimmy Crook holds her gaze for egocentric line after egocentric line. He's only a bass player. Hardly writes any songs, three co-credits across seven albums. Dennis has read the small print on each and every cover and inner sleeve. Jimmy Crook has enjoyed one hell of a charmed life. Dennis thinks Mary is too smart to be taken in. Mr Californian Suntan making eyes. He should put the dark glasses back on; he wears them on three of the album covers. She is staring back, matching his stare with her own. Even smiles back a couple of times. Dennis doesn't like

Jimmy Crook Shows Up

it. The most famous man to set foot in Charmouth; they are all watching him drooling over Mary. Dennis too, although he seethes inside. Mary's hopeless boyfriend, Jason Hardcastle, grins the biggest smile in the room. Beaming at the bass guitarist. Charmouth's own lady's man giving come-to-bed eyes to another fella. Mental. Is he pimping Mary out? When the song is coming to an end, Dennis calls out across the room. 'Neil, Jason, you guys should do Crazy Darkness.' He wants Jimmy Crook to fade into the background. Thinks about putting Templeton Ca. on the deck. Laughing Llamas can go fuck themselves.

2.

One year to the day he has lived with Annabel, with Antonella Vitale as her passport evidences her true name to be. She has not told him this directly. Not even indirectly. He took a quiet look while she was working at the polytunnel farm. He doesn't think she does it to deceive him. Calls herself Annabel in the way that Thompson—possibly his proper name—was long ago known as Pretty and more recently as Major. Annabel is a good name. Antonella sounds like a mobster's wife. His lady-friend has chosen well. Her hippy name the better of the two.

There are nights when they talk and talk into the small hours. Particularly so in the early days; the work exhausts her more now. She is a supervisor, directs planting. Seems to know what there is to know about every salad plant under the sun. Annabel has got old Mr Garside, the tomato farmer, doing chilli peppers. Shown him how to grow bigger marrows—prize-winning big—but neither Garside or Annabel has any interest in parading vegetables, and she has explained at length to Dennis that she never tried growing them in America. 'Tasteless gourdes,' she calls them. 'The very biggest has the nutritional content of a lone pea.'

The talking has been an education to Dennis. Annabel told him she was born of two storms. One raged across the New England coast for the duration of her mother's labour. A hurricane so destructive it damaged the roof of the very hospital in which Annabel—as he thinks she was not yet called—emerged into the world. The second storm lasted eight years, the duration of time that her father lived in the same house as her mother. She and an older brother heard the drunken shouts. Saw the broken furniture in the mornings after their rows. America went to war in Europe and Japan while, back home in folksy little Providence, Rhode Island, her father and mother had no need to join the wider conflict. Theirs was plenty.

'A child of a post-war broken home, it was a sorry state for a girl to grow up in,' said Annabel. And to him, she sounded to be pitying another person, as if she had disassociated herself completely with the girl she once was. Antonella, not that she ever disclosed the name. Those early years were not pleasant to recall. Memories of a mother with two black eyes. When the father had gone—'He joined the Boston police; eyesight too poor for the army, fine and dandy for policing that sorry city'—and the rump of the family moved from house to flat, her memories flowered. 'There was a real nice woman in the flat below. I call it a flat but really it was a proper house divided into two. We were upstairs, Miss Brambilla down below. Miss on account of never marrying; we thought she was a hundred years old but maybe she was no more than eighty. Wrinkles on her face that parted or narrowed with each smile or frown. A lot of smiles, Miss Brambilla, a thoroughly good soul. May she rest in peace.'

This gave Dennis pause for thought. They both know from bitter experience that death is a harbinger of even more tumultuous feelings than the drugs she keeps on using. He sticks to pot. Annabel's use of acid, or whatever it is she takes, scares Dennis. He hasn't raised it; prefers to say he is free and easy. And wherever the drugs take them, it has none of the weight that death does. Whatever the doors open out on to, it is not the actual abyss. That is the trip they both avoided. Annabel didn't intrude upon his grief when Zoe Carmichael died. She took it seriously enough, gave him space. If she saw a connection with her own Miss Brambilla, she didn't mention it. He thinks she never understood his attachment. She never met Mrs C, never saw that Zoe Carmichael was the one who willed it. She needed him, needed Dennis. That's what losing a son must have done to the poor old lady. He was only riding the wave, being there for her, although he felt the warmth that she would have preferred to give another.

The other Mrs C—or Miss C to be more precise, Chadwick, the unpredictable warden of Plaza Court—had an interesting meeting with Annabel back in April. There was a leaving do at the Sea Shells Café, for Tracy who was moving back to Plymouth to look after her mother. Diane Smith, from Weymouth, covered for them at Plaza Court so the team of four could spend time together. Give Tracy a decent send off. Without any prior agreement to do so, Lorraine called

Jimmy Crook Shows Up

in at Croft Road fully half an hour before they were all due to meet. It's a flophouse, anyone and everyone comes by. For an hour, or for a week, he never puts a limit on their stay. Nevertheless, Dennis wore a look of surprise, just about remembered to shut his gaping mouth, when Lorraine Chadwick came knocking.

'I thought I'd meet your young lady,' she said on the step. And Lorraine never used the word young when referencing Annabel at Plaza Court. 'You still have that woman living here, don't you, Dennis?' He struggles to explain exactly why he dislikes her every word so intensely these days. She who he once looked up to.

Annabel was in the garden, planting or weeding. She has refashioned his mother's vegetable plot, does not like to waste fertile soil. Garlic, celeriac, other plants which Dennis had never previously tasted, are now abundant in his garden. 'Come and meet Lorraine,' he shouted.

It was not cold but the summer dress Lorraine wore seemed out of place. The neckline plunging; hem well above her unstockinged knees. Miles above when she sank onto his low futon. 'I just know she's been dying to meet the other woman in your life,' said Lorraine while Annabel was in the kitchen washing her hands.

When she came in, his lover was wearing jeans and sweatshirt, black hair in one large plait down her back. 'Hello, Lorraine. Denny has told me so much about you.'

'I'm sure I'm not as bad as he says.'

They shook hands and Lorraine held on for the longest time, looking searchingly into Annabel's green eyes. Perhaps she saw it, perhaps not. The temptress who beguiled the man-child, Dennis. Annabel was fairer of skin at that time of year. She tans well but this was early spring. 'Dennis has told me only good things about you, Lorraine. He says you taught him everything he needed to know about working with the elderly. Learnt it all from you.' Annabel displayed a seldom-used gift for lying. Or perhaps Dennis has said it at some point. He often thinks she was a better manager three years ago. That she's lost it.

'And I'm sure he's learnt a lot from you,' said Lorraine.

'Yes, we're good for each other.'

Dennis liked Annabel's breezy reply. He offered Lorraine a drink.

'Can I trust you not to drug me?' said the warden with a smile. It drew no laughter from her hosts.

The three of them duly shared a pot of tea. Dennis near silent as the two ladies talked about him. Lorraine—inappropriate as only she knows how to be—told of her concern for him back in nineteen-seventy. 'He was a little lost child. I expect he's told you. A real tragedy losing both parents on the same day. We all felt for him, I'm sure.'

Dennis cringed inside, wondered if Annabel would hold it together. At Plaza Court, he has breathed not a word of Annabel's own connection to the events that orphaned him. Not shared it in Charmouth, not even with Mary. She lost a husband that day, twentieth of January, nineteen-seventy. Lorraine's words were sympathetic while her tone suggested a kiddie losing a pet hamster.

'I was so pleased when I heard you'd come and taken him in hand.'

Annabel shot him the quickest glance; they both knew it was a lie. This woman was jealous of a female social worker sitting too close to him on the office desk. They've laughed about it more than once, she even asked Jane to tell the tale during a social visit.

'Lorraine was great to me back then. A big help before I'd grown up,' said Dennis, keeping it light.

'I was that, Annabel,' his manager chipped in. 'There was crying some days but he could always get a hug from Auntie Lorraine.'

Dennis nodded politely at this regretted truth. Annabel changed the subject, asked Lorraine about her family, she didn't bite on the bait. Has only a cat waiting for her at home in Maiden Newton and an ageing mother somewhere up north.

Lorraine asked about the vegetable plot and Annabel filled her in. Still the silly fool had to smile an aside to Dennis. 'Not growing any marijuana, then?'

Dreadful. Said it with a hard jay, hasn't a clue. Dennis shook his head but couldn't laugh—not while the butt of the joke was in his house—and after a brief silence, Annabel said, 'You're not a hippy, Lorraine. Does the way we live offend you?' The question seemed to startle Lorraine, and Annabel was only raising what was in her every sideways glance.

'I just want people to be happy. This little mister, in particular,' she said, putting a flat palm up to Dennis's cheek as she said it.

Still public property, he thought. A national news story, milked for a month in the local rag and everyone wants to say how they were there. Condemning or supporting. A bit of each from quite a few.

He wished that she had never come round at all. Her presence seemed to diminish the job he does, shrink his working worth by having so hapless a boss. After thirty minutes, he and Lorraine took

Jimmy Crook Shows Up

themselves to the fish bar. The four who are employed at Plaza Court—Tracy off the payroll the following day—sat at one of just three Formica tables which turn a chippy into a café for those who can afford nothing better. Lorraine regaled Tracy and Alison with tales of the meeting.

'He's found himself a handsome woman,' was the highpoint; 'Sturdy from tilling the soil,' the low.

Nowadays he thinks her calling in was a good thing. Annabel saw more than Lorraine that visit. His odd status in this corner of the world, noble and pitiable. Never evident at his parties—they are looser, freer, unencumbered—but those are the qualities lent to him on every walk down Charmouth High Street.

* * *

One year to the day, Dennis and Annabel have been lovers. Exclusive lovers unless you include the eleventh party. The hashish had disagreed with Dennis that night and a hippy from Exeter did stuff to him, sexual stuff. He was trying to sleep. The girl came into his room without invite, Annabel's whereabouts unknown, the wrong end of a tab of acid, probably. Tripping, well out of it; she does more of that than Dennis likes to think about. The girl from Exeter did it all to him, not the other way round. Went on top. And whatever he did, it was because he thought she was Annabel. Although he also knew she was a hell of a lot slimmer. He thought the hash had made him perceive it that way. The girl's name never found its way into his head. No one could count a coupling like that, surely. True to each other they have been. His thoughts of Mary are not a breach in or of themselves. Imagining something isn't the same as doing it.

Or has Annabel been less exclusive? Dennis has worried about it more than once. Herbie was his biggest doubt but unless they got up to stuff while he was out, she has been true to him. Herbie plain said that he and she hooked up one way or another—probably in London—before she came to live in Charmouth. Maybe in America, only Dennis can't work out a plausible timeline for that. Annabel has received a couple of postcards from him, Herbie's back in Canada now. Quebec. Strange how jealous he feels and she talks about him like a pet project. Helping draft-dodgers is a hippy's only obligation. Dennis agrees in principle. A better class of deserter would have worn underpants at breakfast. And she's been to London twice without him; he only went up this last time. The Llamas. No reason to think she was untrue; stayed in a hippy house so he can't discount it.

Dennis and Annabel tell each other they are not possessive. Say they happen not to need anyone else. He doesn't really know what he thinks about free love; still harbours stronger feelings for Mary Bredbury than he has been able to tell her, or admit to his actual girlfriend.

Between parties, and if nobody is flopping, he and Annabel could be a regular husband and wife. Dennis watching rugby on a Saturday afternoon, Annabel mending clothes. His late mother's sewing machine has returned to this world; he never threw it out because he hoped to get a couple of quid for it. Now it has magicked up new curtains for every upstairs room. She's very practical: vegetables that cost no more than her attentive labour; homemade jam.

One day, earlier in the summer, a letter arrived addressed to Antonella Vitale. Dennis decided to leave it on the mat, he was unsure how to approach this other version of Annabel. Chose not to confront the matter at all, left the letter where it landed below the letterbox. She would share the news it brought if she wished.

He thinks he called it right. When he returned from his shift at Plaza Court, the letter was no longer on the mat and his almost-common-law-wife chose not to mention its arrival, its content or the name on the envelope. Not so far and it's been a month.

Dennis took a little look in one or two likely places the next time she was working and he was not. Her underwear drawer; beneath the sowing machine. Never found the letter, never learnt who from her other life was calling, chasing, wanting to know when Antonella Vitale would be returning to America.

He once thought he and she had a shared past, their connection to a singular tragedy. That is not, he has subsequently learnt, quite how it works. The arm around the shoulder is welcome, and still the suffering turns out to be a most solitary activity. Always done alone. His, hers. It lives in the house unspoken, the most voluminous silence. Takes a few hours off on party night.

* * *

Ha! One year to the day since Dennis became the talk of Charmouth for a reason other than the tragedy that ended his parents' lives. For living with a woman, unmarried. An older woman, if not quite as old as first he feared. And not even a local woman. Not of Charmouth, Dorset or even England. He bagged one more exotic than any of that.

Jimmy Crook Shows Up

Quite a lot for a tiny seaside town to get its collective head around. And now they can add the visit of Jimmy Crook, whatever way it turns out. The man in the top hat will mean nothing to the old folk at Plaza Court; Lorraine has likely never heard of him either. He's no crooner, an impromptu rendition of Charmed Life aside. But everyone under thirty will have tapped their foot—the dashboard of their car—along to his chirpy bass playing on the Llamas' biggest hit single. I Can't Pick It Up with My Chopsticks reached number two in the pop charts, still in the top ten at the time of Dennis's first party. He heard Mary's church-going mother singing along to the chorus when it played on the radio. Won't have had a clue that the words extolled Annabel's funny drugs: subtle reference to an acid tab beyond the reach of the said utensils, the hard stuff which Dennis never touches.

Will he become known for this turn up? Having the famous rocker hang out on Croft Road. If the big-headed old letch doesn't behave himself, Dennis is not sure he even wants to be. Jimmy Crook doesn't just stare at Mary. He has sent Jason on some pointless errand for plectrums. His eyes watch only her chest, like he's got to check her free roving breasts never escape the loose-fitting T-shirt. Catch them if they do. That's what Dennis reckons. He's been watching Jimmy ogling Mary for about forty-five minutes.

Dennis has put his drink down. Not in the mood for any of it. Annabel is still beaming, walking around. Talking with everyone about the Llama who is amongst them. Why can't she see what he sees? They have been a couple for a year to the day, and she has allowed Dennis to examine her private places with an indecent curiosity when it is the two of them alone. He doesn't try it on when the room is humming, knows the beginnings and the end of privacy. And nor does he sniff around other girls, not in the literal way this weathered-faced Californian is doing. Daisy might have been the exception, the girl in the see-through waterproof but that was explicable. A shop window display. Mary's T-shirt is just a kid experimenting, trying something a bit freer. A million miles from Daisy's stunt, it really is. Jimmy Crook has no excuses.

And now he has an arm around Mary Bredbury. 'You live in this little place then, chickadee?'

How long is it taking Jason to locate a fucking plectrum? Get one in here, the guitar too. Crook needs something other than Mary to occupy his invasive hands. He can sing another ditty about his unjustifiably charmed life. Dennis would rather that than this pawing.

The Flophouse Years

'I'll be getting out soon,' Mary tells Jimmy. 'Can't stay in Charmouth forever.'

Dennis thinks the opposite. Expects to live here for as many years as this world has in store for him. This house, Plaza Court. He has never wanted more. Everything going swimmingly except for Jimmy Crook proving himself a pain in the arse. And he has Annabel, at least she seems beyond Crook's compass. He was never sure she would stay a month and here they are.

* * *

It is a year minus one day since Dennis learnt of Annabel's connection to the tragedy that ruptured his life. She was on another continent when it happened. It is a source of confusion within him that his lover's former husband was also a member of the religious sect which snagged his parents. The whacky cult that turned around his father, Peter Harris, that was the man's true name. Kids believe what their parents tell them, then somewhere around their fifteenth birthday they spot that it is all shit. He and Annabel were once believers, if only on the coattails of the more zealous. Dennis, by that time an adolescent doubter of all things parental; Annabel said only that she was never comfortable with all the practices of that strange faith. Dennis knew enough to guess which one she disliked the most; he has never sought clarification. They were both estranged from every tenet before the fateful day. January the twentieth.

Nowadays Dennis thinks of his late father with contempt. Or not at all. That is not so easy but, once or twice, he has gone more than twenty-four hours without bringing him to mind. He is sure he has. Dennis never pours such scorn upon his mother's memory. She wasn't much but he doesn't hate her. He wonders which way Annabel feels about her ex. The husband who made her a widow before she got around to divorcing him, or he to divorcing her. She hasn't said quite how it was. Never even told him the man's name, and that seems to be a testimony to her privacy. Said only that she had moved out some months before it happened. The tragedies. A very quiet lady on the topic of personal traumas experienced. Draft dodging and vegetable growing she can jabber on about for hours.

Bloody Crook-cock is whispering into Mary's ear, even making her smile in reply to whatever drole chat-up he has rehearsed. Dennis really hates the fucker. It is not an emotion he regularly tunes into. The hatred has entered his bloodstream of its own volition, a reaction.

Jimmy Crook Shows Up

Why doesn't Jason do something? Dennis would not leave Mary to the mercy of the old playboy if she were his girl. He'd take her far away from the bass player's pernicious reach. A walk on the beach: head into the sunset with the pretty girl.

* * *

One year to the day since Dennis wondered what having sexual intercourse actually felt like. Worried that no girl out there would allow him the chance to find out. Annabel let him in, has continued to do so. They give it a go most nights of every week. More than got the hang of it, he's quite experienced in his own estimation.

And now Jimmy Crook is at his party. The famous dude exudes a carnality that embarrasses Dennis. Doesn't await the acceptance of others; the man has a presence, a push into the consciousness that is visceral. Lips and eyes always moving, rolling, expressing a warmth of feeling, one way or the other. Towards himself or a young girl's tits. It's there for anyone to tune into, he stirs the humors of all in his ambit. Having this irritating prick at his party could lead to a picture in the local paper. Requires someone with a steady hand, still sober enough to take a decent photograph. Not many of them left by this time. Dennis has scarcely drunk a thing but he won't be snapping any pictures. Not for the Bridport Clarion, no kowtowing to the letch in the top hat by Harris. Not given who he keeps staring at. Putting a hand around her waist. Dennis would like to wind up this party and it's barely in full swing. New arrivals every few minutes. Laughing Llamas back on the deck, a group of four girls are dancing in the corner, casting glances at their idol. More suitable groupies than the one he seems set on. The dirty rocker has his bass-string-thwacking hand on the back of Mary's head, draws her in for a kiss she is not doing enough to get out of. Jason Hardcastle has re-entered the room with a clutch of multi-coloured plectrums but still he does nothing. Nattering with Annabel, pretending not to look. Christ and the apostles and all their ugly maiden aunts, this party would be a fuck-sight better if Jimmy Crook had never come near it.

3.

'What's going on, Mary?'
  'I don't know. Stoned, I suppose.'
  'You're not that far gone.'

The Flophouse Years

He virtually pushed her into the garden. Stupid Jason should be doing this but he's gone the other way. When he left the lounge, Jason was telling the bass player—who is not God by a long chalk, by all the chalk in the Dorset Downs—that Mary is a good lay. Jesus! Dennis doesn't want to hear that, doesn't care to know that Jason knows. What an outrageous thing for the little shit to say about his girlfriend. Supposed girlfriend. To a narcissist twenty years their senior, a free-love hippy with an unruly cock. Dennis can imagine that it's true, that sharing flesh with Mary Bredbury might be a most memorable pleasure. And she probably knows what she is doing in that department, seems to have spent the year since he missed his chance, gathering experience after experience. At least, he thinks that is what she has done, he's never asked her directly. Or even approximately. He tries not to think about it at all. He doesn't know what it feels like to make love to Mary. It is karmically unfair that Jason does. Dennis hit an unlikely jackpot with Annabel, she's great with him. Upstairs. He doesn't want to compare and he never tells another soul about it. How their bodies entwine. It's a private matter. Some things should be kept in the wrapping paper, uncovered only when one is alone with one's girl or one's thoughts. Now Dennis is trying to avert a disaster. Mary may have lost her innocence many months back but Charmouth boys don't count for much on the big clock. The life changing never-go-backs. People are bound to talk about it if she goes upstairs with Jimmy Crook. He is to be repulsed. Must be. Why can't she see how repulsive he is?

'It has nothing to do with you, Dennis.'

'What would Stephen say if he was here?' Stephen Bredbury is away. Camp America. Working as an activity organiser for the deprived youth of Philadelphia—God help them—an ocean between him and his sister.

So strange that it has come to this, a circle turned in twelve months. Dennis really thought Mary was acting on alcohol twelve months ago, when she offered herself to him. That was it: she offered and he said, you've drunk too much. He thought she was making a decision she would later regret. With or without alcohol—probably a few of each—she seems to have made several similar decisions this past year. Regretted Gordon Stickland and will surely feel the same way about the pimp, Jason Hardcastle, when the penny drops. She has discovered herself in this year. And she thought he was rejecting her looks twelve months back, said it to his face a few days later. Daft. No

Jimmy Crook Shows Up

man on Earth would reject Mary on those grounds. Impossible. She's figured that much by now. Knows she turns heads. Seems to be enjoying the attention; a rock god smitten. Looking at her with a deeply carnal interest, the fucker has no other setting. You can smell it on his person, untidy hair framing his weatherworn face, the creases of his smile. Half hobo and half dandy. Mary could be the first girl who tells him no but that would not be in the spirit of this hippy party. A Llama among them. Everyone seems hell-bent on giving Jimmy Crook whatever he wants. Scrumpy cider, plectrums, fawning compliments. The pretty young girl. Everyone except Dennis Harris.

'Don't do it with him, Mary.' She has narrowed her eyes like she hates him again. They got past this months ago. Well past, fallen back into friendship, that's what he thought. He hasn't judged her behaviour with the Charmouth boys. Having Jason Hardcastle for a boyfriend isn't something that sticks anyway. Girls and boys in Charmouth try each other out for a bit. Do so unless they are damaged goods like Dennis Harris. The Dennis of his fledgling years. She is not the first to do the rounds. It is Crook that will tarnish her. Make everyone see Mary in a light that is not her. He thinks his intervention today is a still better deed than not taking advantage of her at his fourth party. A year ago, exactly.

'Nothing to do with you, Dennis. Nothing.'

'In Stephen's absence think of me as an older brother, Mary. I'm counselling you to hold on to your self-respect.'

It could be the pot but it's probably his prissiness, Mary is virtually pissing herself laughing at poor Dennis. She's seen orgies at one or two of these parties. Disapproval and fascination might be cousins, Dennis has thought that before. He initially felt he was not cool enough for it but since living with Annabel he wonders if it's wrong. If all this free love twists people up while they pretend it doesn't. He has never stopped anyone from pairing off, thought himself the matchmaker because it happens at his parties. Creating the vibe that leads to a few twenty-minute shags. It seems a popular activity, although Dennis was too out of it to take in exactly what was happening the only time he had in on the action. And now there is a very particular match which he seeks to obstruct. Not cool of him, it simply needs doing.

'What I do or don't do with Jimmy Crook is my business, not yours,' she snaps.

'Business? It's not business, he's trying to exploit you, Mary. He wants to use you, not to cherish you as a person who truly loved you would. Don't do it. Stephen isn't here to caution you; think of me as Stephen, please.'

'I do, Dennis,' she giggles. Takes a moment to control her laughter. 'You're just like him: a sniffling little hedgehog interfering in something that doesn't concern you one jot.' She glances down at her own legs, short shorts covering her. Goose bumps in the garden. Runs her right index finger along her inner thigh, scratching at an insect bite. Looks up at Dennis while she scratches, and he quickly looks up from the legs which transfixed him. 'A hippy when it pleases you, a parent when it doesn't. Well, we don't have a daddy either, Dennis. Not since I was pre-school. Stephen has an excuse for trying to mollycoddle me, you really don't.' She has desisted scratching, pushes out her chest and again Dennis watches the movement of Mary's body, the tremble within her T-shirt. 'I'm going back inside; leave me alone.'

He follows her through the kitchen door where the pair of them run straight into Annabel and Jimmy Crook.

'Denny, please, stay and talk,' says Annabel. And then she looks at the big name. 'It's his party, you know? He put the place on the map. I think Dennis is feeling starstruck.'

This sets Mary off into another fit of giggles. 'Starstruck,' she splutters, pushing him towards Crook with both hands.

'Go and find Jason,' Dennis whispers to her. They can go upstairs and use his boxroom for all he cares. Just don't do it with Fake-God. That's the disaster he's trying to avert. Hardcastle only a minor mishap.

'What's the lowdown, man,' he says to Jimmy Crook. 'All good?'

'Yeah. Just happy to be here, brother.'

Crook watches Mary's rear, the backs of her thighs, as she walks through into the lounge. Dennis realises the man's top hat must be back there too. He is no longer on stage. Looks drawn, aged, beneath the fluorescent lighting of the kitchen.

'See you shortly, sweets,' calls Jimmy Crook as the girl disappears from view.

'Okay boys, chat away,' says Annabel, and she follows Mary.

Dennis and Jimmy stand alone in the kitchen. 'It's probably not a big deal for you,' says Dennis. He is contemplating how to implore the oversexed idol to leave Mary alone. It could backfire, make it more likely still that he does to her what she seems incapable of stopping of

Jimmy Crook Shows Up

her own volition.

'I wanted to talk with you, man. Dennis. I know the weight of it all, yeah. I know because my friend Shannon told me all about Annabel. You dig what I'm saying?'

'No,' says Dennis. 'I don't dig. Not sure what you're on about. Who's Shannon?'

'She's not here. She's a great friend of mine. We go way back. And Shannon knows Annabel from back in the States. Reached out to her right after it all went the way it went. You dig what I'm saying?'

'Yeah.' Dennis scarcely understands a word, it's just that saying no doesn't sound true hippy.

'When she got out of the clutches, you know?'

'The clutches?'

'Well. I gather you were in the same boat. Was it your parents? You're only a kid.'

'Sorry? What do you know? It's...I'm not sure...personal shit and everything.'

'I'm sorry, man. It is personal shit. The heaviest. Were you ever in the group? One of Toogood's chosen travellers.'

'Yes...' He scratches his ear. 'No...it was different then. I wasn't a grown up. I had nothing to do with the shit that happened. My dad told me about it. I heard some of the Toogood tapes but not so many.' As Dennis rambles, he notices that Jimmy Crook is paying him the closest attention, listening hard, searching his face as he does it. 'Does it mean something to you, Mr Crook? A connection.'

'I'm Jimmy to you, friend. No, not personally, man. I never paid them much attention until after it had all come to a head. A lot of survivors showed up at Haight-Ashbury, I can tell you. All around the Bay Area. You could expect that, I guess.'

'They weren't the same. None of the Themagins were druggies. Clean-living idiots, the lot of them.'

Jimmy Crook laughs appreciatively at Dennis's observation. The hippies and the religious cult to which his parents belonged have little that is obviously in common. 'And that might be the weirdest, Dennis. Those guys believed in horse-feathers like no normal person can without breaking their brain on acid first. LSD could do it. Big trips. But those guys were as straight up as the Mormons in Salt Lake City...'

Dennis cuts him off. 'I'll tell you my personal view, how it was for me. When I was a kid, a youngster, I believed my father was God. Not literally, not different from the way quite a few kids probably do. But

The Flophouse Years

he was smart, showed me stuff that seemed important. And it all felt even more important for how he showed me. You get what I mean?'

The rock star nods.

'I kind of took up three religions on account of my dad. He was a born-again Christian for a time before the weird stuff. Then that, the Themagins. But the other, the third, was the cult of Peter Harris. Just me in that nutty sect, Mr Crook. I didn't think my dad could do wrong, not until the very day I realised he couldn't get a darned thing right. Brainwashed from birth. Maybe every son feels the same. It only matters when the change comes, turns you round the full one-eighty degrees.'

'Jimmy.' The man slaps him on the shoulder. 'I'm Jimmy to you, my friend. I dig you. All that you've got going on here.'

'I lost my faith long before my father died. Lost my faith in everything. I like the hippies but that's because they say anything goes. People come here and do drugs, and some come here and don't do drugs too. Both are cool, cool with me. I'm not for forcing anyone, Jimmy.'

'Right on.'

'I can't force you to do anything, Jimmy. But if you are my friend, want to listen to a word I have to say, leave that kid, Mary, alone, man. She's a bit mixed up. Still in school. Doesn't need you messing with her mind. Or any other part of her come to that.'

'Sorry, man. Is she your girl? I thought she was with…'

'With Jason? Might be. It's a mess. He's not good for her either but he's her age. Close enough.'

'Age? I thought you said anything goes, man?' Dennis is shaking his head at the rock stars objection. 'Age? Christ, Dennis, you've got a thing going with Annabel—I am told—and she's even older than I am. I smell hypocrisy in your demand.'

'Jimmy, I'm asking you to leave Mary alone. I'm a friend of hers and she's not in the right headspace to…' He's not sure how to persuade him, and nor does he believe Jimmy Crook to be younger than Annabel for one second.

'Oh, fuck it, man, I came here as a favour to Annabel. To my friend, Shannon, really. I didn't come to argue with you. I'm on your side. Girls throw themselves at me and I dig that. I've got something they want. You can judge me but you're only being small town. The world will just keep on turning around, man.'

'I'm asking you as a favour. When do you go back to London,

Jimmy Crook Shows Up

Jimmy?'

'Taxi's waiting, man. Sooner I go back the less this gig costs me.'

'Is that right? You have a taxi parked up here?'

'I'm not waiting on taxi's when I've had enough...'

Now it is Dennis who laughs. Laughs at the Llama. 'I didn't know hippies did that? We have a jar here, a from-each-according-to-his-means jar. You know what that is?'

'Christ, Dennis. I brought bourbon.'

'That's not what I'm saying. This is a flophouse. Any hippy can stay. Some who aren't yet hippies have tried it. An education. It doesn't run on arse wind, Jimmy. You're the first guy who I've ever heard of who has a taxi waiting while...'

'Fuck you, man. I'm in the biggest band on the West Coast right now. We did the headline at the London Music Festival...'

'I was there, man. I know who you are. I'm a fan. But you know what I was saying about my dad...'

'Yeah, sorry man. You were in the middle of saying...'

'I thought he was God. But nobody is. I thought you were a sort of god when I first heard your records but I shouldn't have. I already knew that there really isn't one. Gods are nothing, just made up by normal people not thinking straight. Imagining a help that never comes. False promises. That's what my dad taught me. I'm cut up that he never spotted it himself. Went to his grave in thrall to a charlatan.'

Jimmy Crook looks through narrowed eyes at Dennis Harris. 'I wish you well, friend. You've been through some shit. I have kept my taxi waiting long enough, I do believe.' Dennis nods solemnly at Jimmy Crook who seems no longer able to look him in the eye. 'Interesting meeting you, what's done is done.'

'Yes,' says Dennis. 'Maybe I'll see you again.'

The bass player leaves the kitchen, goes through into the lounge. Dennis wants to follow while knowing how uncool that might look. His friend, Mary, is in there, Annabel too, but the latter seems of only passing interest to Jimmy Crook. Within a minute the famous man comes back out of the lounge. Top hat perched jauntily on his ruffled up black and grey hair, a jacket in his hands. He glances down the hall at Dennis, says not a word and leaves the party. Departs from number three, out to where his taxi awaits. A drive with bourbon, then a bed in one of London's finest hotels.

Dennis raises a small glass of cider to his lips. Toasts the closing door.

The Flophouse Years

* * *

Annabel gives him the most questioning look. 'I thought it would help,' she says. 'You are such a big fan and I knew he would want to talk about it. Shannon told me he's really obsessed.'

Dennis feels like a fraudulent hippy. Or the most genuine. He can't work it out. Everybody wants to tune into the vibe, dig each other and form a big head of likeminded love and peace. It doesn't happen like that and, surely, they all know it. Ban the bomb? Of course, those damn things need banning. When did a bomb ever do the world a pinch of good? But Jimmy Crook counselling him about the tragedy of his parents passing? Doing impromptu social work just before fucking a girl Dennis expects to think about every day of his life and Crook forgetting her by the following morning. No! No! No! 'He's a great bass player, Annie. Knows nothing about what went on that January. He's on an ego trip, that's all. Probably hopes to write a song about it.'

'Would that be so bad? Something to hold on to.'

'It would be a pile of shit. If I wrote a song about it, it might be a pile of shit too, at least it would express how I felt. A guy who was there. Crook was after everything he could take. I didn't...'

'You've got him wrong, Dennis. You're in some weird mood tonight.'

She might have that right. Dennis is certainly not looking to argue with Annabel. It was like an anniversary present: a member of his favourite band showing up at his party. Unbelievable on a lot of levels. He turns his back on her and takes to the stairs. He hears groaning in the third bedroom; someone's at it already. He would hate it to be Jason screwing himself into Mary, knows worse things could happen. On opening his own bedroom door, he peers into the gloom. The keep-out sign has done its job.

Dennis lies on the bed and tears come to him. Why the fucking stupid chauffeur-driven hippy thinks he can just start talking to him about his parents makes his blood boil. The sheer arrogance of Jimmy Crook. Kids treat the Llamas like gods and then the stupid fuckers think it's more than a joke, more than an aberration of the vibe. Annabel is thirty-six, just days off thirty-seven: her passport reports this, it is unspoken between them. Many of those years must belong to Antonella Vitale. He doesn't know when she adopted her current name. The day she met him, for all he really knows. She chose

Jimmy Crook Shows Up

hippiedom because it's lighter, a laugh. The other world can be completely unbearable at times. He's felt that and surely her experiences are on a par with his. Not that they have ever compared notes. Not really. And now she has given way to this other magical thinking. There is no doubt that he, Dennis Harris, is a bit fucked up by all that's gone before. She offers him the touch of Jimmy Crook's shirt hem, fingers upon the rim of God's top hat. Can such a thing correct the errors of being born into a shit-filled world? What the hell can a man like that do. Say, 'Far out.' That doesn't bring back the dead, not even close. Dennis knows his life is far out, he has spent every day since the twenty-first of January, nineteen-seventy, trying to find his way back. Jimmy Crook cannot help him with the project. His cock does not point the way, he has no special powers. His singing tonight was pretty shit too. The bastard bass player wanted to mess with his mind and shag his best friend while he was at it. It might be the vibrations of bass notes, the way you can feel them through the frame of your body. It could affect a man plucking away next to his big fat speaker for the duration of his adult life. Can't help himself from shagging-shagging while not helping anyone at all. The bass notes have stirred the man's baser feelings. Lust seems to be our bottom line. Dennis feels it and he's one of the good guys. Keeps the lustful feelings to himself for the most part. Mary looked gorgeous tonight. The T-shirt and everything. And Dennis thinks his actions have let her know that she is his best friend. That he never rejected her, simply wanted better for her than he could offer. Annabel and Crook and the lot of them have got the Dennis-is-fucked-up part of the equation right. Knowing someone has a few screws loose, diagnosing that Harris is hurting, none of it changes a damn thing. There is no real value in naming the ailment when the drugs don't work.

He turns over on the mattress he lies upon, face into the pillow. Click of the door, Annabel is in the room, undressing beside him. Dennis is not interested tonight.

Why invite a shit like Jimmy Crook? It ruined his sixteenth. Dennis wants to forget about this one from start to finish. Stupid fucking party.

The Flophouse Years

Chapter Four

Antecedents

Part One
1.

I know a lot more about space than my physics teacher but I keep it under wraps. Don't say. The stuff I know might be top secret, although neither Mum or Dad have said so. And they have changed their names now, they're not Mum and Dad anymore. I'm not the only one. Dennis is my name at school, at home they call me Ancient. It's a good name, connects me to the past. I didn't like it at first because it makes me sound old, but Dad has explained it—Dying Star has explained it, I should say—I will be a very important person when I grow up, when the revival happens. When they come to fetch us. Dying Star is a good name: it's not about dying at all but renewal. A dying star takes on another life when it implodes. It gets reborn and I don't think my physics teacher even knows that. I call my mum To the Ship now. That's a weirder name than Ancient. I don't like that one much because it doesn't sound like a name. I don't say their new names when I'm hanging around with my friends. Friend. Stephen is the main one. This lesson is about planetary motion and I don't disagree with what Mr Whittaker has been saying so far. If he gets into the tricky stuff, I think I'm going to let him tell the class rubbish. Dying Star said I'm not to tell anyone that I've been chosen—not yet—and if I start talking proper science it might give it away.

The important point, and I won't make it to the class but I am whispering it to Stephen, is that the laws of planetary motion—which Whittaker's talking about—also apply to comets. That is, they move faster when they are near to the sun and slower when they are further away. If you look at the orbit of Mercury or Earth—any of the planets—the near and far is quite a small difference. We speed up and slow down but not by much. Haley's Comet goes out further than Neptune—not as far as Pluto but only one bus stop from it—and then it comes up closer to the sun than the planet Mercury. Goes hell for leather when it's swinging round our star. It speeds past really fast for the bit that we can see from Earth, the time when it is backlit by the sun. Comets pass by Earth more than you might think. They come and say hello. Planets and stars are much, much bigger. Comets are just big balls of ice but there could even be people on them. Not people like us—better than that—the sort that could teach us everything we need to know. How to do better than this sorry life. Never die. I don't mention the people to Stephen. It's probably true but I've not learnt how come yet. How they can live on ice. Dying Star knows all about it. To the Ship as well, I expect, but she doesn't talk about space so much.

'Harris! Head up, mouth closed. Pay attention to the lesson.'

Now I'm being done for whispering. It's not fair at all because I was telling Stephen physics—how comets speed up—not talking about football or telling a dirty joke. That's all you ever get from most of the boys in our class. Stephen's a cut above. Worse than me at football and fighting.

Mr Whittaker says if I can 'keep my trap shut' for the rest of the lesson then I won't have lines to do, but if I can't, I will. I nod. Dare not speak or he'll give me the stupid lines. Half the class laugh when he says 'trap shut,' but I don't think teachers should talk like that. It's too casual: if he speaks like that then the children who he is supposed to be teaching will do the same. Talk casual or worse. He should be setting an example. A lot of boys in the class swear. My dad used to talk very casually when I was young, I remember him swearing at Mum. I'm right to call them Mum and Dad when I think about this; their Themagin names—Dying Star and To the Ship—came much later.

Nowadays, Dying Star doesn't swear at all.

I think our family was quite an unhappy one before we found God. And it took us three tries to get it right. To sort the wheat from the chaff. Just trying seemed to stop the swearing, even when we hadn't found the right tramlines. I think that having no future to look forward to is the reason why people swear. Frustration that time is running out. I know it isn't; time will go on forever, we simply need to know how to stay in the picture. Follow the trajectory. Like following the path of a comet. They go on and on, been doing it since time

Antecedents

began. It should make me serene, satisfied, happy. It's what everybody wants. The trouble is, a lot of the ignorant kids in school—all of them except Stephen, in fact—take their frustrations out on me. I think it happened to Jesus too. I don't actually want to become as famous as him; I'd get really embarrassed if people started singing hymns about me.

* * *

All the boys say school dinners taste like dogshit but To the Ship's cooking is mostly worse. When Dying Star gets in a buoyant mood, we have fish and chips. Not much money for it though. Dad doesn't earn like he used to. This lunchtime Stephen says the dogshit is worse than usual but I don't really notice. It's only Earthly stuff, nothing of cosmic importance. I can't tell him that. Not yet. He says my parents are weird and calls them Mr and Mrs Harris. I don't put him straight; he doesn't know what they really are. Wise not weird. It's only cottage pie we're eating. Peas and meat and carrot, mashed potatoes on top and the dinner ladies have made it go crispy brown. I like that a lot, it's a clever flourish. 'If your dog's shit is like this, I'll eat its turds for you,' I tell Stephen. He gives me a funny look. Because he doesn't have a dog, I suppose, but I was only making a joke. Didn't know Mr Whittaker was standing behind me. It's his turn to walk around all lunchtime checking that we're behaving properly. And he's a stickler about actual swearing even though he can talk a bit casual himself.

'Lines Harris. Lines for your language. I must keep my vocabulary simple at all times. That's what you've to write. Two hundred times. Now repeat it back to me, Harris.'

'I must keep my vocabulary simple at all times,' I say. He nods. 'I was defending school dinner, Mr Whittaker. I shouldn't have sworn but I was only saying how much I like this.' I put my forefinger on the rim of the dinner plate.

'You like Mrs Beadle's cottage pie?' he says, pulling back his neck like I've said the daftest thing possible.

'Yes. It's decent.'

'No accounting for taste.'

I wonder if Whittaker should do the lines. A teacher who rubbishes the food that the school serves up, it isn't right if you think about it. He's another ungrateful soul in a world full of them. That's another reason why we need to start over. Dying Star says it all the time and I've figured it out for myself as well. Part of the problem is everything we see on the news: all the strikes and the different countries threatening to go to war. It only happens because everybody wants more than they can have, I'm sure it is. If we were all content with what we've got, we'd get along famously. The pie's not too bad. And we will all get along one day, making it happen is what religion is for. I haven't figured out how to make everyone else see it. Dying Star will help me, of course. And Number One has all the answers. I've simply not heard him say them yet.

* * *

The weather isn't so bad outside. We're not allowed a football in the quad in case it breaks the windows. We put socks inside socks, dozens of them, wrap them up into a very firm round sock-ball. Play footie with that. I have to go into the art room to do my lines before I can join in the game. Two hundred. When I'm in there, I cheat. Hold two pencils together, one on top of the other so that I only need to write it one hundred times. It still takes a while; I can't write as quickly doing it this way. Better than half pace, it's worth it. I've practiced quite a lot at home—some of the teachers give out lines for no reason at all—I'm pretty good at double writing. I could stay behind and do them at the end of school, join the kickabout, but then I'd miss the bus and my home is miles too far to walk. When I got an actual detention, at the start of term, Mum was a bit cross. I arrived home about two hours late because it's a crappy walk along the main road. No footpath, so I had to stop and stand in the verge every time a car passed. She said it was dangerous and I should have phoned her, the snag was I didn't have money for that either. And I don't see what she could have done. We don't have a car. Not these days. She never actually sounds cross but she told me to do whatever the teachers want. She said they can't help it if the rules and punishments are not very fair. It's the state of the world. Dying Star laughed. He didn't tell me that I should do different but he's more rebellious than Mum, than To the Ship. I think he is. He says the rules wouldn't be unfair if the right people were in charge. Won't be when they are. I expect he means God. God's mates. My dad has probably listened to all of the Toogood tapes, understands how it will pan out. I've only heard a couple. He says I'm too young for most of them although I can't see what difference my age makes. Fifteen at the end of the month.

* * *

Antecedents

I got the lines done quite quickly. I'll find Mr Whittaker as soon as the bell goes. Right now, I'm in the quad, playing on the same team as Stephen. We usually lose because Gordon—who picks the teams—puts all the best players on his side. He's running at me, dribbling the funny sock-ball. I have to tackle him but I'm not such a good player really. I lunge for the socks and Gordon tumbles over my leg. Lands on the tarmac quite heavily. 'I got the ball,' I shout and run to kick it. Before I've even done that, he's stood up and grabbed the back of my pullover. Pulls me down onto the hard surface. He's a right bully, Gordon Stickland. You shouldn't fight about tackling. It's just a part of football. The big snag is that I can't fight back. Don't know how and I know it's wrong, as well. Principle and practice. He sits on top of me and starts punching my face. Not hard, I suppose, but the sound is a bit sickening inside my head. Crunchy thuds. And my nose is bleeding now. Some girls come and tell Gordon to stop, that it's not a fair fight against a weirdo. I should tell them that Gordon is the weird one, not me; thinking that a swing of the arm can settle anything is obviously stupid. None of my classmates know very much yet, they've still to learn that everything they do resonates somewhere else in the universe. We lay down footprint after footprint which will be counted, tallied at a later date. Stickland will get his comeuppance.

Fighting is properly wrong and that's why it hurts so much. I'm not weird. A bit of a martyr, I suppose. Mrs Reece, the RE teacher, bangs on about Jesus every lesson. I like the stories—miracles sound neat—lately I've been learning he got it wrong. Not much point in raising the dead if you just do it once and then skip off back to heaven. That's only showing off. Doesn't help those of us still left here.

Now Stickland has gone back to playing sock-ball, I can go to the medical room. My nose is a right mess. Stephen offers to come with me and then, before we've left the quad, Gordon shouts at him. Tells him he has to stay and carry on playing the game or else the teams won't be fair.

* * *

To the Ship asks me loads of questions. I don't like answering them, it's all bother. My nose isn't broken, Miss Rogers said that at school. Stickland got a detention for fighting and I caught the school bus. I forgot to give my lines to Mr Whittaker but I've felt woozy all afternoon, so I'll explain that I was unwell. It should sort itself out tomorrow provided Gordon doesn't get after me again. He should see it was his fault. Tackling is what you're supposed to do in football, I'm right about that. I explain it all but To the Ship doesn't get it. Isn't interested in football.

'Don't play it if it's a violent game.'

Opting out might make me more of a target. That's how bullies choose who they're going to fight. Stickland never beats up his own team. I don't know if I can tell her this. She doesn't need to know about the hard time I get at school. She might take me out altogether and that could be an utter disaster. Dying Star talks about home schooling more than To the Ship but I don't think either of them can teach me to pass exams. Dying Star teaches me things that are important but not anything that will help me when I have to get a job.

Dying Star arrives home from the petrol station. He works as a pump attendant, used to have a better job a year or more back. Earned a lot more selling insurance—that was before he found Jesus—and long before he gave up on Him because Aris Toogood is even better. He's much less fussed about my nose than To the Ship was earlier. 'Earthly bodies,' he says with a wave of the hand.

He says that what we look like is unimportant in the long run. The eyes that we see with are unimportant. They won't outlive our souls but our souls will outlive our eyes. It makes sense although I can't imagine not being able to see. It's good that he's not worried about my bloodied nose: I don't like bother. And smelling is nothing like as important as seeing. Mostly, we only ever smell farts and the sulphur powder that Miss Tinsley gets out in chemistry lessons. Just things that are rank.

To the Ship has boiled up some barley for our tea-time meal. It looks more like a pudding, could even be a little milky, but there is salt in the mush. I eat it because I'm very hungry—and not eating is petulant, Dying Star says so—I was sick in the toilets at school, after the fight which I barely participated in. Themagins like me get a pummelling because we don't fight back, not that there would have been much point against Gordon. He's got about six inches on me. Toughest lad in fourth year.

Dying Star says that a couple of our kind are coming down from Bristol this evening. When this happens, I usually go straight up to bed, unless he invites me to join them. Some of what Themagins do isn't really for children, that's what Dying Star says. In September, an American couple brought their boy along. Me and him had to occupy ourselves all evening. He slept in a sleeping bag on my bedroom floor.

Antecedents

I think his parents did the same in the lounge.

While To the Ship is eating her barley, she hums. She's started doing this quite a bit lately. Dying Star ignores it. At least, I think that's what he's doing. He certainly doesn't join in. I recognise the tune: the theme of a space programme on television. I only know this from other kids at school. We don't have one, no TV in the Harris house; Dying Star is proud of the fact but I miss it. He plays his spools quite a lot—tape recordings—mostly of Aris Toogood, and he has a couple with country and western music on as well. They're a bit shit but I never get to hear any proper pop music. Stephen tells me about it—what's in the charts—and I don't know whether to disapprove or say I like it. I've seen some record sleeves in the library. Hippies look good to me—their hair—and I've read that they are against war which is the same as us Themagins. It might be because I'm thinking about this, that I ask Dying Star if he thinks hippies are all right. We all want peace.

'We see the futility of war, Ancient. I think those hippies are mostly just too scared to fight. They don't look past their own earthly fears. Dodging the draft. Don't misunderstand me, son, they could mean well—I've never met any—but it's clear to me they're just lost souls at the bottom of it. Drugs and waving around on a hillside while a few longhairs make a racket on guitars: that's not the road to eternity. It's nonsense. I will grant that they are right to challenge why everything must be like it is; they've no doctrine, that's their weakness. No real idea of what the better life will look like.'

'I think they want it here, without going far away to other planets and places.' I don't mean to start an argument, it's just what I've learnt about hippies. Stuff I've read in the newspapers at the library. Hippies in communes living by their own rules.

'Then they are fantasists, Ancient. They want to find something good in this purgatory. Do you think their wailing guitars are good? Women parading with their braless breasts wobbling about under their blouses. Is that good?'

I shake my head although me and Stephen go in a newsagent in Bridport where the girl who serves us dresses that way. Serves him, I never have any money. It looks pretty good but it might be wrong as well as good. It is wrong, I suppose.

'There is only one way off this Earth, Ancient,' says my father. He has said it lots of times but I don't understand the detail. Dying Star laughs at American space travel, the Russians too. He calls them

The Flophouse Years

amateurs.

* * *

I am still up when the couple from Bristol arrive. They're younger than my parents and the man looks like a hippy—long hair, a thick band of red ribbon holding it across his forehead—their names are Ganymede and Burning Rock. I know all about Ganymede. Not the man, the moon: it's one of Jupiter's. The most massive moon in the solar system, bigger than the planet Mercury. Burning Rock is a funny name for a woman. Ganymede has a jacket with tassels coming off the sides of each sleeve. A cowboy jacket, I think it's called, it looks odd with the headband. She wears jeans and a green sweat shirt. Normal clothes. She shakes my hand like I'm a grown up. I think it's about time but most people don't. She shakes it quite hard, and the way her sweat shirt moves makes me think she might not be wearing a bra underneath. It's only a hunch, I can't see through the fabric or anything. When Dying Star says they've to perform some rituals, I sense it's time for me to go to bed. Or at least, up to my room. I glance at the staircase and To the Ship nods. I take myself up. My father is already setting up the tape recorder on the dining table as I glance over my shoulder from the stairs. I look at Burning Rock mostly, my father is just in the background. She has short black hair and it curls around her ears. Her face is actually the nicest one I've ever seen. Can't stop looking.

I have a few books in my room. Astronomy and some old kids' stories that I've not thrown away. They're a bit dumb but I've finished my library book. I can hear the voice of Aris Toogood carrying from down below. I think it's one I've heard before, about how we have a collective mind. He uses that word very differently to the word brain. We have one each of them but share a mind. That's how I understand it anyhow. I try to ignore the sound; I will be allowed to join in the rituals when I'm older. Dying Star says being curious about things which I'm too young to understand is precocious. That means it's a bad thing. I begin by reading my astronomy book but it isn't as interesting as all the facts Dying Star knows or all the things Aris Toogood says. I like the pictures of Neptune and Saturn. Then I start getting into my pyjamas; it's early but I know not to go downstairs when the adults are communing for Themagin. Not until I'm old enough.

I can't see Burning Rock because I'm in my bedroom, but I sort of

Antecedents

can. Just with using my brain—memory of twenty minutes earlier—I picture her face. I find myself thinking more and more about her as I'm changing into my pyjamas. It's a funny kind of thinking although I'm sure it's just the same thing that all the other boys in school do. Picturing what she might look like without the sweat shirt on. Or the jeans. That sort of thinking. Dying Star has talked to me about it, says all boys think this way but I'm not to. A different destiny. I'm Ancient and he says that means I've to save myself. I didn't understand what he was even talking about when he first said it over a year ago; however, Stephen's mum is really religious. Just Church of England, not an interesting one, but she's talked to Stephen about the same subject. The facts of life talk, he called it. She told him that physical love is one of God's gifts to his children, so it's disrespectful to squander it. Stephen laughed when he told me, said he doesn't believe in God anyway. Says boys who play with themselves are dirty, so that's the only reason why he won't. I didn't really understand everything he said but pretended that I did. I got the gist of it. Stephen doesn't take his mother's religion as seriously as I do my parent's beliefs. It's only the Church of England, so he's right not to, I suppose. What they say in clapped-out old churches doesn't really matter. I don't tell anyone about our beliefs. Not even Stephen. Themagins are not very well known but there has been the odd article in the newspapers. They call us a cult. I raised it with Dying Star. Asked what they meant.

'Ancient,' he said, 'people who have not been chosen simply hate those of us who have.'

I'm on the right side and that's the important thing.

I get under the covers with my astronomy book. Try to put Burning Rock out of my mind. When she shook my hand, she put both of hers around mine. Her hands were really warm while mine are actually quite cold. Living in a cold house does that. Dying Star doesn't earn much these days. Not enough to buy coal. I imagine what it would be like if Burning Rock put those warm hands on the most private part of me but as I do this, I feel really guilty, I'm being terrible. Burning Rock is one of us, she's come here as a friend. She and To the Ship, Dying Star too, had a little hug. Not just shaking hands. I hop out of bed and go to the bathroom. I'm not going to think about her anymore. I'll just read astronomy when I'm back.

On the landing I can hear the voice of Aris Toogood talking about all the different worlds which are dotted across the universe. I stand stock still before going into the bathroom. Stephen calls our ground-

The Flophouse Years

floor room an open-plan. I think it's just a room, not much of a plan about it, it's the only one down there except for the little kitchen. The sound of the tape recorder carries up the stairs and I can hear the four of them humming now. Not the TV theme that To the Ship hums but something simpler. It's like a four-note scale going up and down. I don't know which notes. They are all doing it in time with each other. In harmony.

In the bathroom I try to do a big job. If anything can stop you from thinking about girls without clothes on, it's having a big shit. They are completely incompatible. One's gorgeous and the other is horrible. Aris Toogood often talks about the promise of a land with a God who truly cares about us. He doesn't spell it out but I think the point is that this creation, the one that the Christian God made on Earth—good enough for Stephen Bredbury's mum by all accounts—is a pretty poor show. Shitting: what sort of God makes everybody do that?

I flush without looking at what it is I've ejected. Barley and any school dinner I hadn't already chucked up. When I'm walking across the landing, I can hear a male voice and it sounds like arguing. It must be Ganymede; I think it's the women he is arguing with, only I can't really be sure. They've stopped listening to Number One. That is another name we use for Aris Toogood. In fact, Aris is what his parents called him, same as we all call him now. Farsighted parents. Mine only came up with Dennis first time around.

Maybe they weren't arguing. As I go into my room, I hear music carrying up from downstairs. I think it is something of Ganymede's because it's not Country and Western. In fact, it might be the hippy music Dying Star rubbished earlier. It can't be a record because we don't have a record player to play it on. I wonder if Ganymede, or even Burning Rock—who I am trying not to think about—has brought it on a spool. I can't see how else that kind of music can be playing in our house.

* * *

I think the music has been playing for hours but when I put my light back on, I can see from my clock it has barely been one hour. I like how it sounds and maybe Dying Star has come around to it as well. I wonder if they're doing the hippy dancing downstairs. It's on loud enough for that sort of party, a wonder the neighbours don't complain. I decide to take a look but I get out of bed quietly. Stealthily, Stephen would call it. He wants to be a private eye and they have to do this

Antecedents

apparently. Sneak up on people to see if they're misbehaving. I open my bedroom door very, very carefully. Make no sound at all. As I pull the door an inch or two, a squealy high electric guitar plays lots of fast notes while a cymbal taps out time, and over the top of it I hear a man grunt. I don't know if the grunting is on the record or in the living room. I walk the first steps to the corner in shadow, then I duck myself down low to peer over the banisters and into the room below. It's fairly dark, they have a couple of candles burning and a lava lamp which I haven't seen in an age. They're all lying on the floor and as my eyes adjust to the light, I can see that the men are lying on top of the ladies. They've got nothing on. Not a stitch of clothing. I squint a bit. I can tell which one is Burning Rock because she's got short black hair, while To the Ship's is pretty long. Ganymede is on top of my mother. Doing all the sex stuff by the looks of it. Hips on hips, his bum facing the ceiling. My dad is giving the same to Burning Rock. I suppose this is the stuff I'm not old enough for. When the American kid stayed in my room a couple of months back, he said that Themagins are all sex-mad. I told him to shut up, didn't believe him at the time. He was a weird kid and I thought he was just being nasty. I'm a Themagin; that boy—he called himself Danny but Galaxy was what we all called him—told me he didn't believe in it at all. He wanted to leave home as soon as he was sixteen. I said he might grow to like it the same as I have. Ancient's not a bad name. He is a year younger than I am. I think his family have taken themselves back to America—it's where Aris Toogood lives—and Danny looks to have been right about the sex-mad stuff. I still like it if it means I'm allowed to do that with Burning Rock. I'd definitely give To the Ship a miss. I expect that it's taboo, after all, she is my mum. Our beliefs are a bit different from the Church of England but they aren't completely off the wall.

* * *

I'm finding it really hard to get to sleep tonight although I'm barely thinking about Burning Rock now. My dad's done all the stuff to her that I'm not meant to think about. When I'm old enough I should probably find a girl my own age. I think I might be too nervous to do any of it to Burning Rock. I actually went red in the face when she shook my hand. I don't think I'm suited to girls that pretty. Shaking hands isn't even sexy, I just couldn't help blushing. The music has stopped now and they have another tape of Number One playing. I know this one—Dying Star has let me hear it—all about the places we will reside in the future. Aris Toogood says that They will come and collect us, They don't want us to suffer alone. It's a comforting message. When I think about Them, I always imagine that They have long necks, kind of like dinosaurs but with kindly faces that lean into us and smile benevolently. Dying Star says They won't look like anything, They will be rescuing our immortal souls not our transient bodies. It's all right for him: he's lain his transient body on top of Burning Rock's breasts, found out what that really feels like. I'm not ready to do without mine. Not yet, not when I haven't used it properly even once.

Long ago, before my parents took up their current names, we lived in Honiton and had a cat. I can't remember Lancelot very well, I think he was black and white. Wash-a-lot was my dad's joke name for him. Teasing cats is funny—not wrong—because they don't understand the words we use. This was a long time ago when I called Dying Star, Daddy. Dad came later and then Dying Star. We had a white car which he used to clean every weekend. He sold insurance back then and he was good at it. Sold the stuff by the truckload. He's good at anything he turns his hand to, my dad. To the Ship told me—this was a conversation just a few months back, a reminiscence—that she was surprised when he announced he wanted to go to church. My mum was the more religious of the pair. Had been up until then. She said they never went at all for the first six or seven years they were married—never bothered about God or any of it—but her parents had raised her a Baptist. 'We went to chapel when I was a girl and that never really leaves you.'

Dad chose for us to become New Pentecostalists. Guitars in church, speaking in tongues, it was tonnes better than the tepid rubbish Stephen Bredbury's mum has to put up with. The Church of England is all boring hymns being discharged like a toxic gas from church organs; the interminable sermons which just tell you everything you can't do. I think my Mum and Dad both liked the Pentecostalists. To the Ship said—in our talk—'The Sunday services were uplifting.' I can remember it a bit. I was young but I think I've always grasped religion. I don't know if I've been touched by God. Probably. I used to think a lot about all the things that Jesus did; nowadays, I can see it's a bit lame that all the miracles happened so long ago. He ascended, which might be the same trick the Themagins are going to do. Living on after everybody thinks you've died is a great idea. In an RE lesson during my first year at secondary school, I raised an important point—that

Antecedents

Jesus plans to come back—and children laughed. Stephen Bredbury too but I don't think his mum would have done. Even the Church of England thinks He's not really dead. Mr Crossland, the RE teacher was going on about Easter and I said He was coming back again, that it would be glorious. I'm surprised no one else agreed. You'd think there would be a few proper Christians in a class of thirty. Of course, I don't expect any of that to happen now that Aris Toogood has told us different. Plan B. Back then, Mr Crossland just nodded. 'I hope so.' I even thought his little smile was quite tell-tale. Not a proper believer and he was meant to be teaching the subject. I didn't tell my dad about the lesson but when he started getting other ideas, it made sense to me. The second coming is a great idea, the snag is that Jesus isn't reliable. Left it far too long. I don't think the kids who laughed saw that though. They were just being daft. Larking about instead of taking important stuff seriously.

Back in Honiton, when I was still in primary school, before I had heard of Mr Crossland, we had a bigger house than this one. Detached. My dad asked everyone from church to come around for bible study. They came but it was another of those things where I went up to bed and missed out. Not that it mattered: the bible is quite boring and riddled with flaws. I wish it was only the bible they were studying downstairs tonight. Themagins don't touch it, not since Aris Toogood pointed out how backward looking it is. A book about what every-one thought when no one knew any better.

I even think screwing is the very worst thing about Themagins. I didn't believe it until tonight. I know Dying Star and To the Ship do that stuff together. They did it a long time ago when their names were still Peter and Sally, it's how come I'm here. I'm not stupid about sex. Nearly fifteen, might have been the last in my class to know but Stephen has told me the stuff which our biology teacher papered over. She talked about reproductive organs but never said what the man has to do with his. I know now. I expect Ganymede and Burning Rock can do it too, make love. I don't know if they're married but he looks like a hippy and I've read in the library that they don't even bother with weddings. Just get on with it. I can't do it because I'm too young; I can see that Burning Rock's pretty face is the sort you'd want to look into if you had to do that stuff. And I can see why Dying Star isn't bothered about sharing To the Ship, she's nothing special. Why Ganymede lets Dying Star lie on top of his wife—or his hippy girlfriend if that's what she is—beats me. I wouldn't. Or maybe I would. Possessions and possessiveness are irrelevant. Shameful. Aris Toogood says so but I've not thought a lot about that before. I don't have many possessions. Just a few bits and bobs. A book about astronomy. No girlfriend and I can't work out if they can even be a possession. Probably not. My books can't walk out on me but girls are a different prospect entirely.

In Honiton, I had toys coming out of my ears. Wardrobes full of them. I've kept some of the books but a lot of it was baby stuff. I think Dad earned a lot more money than Dying Star ever has, which is probably because he used to think possessions were worth the effort. He thought all sorts back in those days.

When I was about nine-years old we drove out one weekend to look at a house which was up for sale. I'm not sure where it was—stuck out in the countryside—it was huge. I don't know if it had a priest hole but it might have done. A tennis court certainly; I walked all around it while Dad and Mum were talking to the owners. When Dad was driving back to Honiton, I asked if we would buy it. 'Just a little recce today, Dennis,' he said. He went on to explain he didn't have quite enough money for such a big house but he was working on it. 'With the Lord's help, we'll get there,' he said. And the Lord was still giving us a leg up when his mother died—my Granny—so we moved into this house. Three Croft Road, Charmouth. I can remember that Dad—still his name when we moved—said we were selling up in Honiton so that we could invest the money from the other house. I thought we were going to live here for a year or two and then get a house with a tennis court. I even think he said we would. A bigger house definitely, with or without the tennis. I get why the Themagins are against that stuff—can't take it with you—but it might be nice to be very rich just for a short time. I think everyone should get to have a go at the big houses. Take turns.

When we moved to Charmouth, into this house—Granny's house—we left the Pentecostalists church in Honiton. It was too far to drive every Sunday and there was a similar one in Lyme Regis, the next town along from Charmouth. Dad started saying they were insincere in the new church. I'm not sure why in particular but I remember there was an old lady who used to bang a tambourine throughout the hymn singing. It might have been that. Mum suggested we just drive back to Honiton each Sunday but Dad wouldn't have it. The thing is, I used to get very, very car sick. I think I'm the reason Dad gave up the church he liked, and he didn't find another easily.

Antecedents

We tried a little chapel in Chideock, I thought it was a bit boring. Everyone there was very old. It was around that time that the three of us, me and my mum and dad, went to Exeter Racecourse where an American evangelist gave a talk to a massive crowd. It was amazing. Thousands of people, the sun shining down on us. Evangelists can do that, fix the weather. Both Mum and Dad loved it. They were baptised again, it was something the preacher encouraged. He talked about a nuclear war that is going to happen and said it would be everybody's fault. He said that we have it coming, don't deserve any better. Mr Toogood says the same. The American evangelist said that if it happens—wipes us all out—when we haven't squared it with Jesus, we would not make it into heaven. You couldn't get baptised often enough in his book. I liked that Mum and Dad got done again but I skipped it. I hate the full immersion stuff, I'm not even keen on washing my hair. There's no baptism in Themaginism. That's a plus. I was twelve at the time: the nuclear war wasn't going to be my fault and I reckoned Jesus would see that.

It's quiet downstairs, so I step back onto the landing. Still doing the stealthily thing, treading softly. I've stopped thinking over the past although it is the only way I know to get out of the present. I want to know if Dying Star and To the Ship have gone to bed. I think I'll sleep better if I know they've each stopped humping the wrong one. I even think my parents are a bit old for any of it, I expect Burning Rock needs to do it. She looks to be a very sexy age. When I look between the bannisters, I see the same shadowy candlelight as before. The four are sitting in a circle holding hands, heads bowed. I don't know what it means but they've not put their clothes back on yet. Nude as bathtime. I stand upright, try to get a better look at Burning Rock and she lifts her head. I see her breasts which was what I wanted. I don't think me looking is any worse than the stuff my dad has been doing to her. I've not heard the grown-up stuff on the Aris Toogood tapes, so I could be wrong. She sees me and winks. I slide straight back into the darkness. Go to my room. I hope she doesn't tell the others but maybe she has to. No secrets between Themagins, that sort of thing. I get under the covers and my heart is pounding. For a minute or two, I wonder if Ganymede will come and thump me for looking at his wife's breasts, then I think that if he is like that then he would have battered Dying Star for what he did to her. I don't have a girlfriend whose breasts he can have a shifty at in recompense. I suppose my dad was doing swapsies. It must be on one of the tapes which I'm too young to listen to. Number One says they should do it, I guess. Not that I can go and have a look mid-ritual, it might be bad. If Burning Rock tells my mother, she won't do anything tonight, I'll probably get a big lecture tomorrow though. Dying Star could go either way. He might go frothing mad at me—disobedience is a bad thing these days—or he might invite me down for another look. When I told him that Buddhism sounded interesting, he said the strangest thing. 'Find a temple and try it.' He's unpredictable.

I think I'll just sleep now. A wink might mean she's keeping it secret. She was nice when she shook my hand. Looked searchingly into my face with her beautiful green eyes. Her breasts looked great too but I'll never sleep while I'm thinking about them.

* * *

Sleeping doesn't happen for me at all tonight. I can hear some more moaning from downstairs. Sex groans, I think. Mostly Dying Star. I know what his grunting sounds like because he and I dug the garden over before school went back. I'm not taking another look at them. If it was just Burning Rock, I definitely would, but seeing my dad's buttocks pumping away on top is actually very dismal.

It was less than a year ago—it might have had something to do with the Racecourse event, or maybe not—that we became Themagins. Dad was very excited for days and days before I learnt why. Maybe it was months. He'd given up selling insurance quite soon after we moved here. His first plan to save for a massive house seemed to have gone by the wall. We had passed the two-year mark. I didn't mind much because I like Charmouth—living close to the sea—and Stephen Bredbury is a good friend. Around the time Dad stopped selling insurance, he also gave five thousand pounds to the Resurrectionists—this was the church in Chideock full of boring old people—and announced he was going to be a preacher. Something went wrong. I think they wouldn't let him because within two Sundays we stopped going there altogether. I don't know if they gave him his money back.

We drove all the way to London, or nearly to London, a place called Woking, where there was a house group of the new lot. I was sick twice on the way; Dad said it was an opportunity we couldn't miss. I didn't know the name of the new religion yet and no one said it on the day. The newspapers said that Themagins were lunatics when they first took off in America; that was years ago when I was small. I'd never heard of them at all back then, recently I've looked them up in the library. It's a lot more complicated than the papers say, sounds a bit crazy until you realise that it's true. That Mr Toogood knows what's really going on.

The house group seemed to be mostly Americans. At least all the ones who did the talking. I can't tell the difference between Brits and Yanks unless they speak. This lot were very different from the Pentecostalists. Space rockets versus donkeys. It was also the first time I heard a tape recording of Aris Toogood. He wasn't in the room but the recordings are the same thing really. He was doing the speech about 'having friends everywhere.' Dad was nodding along and I was quite confused about it; I wasn't even sure if it was a good thing. Dad has always criticised Harold Wilson for his "friends". I didn't really understand the point with Wilson but thought it meant they gave you money you didn't deserve or put in a good word for you that wasn't even true. The more I listened to Aris Toogood's tape recordings, the more I realised that his friends are not at all influential on Earth—not yet—whatever power they wield in the wider universe. We are not alone, that was the real message. And these are not Martians who might attack us with flying warships. Science fiction is much gloomier than reality.

Dad was listening so intently that I couldn't catch his eye. Wasn't sure if he thought it was good or if he would complain about it in the car on the way home. Mum kept smiling at me, she tends to do that whether it is raining or beach weather. I remember about half the people there were like my dad: serious faces, nodding sagely. The other half were all smiles. It might have been because they thought it sounded far-fetched or it could have just been because they liked the idea of friends in far-flung places. I feel exactly that way now that I understand it.

There was food at the do in Woking which I remember enjoying. Sausages on sticks mostly but there were some sandwiches as well. I liked it, although I think all church food is about the same. The denomination doesn't make a scrap of difference. I'm not an expert but I'm experienced.

I can't really tell if Dying Star has become one of the relaxed smiley ones these days. You'd think he would be if he gets to screw Burning Rock. He says to me that we are living through the last days on Earth, that it won't be habitable at all in twenty-five years because the oil will run out. I think driving cars is pretty new, we managed without them before. You'd think we could manage it again. I suppose I'll move planet if my parents do. And Earth is old hat, the new one sounds a lot better than this when Number One talks about how harmonious it will be. It's funny, just as I think about this, all the grunting, even the humming and the hippy music, has stopped.

Peace on Croft Road.

I think I can sleep now.

2.

I'm not playing footie this lunchtime. Not giving Stickland a chance to start on me again. Stephen's a decent sort and he walks behind the science block with me. Just talking. I've been in a crummy mood all day, didn't get much sleep. I want to tell Stephen why not but I can't because Themagins are very private. Not with each other, not at all judging by last night. Just with those outside the circle. Dying Star says we are misunderstood by the ignorant world but I'm no longer sure what to think about it. The world doesn't know the half of it.

'Your nose doesn't look too bad,' he says, 'but your eyes are a bit bloodshot.'

I tell him that I hardly slept because my parents had friends around the house and one of them was a looker. I tell him that I was watching from the landing. I know that sounds like I'm a voyeur and it wasn't like that at all. Stephen doesn't say anything about it and I don't want to say Burning Rock was stark naked because he'll get the wrong idea about her. I don't think she's very slutty, probably only stripped because the others did. Because Aris Toogood told them they had to. I don't use her name either. She is sure to have another one—her pre-Themagin name—but I haven't the first idea what it is. Was.

'So, you fancy her then, Dennis? She has a husband and she's loads older than you are.'

I seem to have said a bit much about Burning Rock, although I called her Susan. It could have been her name once, quite a common one. Earlier this morning, in the form room before Whittaker got in, Gordon Stickland laughed at me when I said I liked Laughing Llamas. They're from California. Hippies. I haven't any records or anything but I've looked at their record sleeves in the library. I can imagine I would like the music. Gordon said hippy girls are all tarts, that free love is prostitution on the cheap. I didn't argue, I think I went red when he said it. Laughing Llamas are five men but Gordon might have thought

Antecedents

one of the guitar players is a girl, or even the bass player. The ones without beards. If I'd pointed it out, he would probably have started fighting. My dad said the hippies have it all wrong, wonder if he noticed that Ganymede and Burning Rock looked like hippies. He got on famously with them. With her. And although the hippies have not signed themselves up to go to other planets, other solar systems, like the Themagins are going to, my library reading suggests that they'll try anything. It might even be what Burning Rock was doing last night. Trying sex with a clapped-out oldie. My dad.

'I don't fancy her,' I tell Stephen. 'She was just nice.' I hope that settles the matter. I ask him if he's finished his English assignment. We had to write an advertisement—catchphrase and all the blurb— that we'd made up ourselves and then explain why our promotional campaign would make people more likely to buy the thing we'd chosen to sell. Better homework than usual; I did an advert for cars that are faster than other cars. It would appeal to quite a lot of people.

'I don't know why Miss sets us those assignments,' says Stephen. 'I think she's trying to be modern.'

'What do you think she should be making us do?'

Stephen is a bit of a weird kid. He gets top marks in Latin but not much better than me at anything else. Always does his homework.

'She should be teaching us to write business letters. The girls will mostly be secretaries and whatever you and I do, we will most likely have secretaries who take dictation.'

He could be right. Definitely thought about it more than me. I'd like Burning Rock as my secretary but I don't say it. Another Themagin secret.

* * *

Back in the house, only To the Ship is home this evening, my father working late at the petrol station. I think we need the money although I'm becoming more and more uncertain about everything nowadays. I thought I knew what was what but the visitors last night have thrown me. The stuff in the papers didn't worry me really, I've never read anything saying that Themagins are sexy. Didn't believe the American kid until I saw it with my own eyes. I like the idea of doing it with someone like Burning Rock; I think it would be best if she took a bit of an interest in me first. Not just following what a tape recording is telling us to do. That sounds a bit stupid actually. It's like Toogood is a farmer trying to breed sheep.

'Mum?'

'What is it, Dennis?' Then she laughs. 'Ancient, I should say.'

'Who were those people last night, Mum? To the Ship.'

She puts a hand up to her mouth. It looks like she is stifling a burp although I can't think why. 'Friends. You know, people like us. Dying Star only gets on with Themagins these days.'

'Did he get along with them? With Burning Rock and Ganymede?'

My mother looks away as she answers. 'All right. We got along quite all right.' I know what it means. Wonder if I should tell her that I've figured it all out.

'Ganymede looked like a hippy.'

'How people dress and what is in their soul are two different things, Ancient. You shouldn't judge someone just because they have long hair.'

'I'm not judging, Mum. I don't mind it.' It wasn't an accident that I called her mum that time. I'm pushing her buttons.

'And Ganymede is not a hippy. He likes some fashionable things. Hippies have it wrong; that isn't only your father's talk. Aris Toogood too...'

'Where, Mum? Where is that on the tapes.'

'It's not on the tapes. Your father has it on good authority...'

'Not on the tapes...'

'It's probably on other tapes. Not on the ones that we have.'

'And Ganymede isn't a hippy?'

'No. He would have said if he was a hippy. Themagins are completely different.'

'A boy at school says hippies are like prostitutes because they do free love. Don't wait until they are married.' I know I've gone bright red in the face, it's just that my mum needs to explain a lot of things to me after last night. I don't know if Gordon is right, or Toogood, or plain old Mrs Bredbury and the boring Church of England.

'Well, they certainly don't wait for marriage, Ancient. That doesn't make them prosti...doesn't make them what you said.'

'But Ganymede looks like one. Him and his wife might be hippies.'

'No. They're like us, pretty much. Very, very similar to us.'

'Did he say that,' I shout. 'Did he say that he doesn't like hippies. What did he say, Mum? What did you do with him?' I blow my top at her; it might be because I haven't slept. I'd be too scared to shout if Dying Star was home. He isn't strict but he might get mad like he used to, I really wouldn't want all that again. To the Ship has gone red in the face, me too but in my case it's the shouting which has made it happen. I expect she is thinking about what she did with Ganymede. It's definitely something to feel embarrassed about. Doing toad in the hole with a man she isn't married to. While the one she is married to is doing the same to the next girl along.

'It's grown-ups' business, what Themagins do of an evening, Ancient. Preparation for better times...'

'And I'll be a grown up very soon, wont I? Tell me what you do? That's all I'm asking.' I say it more calmly, if she doesn't give me an explanation, I might give up on the lot of them. Last night was actually weird, that's why I wouldn't tell Stephen. If Themagins are too freaky, I'm going to try the hippies instead.

She narrows her eyes just a little. I think she suspects something. Might think that someone has told me. I hope Burning Rock never told her I was watching. 'We are all one, you know. All of us. Being individuals is a fallen state. We have to prepare to become one again.'

'How? What do you do?'

'It's like meditation, Ancient. Mind and body. No more questions, please. If you ask Dying Star, he might be able to explain it better than I can.'

I reckon my mum knows I won't ask him. I've been looking up to my father all of my life. He's brilliant at something but these days I'm at a loss to say exactly what it is. I liked the look of Burning Rock before I knew she was a free-love type. I know sex is wrong unless you're properly married but all the kids at school get the same feelings. We just have to control them. Finding out that Dying Star doesn't—that he tells me hippies are all wrong and then goes and does most of what they do—I don't know if it's preparation for anything. He might be having too good a time for it to be serious and worthy. Could be the Church of England is boring because God likes it that way.

Meditation, my mum called it! The Buddhists do proper meditation. She does it with a stranger's big willy inside her and I don't think it counts.

Part Two

3.

Sharon Leeson has invited me to her party. Stephen must be wondering how I've wangled it. No invite for him. Sharon is in my night class, the Care of Elderly People course that the council has sent me on. They used to call it 'Care of the Elderly,' but now we always say 'People'. We don't forget that they are people like us. Not old junk. It's the main point of the course. Sharon is an auxiliary nurse at the cottage hospital. It was where they used to send anyone with TB until about five years ago, now it's full of old people instead. She says that hers are all dotty, can't think straight at all. Mine—in the flats—can be a bit forgetful but they aren't half as bad as her lot.

Stephen and I both remember Sharon from school, even though she was in the year above us. We remember her pretty face and her short skirts. Everyone had to sit cross-legged on the gymnasium floor for assembly and I looked nowhere else. At evening class, she usually wears jeans and she has been nice to me all term. We sit together if her friend Alice isn't in. Alice works funny shifts, can't get every Wednesday evening off like I can. A private rest home, they're the worst. Mine's council, and my manager, Lorraine, is brilliant. She's not what you would call sexy but I can imagine it would be all right.

The party is all over the ground floor. Mostly just young people stood around with tins of beer and then there are a couple of kids necking on a sofa. Not me, obviously. I like Sharon loads but I've no chance.

There are lots of Christmas decorations up in the Leeson house. I think something in the dining room got torn because two or three lads were mucking about. Sharon doesn't seem bothered; I guess her parents are easy going. They must like her a lot, allowing her a party like this. Beer and teenagers, it's not for the fainthearted.

Seeing all the tinsel and what have you brings home the simplest truth for me: there are no decorations in the Harris house; no Christmas for Themagins. Not that I believe any of that shit. I even think Mum guesses that I've stopped; I tell her to call me Dennis like everyone else does. There's no talking to Dad, to Dying Star. He's completely hooked on his off-to-the-stars nonsense.

I brought four tins of beer here but they've all been filched. I only drank one, so I've picked up a bottle that someone else brought. I guess it will be okay: you take mine, I'll have yours. It might be what everyone does; I'm new to socialising outside of a classroom or the old people's flats. I try sitting next to the speakers. The music is on really loud and I like it that way. You can feel the sound waves, physically feel them rippling on your skin. A girl who I don't know starts talking to me. I can't hear a word but it feels good that she's trying. Chatting

Antecedents

me up, unless it's some diatribe against me which I can't hear. I nod and smile, seems the right thing to do. Before I've figured what she wants, her mouth has clamped itself upon mine. Very good. I've been hoping to have a go at this for some time. Kissing. I hold onto the back of her head but not as fiercely as she does me. Then I feel her tongue on my own, momentarily inquisitive and then it starts rooting around. Counting my fillings, I expect.

I don't know my new girlfriend's name yet and she's not much of a looker, not that I should be too choosy. She's only getting me. That is, if she wants me. She might be very drunk and this is to make some other boyfriend in the room jealous. This thought frightens me slightly because I've still not learnt to fight. I believe in it a bit more. Not that punching is any kind of a good thing, just being as clueless as I used to be is a recipe for disaster. Don't fight back and you'd come off worst in a ruckus with your granny. Not me because mine's dead, but back in school I let kids take advantage of me because I was a Themagin. They didn't know that, of course, they just thought I was as wet as Christmas.

When we have a little break from kissing and this girl is whispering something unintelligible into my ear, I try to lead her away from the speakers. She takes my hand, even puts the fingers of her other hand over the rim of my belt, an inch down my trousers. At the arse side, thankfully. I like it but she's going a bit fast. Never been kissed before, me.

'What's your name?' I try.

'You're Dennis Harris,' she replies, although I actually knew that.

I lead her out into the garden. This might be a stupid thing to do. It's bloody freezing out here and not much chance of getting it on, as my hippy friends say. Not that I know any but they're my tribe now. Stuff the Themagins. 'I know that. But I don't know you.'

Now she starts kissing me again. It's good. Cold outside but I put my hand up her jumper—feel her bra which is another first for me—she doesn't stop me. I might have to ask Sharon what this one's name is later. We can neither talk with a mouth full of tongue.

* * *

Loads of cars have come and gone, all the parents who take the time to collect their kids. Sharon says we can stay as long as we like, us without homes to go to, parents who don't care much. Hers have come back from their drinks evening and then they went straight to bed.

The Flophouse Years

Sharon turned the sound down. They like it if their children party late, that's what she told me. They hope to have a Christmas day lie-in after years of getting up early to give out presents. Sharon is eighteen and Chrissie, her sister, fifteen. Julie—who might be my girlfriend—is a friend of Chrissie's, which is why I didn't know her. A couple of years younger in school. She's gone now. Her parents are much more interested than mine. And there will be no early rising for me tomorrow. No presents in the Harris house. The garage is closed all day—no work for my dad—and Themagins can't abide Christmas. Jesus got it wrong, apparently.

Sharon is handing round mince pies and I take two. It might be rude, it's just that I get none of these at home. Number three Croft Road. A long time ago it was my granny's house. I used to love visiting when she was alive; I think it's a shithole now. I say thank you to Sharon, don't mention the shithole. I asked about the girl I'd snogged as soon as she left, and Sharon was funny. 'You should get the name before you start sharing germs, Mr Harris.' Told me it was Julie Davies. Sharon was only being funny; she wasn't telling me off. Julie lives in Lyme.

In the garden—before I learnt her name—Julie told me it was too cold to be unclothing her. I was embarrassed when she said it; I just like her, I'm not a monster. But the next thing she asked was if I could point out the comet. I thought it was a weird thing to ask. I didn't know her name and feared she knew I'm from a family of nutty Themagins. I told her it was way too late. You can only see the comet shortly after sunset, before it slips over the horizon. I asked her quite directly why she thought I'd know about comets, even though she was right and I do.

'I remember you talking about planets and the moon when we were at school,' she replied.

That threw me. She had already told me she was there. A year or two below was already my best guess and different year groups hardly ever mixed. It turned out that she was one of the kids who hung around near my crowd on the sports field when it wasn't muddy, when the teachers allowed it at lunchtimes. I remembered the little gatherings but not Julie. Didn't stick in my memory and she seemed all right tonight. I think I only remember the prettier ones, the Sally-girl. In fact, we were all slightly odd kids, boys and girls. Not the cool ones, not good at sport or anything, and mostly well behaved. It was only in my last year or so in school that me and Stephen went near girls, and we probably just went red in their company. Didn't speak, couldn't speak, or if we did it was rubbish about space. I think he's still the same. Most of the boys talked about what they'd like to do with Sally Dunlop—not if she was present, of course—and that was cruder talk than I ever engaged with. Thought it but didn't say. I think tonight is the closest I've ever come to any of that, and I'm still a long way off the real thing. 'It's called Comet Tago-Sato-Kosaka,' I told Julie. She nodded like she'd heard that before. 'It's just a big chunk of ice. Maybe a bit of rock thrown in. It hurtles around the solar system for thousands of years before coming back.' I chose not to tell her that my dad calls it Comet Toogood, calls himself Dying Star. She has no need to hear what Themagins think of comets. If she turns out to be one then she quite simply isn't my girlfriend. I'll keep her if she's normal, it's my only condition.

'Done your assignment?' Sharon asks as she slides down next to me on the living room carpet.

I can't answer straight away because I've a mouth full of mince pie. It's totally brilliant that she asked me to her party. I've been a bit of a weirdo since I was about twelve. It's having freaky parents that's done it. I'm trying to be more myself now. Say what I think, not just a rehash of what I imagine my dad would say.

'Marginalisation. It's shit for the elderly but they aren't the only ones,' I say.

'Don't be the sort of kid who feels sorry for himself once they've had a few beers,' says Sharon.

I put my hand on top of hers, I think she knows I'm not being forward, her being older than me and everything. 'I'm not,' I tell her. 'It's just interesting. People with economic power get influence beyond their money. The text book says that the unemployed don't even vote.'

'They feel disenfranchised, so they act out how they feel,' says Sharon. I think she has a better understanding of sociology than I do. Can't remember what the big word means but she's bound to be right. The thing is, I wasn't bad at school, it was just that I often got confused. Some of the things which I grasped, I then let go. Learnt for a test and forgot ten minutes after I'd put my pen down. My dad telling me all teachers are propagandists was no help at all.

'Will you always do it?' I ask. Sharon looks at me like she's not understood. 'Nursing. Working at Perrymount.'

'Oh, Christ, I hope not,' she giggles. 'Mum wants me to get trained up, be a proper nurse, and I might. Emptying bedpans is not going to be my life. Not the next forty years, Dennis. Surely not.'

I nod along at that; I actually don't mind it at Plaza Court but currently we've only got one shitter. She says Perrymount reeks of the stuff. 'Isn't it worse for the qualified nurses? Watching operations and passing the doctor the tools.'

Now she laughs at me. 'Utensils,' she says.

'No one amputated a leg without a decent saw.'

Sharon puts a hand on my uncombed hair. 'You're funny.' I think she means it in a good way. 'Mum says I'll only work until I get married, that I should stop if I have a family. I tell her she's out of date; nothing is how it was when she was my age. Girls should have careers. Of course, I would stop work to marry Danny Clare if he asked me.'

I laugh like she has said something funny while thinking it pretty tragic. Danny Clare is a hopeless pop singer; I thought only much younger girls—Stephen's little sister, Mary—liked that rubbish. Sharon should know better. 'Rich people like that don't live down here,' I tell her. 'They go for the swanky houses in London.'

'That might be what I'm after, Dennis. And anyway, Danny had an impoverished upbringing. He only has a lot of money because he's such a good singer.'

I know what she says is technically true, a poor Irish kid before he started selling records; his picture gets on the front of magazines aimed at teenage girls. Not about to whisk her away from Charmouth. Danny Clare's never heard of Sharon Leeson and she looks great to me, probably only average to the likes of him. I'd tell her but I don't wish to sound cruel. 'Do you want to go out with me while you're waiting for Danny to show up?'

Now she punches me on the upper-arm. Not hard-hard but a proper punch. 'You and Julie are a thing, aren't you? Kissing all evening from what I saw. You can't be asking me out, Dennis. It's not right.'

I suppose she has a point. Sharon looks tonnes better than Julie and she's older, might let a boy give her more than just a kiss. Unless she's saving herself for Danny Clare. I shake my head anyway, tell her I was joking. I know my place in this world.

4.

'Come down if you want some bacon,' shouts my mother. I've slept in

Antecedents

dead late because I had to hitchhike back from Bridport last night. Get home from Sharon's party. No one gave me a lift for an age. We don't usually have bacon for breakfast, so a tasty sandwich must be my Christmas treat. A snog with Julie as well, the wisdom of which I'm having second thoughts about. She's a kid and not a very attractive one. I'm working at two o'clock. Lorraine says that I'm great, I volunteered for today's shift. She must think me very dedicated giving up my family Christmas for old people. Doesn't know the half of it, and I won't be filling her in either. In the Harris house, we don't even have a telly to watch the programmes everyone else talks about.

When we are eating our sandwich—and it tastes pretty good, which is not something I say much around here—my dad starts to talk about where they were last night. I say, 'Yeah, Mum said you had another Themagin thingy to attend,' and he kind of explodes.

'To the Ship! Your mother's name is To the Ship. You know that much, so don't act like you are ignorant, Ancient.'

He's going baboon-bonkers but I'm not bothered. 'Dennis,' I say, 'I like Dennis better.' Dad just carries on, it's like he doesn't really hear me.

'We don't have thingies. Maybe you were at a thingy last night. Whatever it was, it kept you out later than it is wise to stay out, Ancient. You're a man now, making your own decisions, but you were very late home. I can't say I'm not disappointed in many of the choices you're making, Ancient. Everything is coming to a head. Important things. Ganymede and Burning Rock—you might remember them—have left for America. Meeting Aris Toogood as we speak, I understand. We believe this to be the one we have been waiting for. Collection.'

I try to look him in the eye while I'm eating my sandwich; everything his stupid mouth spouts is crap. He should just shout down the toilet. When I was a Pentecostalist, I think I believed Jesus would come back. He had already done the resurrection trick once, so why couldn't he pull it off again. Plausible. Come back, do a few miracles to show it wasn't a fluke first time, and then decide who makes the grade and who doesn't. Heaven or hell: the great Christian gameshow. That was easy to buy into until I started doubting if the first back-from-the-dead stunt happened quite the way the bible reported it all. There are a lot of myths in history and I think they go that far back. Aris Toogood's contention is a million times stranger, and even the Christian story is a bit of a stretch. A life form from a better planet than this one is about to show up and whisk us off for the good life on Zog or Halley's Comet or wherever this new place actually is. That's Themaginism, the top and bottom of it. I think it all works like the emperor's new clothes. Someone brighter than my dad told him it was true and he's scared to contradict them and look an idiot. Same as in the fairy tale, it cuts both ways. You're going to look an idiot sooner or later. And I'm an idiot because I get earache off my dad for not being a dedicated Themagin. The wife swapping stuff they do—preparing for when we are all one—I wouldn't mind all that. Except that I've decided never to make love to a total fruitcake. Sharon or Julie, maybe Lorraine, would all be okay—pretty brilliant probably—but I definitely won't be making love to any Themagins. Got to put the bar somewhere.

'I'm sorry I shouted.' This is a rare admission. My Dying Star of a father is actually apologising while I remain wary. This crab bites when he's smiling. 'I think it is normal for teenagers to question what their parents are doing with their lives. Think about it, Ancient, can you imagine if I'd still been selling insurance when you got to this age, sixteen, seventeen...'

'It's seventeen. That's the one I am.'

'...Yes. You'd have had a field day. My pointless life. Getting people to pay money for premiums, to bet against the accidents that might befall them. Now that's funny...'

'So, Dad—Dying Star—how does filling petrol tanks beat that again?'

'Ancient, Ancient, you know that my current job is not something I am in any sense dedicated to. Our family needs the few pounds that I make; it's a mindless job. Money for food to get us by. The core of my life is learning from Mr Toogood, preparing for the great journey to come.'

'I've got a job at the flats. The council pay me pretty well. I'll be on more than you when I hit twenty-one, get the full whack. I don't think it's mindless. The elderly ladies and gentleman all seem to appreciate the helping hand. Having things done for them...'

'Ancient, yes, I like your job, I'm very proud of what you're trying to do. However, I'm afraid these are not normal times. None of the old folk you work with will be able to come along. Far too frail to join the movement. It's honest labour but it's futile.'

'You've put all your eggs in the wrong basket, Dad. If Mr Toogood's magic spacecraft fails to materialise then what? I'll be appreciated and you'll be a petrol pump attendant.'

My dad literally looks down his nose at my put down of his beliefs. 'It's here, Ancient. The ship of plenty is on the approaches. And there is room aboard for you.'

I get up. My bacon is finished. Gone. I downed it while forgetting to enjoy it, couldn't think about it once he'd started blathering. I don't reply to his bullshit. There is no point with some people. I just grunt something that isn't even a word. That's how my father makes me feel: like a pig contemplating a packet of bacon rashers. I can't tell him about the emperor's new clothes. Tell him he's naked. You've got to see it for yourself. That's what I think. I saw through the lot of them a couple of years ago, decided it's mental dung. Didn't really dare argue about it until I left school, got my own wage. It's the disenfranchisement thing Sharon was talking about last night. I thought my dad talked a lot of twaddle and at the same time I feared it was me not understanding properly. Once I saw I could make my way in the world without him, he became a joke figure. Thinks his petrol-pump job will get him to the stars. I arrive in my room and slam the door shut. Christmas! I pull a copy of Newsweek from between my bed and mattress. It's daft that I have to hide this stuff. I nicked it from the library, and Mum and Dad don't need to know that. I could buy it with my pay, it's just that I'd seen no one move this copy in days. The library has plenty of magazines without this one. I start reading an article about Vietnam, everything I read on this subject puts me on board with the hippies. South East Asia is nowhere near America, they shouldn't even be there. Why Dying Star sticks to his Toogoodian horseshit beats me. I think it's pride. He can't bear to say he's been chasing the wrong hare; no prizes in the offing for that stupid greyhound. Of course, if the spaceship honks its horn, I'll have to eat humble pie. Eat my copy of Newsweek.

I reckon I'm in the clear.

5.

There's a tree in the foyer and a bit of Christmas bunting all the way down to the office. Not much really but more festive than anything back at Croft Road. Bugger all at number three. I'm doing boxing day breakfasts on top of the afternoon-to-evening shift that I put in yesterday. Lorraine Chadwick, the warden, was rostered for this one. In fact, she says she will be on the end of a phone if I need any advice, any questions at all. She asked me if I could work the shift for her by telephone yesterday. She has family down from Liverpool or some such, thought they were coming for two days, and now it turns out they're staying for three. When I told her I could cover it, she said she could kiss me. I felt embarrassed. She's a lot older than thirty by my guess but I wouldn't mind if she did. Her shape isn't bad for her years. The face can be a bit stern and I don't expect she was being serious. She isn't married, so it's hard to tell. Funny contrast: Julie is too young—I'm worried that she's told her mum I had my hand on her bra—and she's only two years my junior. Lorraine might be twenty years older than me. I'll find someone in the middle sooner or later.

I'm making bacon sandwiches in the central kitchen—cook doesn't get in until ten-thirty—when they're done, I'll whiz them around the flats. Mrs Johnstone will just have half a grapefruit. I think mine are easily as good as the sandwiches my mum made yesterday; I might be a better cook than her. When I've done this, I've only to sort out a small amount of laundry, then I'll do a round, a slow one. A bit of company for everyone. Mostly I'll stop to chat with the ones who don't have family round. About half of them judging by the breakfast list. And the car park.

* * *

I like Mrs Carmichael, she's more with it than most. That's why I leave her flat until near the end, spend as much time as I can with her. I'm not neglecting the others and I don't have favourites, it's just that she's interesting.

'Working all Christmas, Mr Harris?' she says.

'It's that sort of job, Mrs C. You guys are here all the time, so one of us needs to be.'

'Guys? I think you will find I'm a gal, Mr Harris. Some might say a lady but I would not wish to labour the point.' She wears the faintest of smiles as she says it, and I grin back. The admonishment is just Mrs Carmichael having fun.

'You're right. It's the way we say it these days. Don't use the term ladies and gentleman so much.'

'And by one of us, you are lumping yourself together with Miss Chadwick and the other girl, the one who's always talking about her dog.'

I don't work with Tracy—we're on opposite shifts—so can't say if she has a point. Mrs Carmichael is no fan of hers, I know that much.

Antecedents

'Yes, the staff.'

'Odd though, Mr Harris. Us and them? You see, I believe you will grow old and become a them, or more probably see the folly of your current division.'

I stop smiling because she's actually making a clever point. I hope I haven't offended her; I probably did say it a bit stupidly. 'You're right, Mrs C. I think I learn more from you than I do from the night classes. Not that I mind them. Learning new stuff is good.'

'You think a lot, Mr Harris.'

'You know, you can call me Dennis. It's what everyone else says.'

'I can but I choose not to. You call me Mrs Carmichael when you can be bothered to say it out in full.'

'Because you're an old lady…a quite-old lady. It would be a bit off for me to use your first name. My being a teenager…'

'Off? Off the mark. A little impertinent. Is that what you're saying?'

'I guess.'

'I don't see what age has got to do with it. Perhaps we shall refer to each other by our Christian names when we have got to know each other a little better.'

'Okay.' I am really stifling a laugh. I know her well, help her out of bed in the mornings if she's struggling. She's the one who usually likes a bit of formality and I get that. I'm not trying to make her say what she doesn't wish to.

'Mr Harris, did you have a pleasant Christmas?'

'Yes. I guess.'

'You were here yesterday, and again today. You must like spending time with old ladies.'

She doesn't say it like a question but she's angling for me to talk about myself. I know it. 'Ladies and gentlemen. Yeah. It's all right.'

'Have we been the highlight?'

I laugh a little at that—not openly—it's a pretty funny notion. 'I like working here. A Christmas eve party was the best bit. People my own age.'

'I'm pleased to hear it, Mr Harris. You have told me before that you have no brothers or sisters.'

'No. It's just me.'

'Your parents must miss you if you have to work throughout Christmas.'

'They're not really into it.' Mrs Carmichael looks a bit confused and it might be because of my modern language. 'Christmas isn't much of a thing in our house. We're not Christians.'

'Good heavens, you don't still celebrate the old pagan ways, do you?'

I crack a smile at that. They might as well be pagans or devil worshippers; I don't discuss my parents' beliefs at work. Ever. Mrs Carmichael might be more understanding than many. More than my friend, Stephen, frankly. When I told him that my parents were Themagins, he went right round the bend. 'Why haven't you told me before now,' he shouted. 'I've been around your house and I never knew.' Said it like he could have caught it. Themaginism: the Harris family's very own leprosy. 'I'll still meet you, Dennis; I feel sorry for you having parents who do that. However, I'm not letting myself get brainwashed. No way.' I told him it's nothing like that. Nutty, but not anything to be scared of. Stephen said, 'Are you sure you've stopped? You're not secretly still one of them?' He seemed to think I might be Lucifer and, honestly, Themagins are just hippies with space rockets. They won't admit it, of course, have to pretend they're better, or purer. The hippies think we're all animals and might as well live that way. Free and easy, do what you please when you please. And with whoever you please. The Themagins have to invent a bunch of aliens who are going to transport them to the planet where it rains milk and honey and we will all live in harmony. For them, wife swapping is just practice for heaven further along the galaxy. Of course, I haven't told Stephen that part because it's far too embarrassing.

'My parents don't celebrate Christmas, Mrs Carmichael.' I know better than to shock old people with the name of their daft religion or their perverse sexual practices. Not that Themagins are at it night and day. About six times a year by my calculation. I'm not counting and I don't watch—catching them at it once was more than enough—but my dad grunts like a hippopotamus. Forty-four, he is. Ought to have given sex up altogether by now. Mrs C just gives me a long stare. 'We don't do presents or anything. They don't think it's very sensible. A waste of money and they're not fans of Jesus.' She's still staring. 'I don't mind it. Christmas must be more fun for people who do that stuff. Sherry and presents.' She still looks at me, I feel like I'm confessing to being the weirdest kid in Dorset. Possibly I am but I don't think it's my fault. 'I'll probably do all the tree and lights malarkey once I have a place of my own.'

'You are telling me that you wish they celebrated Christmas as others do?'

Antecedents

'Yeah. I don't really get on with them. They're not normal.'

'Well, Mr Harris. I'm sure they are very fine parents. After all, they brought you up to be the boy you are. Normal isn't everything you might think; it can be an embarrassment for children when their parents don't behave as other parents do.' I nod along to this. It's a bit of a lecture; whatever she says I won't be telling her the detail. It's not that I don't trust her, I simply don't share that stuff. Regret that I told Stephen as much as I did. 'Tell me, Mr Harris, were you excused religious education lessons in school? Due to your parents' beliefs.'

'Oh no, Mrs Carmichael. We belonged to a church when I started at grammar school. I paid a lot of attention. I've got the O-level.' This is totally true. And Dying Star says that I passed four O-levels when I really passed five. He won't count RE—calls it all make-believe—and I worked as hard for that as for the others. And he counts physics and then believes his own crap about people living on comets.

'So, you know all about Christianity, you simply don't believe in it?' she asks.

'I think I do. I mean to say, I believe some of it. Jesus was good, we should listen. I'm not really a bible reader these days but I'd send my kids to Sunday School if I ever had any. Not a zany church; there are too many of them. Church of England probably. Something to believe in without going overboard about it. It's my parents who are strictly against that stuff.'

'And what are they in favour of, Mr Harris?'

'This and that. I need to go and check if Cook needs any help fixing dinner.'

* * *

This evening could be a nightmare. Not literally, all stuff I can handle, but another couple have come around for supper. Themagins. I'm going to give Julie a call; I got her number from Sharon's sister. If she wants to meet up, that'll be great. I don't know if I should promise to keep my hands to myself, maybe she liked it as much as I did. Staying away from my own house, just in case Dying Star and To the Ship— daft bloody names—start on their ritualistic shit with another couple, is all I'm really aiming for. I'm going to phone her from the box on the corner—use a pay phone—can't have my parents listening in to my personal calls. Before I've even left the house, the Themagins arrive. I have to laugh. This pair look way older than my own sorry parents. Saggy tits for my dad tonight.

The Flophouse Years

'Oh, sorry Dennis,' says Julie over the phone. 'My auntie and uncle are staying over. I think I'm expected in.'

Not a total rejection, so I can't have been too far out of order in Sharon's garden. 'If I walk around, could you pop out for an hour or so.'

'Where will we go? They won't serve me in the pub, Dennis.'

'Nor me, half the time. We can just walk around.'

She agrees and I get her address. Julie lives in Lyme and I'll take the coastal path. I've a decent flashlight, the one I use to read in bed. Pretty sad that I still read under the covers at seventeen. And it's Newsweek not pornography that I have down there. I'm glad I've someone to meet up with, I've had nights when I walked around Charmouth on my own just to avoid listening to the sounds downstairs. Themagins mating, that shit.

Julie Davies is all right.

* * *

The walk along the coastal path is eerie. There's a decent moon so I keep the flashlight in my pocket. If it clouds over, I'll need it coming back. As I leave Charmouth and go past the beach huts where four or five kids are playing, chucking stones in the water, I can see the comet near the horizon line. It's called Comet Tago-Sato-Kosaka, named after some Japanese astronomers who saw it coming. Big telescopes can pick them up in deep space and monitor their trajectory. And comets always come up close to the sun, they have the strangest orbits. Ninety-nine percent of the time they are going dead slow out in the cold of the Kuiper Belt or thereabouts, then they speed up for a quick waltz around the sun which frazzles them. Some fade because they lose a lot of mass when they are near our star. The heat burns it off, that or the solar wind. The tail just comprises crap that is falling off it all the time. All the time it is near the sun. When they are heading away from the sun, the tail is actually in front. A comet's nose but no one calls it that. I don't think comets even have tails when they are just swanning around deep space. Nothing blowing the dust off.

Back in the pagan days which Mrs Carmichael rightly thought my parents to be stuck in, comets were a big deal. Stars don't move, not relative to us. The moon and the planets have fixed paths and we can keep track, figure out where they will be next week or next month. It's funny how long it took for men to see that it was only the moon going around us, everything else goes around the sun. All that business with

Antecedents

the Pope berating Galileo for getting it right, makes me think we are born big-headed. It took the cleverest scientist to see that our baby-like assumption—the idea that we are at the centre of everything—is a dumb one. Comets must have upset them big time in the old days. Something unknown entering the visible sky. You see, they didn't know that there are lots of things up in the sky that are too faint to see unless they chance to come up close. Those old pagans didn't have telescopes, no chance of working it out. Comets get brighter and brighter as they close in on the sun, but they can be difficult to see because they are only in sight near sunrise and sunset. They are there in the day too, obviously, it's just the brightness of the sun that makes it so we don't see them. And after five or six weeks swinging by, they go back to the outer reaches of the solar system. Where they belong and we can't see them. Druids and the like—the most knowledgeable people in a dimwit age—must have tried to explain comets to the kings and queens and anyone else who asked. It was crafty of them to say that comets were messengers; that's been the folklore since anyone had the words to describe them. Comets bring news, the war to come or the birth of a messiah. It gave the druids a hold over the kings and queens. They believed whatever the druids said the message was. The star of Bethlehem might have been a comet, although the idea that any kind of star can lead you to a stable is daft. I'm following one to Lyme, the comet leading me towards Julie Davies. A girl I can kiss but not much more, not without risking big trouble. Although there were kids at school who did it. Probably did it: loads of boys boasted that they'd had sex with this girl or that. Sally Dunlop mostly. I believed one or two. They might have fooled me or I might be the last boy on Earth to get in on the action. Last in Dorset. It won't be tonight. Me and Julie will just walk around Lyme Regis—she can tell me what a normal family Christmas is like, I want to hear it—a cold night in thick coats for us.

The sea is splashing on the rocks, heavy waves, a big crashing thump as if the stones that line the shore are hollow. I feel the spray once or twice. It's about a dozen feet below me at this point but very rough out there. I can see the lights of one or two boats. Ancient people—not me, the proper ones who lived long, long ago—thought that the stars in the sky were boats on an ocean up above us. It's rubbish and yet I like it as a way of thinking about the stars. The universe is a swirling ocean, although it turns out to be full of nothing. Ours might be the only planet with water on it. The others—Mars and

The Flophouse Years

Venus are the nearest—don't look a bit tempting to me. Inhospitable: it says so in my old astronomy book. When I walk along this coast I come to a cove or a town or a beach every two or three miles, more frequently than that on some stretches. If you could walk across the solar system—which you can't but it's fun to imagine—at a rate of fifteen miles a day, seven days a week, you would arrive at the moon after about fifty years. And let's face it, you would be much slower than that if you were carrying sandwiches to last until you got there. There are no cafés or service stations on the way. It's amazing that we've landed on it, and we're sure to get to Mars next. Amazing and pointless. Going to deserts which are dryer than we can imagine. This is our planet, suits us well, even the rain is a good thing. The grass really isn't greener on the other side. No grass at all on the moon. Nothing between here and there, and it's only a big lump of rock when you finally arrive. Moon, Mars, any of them. It's all gas on Jupiter and Saturn, we'll never land a spacecraft there. Never ever. We are on our own. Maybe God sent Jesus but I don't really think so. I just said it to Mrs Carmichael because I don't want to fall out with her. If God made the universe, He must have been smoking what the hippies smoke.

I believe we are better off not thinking about it too much. Dying Star can't spot that selling insurance is better than squirting petrol into other people's cars. It pays more and you don't come home stinking of oil: obvious and still he can't see it. Scrubs up if he has to screw someone else's wife for the greater good of humanity. The Pope was the warped thinker when he threatened Galileo, and Toogood and my dad are in the whacky chairs today. Think straight or don't think at all. The latter is probably the safer option but the cogs in my mind just keep on going round and round.

* * *

When I knock on the door, Julie's little brother answers—or cousin—I don't know the Davies's at all. 'Your boyfriend's here,' he shouts up the stairs.

'Don't leave him out in the cold,' says an adult's voice. A man.

'Come inside, mister,' says the little kid. He's no more than eight and pretty funny with it.

'I'm Julie's dad.' The man whose voice I heard is in the hallway, smiling at me which I take for a good sign. 'What will you have?' He takes hold of my elbow, guides me into the kitchen. They have a table crowded with every type of drink, the alcoholic sort, for the most part.

Antecedents

I can hardly take them all in.

'Double Diamond,' I say. Beer in the tin, trustworthy. There are lots of bottles that I can't identify. Pernod and Vermouth; I'm none the wiser for reading the labels.

'A Double Diamond coming up. Find yourself a chair, sonny m' lad, Julie will be down in a jiffy.'

When I step into the lounge a sister or cousin or the like, stands up from her armchair and gestures that I should sit. 'Thank you,' I tell her. The house is really crowded. There is a man older than my dad sitting on a stuffed footstool. I don't think it's always this crammed, just visitors. Normal for Christmas everywhere except number three Croft Road.

'What's your name, young man? asks her father as he hands me a glass filled with beer.

'It's Dennis Harris,' says the girl who gave up her seat. 'Julie's boyfriend is called Dennis Harris.'

I sound to be a bigger fixture in her life than I know myself to be. At least they seem happy enough about it. Whatever she's said about me, I still get a beer.

'Happy Christmas, Dennis Harris,' says her father, raising his own glass from the coffee table.

'Yes, happy Christmas to you all.'

Julie comes into the room. She wears a green skirt and she's a bit podgier than I realised two nights back. The lighting in here is very sharp; I knew she had spots but there are actually loads of them. 'Dennis,' she says, and she slides into the armchair—it's a big one—putting her bum beside mine. I think we are indecently close but that might be the way of big families. A bit of my beer spills onto her skirt. It happened because of how she leapt on me but I say, 'Sorry.' I've got manners.

'Daft thing,' she says, leaning into me and kissing my lips. I think my face has turned a shade of crimson. There's no kissing in the Harris house, not while my generation is in the room. They do worse when the lights are down and Aris Toogood is talking on the tape machine, but I've determined to think about none of that tonight. I wish Julie looked more like I remember from Christmas eve although her skirt has ridden up which could be good or bad. The back of my hand is touching her thigh. I raise it up out of the wedge between us. If this lot are Themagins, I'm probably going to have to screw her.

'Give over, Julie. You're squashing him,' says the man on the footstool.

'Boys like that,' says the sister or cousin. She looks about twelve, shouldn't know about that stuff in my estimation.

'It's all right. Are you comfortable, Julie?' I've never had a girlfriend before; it's just dawning on me that getting to know the family must be part of the deal. I wonder if I dare bring her back to my house. Meet the freaks. Only when Dying Star has no visitors of his own, obviously.

'It'll be all right for a bit,' she answers, 'but we're going out soon. Can't kiss properly in front of you lot.'

'Ooh!' say about four family members in unison. They think it's funny, don't know that I had my hand up her jumper two nights ago.

'Dennis?' says a woman on the sofa. The girl who gave up her chair for me has draped herself across the woman's lap. Too big for it in my view but she's there.

'Yes,' I answer. My voice quavers a bit. Something in the way she said my name has unnerved me. She said it very slowly.

'We've not met. Do you live in Lyme?'

'In Charmouth.'

'Oh. Has your mother dropped you off?'

'I walked here.'

'See!' says Julie. 'He'll do all that for me. And miss all the tele programmes.'

'And how old are you, Dennis?' continues the woman. I've worked out who she is for myself.

'I'm seventeen, Mrs Davies. Is that all right?'

'Of course, it's all right, Dennis. You're as old as you're old. No doing anything about that. Just don't break our Julie's heart, all righty? She's my special princess.'

'I'm your special princess,' says the wriggling twelve-year old—or eleven, or thirteen—I'm guessing.

'You are too but there's no prince on your horizon, Sandra. That's why I'm bothering about Julie.'

I can't say anything to this. I'd not seen Julie in a proper light until ten minutes ago and now her mother is talking like I'm going to carry her off on a white horse. This is probably normal madness, not like Dying Star and To the Ship, whose names I dare not say in this household. It is crackers, for sure. We will walk around Lyme Regis, not marry. We might snog, I'm a little less keen now I've seen her face properly. I drink a long draft of beer. Raise my glass to Mr Davies. 'Thank you. This is great.' He smiles back but I can't tell what he's thinking. 'I'm a care assistant, not a prince,' I tell the nosy lady. I've no intention of breaking Julie's heart but she's the one kissing me in front of her family. The one who started on me at the party. If it all ends in heartbreak, the cause will be her own inflated expectations. I'm not worth much, it's daft getting excited over me.

'Oh,' says Mrs Davies, 'Julie said you were in sixth form.'

'I didn't,' she protests. 'I said I knew him from school. I didn't say he was still there.'

'I work at the old people's flats, the housing support project.'

'Where is that?' she asks.

'Behind the Co-operative stores. In Charmouth.'

Mrs Davies nods, seems to be weighing me up. 'You're a caring soul then. Not so many boys do that kind of work.'

'They need more males,' I tell her. 'Some old men don't like being bathed and dressed by girl care assistants. Get embarrassed by it. Lorraine said she was delighted when I applied for the job.'

Mrs Davies nods a bit more. 'Who's Lorraine, Dennis?'

'The warden of the flats. I've learnt all sorts from her.' I want to talk about this—looking after old people is what I'm good at—Mrs Davies no longer looks terribly interested. She's found out whatever she was after.

'If you can be back here by eleven, I can run you home, luvvy. Save you having to walk it. Don't want you getting knocked down on the road. A lot of young drivers really put their foot down this time of night.'

'It's all right...' I'm about to tell her I use the coastal path; think it might sound odder than a boy working as a care assistant. She's shaking her head; I shouldn't refuse. 'Thank you, Mrs Davies,' I say.'

'I can't drive you,' says her father. 'I'm going to be pie-eyed drunk by eleven o'clock.' He splutters away at that, laughing like it's the funniest joke ever told. Only little Sandra joins in and she's drinking orangeade judging by the colour of it.

* * *

When we are walking towards The Cobb, hearing the constant rattle of the ropes upon the masts of boats as they tremble in the strong wind—there are many moored in the small enclosed harbour—I say, 'Your family were a bit much.' I mean it nicely. Mr Davies gave me a beer. Never expected that and it was very welcome.

'Don't be mean,' says Julie. 'They're great. We're a great bunch.'

The Flophouse Years

I have my arm around her shoulders. She looks better when the lighting is nearer to nothing and I want to be friendly tonight. I'm here to keep clear of the home her mum wants to run me back to. 'Yes,' I tell her. 'I'm just not used to people like that.'

'Normal people?' she answers. I have to laugh: Julie is spot on, I'm not familiar with that sort whatsoever. 'My family might not be rich but they all care about one another.'

'Yes. They're really nice—I meant the fuss they made—I like them. Your mother thinks I'm your prince.'

'What if I think it too, Dennis? Every princess wants one.'

Oh shit. I'll play along for now. Let her down gently in the new year. 'But I'm a care assistant. Not sure what your mum made of that?'

'You're working, Dennis. You're dead grown-up. I like that. Will you get a car?'

'I've not learnt to drive yet, Julie. I suppose I might.' Might not is the more likely option, not sent off for a driving licence yet. I don't need much outside of Charmouth; I live there, walk to work. If my parents chugged off on their spaceship, it would be the perfect spot for me. Julie seems to know what she wants but I'll not be buying a car just for her. 'Do you have plans? What are you good at in school?'

'I'm not much good at anything, Dennis. Bottom sets. Miss likes my sowing. I'm quite good at that.' As we walk around the cold little town—noise coming from the odd pub, a house party on Sherbourne Lane, nothing me and Julie can join—she snogs me now and then, which is all right but I'm starting to think of it as practice. If I remember what she looked like in the sharp lighting of the family's lounge, it all feels a bit grimmer. 'What's wrong with you tonight, Dennis? You talked a lot more at the party two days ago.'

I don't think I actually did. There was music blasting away so no one really needed to talk at all. She's right about my mood though. I keep thinking about her family: the normal ones. All crammed in the lounge together chatting and supping from tins or glasses. A good time. My sorry lot might be listening to Aris Toogood telling them how to prepare for the extra-terrestrials. Visitors expected from a planet only Aris has the phone number for. They might be doing God-knows-what on the lounge floor. Dirty bastards. None of it's normal.

I give her a big snog. It stops her telling me to talk when I've nothing I want to say. And kids my age are meant to be doing this. Necking and angling for a bit more.

Antecedents

* * *

When Mrs Davies is running me home, I have a little panic that she will expect to come in. To meet Mrs Harris as she calls To the Ship. Not that my mum would correct her if she did; Dying Star might but not my mum. I sometimes think she only believes it to keep my dad from going even more mental. My real worry is that the pair of them might be rolling around on the living room floor, stark naked. Not just the two of them either, the two old duffers who have come a-calling could be doing all the randy sex stuff with them. I decide to tell her they'll be in bed and pretend I use a back-door key. I'll stand in the garden until I know Julie's mum has gone and then walk around Charmouth until one or two in the morning. That's my plan. I'm not catching Dad at it. Haven't since I was fifteen but even hearing him grunting on the job knocks me sick.

'What does your father do?' asks Mrs Davies.

'He works in a garage.' I could specify that he does the lowest job a garage has to offer. Choose to spare her the detail.

'You didn't fancy going into the motor trade yourself?'

It's a dumb question but not Mrs Davies's fault. I'm even misleading her a bit. Pump attendant is not close to being in the trade. Apart from a few old ladies everyone can fill up for themselves, it's what they do at most petrol stations. My dad stands out in front like a little lost windmill just so Hodder's garage can charge a penny a gallon more for petrol. It's pitiful if you think about it. I've seen him, the garage is on the edge of Bridport. His job consists of doing what doesn't need doing; paid a pittance and it's worth less than that. I've a suspicion—based on her motor-trade question—that Mrs Davies doesn't want her daughter dating a care assistant. She probably thinks it's a girl's job. No worries, I reckon we will have finished with each other by the second of January. She can have her Christmas romance and I'm getting the hang of kissing, she let me put a hand on her waist, so I felt the skin underneath her clothing. I liked it and she might have let me go a little further. Only a kid so I thought it best if I didn't.

As we enter the main high street I say, 'You can drop me here, Mrs Davies. Croft Road can be tricky to turn a car around in.'

'Oh, you drive, do you, Dennis? I never asked.'

'No, but people say it's tricky.'

She takes my word for it, sets me down by the chip shop. Closed of course, it's Boxing Day. A shame, I'm starving hungry. There was lots of food at the Davies's house but I didn't take any. I don't like people guessing how crummy my homelife is. Barley on Boxing Day. Without Plaza Court lunches I'd probably have starved to death. I've got some digestive biscuits in my room that I'll eat when I finally get to bed. I bought them from my own wages; keep them hidden from Dying Star, from To the Ship. I think they'd steal them if they knew they were up there. They're not the sort to get into a sweat about morality, bother about stealing or any of that. They think it's just them heading for the spaceship and tough luck for every bugger else. That's the long and short of Themagin theology. The sum total.

6.

I'm off work tomorrow, so I will definitely be out tonight. No idea where to, I simply can't stand staying in. I asked my dad how he was going to see the New Year in this evening. 'Will you be doing it in style?'

'Yes, Ancient,' he beamed back. I said 'Dennis' under my breath. Check the birth certificate: I'm right, he's wrong. 'This is going to be quite a year, this nineteen-seventy. A lot of people are going to find out the truth this year. You too, Ancient. You really are.'

I wish I hadn't asked. When he gets this excited, I wonder what he's thinking deep down. Exeter City fans do it on first-round Saturday. The FA cup. 'This could be our year to go to Wembley.' They say all that kind of crap, kidding themselves. City are rubbish, and still I'd bet on them winning the cup way ahead of a bunch of aliens coming to fetch Dying Star. I'd like them to do it though, take my dad to Pluto, or further afield if there's petrol in the tank. He's earned himself a hearty good riddance from me, Dad's a total embarrassment.

I broke a heart on Tuesday. Unintentionally. Missed out on a New Year's party too. I reckon it would have been a lousy one. I saw Julie in Lyme one last time, it was all right but she started getting a bit strange. Wanted to call me a baby name, one she used to use for a cat. The cat's dead, so that made it doubly freaky. Buggums or Snuggums, I hate that shit. Dennis is my name. I nearly said it sounded worse than Ancient, glad I didn't because there would have been no explaining it without saying way too much. Julie said we should go to a New Year's Eve party at her friend Debbie's house. The trouble was, there will be no beer there. Children playing games and finishing at ten. I'm not into hunt the thimble. Laughing Llamas were on the record player at Sharon's on Christmas Eve, not kids' rubbish. I told her this, that the

Antecedents

party would just be silly school girls. She said, 'If you loved me, you would go.' I tried to reason with her. I don't know who I love really. I liked her a bit but it wasn't love. I'm keeping that back for someone I'm more on a par with. Two years younger isn't a lot but Julie's thick with it. I tried to explain it, used better words than I just have. She ran off crying. I followed; it was dark and I was worried she would do something stupid. Then she just ran around the back of her own house, so I left. Couldn't come to any harm there. It's for the best, I think, although I haven't a better party to go to. Me and Stephen are going to try and get in The Crown. Stay for the lock-in if they're having one.

* * *

Stephen is in lower sixth, he's very thin and wears wire-rimmed spectacles. I look eighteen although I've ten months to go. He is why we weren't served. The bar lady asked him his age, didn't ask me mine. Stephen said, 'I'm nineteen, missus,' and that's a decent answer, making out she was way off the mark. Saying you were eighteen yesterday, or something like that, would never work. The problem was that the lady laughed. I don't know why really, maybe because Stephen is wearing a jacket and tie, looks like a schoolboy. Not his actual school blazer, just close enough to make him look like what he is. Stephen laughed back. He's like that, can't talk to girls at all. 'No, you're not, are you?' she said. 'I'm nearly eighteen,' replied Stephen. A white flag.

I've bought four tins of Double Diamond at the off-license. The girl who works there knows my name, she's a friend of Sharon's. I expect she worked out that I'm underage, mates help each other so she didn't say anything. I'll share the beer. Stephen means well but he's about as cool as bad breath.

It's not so cold tonight and I tell him we shouldn't open them yet. We can drink beer down by the sea if we need to, but I'd prefer to gatecrash a party.

'We don't know anyone having a party,' says Stephen.

'Noise, music, parked cars.'

'What if there are rough sorts there?'

Now I laugh at him exactly like the bar lady did. 'That's what they'll be thinking about their gatecrashers, isn't it? They might worry that we're going to get drunk and smash the place up. Not that you and I would do any of that.'

The Flophouse Years

'I certainly wouldn't, Dennis. I shan't be kissing girls either. Not one's I've never met before. It can result in disastrous affairs, you know?'

I carry on laughing. He's trying to have a dig at me and Julie. Jealous as hell, I'd say. Stephen is a mouth virgin, not even kissed a girl yet.

It takes only minutes to walk up and down the main street of Charmouth. I lead us out of the village, up Green Pit Knapp. Head for the country. There might not be any parties, not many people living there, I just think it's worth a punt. Stephen follows me. He has nowhere else to go.

We come to a barn by the road side, hay still stacked in bails along one wall. 'Why don't we drink our beer in here?' he asks.

Funny that he calls it our beer when I'm the only one earning a wage. 'Not yet. We'll need it to get into the party.'

'Party,' he mutters. That's just typical Stephen. He criticises my choice of girlfriend—said she wasn't pretty enough, but he remembered her from school which is more than I managed—and he can't actually get within twenty yards of a girl. They run. He's mostly interested in biology, talks about dissecting animals and how easy it is to kill a person if you cut off the blood supply to the brain. Not chatting up talk in my book. Or any book written by a normal person. And he keeps going on about Themagins. I've not even told him the half of it. As we are walking in the dark, my flashlight alone guiding our way, he asks me, 'Is there any kind of New Year festivity in your house, Dennis?'

Stephen lives with his mum and his two little sisters. Their dad left years and years ago, I think. Long before I landed in Charmouth. Mary, the older of the pair, is fourteen; I sort of like her better than Stephen these days. Sort of because she's still a kid. Mary has a lot more gumption than this chap. And she's pretty—the face, the lot— but she's younger than Julie Davies. It wouldn't be right to fancy her but I kind of do. I think his family is quite poor but they still eat better than barley every day of the year. There isn't a drop of alcohol in his house and the lights will be off at ten-thirty, New Year's Eve or not.

'They have friends round again, Stephen. I hate them. I'm staying out until dawn whatever happens.'

It's far worse than I tell him. Three cars have parked on Croft Road; seven crackpot Themagins have descended upon my house. One of them is Burning Rock. It's been over two years but I recognised her straight away. Still looks good. That stuff sears itself into our brains. I hope there isn't any sex this time; there are so many of them and they don't have even numbers, so they really shouldn't. The odd thing is, I thought she was in America. Dying Star said it a week ago. And she came on her own or with another couple. No Ganymede tonight, not that I mind him so much. Hippy hair. A freak though, all Themagins are freaks.

'Will there be beer at your parent's party?'

I can only laugh at that. 'You don't want to go into my house, Stephen. The lunatics will brainwash you, change your name to Rocket Pants and have you buying a ticket for the spaceship.'

Stephen doesn't laugh at all. 'I suppose so,' he says. 'Right now, we're just walking aimlessly, there are hardly any houses out here, never mind parties. You're right, I don't want to meet your parents. Couldn't you slip in and take some beer. It's your house.'

'I don't know what they're doing, Stephen. Don't want to know. If one of them has brought tins or bottles, good luck to them. I don't share with nutters.' We walk on in silence for a few steps and then I reach into the brown paper carrier bag, pull out two tins of Double Diamond. 'Except you.'

* * *

It's incredible. We've only passed about three farms and now we've come to a big house with rock music and shouting. A handful of people outside. Lots more inside, I expect. Dozens of parked cars. And it's a young people's party but they are probably older than us.

'I'm not sure,' says Stephen.

I tell him we're going in. I'm dead certain about it.

I've put the flashlight into the carrier bag to make it look like we have more than two measly tins of beer between us. We drank the first ones double quick and chucked the empties into a ditch. Goody-two-shoes didn't think we should and then he said it felt good once he'd done it. A spot of littering seems like his full quota of thrills, all he can manage in one night. Stephen is better company than a Themagin but not by very much.

'Hi there,' says a lad on the drive as I ring the doorbell. I recognise a girl in a grey coat standing with him, there are a few others out here too. Jet black hair; her name's Hannah. Two years above us in school; she looked good back then and probably more so now. It's too dark to see. To evaluate, as we say on my course.

A girl I've never seen before answers the door. 'John invited us,' I tell her.

She leans into me and pecks me very lightly on the cheek. 'Gatecrashers? Welcome to my party.'

Now it's my turn to go as daft as Stephen. 'No, there is a John here,' I try. I hope she can't see that I'm blushing, a bit shit at lying.

'I was just telling my boyfriend that we were only a couple of gatecrashers short of the best party ever. Now shut up about your friend John and get yourselves a glass of punch.'

We shuffle into the kitchen; the hallway is heaving with more than a dozen people. I put the torch into my coat pocket, so that I can't accidently leave it behind. The two tins I place on the drinks table show how tight-fisted we are. Nobody seems to be looking except me. The strip lighting in this room is bright. Everything laid bare. There are a few hippies here. Hair really long. The girl who answered the door introduces herself. 'I'm Belinda, I'll let you know. Just so you can say whose party you've gatecrashed.'

'Weren't we in school together?' I want to keep her talking, she looks great. Belinda laughs and tells me probably not. She went to a private girl's school in Devon. She wears a skirt and blouse that look a bit hippy. Not full blown, kind of pointing that way. The music playing is brilliant. It's not as noisy as some but the guitars are just doing bonkers riffs. I love it. Stephen has probably wet his pants, being at an actual party and everything. He wasn't at Sharon's—couldn't have coped—and this is miles better. I'm beyond caring about him. 'Find a girl in a dark corner,' I whisper to him, 'snog and fumble. Six days later, when you've seen her in daylight, finish it.' I'm the one laughing now. And the girls here are way older than Julie Davies, free-love hippies by the looks of a few. Might let us do more than kiss. You never know.

* * *

There's a guy here who calls himself Pretty. It's a stupid name but I'm used to that with Mum and Dad and Burning Rock, the latter scarcely on my mind since we entered the party. One thing about so-called Pretty is that he really isn't. His hair is long, straggly and—I fear sounding like my dad—unwashed. He wears an eye-patch and I reckon there is a perfectly good eye sitting behind it, in fact, I've a notion it was on the other eye when Stephen and I arrived. It probably was; however, I've drunk a bit too much punch to swear to it. The other thing I have to say about Pretty is that I like him. He's telling stories about going to London, going to parties up there. He says they have live bands playing and one time he saw a coloured drummer with an Afro hairstyle. Stephen asks, 'What colour?' and everybody laughs at him. He goes red: I don't know if he was trying to make a joke or just is that stupid.

'I don't mind about the live music,' I tell Pretty. 'I expect records are better because any band would just be locals not rockstars. Not like these Laughing Llamas.' I know that the one we are hearing is by that band. I watched Belinda put it on the deck, recognised the five cool guys on the album's sleeve. We're all down on the floor, cross-legged. She is sitting along the adjacent wall and smiles at me. I think it's good to tell the host it's a great party.

'I'm just saying the rave ups get wilder in London.'

'That might be true,' I tell Pretty, 'but Belinda took a chance letting gatecrashers like me and Stephen in. She's a wild chick.' I glance at her. She has her arm around some other lad but smiles right back at me. I mean it as a compliment, I hope she gets that.

'Yes,' drawls Pretty, 'you and Stephen or a couple of stray sheep. That's all the passing trade around here.'

Everybody is laughing now and I guess it's a pretty funny idea: sheep at a party. I glance at Stephen; no smile on him, looks somewhere between tired and terrified. I reckon his what-colour question really was just dumb. He's a hundred miles from telling a joke right now.

'Half of Dorset only dream of sheep. Just finding a party was a miracle. Our parents' generation raise a sherry in front of the television and listen to blokes in kilts playing the bagpipes. Boring as hell.' Before I ditched Julie, she hoped I would do this. She said that after the kids' party finished, we could go back to hers. It's how her parents see in the New Year, sherry and Auld Lang Syne. I called it right, missing that nonsense for this.

'Ha,' says Pretty, glancing at Belinda now. 'I've got some dried-out sheep shit, the flaky variety. Makes you forget the words to every Scottish song you ever knew.'

He takes out a tobacco pouch and I'm really clued into everything right now—reading between the lines—it's not sheep shit nor even tobacco in there. Stephen leans into me; I feel his breath on my ear. I would rather it was Belinda hovering there.

'Had we best go?' he says, very quietly.

'No way,' I tell him. 'Don't be a dick. Smoking it won't make you forget biology.' I actually wish it did. He's gone on about that a bit this evening but only with a couple of boys. I've been talking to girls. They're older than me which is brilliant. They're me free and easy, all smiles. One of them was pretty interested in Plaza Court—I'd told her where I work—she asked if we kept on to the dead bodies, asked it four times and I'd answered it the first time. I liked looking into her eyes, she's wearing some kind of sparkly make up. The talk was weird but maybe hippies are always a bit that way. I've not done any necking at this party but a puff of dope looks on the cards.

Pretty uses his fingernail to extract a single cigarette paper from a little wad of them and starts to spread his sheep shit on it. I see from the label that it is an actual tobacco packet—ready rubbed—I'm worried that he might not be all he says he is. This might be a roll-your-own we're going to share, nothing more. Then—his cigarette still open, the brown tobacco strung across the wide-open paper—he gets a small tin out of his breast pocket, opens it, and pinches a little of something in there onto the naked cigarette. Makes lip-smacking noises while he does it. Winks—or possibly blinks, God knows what the eye behind the patch is doing—'Pixie dust, people,' he says. 'The solution to all our problems.'

I think the second tin is the sheep shit. The necessary. Stephen is tugging on my sleeve and pointing at the door. No one leaves a New Year's party before midnight and this one is utterly magnetic to me.

'Watch the master,' declares Pretty, as he rolls up the joint. He makes a bit of a pig's ear out of it. The result looks like a tiny sausage, pinched in at both ends. He even twizzles the two ends shut, nothing like a proper cigarette.

'What happened to your eye?' asks Stephen. He's a hopeless case without the punch and he's had more of that than he can handle.

'If your right eye causes you to stumble, pluck it out,' replies Pretty.

'But it's your left eye you have covered.' I don't think he recognises the quotation, and his mother hosts weekly bible study.

'It offended me,' says Pretty, pulling a lank of his own hair through his fingers. 'Having two seeing eyes is passé. And in the world of the blind, one eye maketh a man a leader.'

'But there are hardly any blind people,' argues drunk-Stephen. He hasn't really tuned in; the Pretty guy isn't trying to win a debate, just talking cool.

'Do you think your two eyes can see further than my one?'

'We can neither of us see through the walls of Belinda's house. And you've got two eyes; one is just covered up.'

Antecedents

'It's my dad's house,' says Belinda. 'If it was mine, I'd just turn it into a commune.'

I think this is the coolest thing a girl could say. I learnt earlier that Belinda's mum and dad are divorced. She mostly lives in Axminster with her mother but her dad's gone skiing so she's borrowed his house for the evening. If my dad had bought the tennis court house years ago—and then taken up skiing—I would definitely do the same. Throw the wildest parties while he was away. I'd even let the sheep in.

'Get with the groove,' Pretty tells Stephen. Then he lights up his home-rolled cigarette. Has a single puff on it himself before saying, 'Take the doobie, brother,' passing it to his verbal adversary. That's the hippy way, sharing not fighting. Stephen passes it to me double quick. Thinks we're playing Pass the Parcel, music on the deck so he doesn't have to take a drag. Not me. I suck like a baby on a big fat tit. It's my first time and I'm keen as mustard.

* * *

'Thanks so much,' I say on her drive. Giving a wave to Belinda who stands on the doorstep. She dashes forward, hugs me. Then she kisses me on the lips and I put my hand on the back of her head, keep it there as long as I can, like I learnt with Julie. This one keeps her teeth together.

'My beautiful gatecrasher,' she says when I let her go. She is as drunk as I am. Not that she gives Stephen a second look. Then he and I set off down the lane. It'll take us the best part of an hour to reach Charmouth. The sun won't be up but it is already three-thirty; the dirty Themagins should have turned the lights out long ago. Watching Belinda all night stopped me from thinking about Burning Rock. She's a kind of hippy, wore a headband some of the evening. Off and on, I'm not sure that she's used to it. There wasn't any free love at the party but I could feel something a bit like it in the air. Free drink by the bucketload. Stephen was the biggest prick in the room.

'All the girls were too old for you, Dennis.' He's still at it, pontificating after the best party of his sorry life.

'Belinda needs to dump her boyfriend then she can get it on with me. That's what she wants. Did you see?'

'She's a bit loose. She only snogged you because you're a gatecrasher. She likes them.'

'She didn't try it on with you though, Stephen.'

'No. I'm not so obviously available. You can come across as vulgar,

Dennis.'

I've been hanging around with this lad since we were eleven. Since my family moved to Charmouth. He and I were neither popular in school but my parents held me back. Couldn't bring friends home with them in the house. In Stephen's case, it's all him. His sister is totally normal.

'Were there any girls there you liked, Stephen?'

'Not really. Belinda's friends were all private-school types.'

I don't get what's wrong with that. Parents choose the schools, not the kids. 'There must have been five or six who used to go to our school,' I remind him.

'But not our year. I think when girls get older, they don't mature like boys.'

Can't think what he's on about. Their breasts get bigger and bigger until they turn twenty from my observations. And he calls himself a biologist. Belinda would make a loads better girlfriend than Julie. I didn't get her number or anything and she lives a long way away. I've no work tomorrow, so I'm going to walk back in a few hours. Before she ups and goes back to Axminster where she really lives. See if she's as interested in me as she signalled. The kiss. Her boyfriend wasn't much better than Stephen. Didn't drink a quarter as much as Belinda. The second worst at the party; nothing hippy about him. And I'm a bona fide gatecrasher; she's going to choose me, sure as the comet is turning around. It's what they do, get themselves back into deep space. Cool girls with crummy boyfriends have no choice but to give them the push. Stick up the vacancy sign, someone better might come calling.

7.

When I arrived back on Croft Road, all the cars had gone. I presumed Mum and Dad were fast asleep. Crept in quietly. Took a couple of digestives from the tin under my bed. The second started me coughing but I don't think I woke them. The parents. Slept in a while but not much considering how late I got back. It's eleven o'clock in the morning when I take myself downstairs.

To the Ship has made egg on toast while I was dressing. She got that right; I couldn't feel hungrier.

'Ancient,' says my dad, 'we really need to talk.'

'I'm going out soon,' I tell him. Dying Star versus Belinda is not a contest in need of a scorecard.

'I've so much to tell you after last night, Ancient.'

I'm bleary eyed. Dad doesn't notice that; I think he's in his own world these days. I drank more than I've ever done before—plus two tugs on a hashish cigarette—I think I'm doing well to stand upright. Can't talk about a hangover with my dad but most kids don't, right? 'I need to go out. Meet a girl.' I don't know what he'll think about that, just think my parents should know I've a life outside number three Croft Road. Beyond his obsession with the crazy people, the looney-bin-bound Themagins.

'You saw our visitors arrive, Ancient. One of them, Burning Rock, who you met a long time ago if you recall…' He's the one who recalls that better; I've no doubt about that. '…she came back from America on Tuesday. Ganymede has stayed over there. Both are going around all the house groups, preparing everyone. Mr Toogood says they are here.'

'Who's here, Dad? They all looked like regular people last night.'

'Dying Star is my name, please. The time has come, Ancient, to opt into the glorious future. Finding a girl is what young men of your age are apt to do; however, there's scarcely time to prepare her for the journey. If you'd like her to come and meet me, I can tell her what's going on…'

'Tell me first,' I interrupt. I really can't have him talking daft to Belinda. Cannot.

'It's the comet, Ancient. Mr Toogood said that they would approach with stealth. They don't want the Americans shooting at them. Firing off nuclear weapons at the saviours of mankind. The moon landings have hurried our true friends, he says. Now we are making a mess of another celestial body, it doesn't leave them any choice but to come immediately. Save those who have the vision to go. Faith in a better world than this.'

I look him straight in the eye. My Dad is utterly serious. A grown man and he believes this HG Wells nonsense. I've read the books, took them from the library. Borrowed some, stolen some. Good stuff but it's only entertainment. Not going to happen in this life. All between the pages. 'I'm going out.' I've wolfed down a fried egg on toast in the time it has taken him to tell me this bullshit. Forgot to enjoy eating it.

'You have to choose, Ancient. Are you boarding the ship, or aren't you?'

'If they park it on Croft Road, I'll give it some thought.' I take my coat off the rack and leave. Dying Star doesn't even argue. It's like the power has changed hands. The comet will come and go, expose Dad, Toogood and the entire shower of freaks as the frauds they always were. Deep down, he knows it. I'm sure he does; it's just caught him between dream and reality. Like Sharon Leeson imagining she might marry the singer, Danny Clare. When Aris Toogood's landing party fails to touch down anywhere on Earth, it must all be over. If Jesus sent a note saying, "Sorry guy, the second coming's cancelled,"—and let's face it, not a peep since Saint John plonked the last full-stop on his supposed Revelations—then that lot would fold too, the Christians. And they do a lot more good in this world than the freaky wife-swappers.

8.

We have a tea break at eight, every class. I don't mind night school; teachers treat me better than they ever did at Allington Grammar. Like a grown-up. It's the first time I've seen Sharon since Christmas Eve. She says, 'I hear you and Julie Davies didn't quite hit it off.' An admonishing face, pushed out lower lip, but I expect she'll be okay about it in the long run. Dumped a couple herself and turned them into funny stories.

'Nice girl, just not for me.' If I say she was too thick, Sharon will scold me. And we're not exactly rocket scientists on the care of elderly people course.

'Don't turn into a rake,' she says. I shake my head, want to say it wasn't like that but I think she's starting in on a lecture. 'Poor Julie had never been kissed before...' Sounds unlikely, at Sharon's party she bit down on me like a ferret. '...and she set her heart on you because you're not like the tough boys, I told Chrissie you were a good soul and she said it to Julie. Then you do this...' Julie only set her heart on me because I didn't brush her off soon enough. Snogged her in the near dark first off. I can't say it or Sharon will think I'm a rotter but it's complicated. '...and Dennis, if you sent her away because she wouldn't let you do everything you wanted, I will think it pretty low. Was it that?'

'Sharon, I didn't know what I was doing when I started. I hope she finds a better boyfriend. I don't think...' I let my own head drop. I think my dad got the sack yesterday. Not for stealing or anything terrible,

Antecedents

not turning up for work was enough. The man from the garage came round to our house and they were arguing on the doorstep for an age. The daft part of it was that my dad wouldn't say he was too busy preparing for the end of the world or whatever it is he's doing, and he was too honest to pretend he had the flu. Admirable and tragic, I think that sums up the silly arse. Where it leaves us, I don't know. He can't lose the house—Granny willed it to him—but we haven't enough money for all the bills. I already pay three quarters of my wages for rent and board. If they want more, I'm off. '...I'm a bit preoccupied with homelife, Sharon. I never bother other people with that.'

She puts her hand on mine. It's a nice gesture, I think she just had to get the don't-be-a-cad stuff off her chest. Sharon knows my dad has a shit job—probably doesn't know he's lost it yet—sees that we're a poor family. 'Tell me what's going on?'

'They belong to a nutty religion.' I feel a wobble in my voice. Stephen's the only other person I've talked to about this and I mostly wish I hadn't. 'Dad's on at me about joining, about doing all the things they want to do.' I don't think I can tell her that spaceships are involved. She might think me crazy even though I'm not going.

'It's not the Quakers, is it?' she asks.

I'm all at sea in this conversation, so I nod, mutter, 'Fucking nutters,' although I don't have a clue what the Quakers stand for beyond eating porridge for breakfast, and that sounds okay. Shouldn't have mentioned religion, I can be such an idiot sometimes.

'Do you know the Breakspears? Ginny's a nursing auxiliary at Perrymount, same as me.'

'No. I don't know them.'

'You must. Ginny Breakspear goes to Meetings—the Quaker Meetings—every Sunday. They're a bit funny—pacifists—but nothing to be worried about Dennis. Your parents can't make you believe what you don't believe. And I sometimes think the Quakers are better than my Catholic crowd.'

I just nod. I've made a balls-up of this conversation. 'They've actually split with the Quakers, got their own nuttier little sect.' It doesn't add up after I've said it. I should have told her that I lied at the beginning, it's just that I can't see a way to do it without saying Themagin. The all-having-sex-together shit was in the newspapers at the weekend. And they've got onto Toogood's prediction that the chosen few will get to leave planet Earth before the month is out. Les Grande Vacances.

The Flophouse Years

I'm not saying it.

* * *

The following day Lorraine, wearing a pretty serious face, asks me to come into the office. I'm sure it's okay because she's always praising my work and most of the old people like having a lad around. Odd though, I can't think of anything I've done wrong.

'Everything all right, Dennis?' she asks, and I nod. 'Are you sure?' I am sure, although what I am sure of is that I want to tell her it is when it isn't. My home life—Themagins circling—is nothing to do with Lorraine Chadwick, everything at work is genuinely okay. 'A little bird told me you might have girl trouble.'

I look at her levelly. I'm not going to get embarrassed about this. Tracy, who works the opposite shifts to me, has said that Lorraine likes to know your personal stuff—calls her an interferer—I didn't agree because she's been all right with me. How she knows about me and any girl whatsoever beats me. There's not very much to know: more than nothing but only a little bit more. I shake my head. 'No. I've got no girls bothering me, Lorraine.'

'I heard that you had a bust up with someone. A fight over a girl.'

'You heard wrong, Lorraine. And it's not something that happened in work, so it doesn't matter. Nothing to do with Plaza Court.'

'Don't get like that, Dennis. You know I'm only here to help you. Young lad like you might need your hand holding to get through the modern world. And that Westbrook girl must be a handful for any boy.'

How the hell she knows about Belinda Westbrook, I cannot guess. The girl lives in Axminster in normal times and her dad's house is out in the sticks, no one could see, so someone must have gossiped. I think my face is starting to colour. It was awkward at the time, no more than that. 'I didn't have a fight. I'm not one to fight with people, Lorraine. A misunderstanding is all it was.'

'And do you want to tell your Auntie Lorraine...'

I don't have an Auntie Lorraine. I quite like my manager, Lorraine, not so keen on this nosy parker but it's still her. Need to keep her onside without blabbing. I went to see Belinda again on New Year's Day after the little contretemps with Dad, with Dying Star. There were no cars on Belinda's drive or anything, so when I arrived, I guessed I was too late, thought I'd have to turn around and walk straight back to Charmouth. I'd forgotten to wear gloves and my fingers were

Antecedents

completely numb, wouldn't have known if they'd fallen off. I pressed the doorbell anyway and I could hear it chime in the house. Hadn't noticed the night before, probably because of the loud music, it makes about six different deep notes, all spaced out, after just one push on the electric bell. A doorbell like no other. No one came, so I blew into my hands, did the bell again. Dong, dong, dong. I thought it a shame if she'd taken herself back to Axminster without knowing I'd be her boyfriend once she ditched the other guy. The bell sounded good—rich—reminded me of Belinda's voice which has a deep earthy timbre to it. I pressed the bell-button about six more times in succession, just for the pleasure of hearing the nice chimes. That's when a voice shouted, 'Coming.' Belinda's voice. It was terrific to hear it. Now I could talk to her one-on-one and learn what she thought of me.

When the door opened Belinda stood before me with her hair all mussed up and a thick dressing gown around her. 'Hiya,' I said, then I looked carefully at her. I could see where her robe slid off her right shoulder, that she wore nothing underneath. Quite a bony shoulder. No pyjamas or nightie, not as far as I could tell. It was a long cold walk—her father's house is virtually in Wootton—there and then I decided it had been worth it. Julie was a disappointment when I saw her second time, not Belinda, her face is clever and pretty. Everything a lad could want.

'Can I come in?'

'I don't know.'

With hindsight, that was an odd thing to have said. She positively pulled me in when I gatecrashed the party just the evening before, then this time she was in two minds. I put my foot across the threshold and she didn't stop me. I don't think she felt threatened although I'm a bloke and she was nearer to nude than any other girl I've stood next to. 'Where can we talk?' I asked.

'What have we to talk about, Dennis?'

'Oh, you know.'

I stepped into the lounge which was still in a state from the party. Empty tins and paper plates everywhere. Crisps spilled on the floor. Belinda followed me in. I sat in an armchair and she moved onto a sofa, pulled her legs up beneath her. I could see they were bare under the dressing gown. I loved sitting with a girl wearing so little. I watched her wrap the gown more closely to her body, not that it was cold in her house. The heating was on a really high setting, two seasons warmer than at three Croft Road. 'How can I help you?' she asked.

I didn't have a clue where to begin. I was hoping that she would guess why I was there. 'I came back to see you alone because I really like you, Belinda.' It was honest, a decent first bid. Belinda cracked a smile and I carried on. 'You seem different to other girls. You do your own thing.' I think that's a great compliment. A bit hippy and Belinda had already told me she was that way inclined. 'Life's a jazz combo not a marching band.' I hoped that she hadn't heard the phrase before, might think it my own. I got it from Pretty.

'You came here to tell me that?' She wore a tiny smile on her face but her tone sounded a bit dismissive. It might have been that she had a hangover like me, we weren't clicking like we had at the party. Belinda is all I had thought about since traipsing away from her place in the small hours. And after the kiss on the drive, she must have thought loads about me. It was passionate.

'I can help you to tidy up, if you like?'

She smiled when I said it. 'I think a cleaner is coming later in the week.'

'I can help now, I'm working tomorrow. Won't the cleaner tell your dad what a mess you've made?'

She waved a nonchalant hand; I don't think she cared a fig what the cleaner might say. It was funny, because the way she stretched her arm started to make the dressing gown fall off her shoulder. She snatched it back but I wouldn't have minded if she'd let it fall. 'What's your job?' she asked.

I told her about Plaza Court, that I help a few get their breakfasts, give baths to two men each Tuesday and two more on a Friday. If the shifts don't work out, they wait until I'm next on duty, because they like having a man to help them.

Belinda nodded, said cleaning her father's house is not for me to do anyway.

'I like it if everyone who creates a mess helps tidy it.' I was determined to make her think good things about me. And I don't expect hippies use cleaners; her dad is probably a rich stiff, I guess she likes taking advantage of that. And she might hate her dad on account of the divorce. I don't really know how that works; Stephen never talks about his father, hasn't done it once. 'And Belinda, you look brilliant. I didn't say last night because you had that funny boyfriend, I just think you'd have a better time with me than with him...'

Antecedents

The lounge door flew open and the man I'd just insulted came striding towards me. He was completely naked, tackle dangling about. It was a disgusting sight. 'Why did you let this little peasant in?' said Nuddy Boy to Belinda. Then he grabbed hold of my jacket. 'Out of here, twat-face.'

'Stuart, he didn't mean anything.' I expect Belinda was kind of on my side but this guy's entrance gave me a flash of insight into why she didn't answer the door in a hurry. Easy to guess what she and the swivel-eyed man had been up to: the pair of them in their birthday suits before she pulled the robe on. It should have been Belinda and me spending a morning in bed together if only the world was a decent place. Nothing ever falls into my lap. No cleaner and Julie Davies still the only girl whose tongue has raked across my own.

'We don't need to fight about this,' I said to Stuart. I put up a hand, not really to stop him coming towards me but to hide his ugly cock from my vision. I'm free and easy but I don't like to look at naked men.

He pushed his chest into my outstretched hand, shouted, 'Fuck off,' and butted his head into my face. I turned as he did it and he only caught my cheek. Didn't hurt much.

'Stop it!' I shouted. Or it might have been Belinda. We both shouted together most probably. Me and her were on a wavelength. It was only Stuart who was not for stopping. He's a right nob. 'Do you want me to?' I said to Belinda. 'To go?'

'I didn't ask you to come.' When I thought about it on the way home, I realised her reply didn't come close to answering the question.

Stuart was wearing nothing; I could have leathered him if I wasn't an apprentice hippy. I said, 'I'll go. Sorry.' I was only speaking to Belinda, not to her obnoxious boyfriend. Disgusting and despicable Stuart. And fighting is really not cool. If she was a proper hippy, she would have ditched him for how he was trying to hurt me. Peace is what hippies are all about. Stuart even pushed me to the door. I turned left and right, trying to make sure he didn't wipe his slimy penis on me. I'd hate that. 'Sorry Belinda,' I said. When I was at the front door—the creep still manhandling me—I couldn't figure where the lock was that was keeping it closed. Belinda stepped across me and released the catch. I swear I felt her breast rub along my forearm but it was too frantic to enjoy, and her dressing gown quite thick. When the door was open and I was turning to Belinda to say goodbye—not expecting her to repeat the warmth of last night's kiss,

The Flophouse Years

thinking about it anyway—the naked wrestler pushed me so hard that I stumbled onto the gravel path. Fell backwards. I landed on my arse; it didn't hurt. Then my assailant came out into the front garden—you can bet his balls were freezing, it was still frosty out there, a major contrast from the warmth inside the house—and kicked me about three times before shouting 'Ow' in the loudest voice. 'Ow! Bugger!' he shouted again. He had hurt his foot. Not done any damage to me, with having no shoes on and only kicking like a girl. Pathetic little fighting nudist. I stood up; Belinda had come out in her dressing gown to comfort her boyfriend. Naked Stuart sat on the gravel holding his injured appendage, Belinda slid beside him and put his rank foot into both her hands. Trying to stroke it better like she might have done with a toddler. The man screamed. Yelled blue murder at his girlfriend's kindly touch.

Belinda turned her head to me and said, 'Now look what you've gone and done.' He probably got a broken toe but it was his doing not mine. I think it might be karma although I'm honestly not sure. Nasty karma doesn't sound quite right.

Unimpressed that Belinda sided with horrible Stuart, I just tossed my head back. Not sure I got the gesture right; indifference is the one I was going for. 'Nice meeting you, Belinda. Bye-bye, Stuart,' I said loudly. Then, before I reached the front gate, a car pulled in. I stepped aside as it passed. There was a woman at the wheel. Belinda's mother, I reckoned. She scarcely looked at me. Stared straight ahead at her daughter cuddling Stuart, whose hunched posture just about covered his dick, all in front of her ex-husband's idyllic country house. I don't expect any girl's parent would be pleased to see that, not even if his cock was out of her line of sight.

'And now you've learnt your lesson, have you?' asks Lorraine.

This stumps me. I've told her everything; if she thinks I've something to learn, she hasn't been listening. 'I'll not be bothering Belinda again,' I tell her.

'Nor any older girls, Dennis. Not only aren't you ready, it's not right. I hope I've been a help, now give your Auntie Lorraine a nice hug.' She steps away from the desk and I do to, both in the centre of the room. I let her embrace me which feels a bit daft. This job is important to me. When Lorraine hugs me—this is the first time she ever has—she presses her chest right into me. Squashing her big bosoms up. I have to admit, I don't mind; I imagine the feel of breasts is always brilliant but this is strictly to stay in the office. I'll not be telling Stephen about it. I never told him—or Sharon—about going back out to Belinda's. I don't know how Lorraine got wind of it. If she's a friend of Belinda's mum, she might know more than I told her. I never said that Stuart was in the buff, only that he wasn't wearing shoes. She didn't contradict anything I said; had heard about the bust up out on the backroad to Wootton. Knew it was Belinda's love rivals. And that I had broken the proper boyfriend's foot. She didn't know that it wasn't like that; Stuart's injury was self-inflicted, one hundred per cent. I'm a hippy not a fighter.

* * *

When I do my round of the flats in the evening, Mrs Carmichael is quite funny with me. She makes a point of looking closely into my face. 'No black eye,' she says. I like Mrs C, she's pushing ninety but seems sharper than anyone else here. Staff included.

'All right. What do you know? And who told you?'

'Mrs Chadwick is a better gossip than you are, young Harris.'

'Lorraine told you about me?'

'It was quite a hoot, Mr Harris. Fisticuffs over a girl. I think you're a romantic at heart. I really do.'

'It was a misunderstanding—nothing more than that—a misunderstanding. I thought she'd finished with the last one but I was wrong.'

'I like to think you'd have fought my Douglas over me if you'd been alive at the turn of the century. I was not white-haired back then, you know. Jet black. Nineteen-hundred or thereabouts.' I must give her a funny look because she adds, 'I am only toying with you, young man. Don't blush.' I haven't had flirting from old women before and it's odd. Can't decide if it's flattering or the opposite. If it makes her happy, it can't be a bad thing. That's what I'm here for.

She's still laughing when I leave the flat. I told her what happened up to a point and I am starting to see that it's pretty funny. Stuart's such a moron that he kicked me without shoes on. Without a stitch on but I didn't tell Mrs Carmichael that part. Can't beat a not-fighting-back hippy; lost a fight with a stationary object.

9.

A week or more after that unsolicited hug from Lorraine, Dying Star again asks me to re-join the Themagins. 'A new beginning,' he says.

The Flophouse Years

His constant prattle—quoting Aris Toogood at every mealtime—is really getting on my nerves. Before he asked, he checked if I have a girlfriend. I tried to be nonchalant but had to admit that the answer is no. Before Christmas I'd never had one, now I've dumped one and had a fight with the boyfriend of another. I don't tell my parents anything about my personal life but I'm getting into the game. Love life around the corner, I'd say.

I tell him that I have no interest in the Themagins. I don't know how re-joining that outfit works. Never had a membership card. Dying Star goes into pleading mode. 'Ancient...' He tries to take hold of my hand but I'm having none of that. Not that my dad is queer and, frankly, that might be better than what he is: a pea-brained Themagin. He's trying to manipulate me by acting as normal dads do with little children. I suppose he did a bit of that in the old days. When it was appropriate. A better dad when he was an insurance salesman than a religious freak. As a Themagin, he's insufferable. '...your mother and I will have to go away. Mr Toogood has made that clear. It will be glorious and you coming with us will complete the picture. Our whole family united in the new beginning.'

'How do you unite with others really, Dad?' I'm sick to death of him making out he's entitled to my loyalty when he only thinks about himself. 'I never really joined in a year or two back when I listened to the tapes and tried to believe them. You had people round and united with them while I went to bed, didn't you?' I say the word "united" in a higher pitch. Say it sarcastically.

To the Ship looks up from darning socks. 'What's the matter, Dennis?' Dad makes a funny noise, a sigh but deeper. She corrects herself. 'Ancient.'

'Dennis suits me fine and I'm not going anywhere. Nothing's the matter, Mum and Dad. You go and unite with Burning Rock or whoever you like; I'm not going anywhere. Staying put. I've a job to do for the council. I'll keep doing it. Still be here when you come back.'

'Ancient,' says Dad, 'we won't be coming back. This is for a new life, not a silly Apollo mission.'

'What's wrong, Ancient?' says To the Ship. I think she's upset by my dismissal of her religion. I even think it plays into her own fears. She must know it's all tosh; deep down, you'd think they all do. There is nothing wrong with me.

'I saw you unite with Ganymede. Unite with him on top of you, Mum. And you're worse, Dad.' I probably should have kept all that to myself but her probing has brought it out. If Mum gets upset, she's only herself to blame.

'Ancient, that was long ago and you were too young to understand.'

'What's to understand?'

'We're all going together; we will be one body on the other side of that ocean, you must understand that?' My dad has a stupid answer for everything. 'It's all on the tapes. We have to learn how to be at ease sharing a single body. This is a transient life, Ancient. We Themagins have been seeing passed these restrictions for a long time. Beyond the single pitiful incarnation that Earth has to offer.'

'Screwing is screwing, Dad. And spaceships don't fly behind comets. This one, Comet Tago-Sato-Kosaka...'

'Comet Toogood,' says my dad. It's a reflex.

'...it's just same as all the other comets out there. No spaceship ever came with one before, did it? How can you believe something so barmy? Believing in something which you can't see. It's not normal.'

'Son, truth revealed leaves everything ordinary in a very sorry state. And Number One has repeatedly said that our forthcoming visitors have been here before. Last time was during the time of Christ, They watched on. They know all about us. I'm sorry if it has bothered you, things we've done that you were too young to understand. To the Ship and I have performed preparation rituals with a few couples, as Mr Toogood instructed we must. We're ready for the journey, for eternity. The craft comes next week, Ancient. To the Ship and I both want you to join us.'

'We won't coerce you,' says Mum.

'No ticket for me. Save the money. Buy yourself first class.'

'Your attitude upsets me, Ancient.' Again, my dad is looking like I've given him a hiding, and I've simply reminded him that he's a libertine who has let Mum down. He has no remorse. I thought he'd hit the roof, then he refers to what he did with Burning Rock as if they'd put up a bit of bunting. Mum seems more circumspect. Ashamed. They are both dumb but she's not to blame. Just does what he says; however, being a follower is a pretty stupid course to run your life down. My Dying Star of a father, he's the instigator. Probably his idea to go to the racecourse and watch the ranting Baptist. I think that one was nutty, looking back, stirring up an excitable crowd. This lot, I do not get. Four of them humming in a living room? I bet it's only the sex that keeps them in the club.

'You'll look ridiculous when the spaceship doesn't come, you know? You'll have to beg the garage guy to give you back the pump job.'

Dying Star shakes his head. 'I'm sorry you're not coming, Ancient. I don't like to leave with regrets but we will both miss you terribly.'

10.

I have four consecutive days of seven o'clock starts during the third week of January. My rota is not usually like this but Tracy is on holiday and the only cover Lorraine has been able to get is for the late shifts. On the Tuesday, when I'm eating cereal at about twenty-past six, Dad comes downstairs. I look at him, his hair is a mess and he may not have slept.

'It's coming today, Ancient?'

'It's a pity I'm working. I like little green men.'

'Don't be facetious, Ancient. Today will be the most momentous day in the history of planet Earth.'

I'm kind of proud of my dad. It's a drizzly day on the south coast—he lost his job earlier this month—seems to be spending what little savings he has. He suggested I should pay more board money a week ago and I said a straight no. I only get to keep a quarter of my pay as it is. Beer and books I buy with that, not gambling and prostitutes. I'm seventeen, need to live a little. Still, in this sorry life, he can announce the greatest day since we learnt to walk upright, think that such a thing will have him at its heart, at the right hand of his beloved Mr Toogood. 'Send me back a postcard.' I rise up from my seat and walk to the door. Leave the crazy zealot. I'll be early for work, can't listen to any more of his batshit speeches. Heard too many, I'm sick of them. No one is going anywhere. When I was young, I thought he was brilliant, now I wish I didn't have a dad at all. Not this one.

* * *

Work goes all right but I have a jumpy feeling running through me now and then. Having your dad ask you to quit work and join a non-existent spaceship is disconcerting. While I'm putting old Mr Tufnell in the bath, there is an accident. I have to help him into the water with a fixed hoist. It's just a plastic chair really, fixed to the side of the bath with a turn handle to make it go up and down, a pivot to swing over the bath-side when it's high enough. I raise his legs when I do this. Then I hoist him back down into the tub. The chair has large diamond shaped holes in it, so that the person sitting on it gets water on most of his or her skin; the snag happens when I'm bringing Mr Tufnell up out of the water. I swing it out before it is quite high enough. His scrotum catches between chair and edge of bath. I'd not spotted that his balls were dangling down through one of the holes in the chair that let water through. The poor fella yelps with pain, points at his cock and I realise what I've done, give the handle another half turn, which is enough. It must have hurt like a bastard. If he makes a complaint, I'm blaming my dad. Lorraine may not see it the way I do. I feel really sorry for the old guy. I like him, always call him Mr Tufnell where Lorraine says Tufty, says it to his face and I don't think he likes it. Not as bad as a trapped testicle, I suppose. It was an accident. That's all there is to say really: it shouldn't have happened but it did.

Later, when I'm with Mrs Carmichael, she tells me that I seem very distracted. She's astute, incredibly frail too. Walks hunched over a Zimmer frame at about ninety degrees, can't get in or out of a bath. Tracy gives her a hand every Thursday. Her mind is sharp. Most days of the week she finishes crossword puzzles to which I wouldn't be able to answer a single clue.

'What's got into you today, Mr Harris?' she asks.

I dither, ask her about tomorrow's shopping, and she reminds me that it's not even her day for it. I can't tell her the aliens are taking my parents off planet for a while, I don't believe it myself. 'There was an accident with one of the patients, getting out of the bath. It was my fault; I feel bad about it.'

'Oh dear, oh dear. It is a bad sign when you say patient, young sir. Resident is the term you usually use. Did anybody die, Mr Harris?'

I laugh when she says that. Said it gravely like I might have bumped someone off.

'Nobody died,' I confirm.

'What has gone wrong can therefore be mended. Nothing in life goes smoothly every day. I speak to other ladies now and then, you know. You're very well liked here, Mr Harris. You won't lose friends over a single mishap. Just make sure it doesn't become a habit.'

When she talks like this, I think Mrs C would make a better warden of this place than the proper one. Not that I've anything against Lorraine. I keep on thinking about how she wangled the New Year's Day story out of me—the love triangle, she called it—then gave me a hug that was sexier than anything little Julie Davies mustered.

* * *

I get home at five past three. Often, I'll stay out, stay away, because my parents are both loonies, but today I want to see them. Prove that Aris Toogood is full of shit. They're not at home. Off playing silly buggers, I presume. Dad has written a little note, left it on the kitchen table.

> *3, Croft Road*
> *Charmouth*
>
> *20th January 1970*
>
> *Our boy Ancient*
>
> **We have gone to join the true Ship of Life. We sincerely hope you can join us in the weeks and months to come. Mr Toogood hasn't explained how that will work but it might.**
>
> *Love from Dying Star and To the Ship*

There is a scribbled note next to it in Mum's handwriting. It says that the sausages in the fridge need eating.

Inside me, I've a nagging little urge to ask Mrs Robson next door if a spaceship landed in our street earlier. I can't do it, not laying myself bare like that. I screw up both notes and put them in my trouser pocket. They'll be back. Before midnight, I'd lay a bet.

I leave the house because I'm not in the mood for being on my own. It's ten to four when the school bus pulls in. I caught it every day for five years, now I'm just meeting Stephen. I think I'm as clever as he is, cleverer at practical things like talking to girls. And his home is almost as poor as mine, his mum insisted he keep on studying. She wants Stephen to become a doctor but I wouldn't trust him with a scalpel. Biology teacher in a boys' school, that's what he'll end up. I don't know a lot but I know Stephen Bredbury inside out. He couldn't cope in a co-educational on account of going red when he gets within ten paces of a girl. I'd be an even worse doctor than Stephen, I know I would. Trapping old men's scrotums in bath hoists is not right on any measure, I still feel awful about it. Keep imagining it was my own bollock caught there.

His sister is on the bus too and she greets me nicely. Stephen is the morose one in this family. I walk with them towards the primary school. Mary tells me and Stephen to go on home, she can collect Monica without us. Stephen says, 'All right,' but I don't like to leave her on her own.

'Go on,' she says, 'he never picks her up.' She gestures Stephen.

Antecedents

'Okay, see you back in the house.'

Mary smiles back at me. She's really young but I like the way she talks to me. Parents off on a spaceship changes you, makes you value small pleasantries.

'You won't believe what happened,' says Stephen as we're on our way to Morgan Crescent, the bungalow where his family live. Then he witters on and on about another lad at school called Mathers who briefly had his briefcase confiscated because the teacher suspected he had brought in cigarettes. The fags were in it and he was done for that; when he got the case back, he accused Mr Armstrong of stealing his sandwiches. Copped it for the smokes and then tried to argue that the teacher had gobbled up his dinner. I like the tale; Mathers is a dick, so this, and Mary's pretty smile, are the first decent distractions I've had all day. 'You see,' Stephen explains, 'he was so insistent, in the end Armstrong got one of the secretaries to phone Mathers' mother. He had left his sandwiches on the kitchen side!' Stephen is laughing at his telling and I join in although he's no raconteur. Great to hear about someone having a worse day than me, there is pleasure in that.

No one home at the Bredburys' house, his mum is out at her cleaning job. Mary and her little sister are back within about ten minutes of me and Stephen. I like that, being around people feels good. Monica, the younger one, sings a pop song—Danny Clare rubbish—her voice is really good. Holds the tune nicely. Stephen tells her to shut up so she only goes and does the opposite. Even starts strutting about while belting out When the Saints Go Marching In. Top of her lungs and she plays a pretend trombone while she's at it. I think it's dead funny even though I kind of hate this song. Her school uniform is blue and she's so thin she might blow away. I think she's going to look like Mary when she's older. The same fair hair.

Mary talks to me a bit. Always has. 'Haven't you got a home to go to?' It's all very good humoured. She thinks girls and boys should argue as a way of not ignoring each other. The home I have to go to is crap at the best of times, empty until my parents give up their charade. Can't talk about any of it with anyone right now. I just smile at her.

Stephen and I play Subbuteo. It's funny that he's so good at this game—football by flicking plastic models across a green baize—and he is also the worst kid on a proper sports field by about a hundred miles. A hundred light years. Easy for him to be better than me at this fiddly game: I don't have a set to practice with.

Mary comes into the lounge, we have the Subbuteo cloth laid out on the carpet, and asks if I'm staying for tea.

'Has your mother asked you to ask me?'

'I'm asking you, Dennis. I'm making tea. Mummy won't be home until late. She's meeting Mrs Chidgey from church this evening. Her friend. Won't be back until after nine.'

It's a lovely invitation and Mary might be a better reason to stay than Stephen. He must have known it's a kids' house for the evening but never even offered. 'Yes please, Mary. I hope you're a decent cook.'

'Cheeky what's-it. I'm top girl in domestic science.'

'I look forward to marking your work,' I tell her.

Mary leaves and Stephen says, 'Don't do that.'

I stare into his face. What am I supposed to have done?

'My sister is even younger than Julie Davies. You can't just use girls, you know?'

This bloke is ridiculous. My parents have buggered off on a spaceship, or they're pretending they've done it which is a crazy-weird game to play on their only son. I'm having the most miserable day and his kid sister treats me nicely. Then I can't be nice back without getting a scolding from the very Stephen who I long ago rescued from social death as an act of pure charity. Sweet Jesus, take me to a better world.

* * *

'Really good food. Ten out of ten,' I tell her. Stephen keeps looking at me like I'm a cad but I just like his sister's cooking. It's not flirting. She looks very nice, actually, but I'm not interested in a girl as young as her. I was sniffing around Belinda Westbrook three weeks back and Lorraine told me that she's twenty years old.

'Mary,' says Stephen, 'I absolutely smashed your new best friend at Subbuteo. Eight-nil.'

He's a dick. Poor Mary has gone bright red and she's known me forever. I think it's something girls do when they get to her age. Start imagining their older brother's friends would make good boyfriends. She tells him to shut up which is about right.

'What goes into a casserole?' That's what she's made and my mum has never made anything half as good as this. Mary served it up with mashed potato on the side and she has done it really fluffy. Creamy, I'd say. A great little cook.

'Chicken and leek and carrot. And for the record, you're not my friend. You smell.'

Antecedents

That's just her being a kid. I'm pretty sure that I don't. 'You're cooking smells better.' I'm not picking a fight with her. With Stephen, perhaps, not with Mary.

'You smell like the casserole will when we all woosh it down the toilet,' says Monica. An unwelcome contribution. It's great having a meal without any of our parents present but this family are a bit immature. I don't blame Mary, Stephen goaded her into it. Monica is daft as flypaper: funny-daft and she sings well. There is really no guessing what she will say next. 'When we shit the casserole out of our bottoms,' she adds, as if we needed the clarification.

'Monica Rose. I'm going to tell Mummy what you said!' This is Stephen reprimanding his sister. If he could talk and listen at the same time, he'd figure out what a prick he is.

I decide that the girls are the grown-ups around here, they can handle the talk Stephen can't. I relate the incident at work. Try to explain how hard my job is, that half a twist on the bath-hoist handle made all the difference. Trapped the gentleman's private parts and caused him terrible pain. An accident, not intended.

'Did his willy come off?' says Monica.

'No, it did not. Nothing like that. Just think about it though, for us, getting in and out of baths is dead easy. For people who can't even walk, it's a worry. Needs a clear plan.'

'Needs a care assistant who pays attention,' says Mary. I feel stung but she's probably hit the mark.

* * *

When I arrive back at Croft Road—it is just before nine o'clock—there's still no sign of Dying Star, of To the Ship. I hate this. I know it's a trick. I'm worried that they'll come back tomorrow or in a week and tell me that they've been to Jupiter or somewhere like it. Then they'll get cross with me when I tell them they haven't really. Dying Star will; To the Ship will struggle not to smile. If an alien spacecraft really did land here, or anywhere on Earth, it would make the news. I actually put on the radio just in case. It tells me that bus drivers are threatening to strike; buses are not spacecraft. Inflation figures are worrying the Chancellor of the Exchequer; numbers are numbers, in my book, might mean I get a better pay rise later in the year. Someone has vandalised Karl Marx's grave; he's long dead so I can't really see what the fuss is about, I suppose it upset his children, or grandchildren. Whatever he has. That's the lot. The weather follows and it certainly isn't raining spaceships.

I couldn't tell Stephen anything about what's going on in my house. He's such a wimp, he would have told his mum, or criticised me for not going with them to prove whether it is true one way or the other. I didn't even want to tell him. I wish none of it was happening. While he was washing the pots, I thought about telling Mary. She would have sympathised with me, I reckon so. The trouble is, her and Monica are close and the youngest is actually berserk. Keeping it to myself was the right thing to do but now, all alone in the house, I feel like the weight of my wayward parents is heavy on my shoulders. It must be the same for parents when their kids run away from home. I've a mind to do just that once they are back here, let them worry about me. Boot on the other foot if I run away and join a hippy commune. The trouble is, I'd lose my job if I didn't show up for work—just like my dad lost his—and it's too important to me. Threw his job away for the stupid Themagins, God knows what he'll do when they come back. I think Hippies are great but not something to chuck everything else in for.

I go to bed at half past nine. I've two more early shifts to get through before I can get a lie in. They're probably at Burning Rock's house wherever that is. Sleeping on the floor, or Dad sleeping in bed with the sexy woman. It's not right, Themagins should be stopped. I think some of the papers said that. Called them an affront to public decency.

11.

Wednesday morning starts the same as Tuesday except that Dying Star is not here to put me off my breakfast. I eat it all today, no need to rush from the house. I try not to think about my parents but when I fetch the milk from the step put it into the fridge, the sausages remind me of To the Ship. They've gone completely rancid, smell like little Monica's description of me, although she was just kidding. There are four sausages left in an opened packet of eight. When I examine them, I see maggots crawling all over the ruddy things. This was what my hopeless mother implored me to eat yesterday. Left a note to that effect. I throw them in the outside dustbin—can't have maggots in the house—then I put a load of washing in the twin tub. I'm giving it a quick go before I set off to work. Mum usually does the laundry but I do all the old peoples at Plaza Court. When they come back, they'll see how capable I am. No need of parents any longer. I spilt a bit of casserole on my work trousers yesterday. I've another pair for today, I could leave the washing for a week or more but I don't want To the Ship saying I can't manage. They can live on the moon for all I care, I'm better off on my own. I go back to the fridge and realise nothing is cold inside it. It's a cold house but the fridge adds nothing. There's a pool of water beneath it. Not working properly at all. Everything is broken, worn out, done for. I'll see if I can fix the fridge when I get home from work mid-afternoon. I can change a fuse; no idea how the cooling mechanism works if that's what's buggered. The whole lot of it is coming apart, that's the state my stupid parents have left me in. Gone to space because their fucking house is falling down.

* * *

Work is okay and Mrs Carmichael is really funny with me today. Gives me girlfriend advice which I don't need and can't help listening to.

'You must secure Mrs Chadwick's job for yourself. Girls want to marry the manager, not the hired help.'

'If I stage a coup, have I got your vote?'

'Of course, Mr Harris. For I am the girl you are going to marry.'

The way she says it cracks me up completely. We both laugh like lunatics in the asylum, like the nutters my dad used to tell jokes about before he became a po-faced Themagin. I think she learnt from Lorraine that Belinda Westbrook is about three years older than me; however, Zoe Carmichael is seventy further up the road. I tell her that as a woman of experience, she shouldn't toy with one as young as me.

'Ah. That's funny,' she says. 'Very, very funny.' Then she goes quite serious and says I am the only person here who talks to her like a grown-up. Lorraine does baby talk. Calls her Duck Egg while I always say Mrs Carmichael. She makes a good point. Lorraine is all right but she thinks the world revolves around her. When I'm in here it revolves around Mrs Carmichael. That's the way it should be; I do what I was taught in the night classes.

* * *

Lorraine comes into work later than usual today because she's covering up until ten in the evening. Tracy is on holiday. We only cross over for the half hour before I go off shift. I tell her how everyone is. Mr Tufnell told me he's fine now. No ill-effects, so I don't mention trapping his testicle in the bath hoist yesterday. Lorraine thinks I'm a decent care assistant and I'd rather not have any black marks on that front. I'm after her job in my pursuit of Zoe Carmichael. It's a funny old world if you let it be.

The Flophouse Years

As I'm walking out of the door, Lorraine says, 'Dreadful business about those Themagins.' I keep walking, pretend not to hear it. I've never told anyone about my parents except Stephen Bredbury. I still don't know how she figured out I got into a fight over Belinda and now she's cottoned on to this as well. I need this job but I don't want to become a laughing stock. If she tells Mrs Carmichael that my parents are in the wife-swapping business, I'll be livid. Handing in my ruddy notice.

* * *

I go straight home but I don't expect anyone to be there. Whatever stunt they've pulled, they're really dragging it out. That's obvious. When I open the door I shout, 'Mum, Dad.' No reply, so I try, 'To the Ship, Dying Star.' The house stays silent. I imagine they're in a bed and breakfast in Plymouth or even up in London. A bunch of naked Themagins humming together on the bedroom floor. Burning Rock there with her knockers out. All the blokes far keener to give it to her than to their proper wives. I really hate my parents.

I put the kettle on then find myself banging the beaker on the kitchen side. Making a racket. I'm annoyed that they've left me. Angry actually. I'm old enough to cope but it still isn't right. The kitchen's a mess, a big puddle by the broken refrigerator. The water looks brown. I'm not in the mood for cleaning up, so I go upstairs without even making the drink I'd planned.

I never ever go in my parents' room but decide I will now. I think Dad might have a picture of Burning Rock in there. Naked nuddy porno pictures showing everything she's got. I don't know why I think it, I just do. He's that sort of pervert, isn't he?

When I open the door, I stop dead in my tracks. Dying Star is lying on his back on top of the counterpane, Mum has fallen off the bed but her legs are still on it, head squashed sideways on the floor at ninety degrees from her shoulder, left cheek on the carpet. They are wearing nothing. My mum's breasts look like the suet dumplings she made for tea a couple of weeks back. The same floury white, the same misshapen oval. I know from the lifeless pallor of their faces that they are dead. Gone from this life. I've seen it twice at work. Only twice before but it's enough. My father could be at peace—I feel only shock—for Mum it looks like pure anguish, face squashed and contorted. I slump to the floor and try to think straight. I can't. I reckon my parents have been here all along. They were in the room

Antecedents

next to me when I was asleep last night. They must have been lain out dead like this before I even went to Stephen's house yesterday evening. It's awful. Just awful. I rush to the bathroom and chuck up. It's not only breakfast cereal and liver from Plaza Court lunch club. Casserole comes up. Everything I've eaten in the last month. I miss the bowl for half of it. I don't like them but it's put me in a right state. Dead isn't close to being on a spaceship. Tears are flooding down my cheeks. Maybe they were unconscious when I came home from work yesterday. I don't know but they might have been. I should have checked all over the house before I went to see Stephen; I was too stupid to think of it. It's like I half-believed Toogood's crap, thought they could be somewhere other than this Earth without thinking it was this. That they are nowhere at all. I can hear crying, wailing, but it's only me. And now a hell of a lot more food comes up. I don't know when I ate whatever it is I'm puking now. Stinks like maggoty sausages and I never touched them.

* * *

I probably should go back in there. At work we wash them, make the body respectable before family come in, or the undertaker arrives. I can't do it. I've got to tell somebody what's happened but I don't really know what's gone on myself. I think it's the police I need to phone. Be honest with them. If they think it's my fault—waiting and waiting like I did—I'll just have to accept the consequence. It won't be worse than this. Nothing is. I'm not going back in their room; the police can arrest me for leaving them in the nude if they have to. I wish I hadn't looked in the first time, except then I might have gone on living underneath their dead bodies forever.

'Operator, police please, I say.'

When I am speaking to the right person, I say that I have found my parents dead in their bed. The woman on the other end starts to sound panicky, asks me a lot of unrelated questions. 'When did they last see a doctor?' I don't know the answer and it's far too late to start fussing with that now. 'Are you certain there is no one in the house with you?' I say a straight no to this one and then feel scared just thinking about it. Could there have been someone else involved? I even wonder if Ganymede has been in and murdered them—I can see why he might do that to my dad but not to my mum—and the last I heard he was in America.

'Officers and an ambulance are on their way, Dennis,' she says. She took my name right at the beginning, uses it nicely even though she's not very good at her job. 'Is there anything else you need to tell me about them. Any background information that might help us?'

I say what I never say. 'They're Themagins.'

'I see,' says the lady. 'I see.' The way she says it makes me think it's made things clearer for her but the sheer confusion of telling another living soul their stupid religion sets me off crying again. Crying as if I'm half the age of Monica Bredbury and I'm a grown up. Supposed to be. Left school and seen dead bodies before. It's because they're my parents that I can't handle it better. I never cry at anything, not until this. Finding dead parents is the worst.

* * *

My house is crawling with policemen. I think there are four in the bedroom; I'm not going in there. Before he entered, one of them said to me that a police surgeon will be here soon. 'Can't move the bodies until then, mate,' he added. They are my parents, not just bodies. I don't ever talk like that at Plaza Court. And it's pretty late in the day for a surgeon to be trying his tricks. Dead and gone, I saw that quicker than I could believe it was possible. Door only half opened. They are not really old, only half the age of Zoe Carmichael. Every single thing about this is wrong.

I'm in the sitting room now and a policewoman is talking to me. Asking questions about 'Mum and Dad'.

I think calling them by their stupid names might be more respectful. I tell her that they've changed them: one is To the Ship, the other Dying Star.

'They'll always be Mum and Dad to you,' she replies.

'Their gone,' I tell her, telling myself too. Trying to take it in. 'I don't have a mum or a dad anymore.'

She tells me that her name is Sergeant Ash. 'You can call me Susan,' she says, 'if that's easier.' I don't see why it would be but I know she's only being nice. Names are only words. Sergeant Ash sounds a bit like a spaceship name and so I use Susan like she said I could. She's real police, wears the uniform, not just answering the phone like the earlier woman. 'We think your parents may have died on Tuesday, Dennis. That's when the others took their lives.'

'What others?'

'There were a hundred and seventy Themagin suicides in the United States, Dennis. Before today we knew of only twelve here.'

Antecedents

'Here in Charmouth?'

'In England.'

'Why did they do it?' I ask.

'Dennis, we were hoping you might be able to help us with that.'

This stuns me for a second. I drop my head but then look up into her face. I know that tears are still streaming from my eyes, I don't really feel ashamed of it any longer. It sounds like lots and lots of people have died. It's immensely sad and, to my mind, it's completely mad with it. All those people have played a joke on nobody but themselves.

'Dad told me they were joining the spaceship on Tuesday. Said it had come behind the comet and all the Themagins were boarding. I think yesterday was the closest Comet Tago-Sato-Kosaka will ever come to Earth.' Susan nods her head. Listens to me really attentively but I still think what I'm saying sounds daft. A load of Themagin rubbish. 'Aris Toogood is the leader...' I've never pictured him before and now I find myself wondering what he's really like. Is he laughing about the silly followers who died because he told them they should. 'Is he dead?'

Susan nods again, I think she even mouths the name: 'Aris Toogood.'

'He's dead?' I repeat.

'He is, Dennis...' This is shocking, I thought he was a conman, not a believer at all. '...he left a message addressed to President Nixon. "The immortal souls of the Themagins have now joined the craft that has come for us." Something like that.'

The police woman sits quietly for a moment. Maybe a few minutes, I'm struggling to take in what she has said. Toogood going seems to make it more likely to be true but it can't be true. Spaceships are all science fiction except the Apollo ones. Then, speaking very quietly, Susan asks the scariest thing. 'Dennis, did your mother or your father ask you to take the poison?'

'What poison?' I hear my voice trembling, can't control it all of a sudden

'There will be a post mortem but from what we've learnt so far, they all died by the same method. All twelve we know about and the news from America is saying exactly the same about the deaths over there.'

'What!' I shout. 'I heard the news. I listened to the news last night. No spaceship, no...' I feel like there must have been other news that came on after the weather, after I'd turned the radio off. I'm crying

The Flophouse Years

about this but anyone would. The BBC playing tricks on me.

The police lady puts an arm around my shoulder. She's just being nice, not into me, I'm sure. She's probably very stern, police officers always are. I appreciate that she's trying to help. 'It was on the news this morning, Dennis. You might not have heard it. Not last night. No one knew then, different time zone in America. I know you're upset.'

Bloody right I am but I know it isn't Susan Ash's fault. It might be mine; I've already told her that I slept here last night without looking in their room. She hasn't arrested me, not seemed very bothered by it. 'Poor boy,' was all she said.

'Couldn't anyone stop them?' I ask. 'If you heard reports from America.'

'It was too late, and we couldn't trace people. We don't have any information about Themagins. Nobody had assessed them as dangerous before all this.'

She says it very calmly; it might be that which makes my blood boil. I like her; feel ashamed of how I'm behaving. I just shout at her really loud. 'My dad isn't dangerous! He's stupid! Stupid, stupid! He never hit me.'

'No. I'm sorry, Dennis. I mean that we didn't know they were distributing cyanide amongst the group. Did he...' She pauses and I look away. She's not cross that I shouted. I think if one of the policemen had stayed with me instead of the woman, he might have bashed me with a truncheon for my outburst. Or I might not have told a man that Dad's a moron. I always wanted to hide that from the world, it's easier to trust Sergeant Ash. '...in America some children have taken it. With their parents. Did your father ask you to take anything?'

'No.'

I've slumped forward on the settee now. I feel shivery, won't shout. This woman is hugging me like I'm about eight which is probably what I sound like. All my daft crying.

'He never told me to drink anything. My dad wanted me to go to the spaceship but I told him there isn't one. They never told me they would be taking poison.' It comes into my mind that the sausages could have killed me if I'd eaten them. Then I would have joined them wherever they are. My penny-pinching mum buys old food because it's cheaper, not a murderer, just a shit cook. 'They never forced me to do anything. I thought their beliefs were stupid. I never met one who seemed nasty or anything...' I trail off as I speak, realising that this might be a big mystery to the police. They're probably finding out about Themagins for the first time. They're nothing like normal criminals. There are hours of tape recordings in the cupboard opposite the settee on which Susan and I sit. Aris Toogood telling everyone what he thinks about this world and the next. The late Aris Toogood. I think he tells everyone to have sex with each other too. I've not heard it, just expect something like it is in there. I wonder if I should tell Sergeant Ash they are there. If they are evidence of something or other. 'Do you know if one of the dead people is called Burning Rock? One of the others in this country.'

'Burning Rock? Is that his religious name?'

'Her name. I don't know what she's called in normal life. She was here a couple of weeks ago. She had just come back from meeting Aris Toogood in America.'

'The distributor.'

As Sergeant Ash says it, I feel a chill. Burning Rock had short black hair, very white skin, the greenest eyes. She smiled at me the last time she was here although I looked through her. Looked at the curve of her chest a bit. She doesn't go in for bra-wearing which isn't even a Themagin thing, my mum always wore one. It was just Burning Rock left it in the drawer. She came back from America without her husband, if that is what Ganymede is. Now the pair of them are probably dead and Sergeant Ash thinks she might have brought the poison that killed my parents. I think it would have killed me if I'd told Dying Star that I wanted to go on the comet with him. I slide down from the settee and onto the floor. I don't cry now; inside I feel like I've become someone else. Someone stupider for the afternoon. I know I'm making an idiot of myself, that's simply what having parents like mine does to a boy. Susan has lowered herself to the floor with me. Says, 'It will be all right, Dennis,' but she should see that it won't. My parents have been dead for more than a day and I've lived in the same house as their lifeless bodies. As she hugs me—just comfort—I duck my head into her body, bash it on her walkie-talkie. It's only an accident and I don't really mind. Bash my fucking head in, everyone else has.

12.

My father's funeral was a near silent send off. Not a word about the Themagins and nothing Christian spoken either. I expect he made the

The Flophouse Years

latter clear in whatever arrangements he made in advance. My uncle took care of all of it—my mother's brother—and he didn't even attend the service. Peter Harris lived and then he died; he married and the couple left this life together. A pair of lunatics; however, the man officiating kept that home truth to himself. It stalked the crematorium, made its presence felt in the gaping silences.

My granny—the living one, on my mother's side—Auntie Jean and Uncle Stanley all attend my mum's service. They kept themselves clear of the one that occurred in the same dismal place just thirty minutes earlier. Her no-good husband. Granny wails like a banshee through her daughter's send off, my mother's. I've not seen her in years, I think she fell out with Dad. That was long ago, over something that came before the Themagins, I don't know what. Not letting my mother breathe, I expect. Whatever he wanted he got: doing a job, not doing a job; going to church, joining a crazier one. I don't cry a single tear in either service—I've stopped doing that—I feel like my granny sounds. Run dry is all, the feelings won't leave. There are two hymns in the second service and I pipe up as loud as I can. I've no voice but it is the last thing I will ever be able to do for her. I don't hate my mother. She was a moron and that's not a crime. It gets in the way of being a decent mum. Obscures the view quite a lot. There isn't much else to say about her. Cooked up barley like we were peasants in the Middle Ages.

* * *

I'm living at Uncle Stan's house for the time being. Mum's brother. He means well but I can't stand him. Auntie Jean is better by about two percent. No more than that. He—my uncle—tried to talk me into going back to school but I don't want to. I want to get back to my own home. That's why I'm seeing a solicitor. Uncle Stan is a bit narky about it—that I insist on going to my own house—but he's only looking out for himself really. Everyone is. It sounds nice of them, offering to enrol me in the sixth form in Taunton. That way of life suits the likes of Stephen Bredbury; it's not for me. I've got a job, and I can't even do that while I'm living in Taunton. Uncle Stanley talks about selling three Croft Road—'You'll not want to go back there after such a tragedy'—and then I can pay my way in his household. I think he's trying to pull a fast one. I just say I'm not selling.

I know I'm not ready to live on my own yet. Crying uncontrollably at unspecified times of day is the biggest problem. Auntie Jean is nice to me when I do it and I'd still rather she left me alone. I think it will

Antecedents

all stop once I cease picturing them drinking cyanide. It's a horrible way to go and if they really believed it would unite them with a spaceship hidden behind a comet, they probably deserved what they got. In the papers they speculate that Aris Toogood brainwashed everyone, they even say his tape-recorded voice acted like hypnotism. That makes no sense to me: I heard him and never believed a word of it. When I sort of did, when I said I was a Themagin—aged fourteen, fifteen, no older than that—it was my dad who nearly hypnotised me. Not with sorcery or anything, boys just look up to their fathers. I might make it my life's mission to tell everyone to stop. I'm never having children, or if I accidently do, I'll tell them not to listen to a word I say. It sounds a bit crazy but if everyone did it, we'd have a better world. No more war like the hippies say. Kids probably should listen to what their mothers have to say. I don't think they pack them off to war half as much as their dad's do. But that would be no use with wet blankets like To the Ship. Some mums are faint echoes of their selfish husbands, everyone should speak up for themselves.

Toogood's voice used to drone on and on in our house. Dying Star played the stupid tapes every day of the year.

We are compelled to live apart in our separate bodies but are we not one in our love for the boundless universe?

I don't think I was hypnotised but I can remember a surprising amount. Haven't listened in an age.

> ***Throughout Christendom, we have repeatedly drawn our children's names from the bible, generation after generation. Do we really want to repeat their mistakes, brothers and sisters? Bind ourselves forever to a theology that knows only what it has been through and nothing of what is to come?***

Everything he said was about that irrelevant. I'm called Dennis, my name comes from the Beano not the bible.

'I'll wait in that teashop. See you when you're done in there,' says Uncle Stanley.

I think he's quite resentful that he has had to drive down here, to Axminster, so that I can see my solicitor. He kept saying, 'My chap in Taunton could sort all this.' I think I'm quite smart, figured how all this works. His solicitor might be working for him, even if he took me on as a client. My mum and dad lodged their wills with Barrett's before doing what they did. And Barrett's worked for Granny, my dad's mum,

The Flophouse Years

before that. Sorted everything when number three Croft Road went from her to him. Inheritance. I'm not using any shifty Taunton solicitor when I already have my own.

By rights, three Croft Road is mine. That's what the will says. It's a bit of a house of horrors; if I close my eyes, I still see them dead on the bed, or half on, half off in my mum's case. I want to go back because it's mine and I like Charmouth. No sea at Taunton, and a childless couple make hopeless substitute parents. They're normal and the food is good but I'm not used to their sort of grub. My bedroom in Taunton is shit. It was Uncle Stan's dark room, where he used to develop his photographs and it has blinds up where there should be curtains. I feel scared in the pitched black of night, I haven't told them about it because I'm meant to be grown up. Very hard to wake up on time in the morning, no sun shining in. Uncle Stan has put most of his clobber in a cupboard, tried his best to accommodate me, I suppose. It simply doesn't feel like mine. I like to see the stars out of the window. Always have. No illusions about going to them. None whatsoever.

'Dennis, Dennis, step right in.' The solicitor's name is Mr Goodman. He works for Barrett's but he's not a Barrett. 'Shocking business, I know. How are you bearing up?'

I smile at him and say, 'I'm okay.' I didn't know that I was, but his question is clever. It doesn't really invite a negative reply. I need lifting up and he's trying.

'I do hope everyone is being helpful to you, Dennis. You're at a funny age. Nearly a grown-up and I know too many of my own generation are a but dismissive with teenagers. You'll want to get along in your own way, and you deserve a helping hand while you're at it. If your parents were here, they would give it to you as best they could.'

I'm nodding along. He means well but I think he's rambling. 'I don't understand what I'm allowed to do at my age,' I say. 'Am I a child or an adult?'

'Ha! Old as you feel, eh? A little bit of each. You know the law has changed, don't you?' I shake my head and he's studying the paper in front of him. 'October twenty-eighth,' he says. I keep on nodding, it's my date of birth. 'Later this year you will be eighteen. As of nineteen-seventy, as of the first of January just gone, you are considered an adult when you reach eighteen. It was not so just a few weeks back. The law used to be twenty-one. No one can make decisions for you after that date. October the twenty-eighth might sound a long way off but it will be around before you know it.'

'Uncle Stanley wants to sell my house.'

Now it's Goodman's turn to do the headshake. 'Can't do that, not his decision. If you want it sold, he can ratify that, confirm it's in your interests to do so. He doesn't make unilateral decisions. Do you understand what I mean?'

'I think so.'

'Now, I wrote to you and I believe that you know the content of your parents will. A very strange will it was, too. An awful lot about giving assets for the greater good of humanity but that was assuming no surviving lineage.'

The wording took me a long time to figure out when I read it. Both my Auntie and Uncle said I should ignore those phrases but I couldn't help thinking them over and over. They never forced me for a second and yet it was obvious my parents hoped I would drink the poison. Both did, they signed identical wills. 'They were nuts at the end Mr Goodman. They didn't hate me, didn't hate each other. They did it because they were nuts and didn't know I wasn't.'

He looks at me levelly. 'You've just said more sense about it than I've heard in all the days since this terrible tragedy happened. God bless you, Dennis.'

I don't think God has blessed me. In fact, I'll be happy if He leaves me alone from here on in, but I quite like Goodman saying it. He's properly on my side, I'm sure of it.

When we talk about practical things, he agrees that I can live in the house. A seventeen-year-old can live alone. Anything else and I'll lose my job; Mr Goodman sees the sense in it. My uncle will be my guardian for those months but he can do that from Taunton. He suggests that I speak to Uncle Stanley regularly by telephone. See him from time to time. He also says that if I prove incapable of living on my own then my uncle would have recourse to setting a more conducive living arrangement. I question what this means and he says, 'Look after yourself properly, Dennis. Don't give him a reason to take you back to Taunton. Not unless that is where you'd rather be.' I tell him that I'll try but I need a new fridge. Mr Goodman laughs about that; he can get it sorted, he says. Plenty of money for a few household items. Even for a television, I learn. The solicitor is very surprised we don't have one already. Doesn't know much about how lunatics live.

When my solicitor has talked it all through with me—said everything about twice but only because he wants to make sure I've

The Flophouse Years

understood it—agreed what should happen for the best, and what it is I really want, I go across to the teashop. I tell Uncle Stan that Mr Goodman wants to talk to him. He seems very pleased with that, finally getting his oar in. When we get in the office and Mr Goodman tells him what we have agreed, Uncle Stan turns sour. Turns to me and says, 'You don't really want to live back there, do you, son? It's not much of a house.'

I don't like him calling me that, I'm not his son. And I don't want to live anywhere but number three Croft Road. It's not been a great home for the last couple of years but it's familiar, and I have friends in Charmouth. A good job, my manager has phoned me four times since I've been on sick leave, bereavement leave, whatever they're calling it. I think she cares more about me than my uncle. His saying it's not much of a house might be about right, I still think I can make more of it than it was. A house is as good as what goes on inside it and I won't be holding any Themagin orgies. Working at Plaza Court and watching my new tele will do me.

'I want to be there, Uncle Stanley. I want to go home.'

Mr Goodman writes that down like it's a verdict in court. I think Uncle Stanley can't think straight because he hates my dad, blames him for his sister's death. Everything looks different according to whose shoes you stand in. I only ever wanted to be where I belong.

Chapter Five

Supper Shared

Part One
1.

The music thumps away downstairs but she believes her place is here, with the sleeping boy. This party hasn't gone to plan. Not close. Annabel removes her hippy clothes and slides into bed beside her boy, her Dennis. She got pretty potted after their row. If it even was a row? Everything has a wrap of smoke around it now. What she has in mind seems a pretty universal panacea.

She nuzzles up against his ear, rouses him from his sleep. A hand on his cock should do the trick but it is more flaccid than she can recall ever finding it. The lad is twenty years old. Spring-loaded. He groans, turns his head into her kiss, accepts it. A little blood making its way to the frontline now. 'Let's get you a good party,' she whispers.

He says nothing, she feels his hands upon her, hip, breast, then cupping her mouth. He does that. The thing between his legs grew back quick enough, he is on her in no time. Speaks no words, flesh shared in the time-honoured fashion.

Dennis seemed upset by Jimmy Crook. Resented the famous guy flirting with Mary, when the girl must have felt flattered. Might have won herself a poking to remember if Denny hadn't driven him away. Pissed him off. Dennis thought Jimmy insensitive for asking questions about times past, the crazy religion of his parents. That was the only gripe Annabel got out of him, not one that merited banishing him from the party. Not after the hours of pleasure the bassist has given Dennis. Laughing Llamas—alternately eerie and rocking—are the sound of his parties, month in and month out. He's coming around now, pulls himself properly on top of her. She likes this: a young buck getting into the saddle, riding her. She weighs a little more than Dennis Harris. Quite right too, in her mind. The man to whom she was—for nine years—married had sixty pounds on her. Of course, she was lighter herself back then. A hell of a lot lighter when they first met. That line-backer almost broke her spine once or twice the way he made love. Smash and grab. She didn't complain at the time but this boy's gentility is a welcome change. Passion that sits in the back of his mind, a quiet insistent hum. Marco was different, a sensual driving force sitting in his temporal lobe like a big fatty mass. She thinks Marco talked even less than Dennis. A lot of waiting and watching in the daylight hours; come the night, he turned into Genghis Khan's hornier buddy. In the early days she took it on the chin. Loved him. Her guts twist momentarily with the memory: lover, husband, powerhouse; rotting in hell if there is any kind of justice. She tries to push those thoughts from her mind as this less-demanding boy stirs her own insides, as he writhes and wriggles upon her.

He's whimpering now, seems to be finishing, all done. Plastered himself across her breasts, arms behind her, spent, clinging. Like a pancake that's missed the pan.

'Baby, baby,' she says to him. 'Everything okay now?'

The door opens, light from the landing streaks across their bed. Two girls start to giggle. 'Have you got Jimmy Crook in there?' asks one in her soft West Country burr.

'Hey girls,' says Annabel from beneath her limpet boyfriend, 'I mean this most politely: can you please fuck off?'

They laugh and close the door.

2.

Annabel thinks it was a turning point, the party when Jimmy Crook came. Turned left or right, anything but straight ahead. She has a close bond with Dennis, the closest she has been to another person since turning Annabel. Something has cooled on his part. He still performs sex with little prompting, says nothing derogatory, it simply doesn't feel the same. Not at all, actually. He blames her for something—she is sure of it— exactly what she cannot define. She hears Templeton Ca. on the turntable more than Laughing Llamas these days. Funny how meeting the man from the band has changed his musical taste. Annabel thought Crooky charming but she has started to see he was also a letch. That all men lean that way has long been her supposition. Maybe Dennis is different, he is certainly a gentle soul. Or he might want to do to Mary Bredbury the same thing Jimmy Crook was angling for. It would get it out of his system. She doesn't say it. Senses that he would feel insulted if she voiced her thought. She can see that Mary is slimmer, far more youthful, a step-change prettier than she. Her own bond with Dennis has been the on-off talk of Charmouth. It certainly piqued that Lorraine-woman's interest. His uptight lady-boss.

He and Dennis don't really do free love but nor does she wish to tie him down. Dennis's restraint with Mary, his pursuit of a platonic friendship might be a higher compliment than any man has paid to Annabel. Marco was on her—doing the act—within about two hours of their meeting. Nineteen-fifty-eight. They were not beatniks and the hippy egg was—at that point in time—unfertilised in the world. Lust was Marco's motivator and she allowed it him. Joined in. Let herself be anything he wanted. These musings make Annabel feel a little lost. She wonders if she is in Dennis's way. An older woman fantasy he enjoys but doesn't need. He can get a little unrestrained, now and then. Suggest kinky stuff then dare not try it. Dennis is no Marco. She wouldn't be here if he was.

The flophouse seems less free and easy, less trusting in the weeks after that party. The one when Jimmy Crook showed up. She wonders if she is doing more harm by staying. The monthly parties continue and the Llamas generally make the turntable. None have walked through the door again and nor shall they. They live in California and Dennis drove away the one who came.

Tom Garside pays her in cash—values her work and knowledge—no one is on her case but her visa ran out long ago. As she cycles back from the polytunnel farm this November evening, a sea mist swirls about her, dampens her hair. Forehead salt-licked. Her coat is barely waterproof, the chill of the rain feels to be upon every inch of her. On the country lane a lone girl walks in front of her, head down to counter the clinging rain. From afar, she thinks it might be her, senses she is right as she closes in. The gait of the walk, narrow hips. Annabel pulls her bike up.

'Hey, Mary,' she says.
'Oh, it's you.'
'Where are you headed?'
'Home.'
'Out for a walk?'
'I had a tutorial.'
'Mary, there is no school out here.'

The Flophouse Years

'My teacher lives over there.' Mary gestures inland, there are not many houses where she points. Just one or two. 'She gives me extra lessons.'

'I see.' Annabel has swung herself off her bike, pushes it as she walks beside Mary on the quiet lane. 'Good or bad extra lessons?'

'What?'

'Struggling or...'

'No. I'm going to do physics at university. At least, I think I am.'

'Good for you. One for us girls, that is. Physics, wow.' They step along in silence for a few paces. 'Mary, do you see a lot of Dennis?'

'Annabel, please don't be jealous of me. I did enough of that for both of us,' pleads the younger girl.

'No. It's something else. I'm worried about him.'

'What's wrong? I saw him a week ago.'

'And he was the usual Dennis?'

'Quiet. But he is quiet, Annabel.' They have stopped walking, stand quite stationary, the drizzly rain plasters Mary's hair to her forehead; Annabel's elaborate plait is taking on water. Getting heavier by the minute. 'I've known him forever, you haven't. When he was a child, he was nearly as wonky as my brother. I think it was that pair who got me interested in physics.'

'Dennis was wonky? That's news.'

'He knew the name of every star in the sky, I'm sure he did.'

'I can see how they lost their appeal.'

'And Annabel, when he started having parties, growing his hair longer than anyone else, I was so young that I thought it the coolest thing in Dorset. I don't know now. I don't know which Dennis I like best. The quieter lad who was embarrassed by his funny parents or the party-thrower. I think the first one joined up more dots.'

'I see. You're a clever girl, Mary. And I'm not jealous of you. Who knows...?' She doesn't voice the thought that is rolling around her head. Steals a look at Mary, face as pretty as it is thoughtful. Going to graduate in physics in years to come. What has such a clever girl been doing with these seaside-town deadbeats. Jason Clarke, Gordon Stickland. Dennis Harris even. 'Do you want to drop by, Mary. Come for an evening meal. Just you. Or bring someone if you're seeing...'

'Can I bring my sister?'

'She's young, right?'

'She's fourteen. It would be like old times. We both adored Dennis when we were little.'

Supper Shared

'You won't be bringing Stephen?'

'Ha! He could spoil any party.'

'It's not a party, Mary. Supper. Dennis cares about you, you do him. It isn't my intention to be in the way, Dennis and I just...' Annabel looks up into the rain as if hoping it can complete her thought. '...for supper. You and your sister.'

* * *

That evening she tells him about meeting Mary. He listens to her but says nothing. Not until he mentions the sister is coming too.

'Monica?'

Annabel gestures yes, although she did not know that was the girl's name.

'Sweet.' Then he looks back down at the local paper he is reading.

'Something interesting in there?'

'Same old crap.'

And the next day he barely says a word before heading off for Plaza Court, the late shift. Annabel worries about Dennis. Something has come between them. She thought they shared an experience: survivors of the Themagin suicides. Both had the sense to distance themselves long before the dreadful reckoning, and both had once been closer to the misguided cult than it is healthy to dwell upon. They grieve for those not as clear thinking. And, for Annabel, her own thinking was never clear at all, she realises, as she bumps her mind back across it. She balked at the demands of Toogood. Marco's driven sex was the biggest pleasure of her marriage—not of the whole marriage—of the early days. Going with the succession of men—those with whom she was to later share a spaceship—was plain awful. She wishes she had never allowed any man to do that to her in front of Marco. All a dreadful muddle in her mind. She was not there mentally, that was the way she coped. She didn't think about the man on top of her, or even the teachings of Toogood. She contemplated the planting or gathering in of vegetables while her husband fucked a youngster. Or an oldster. While someone with a serious face lay across her. She wasn't any kind of hippy at that point in time, just wanted a normal marriage while finding hers had long missed the mark.

So, why run from all that shit to the hippies? She never understood that turn of events either. Annabel thinks about plants more systematically than she can manage with humankind. 'We are weird fuckers,' Dennis had said when she tried to talk to him about it. About whether hippies were dropping in or dropping out. Perhaps she should have talked more. What she has been through, all she has lost. He isn't much of a one for opening up, maybe she isn't either. She regrets how much she shared with Jimmy Crook; some tragic truths she has yet to tell Dennis. Guessed the bass player was the man with the Midas touch; perhaps he has been just that. She can see what her lover feels about Mary Bredbury, Jimmy Crook shone his torch all over that important consideration.

'All the old people in bed?' she says upon his return. Dennis shrugs. It's a stupid question but she's trying. They probably should be; Annabel doesn't know what time they turn in. He might have told her months back; she hasn't paid enough interest to his job. He loves it. Used to love it, at least. She wonders how it's going; is he this silent at Plaza Court? Can't imagine him cheering up old folk with the long face and ever-present sense of gloom. She was like it herself straight after it all happened. The deaths. Not for long; threw herself into being a hippy—being Annabel—as a way to be only present, feel nothing for what had gone before. It's like Dennis has gone back there.

'You know we've got Mary and her sister around tomorrow evening?'

'Yeah. Good.' Then he is staring away into space. No television on, not even a local paper in his hands. She has never been more worried about him.

3.

He rises early and takes himself back to work the following morning. Annabel is up at the same time, makes him toast which he thanks her for. She cycles to the polytunnels. Only three or four hours work for her. Less to do at this time of year. She manages a section now, earns a decent hourly rate. A diligent cultivator.

When she returns to the house, a girl and boy are waiting on the doorstep. Not kids, mid-twenties, at a glance. Annabel lets them in: it's a flophouse. She wonders how to manage the evening ahead. The visit of Dennis's friend and her sister. She recognises neither hippy.

Schylar and Hendrika are Dutch—hitchhiking—feeling their way across the south of England. They heard about Croft Road when they were in Bournemouth. A lot of people have passed through, word of mouth scatters the seeds. In the house, Hendrika takes off her coat and sweater to reveal a Llamas' T-shirt. Schylar asks questions, throws out statements, in his clear but accented English.

Supper Shared

'It is all right to stay?'
'If there are charges, we have a little money.'
'Hendrika is a good cook. A professional.'
'We've a pizza and salad planned,' says Annabel. She explains the money jar in the kitchen, the open-ended arrangements.
'I heard there are showers here?' says Hendrika.
'The rubber thing behind the bath taps. Squeeze one funnel onto each nozzle. It's not exactly the Hilton.'

* * *

Annabel starts to prepare food. She has the ingredients sorted, trying for a meal she last made years ago. Thinks over the detail of the process. A mixing bowl with plain flour and semolina measured out, awaiting further reinforcements. Hendrika walks in, long wet hair on her shoulders, different T-shirt. Wearing shorts. Odd for the time of year but the house isn't cold.
'We've some friends coming over,' Annabel tells her.
'That's all right,' says Hendrika. 'Schylar and I are quiet.'
'You can have some food, of course.'
'Let me assist you in its making. I love to knead.'
She proves to be a great help. Annabel has no recipe and was struggling to recall how she ever fixed this meal in Rhode Island. Hasn't made pizza since the world—the corner of it in which she had friends and family—knew her by a different name. Hendrika suggests other items she might add. Herbs. Annabel has rosemary in the garden, mint too although she'd not have thought to use it without this imaginative girl's prompting.
'What is Schylar doing now?' asks Annabel.
'He might be reading. Schylar reads funny books. Comics you call them. Comic strip books. He might take something. He likes to read them when he is on something. I'm not so...what is the word? Enamoured. I am not so enamoured with all the drugs.'
'A time and place, right?'
'I think so. Now is the time for making pizza. Are your friends to be impressed with this?'
Annabel pauses before answering. Unsure if she is implying the meal unimpressive or if her wording was simply clumsy. Second or third language, Hendrika's doing well. 'Not really. A couple of girls Dennis knows. It's his house. You know that?'
'Dennis? No. We were only told how to find the...what is the

205

word…the flophouse. Not the name of the owner. Is he a landlord or a hippy?'

'One of us, Hendrika. He's…' She feels the tug of doubt in her mind as she completes the phrase she was starting. '…my boyfriend. We're a sort of couple.' Couple is how she usually says it, the vagueness is new. She thinks it is the visit of Mary which has prompted her to use the modifier. This planned meal is getting to her and she really doesn't dislike the young girl. Mary Bredbury. Dennis's silences might be the more disconcerting. They are reminiscent of something long ago. Marco throughout the year before he discovered the Themagins. Miserable Marco who subsequently turned the corner only to lose it altogether. She tries to push all that from her mind.

'Then I make the pizza super-nice for your boyfriend. The generous hippy with a house. A nice house, I think. The sea is very near?'

'A quarter mile or so. Hendrika…'

Annabel is tongue-tied again. She wants to warn this helpful girl that Dennis is not himself; she wonders if he is taking some drug or other that is having this effect on him. It is unlikely, to the best of her knowledge he only ever smokes pot. Likes to down the beers too. Hasn't done either of those since their last party. The first of November was a bit of a flop. That was her view. He said, 'Went okay,' by way of summary as they took themselves to bed, a quietened lounge of sleeping-bagged hippies. A couple in the spare room too. Not the old vibe, though. That matters to Annabel. The day she arrived she was keen to meet Dennis. His demeanour throughout the party, his total acceptance of whatever happened, blew her away. It's why she threw her lot in with him. To enjoy life without caring too indebtedly about it. She once thought him the survivor she could learn from.

'We might like to see it. Go and walk down to the sea. Will there be time?'

'It's a short walk,' says Annabel. 'Five minutes there, five minutes back.'

'If Schylar is not in a gibberish state of mind, we will go. I think we can do this and still arrive back in time for the pizza, yes?

'As you please, really.'

* * *

When Dennis returns from his shift at the flats, the Dutch couple are upstairs in the spare bedroom. There will be no walk to the beach this

Supper Shared

afternoon. Schylar has gotten himself into a very gibberish state: backwards down the rabbit hole. Hendrika chose not to say from which drug. Annabel doesn't say it but she envies him the mood, the departure from the anxiety she feels every hour now.

She tells him about the floppers, what is going on. 'Hendrika put money in the jar.' Dennis shrugs, never bothers either way. 'I think they should eat separately. We've Mary and her sister coming, Dennis.'

'No way. No exclusivity Annie. And it will be an education for Monica. She's a spunky kid but needs to meet more hippies than just me. And she knows me more from years ago, when I was a lost kid. Meeting these guys from overseas will be a good thing for her.'

Annabel thinks he has spoken more in this exchange than in all their conversations of the last three days combined. That much is encouraging. He failed to spot that she too is from overseas, will also meet Monica for the first time.

When Hendrika is back downstairs, washing salad—she truly loves preparing food—Annabel asks, 'Will Schylar be okay to eat with us?'

'Yes, he will eat. I think you say, he has duffed up his brain, so we should eat upstairs. He cannot embarrass you up there.'

'No,' says Dennis. 'Guests eat with us. It's a rule. We don't mind what's going on in his head.'

'A hippy house with rules?' says the Dutch girl.

'No fighting and everybody eats together. Two rules.'

'Ha. We can comply with both of these. I like the rules of your house, Dennis. What is the phrase? They have emerged from a healthy logic.'

* * *

Annabel has already set the cutlery out, six places fill the dining table, when the door-bell rings.

'Shall I get it,' says Hendrika.

At the door, she ushers young Mary and even younger Monica across the threshold. 'Who are you?' says the older of the pair.

'Staying tonight. I'm not sure I am really meant to be here; however, I am overjoyed to meet you.'

Monica beams. 'Overjoyed to meet me?' Her hair flaps beside her child's face, two ill-gathered bunches. A floral frock and cardigan clothe her. She is still young, growing to look a little like her older sister. Too young for men to seek out her eyes, appraise her shape, but perhaps they do. She glances round and round the room. Annabel suspects it is her first visit here. She certainly hasn't clapped eyes on the younger girl before.

'Hi girls,' says Dennis.

'I'm glad you two are friends now,' says the younger sister.

Mary pulls Monica into a playful hug. 'Who says we are?'

'Have you heard from Stephen?' asks Dennis.

'Not coming back until Christmas. Mummy hasn't the money for his train fare.' Monica is not shy about her family's poverty.

'Did he tell you he's got a girlfriend?' asks Mary.

'That's news to me.'

'A biology girl,' shrieks Monica. 'What do you think they're like? Girls who cut up rats. He's a freak is my brother.'

Hendrika watches them chat, head tipped to one side. She says only, 'I'll fetch Schylar,' then disappears up the stairs.

'She speaks funny,' says Monica, when the Dutch girl is out of the room, in the room above with her drugged-up partner. The talk coming from up there is unintelligible to the four down below. Language and volume.

'Not funny,' says Annabel. 'Dutch.'

'But her English sounds ridiculous.'

'No,' Mary chides her sister, 'she speaks great. We don't know a word of her language, do we?'

They stop talking, pay close attention to the alien cadences of a foreign language coming from the stairs into the open plan room, a male voice doing most of the talking. He raises his voice to a high pitch and then down to an exceptionally low register. It might be the sound of an orator—an opera singer, even—limbering up.

'I think it is necessary that I apologise for my boyfriend,' says Hendrika as she is coming down the stairs, glancing back as if her partner may stumble, though he does not.

Schylar stopped his strange vocalisations mid-stairs and now he sits competently on the dining chair which his girl has pulled forward for him. Stares straight ahead, zombie fashion.

'Will he eat?' asks Annabel.

'That he can do. Give him a horse and he will eat a horse. I have not known my boyfriend to refuse food.'

'Wow,' says Monica, 'is he always mental?'

'What do you mean by mental?' asks Hendrika.

'Monica,' says Dennis, 'this gentleman has lost the thread for a little time on account of taking drugs. He'll be back with us in a while. You can see why we don't let you take any, my young friend.'

'Oh, God. It sounds terrible.' Then she turns on her older sister. 'You said you did it. Were you as mental as this man?'

Dennis takes it upon himself to walk around the table, to Schylar. 'Hey there,' he says. 'All right there? Can I give you water?' Dennis pours from jug to glass, tries to place it into the Dutchman's hand.

'Thank you,' says Hendrika. 'He speaks English rather well but I think...' She taps the side of her own head. '...forgotten.'

Monica starts to laugh; Annabel surmises there is fear mixed up in there. 'I don't think your Mary took the same as this gentleman,' she says to the younger girl.

'I only tried it because Dennis did. Or rather, Jason.'

'Are you still seeing Jason?' asks Annabel

'God, no.'

Annabel looks closely at the pretty girl who has so summarily dismissed her summer boyfriend. She makes mistakes, learns from them, it seems.

Hendrika rises and says, 'Let me look at that pizza.'

'I thought you were cooking it?' says Dennis to Annabel.

'She knows what she's doing.'

He continues to look puzzled. Looks at her accusingly, she thinks. It strikes her that Dennis would have laughed about it just a dozen weeks ago. It's a flophouse; who cares who cooks the pizza?

* * *

The food is a great success. 'All Hendrika's doing,' concedes Annabel each time someone at the table praises it.

'But you are growing the salad,' says the Dutch girl. 'And you grow it very nicely.'

Mary tells them about her aspiration to go to university. To follow Stephen. 'We're a clever family,' she says, self-consciousness parked off-road for the evening. 'Monica should go too. She's smart enough.'

'I'm not a scientist, nothing like my brother and sister. I want to do drama next year but can't unless fifteen opt for it.'

'What does that mean?' asks Annabel.

'They won't run the course in my school unless fifteen of us choose to do it.'

'Oh. I can see you doing drama. You're a very confident cookie.'

The youngest at table tells the assembled about her part in the upcoming school play, a girl kidnapped by pirates. 'The starring role.'

The Flophouse Years

All the while Dennis, who is sitting next to Mary, speaks quietly with her, and Annabel wishes they were the ones projecting. She wanted Mary here; Monica is only tagging along. The kid is bright but the American gets little from talking to her. Gets a headache; young Monica must have a bright future ahead, bubbly, confident, Charmouth-naïve. She is not what Annabel wants from the evening. Across the table, she notes that Dennis is doing the talking she cannot hear. The majority of it. Young Mary is lifting him out of himself one way or another.

Schylar gives a loud burp and then laughs at himself.

'Excuse my boyfriend, everybody. He is not understanding what is being said.'

Monica laughs at him. 'Wouldn't you like a better boyfriend?' she says.

'At this moment, yes.'

'And you don't take them, do you?'

'Monica, it is a complicated question. I don't consume the ones that Schylar has taken today but drugs can be very enlightening. They release only thoughts and feelings that are already inside us.'

'What, like his burps?' says Monica.

'Perhaps burps, and sometimes insights that are even more profound than that,' says the Dutch girl.

'I do them,' says Annabel. 'Can't help myself but I would never let a daughter your age try them. Not yet. No reason to take drugs so long as laughing at those who do is still funny.'

* * *

The Dutchman burped off and on for half an hour and now he has gone to sleep in the lounge chair. Not much of a guest but that's hippies for you. What happens will. The girl is very nice. They told her not to and still Hendrika has done all the washing up. Monica helping. The little sister seems to have acclimatised to her accent. Annabel is in a foul mood. It isn't like her. She invited Mary here because she thought it might lift Dennis's spirits. That it appears to have worked makes Annabel feel like a visiting witch. The one who put the curse on him in the first place. And God knows, she and Dennis have both suffered enough curses. She has come upstairs to the bathroom, sits on the toilet. Respite from company as much as any other purpose. And she has always been a woman to thrive on the proximity of others. Charmed her way into a supervisor's role at Brigham Farm, the one

Supper Shared

here in Dorset. She pulled off the same stunt at Syrah Nurseries, out in California, before she ever came to England. Knowing her onions helps. She was running from the Themagins; that was why she went out to California. Away from her marriage. And she had done everything Toogood asked of her up until then. Long before he asked anyone to drink cyanide, that was not foreseen. Not by Antonella Vitale; no comet in the sky when she left Rhode Island. He talked about other worlds on the tapes and Toogood even implied they would be going. No mention whatsoever of the circuitous route taken. Antonella used to be a classroom assistant back in Providence, growing vegetables only a hobby in those days. She enjoyed working in schools at the time but no longer wishes to be around children. It might be Monica who is getting on her nerves. On her tits, as they say here. She laughs about that, puts her hand to the said body part. Monica is a gobby girl. Annabel thinks in English-English after living here for eighteen months, although everyone she meets still asks question after question about America. She will always be an outsider. The interloper in Dennis's life. He has told her all about the unseen events at the first party she came to—he calls it his fourth party—Mary was offering herself to him in a pretty blatant fashion. 'She's just a kid,' he told her. 'I didn't want her first time to be a cause for regret.' He explained to her that Mary was far drunker than she knew how to handle. 'I even worried that she wouldn't remember it if we had. That is not the man I am.' And he also admitted she, Annabel, was his first. A lot of boys wouldn't have been that honest. Nor could most have resisted Mary. She looks pretty special. And what of her? Of Annabel waiting in Dennis's bed because she liked the look of him; crossed an ocean to get away from her memories then chased down another survivor when the Themagin-obsessed Daisy told her his whereabouts. Annabel wonders why she has done what she's done. Set up home with a lad who, like her, could have easily wound up dead almost four years ago. Caught up in an inexplicable tragedy. Are they just preparing for the next life? Must first share bodies while apart in order to coalesce harmoniously when one. Aris Toogood's meaningless drivel upsets her; she might not be as free of it as she supposes. Annabel stoops forward and picks her knickers from around her ankles. Pulls them back up as she stands from the bowl. Her skirt falls back in place, she brushes a hand down to be certain. Flushes, steps to the wash-hand basin. A bar of soap, she scrubs herself with the vigour usually reserved for the soil-laden hands of her

The Flophouse Years

working day. Dennis and Mary are laughing, that is what she thinks she hears. It could be Hendrika and Monica. Can't be Schylar: he has won himself a proper headfuck. Brain on vacation for the night. A few hours on the moon. He was sleeping in the lounge when she came up, his body slumped forward. Hendrika lifted him up, leaned him against the chair's backrest. He said—very, very loudly—an odd sounding Dutch word that she does not know, and heaved himself forward again into the awkward slump. Despite the distinct vocalisation, she is sure he did not wake up. The drugs have taken him to an ugly place, at least he is oblivious to Dennis and Mary's latent love-in. And Annabel is all too aware of it. The restraint in their romance is the opposite of hippieism. It is noble.

When she has dried her hands, she slips into the spare room. There is a smart blue rucksack and a dirty green one. The top flap of the latter is open, unbuckled. She slips a hand in, looking as she rummages. No immediate joy, she tries a side pocket. A small medication bottle emerges clasped in her withdrawn hand. She looks at the label. It is not from a pharmacist. Could be in Schylar's hand, his or someone as keen. 'De Shit,' says the handwritten label. Dutch seems to be a simpler language than ever she expected. Every hippy knows what is in here. She tries to unscrew the top. It has one of those damned child-proof screw lids. Quite right with Monica in the house, she thinks. Young girls like that always talk like the drug police when they are on the verge of turning full circle, deciding it's time to love the stuff. The blink of an eye. The top comes off. She tips the bottle on to her open palm. He's got more than forty in here. Whatever the fuck they are. Must be better than watching your boyfriend behaving gallantly with a girl younger, thinner, fairer of face—cleverer, goddammit—than oneself. She pops one on her tongue. Down in a flash. Then she puts seven more in the pocket of her hippy skirt. She bought the pizza ingredients; the flophouse is all about sharing. Annabel's even sharing Dennis with pretty Mary Bredbury.

She leaves the spare room but at the top of the stairs she turns back. Walks into her own bedroom. The sheets and blankets are strewn carelessly about, bed left unmade since both arose this morning. She usually makes it, preparing the meal was her excuse. They have a double bed now, bought it in September. Went halves. She thinks it might have been a mistake. They used to sleep in each other's arms when it was just a single. Now they have a wall of air between them. Of rucked blankets. She decides to make the bed, have it tidy for when

Supper Shared

she takes Dennis from Mary's gaze. Draws him upstairs for herself. She gets confused tucking in the sheets. Thinks she has folded them incorrectly, sideways or longways, tail end at the head so that no one may enter the bed. Fuck, that was weird. Thought she saw a cat on the blanket. A black one, or a blue one. Nope. Whatever this shit is, it is swamping her sorry brain in double-quick time.

* * *

When she returns to the lounge, Annabel laughs at Schylar. The poor fella is slumped over, it would be uncomfortable were he not so strung out he feels nothing at all.

'Looks very sweet, I am saying.'

Now Monica laughs, Hendrika's spoken phrase prompting the reaction. The look on the little girl's face is pure fear. Sharing a room with a bearded man who is not even in it if you think about it for a second or two. Annabel thinks her own phase two—which can't be far off—might make this goody-two-shoes crap in her knickers. Education, that is what Dennis said the flophouse is all about.

'Have you been drinking cider?' asks Annabel.

Monica turns to her with a defiant intake of breath. They seem to be staring each other down. Annabel makes cross-eyes and Monica cannot hold her gaze. 'Mary said I could,' she squeaks out.

Now it's Annabel's turn to splutter with laughter. 'Drink away,' is all she says. Her laughter continues, it has attached itself to some other imagery in her brain. She is here and there, annoyed with Monica's prissiness. Likes looking at the girl though. She has a fine neck and throat. Perhaps it is her youth, Annabel enjoys the symmetry of the lines from her mouth to the small protrusion of her breasts beneath the floral frock she wears. Her neck is not long but it is well defined. A four-carriage motorway comes to mind when looking at that pleasing shape. Motorway, autobahn, and even that isn't a Dutch word. Annabel doesn't know any. Only de shit. There was a time when she called them freeways, has long discovered freedom to be an illusion. The cat is back, on the arm of the chair next to the drug-addled Hollander. 'Hendrika,' she says, 'did you bring anybody else with you?'

'I'm sorry?' replies the guest.

'Annabel, are you okay?' She cannot tell if it is concern or disdain which frames her boyfriend's question.

'I think she brought a cat.'

The Flophouse Years

'There is no cat.'

'Are you okay?'

There is a lot of chatter. Annabel doesn't know if it is Monica or Mary who says, 'Look at her eyes, her pupils.' Smart little fuckers these Charmouth beauties. Now Dennis is in front of her, a hand holding each forearm. 'It's okay, Annie,' he says. That single word sounds like music to her. He abridges her name for affection; usually says it only when they are alone, and here he is using the term in front of the girl with the motorway neck. Not that she matters. It's the other one who would be his soulmate but for Annabel's butting in. That is what this evening is about. Annabel so loving the world she gave her only son. The cat seems to have gone now. She never gave birth to Dennis, either. That thought comes to her late, comes to her as she looks into his face. The face of a modern-day Jesus. He seems unperturbed. Maybe she has created his future with a passing thought: Dennis hasn't worked out his destiny yet; it will come. Annabel tries to reassure the boy that she is right as rain. As all the rain in Charmouth, thousands upon thousands of gallons of it. Salty rain on the windows of the house beside the sea. The words are at the bottom of a well. That happens from time to time. De shit does it. 'Let me get you a drink of water.' The man said that, the one she likes. Jesus' hair. He stands and addresses the room. 'She likes popping things sometimes, pills, acid tabs. Didn't know she had any in today. Do you think Schylar left his tablets out?' This utterance—which has nothing to do with the cat—must have been for Hendrika. She hears the Dutch girl say something in response, doesn't take in her words. A livid feeling courses through Annabel, salt and vinegar, garlic too, pumping through her angry veins. She's in the room and the lad, Dennis—she remembers the name now—a boyfriend, after a fashion, talks as if she's gone. As if she is in the past and he recalling her to whatever the pretty girl's name is. One of them should shoo the cat away, it's on the arm of the futon, might scratch the little girlie with the motorway disappearing into her dress. Can't do it herself, brain spinning on a little roundabout, won't be stepping off for cat shooing. Probably can't walk without falling down. Swinging around on a roundabout does that.

Dennis leaves the room. Gone for water. Water doesn't do anything. Makes the plants grow. That's about it. Annabel no longer looks at the people in the room, they are confusing to her speeding mind. She leans her head back, the swirling pattern on the ceiling is providing more than enough stimulation. She cannot recall seeing it before; it is all off-white, painted long ago. There is a pattern in the relief of the plaster. It's nice, looks like white pineapples. An abundance of them. And that gets her thinking about vegetables. She grows them and then she eats them. It's pretty close to cannibalism, eating your own babies. And plants aren't going to run away. Not a fair fight: she has a spade and they have only their limp leaves with which to defend themselves.

He's back—Mr Loves-Me-Not—and trying to get a glass of water into her hand. Annabel has levelled her head but cannot cooperate, cannot work out what the plan might be. The boy's face is all wrong. The smell is him though, she has definitely slept with him, so familiar is he to the nose. 'Wait.' The word comes out of her own mouth. She hears it and so must he. There is a back of a head now, he is saying something to the room again. That she is all right, probably. When nothing is all right. She is losing the little she has in this life. Her hand goes into the pocket of her skirt and the small quantity of pills she stole come straight up to her mouth. This is going to be some trip. Meet the cat. She tries to take the glass of water off Dennis, some spills onto her skirt and he starts to apologise. Nothing is his fault, he lives in Charmouth, not in the world. Be absolved young Dennis, the cat absolves you. Plenty of water left in the glass and she thrusts it to her lips. Drinks it greedily, washing down all the tablets she took from the child-proof bottle in the gibberish man's rucksack.

There is a shriek of laughter, it must be Monica. 'He's fallen over now,' she says. She finds her eyes closing but it is true. Schylar of no fixed abode has slipped from armchair to the floor of the lounge. A bit of a bash as he hit the deck. A demolition. Annabel has that to look forward to.

Part Two

4.

Hippy gatherings are always a bit like this, so maybe it hasn't been a total disaster. Annabel has got herself fucked-up in company a couple of times before. Monica looks shocked, that bothers him quite a lot. Always a friendly kid, he never meant to scare her. Fourteen-year-olds probably shouldn't be here. Not with the likes of Schylar turning up. Shouldn't, full-stop. Mary can handle it. She might be laughing at him, his messed-up life. Well, why not? He's not really on her level and he knew it years ago.

The Flophouse Years

'I'm going to walk you two back home,' he tells the girls. Hendrika can watch Schylar and Annabel. Hippies sleeping, nothing to watch really. All going on in their own private cinemas. Some shit turning over and over in their brains. Going so fast they cannot also be in the world. That was how he found it the only time he tried. Sticks to pot: a short punt out and an easy swim back to the shore.

Mary has a terrific coat that she puts on. Mustard yellow, not bright. He thinks all the colours close to it on the spectrum are a bit disgusting while the one she has chosen is perfect. Her fair hair sits on the collar, frames her face.

Little sister walks beside her. Mouthy Monica. He wonders if she is over the moon at sitting out a grown-up druggies' party or if she will tell her mother. He and Mary could each get an earful from Emma Bredbury—from Mary and Monica's mum—if she does that. What happens will; there is no changing it from here.

On the way both girls ask him if Annabel will be okay. He thinks she and Schylar took the same drug but no one is worried about the guy. They made no connection with him before he slipped off to the crazy place. Cheerio but be back soon, all that shit. Bit selfish of him: dropping into the flophouse and then wending his way down the wormhole without so much as saying hello.

'Annabel's done this quite a bit. We've all got a lot of crap to get through. It's one way of doing it,' he explains to the sisters.

'All? says Monica. 'You're the only boy I know who owns a house. What have you got to complain about?'

Dennis feels the reverberation of Mary's punch upon her younger sister's upper arm. He agrees with the punch, doesn't say anything in his own defence. His troubles. There is silence for forty paces and then Mary takes a hold of Dennis's arm, leans into him. Monica goes round the other side and does the same. They walk all the way to Morgan Crescent, lucky Dennis feeling the warmth of two girls. One's only a kid, it's Mary he glances at repeatedly.

When they reach the step, Mary has a key, turns to the door and then turns back again. 'It was great to see you, Dennis,' she says. Kisses him quickly on the cheek. He tries to return the kiss, chastely, also upon her cheek and she takes his head in her two hands. 'Annabel's not right for you,' she whispers in his ear, said so quietly that Monica cannot have heard it. Then she rests her forehead upon his before turning to the door. Opening it and retreating into her family home.

'Don't I get a kiss?' says Monica.

Supper Shared

Dennis busses the top of her head. 'Night-night. No telling Mummy.'

'No. If I tell her that you kissed me, she'll make you marry me.'

Monica follows her sister into the house and Dennis laughs out loud. The kid is top of her class at school.

* * *

When he arrives back at the house, Dennis sees that Hendrika has fetched knitting from her rucksack, spread it out on the futon where he and Mary were previously sitting. A cardigan is incongruously around her T-shirt, skinny white legs protruding from the orange shorts she has worn all evening. The needles click. Schylar is upon the carpet still. Snoring. Annabel looks glazed, head tilted back slightly. Dennis takes himself to her, leans in and feels her breath gently pushing onto his cheek.

'She's slept there before,' he says. 'Are you coming up, or keeping vigil all night.'

'I cannot move my man; he is bigger than me.'

'My girl too,' says Dennis. A laugh but it's true. They weighed themselves a few months ago, Annabel not self-conscious at all back then. She's changed, gone quieter. Who knows what she is going through, her incessant need to obliterate an evening. He's not in touch with any other survivors—never has been—feeling down some of the time must go with the territory. He has told his life story to his lover. Not every detail perhaps, not the crushes on the schoolteachers, or even the one on Lorraine Chadwick. All the salient parts. 'My husband went with them,' she told him. No name, no detail of the life she once shared. He thought she would let it all out when she was ready, instead she just flees the world. Drugs are only a minor diversion for Dennis, a hippy accruement. Recreation not destination. He has wondered once or twice if Annabel wants out, wants to leave Dorset and find a climate more conducive to growing tomatoes. He will never leave Charmouth. Doesn't imagine he is staying for the right reasons but he is a part of the town's history. Stick around and he'll be a fossil. The sympathy he receives outweighs the embarrassment he used to feel. He knows his parents let him down, still he mulls over their deaths. Thinks he could have intervened. Should have. How a kid with no life behind him could have guessed what going to the spaceship really meant—the ugly euphemism—never explains itself when he dwells upon it. The truth about their mode of transport has been sitting heavily in his brain since the very next day. A date inscribed on brick. This boy became enlightened on the twenty-first of January, nineteen-seventy. A brick in the brain. On its reverse side the engraving reads, one day too late.

'They will be all right in the morning. It is normal,' says Hendrika.

He takes himself upstairs, uses the toilet quickly then straight into bed. The big double, he keeps to his half. Annabel may be up later, the half-lives of the different drugs which hippies take remain a mystery to him. He can hear water running in the bathroom, the visitor brushing her teeth or whatever Dutch ablutions she gets up to. Then she is in the next room, walking across the floor, once, twice, once more. When he has heard no sound for two or three minutes, thinks that she might have fallen asleep, or at least be in bed awaiting its arrival, he hears the lightest tap on his bedroom door. He does nothing and it comes again. A finger's tap.

'Are you okay?' says Dennis quietly.

His bedroom door opens—a light from elsewhere, from her bedroom, gives soft illumination to the silhouette in the doorframe—the Dutch girl stands naked before him.

'Is this the hippy house they say it is in Bournemouth?'

There is a bemusement in her voice which makes him smile. Life has been too serious of late. He has noticed her slender legs all evening. Sex was the furthest thing from Dennis's mind but he continues to smile and Hendrika enters his bedroom. Pushes the door closed behind her. His own hippy is well out of it, in the lounge below, possibly floating through deep space in her chemically assisted mind; Hendrika's hunky hippy is on the floor down there, the same or worse. These things happen.

'Don't get cold,' he whispers, raising the covers. She has come around to his side of the bed. She is in it; she lies upon him.

In his ear she whispers, 'There is a light.' A nude girl with long fair hair is straddling Dennis, he manages to reach for the bedside lamp, click it on. The sight of her pleases him, she must see the broadness of his grin. He tries to recall the words Mary said to him just thirty or forty minutes ago. The girl is suggesting she may stand beside the bed, something about his height. He is unsure what she wants but happy to try it.

May have to explain this to Annabel in the morning. Perhaps she'll understand without formal explanation, words can be a spider's web. Free love, they've talked about it off and on.

Supper Shared

5.

Dennis is drifting aimlessly in the deepest of sleeps, a shrill scream intrudes upon it, hurries him into a wakefulness which confuses him. The dream slips away in that moment, as if it never was, and still the screaming continues. And then that too stops. It all feels wrong to him—he is sure that he has had a better night's sleep than any in the last month—there can be nothing to scream about. Slept like the world is at ease with itself. If three bouts of love-making with the wildest knitter in town helped him, then thank you, kind lady. It was a pleasure taken and taken again. And now there is a scream in the house. Again. It does not belong. He thinks he should act but feels gravitationally bound to the bed. The girl who has been beneath him, above him, bent over the bed for him and entwined with him throughout the night is no longer here.

He pulls on jeans, a dressing gown for its closeness to hand. From the top of the stairs, he sees Schylar twisting his neck to greet him. 'It is your wife,' he says. 'She needs you.'

He runs down two at a time although he has no wife. Annabel looks to be in the same position she slept in the night before. Hendrika—wearing only knickers, nothing upon her top half—is beside her. She turns her stricken face to his. Tears crowd it.

'She is not breathing, Dennis. Not breathing.'

He crouches by Annabel, hopes to right the situation. Upon touching her face, he feels that she is quite cold. There is no colour in her features. Like a porridge paste. He coughs. A little sick comes into his mouth and he does not know how to rid himself of it. Tries to swallow but barks it back up. Dressing gown duly bemired.

Hendrika puts a hand upon him. 'I'm so sorry Dennis. I did not know.' She is distraught.

'Oh God.' He sinks beside Annabel. Begins to place a hand upon her knee, removes it before it has even touched. 'I'm so sorry,' he says to his girlfriend who can no longer hear him. 'I'm so, so sorry.'

'It is not looking good,' says Schylar. His words arrest Dennis's flight to tears. Annoy him even as he thinks the man's limited English may be the impediment. He scarcely spoke last night. Nothing close to intelligible.

'I must call the police,' says Dennis. 'Fetch them here again.'

'No,' says Schylar. 'Give her more time. Hendrika told me she took my shit.'

'She's dead, dammit. I have to phone the police, don't you see?'

Hendrika nods in agreement. Dennis finds it unpleasant, watching the girl's breasts bob with her head movement. The body he should never have enjoyed while Annabel suffered below. 'It is for the police,' she agrees.

'We must leave first,' says Schylar.

'It is about this poor lady, not about you,' the girl shouts at him.

'It is about her,' says Schylar, 'but still I think we need to go.'

'Will you stay?' says Dennis to the topless girl.

Hendrika puts an arm around his shoulders. 'Of course. Schylar also.'

* * *

The ambulance and police do not take long at all. Fewer than twenty minutes upon the clock face. Just enough time for Dennis to slip some four years into the past, become the lost child of his former life. Hendrika has covered herself more decently than Dennis has seen since she has been in the flophouse. Done so hurriedly, hair askew. Jeans not shorts. The flesh he should never have grasped and grappled with finally removed from his incidental gaze.

Sergeant Ash arrives in the second police car. She has a look of pure pain on her face when she says, 'Hello, Dennis.' He cannot reply. Weeping once more. Losing Annabel to Herbie, or to Rhode Island, he could have withstood. There had seemed less between them in recent months. It is death which is unbearable. Irreparable.

And compounding this are frightening images flashing across the rear window of his brain. He forgets that it is Annabel; thinks it is To the Ship, marooned in his house, stuck fast in a death from which there can be no release. It could be her, this body in the lounge, that is the feeling that overtakes Dennis. Not when he looks at Annabel but it comes on him the instant he looks away. He knows enough to speak rationally, when he composes himself, when the policeman accompanying Sergeant Ash is asking questions, writing down Dennis's answers.

'Her full name is Antonella Vitale, I believe. We all knew her as Annabel.'

In January nineteen-seventy he had felt both conflict and the need to be finally open in revealing his parents' Themagin names to this police sergeant. She attended then as now. And Susan Ash knew very

Supper Shared

little about the Themagin suicides. What she had grasped was only from the national news bulletin. Stories from America, one or two outposts in western Europe. Learning that two died here in Charmouth must have been a surprise, although she took it in her stride. Today there is no embarrassment on Dennis's part in revealing Annabel's other name. It is her birthname, the right one, Antonella, which he finds strange to say out loud. Not a name which he has any objection to. He knows no one else who bears it, and in his mind, it was never her. Never the name of the lady he lived with. It is, however, the one on her passport. It is true, not Themagin nonsense.

Susan Ash is the same sympathetic soul she was when he last was in this state. Seventeen, twenty-one, he cannot possibly grow up while those close to him keep choosing to do this. To opt out. When he tells her that Antonella Vitale was once a member of the Themagins—had left to become a hippy before the comet's arrival—she is shocked. 'Why did I not know that, Dennis?' She says it as if she has been watching over him, although he cannot see how she could have done so. She has remembered him, no doubt, her first visit was an exceptional one. Dennis knows himself to be in need of greater vigil than her sporadic thoughts. Perhaps she sees it too. Crossed fingers will never save the cursed.

'Who was in the house last night?' asks the policeman who accompanies her. He is doing all the writing.

Dennis tells of the two sisters, confirms that he walked them home while his girlfriend slept in the armchair.

'Fourteen?' says Sergeant Ash. Dennis hears accusation in her tone.

'They didn't do any drugs. I didn't. She didn't.' He gestures Hendrika.

'My boyfriend was here but left in the night,' she says. Dennis hears no quaver in her voice, detects no lie although one has wrapped itself around her words like a cobra.

'Left in the night,' Sergeant Ash echoes back. 'Why do you think he left in the night.'

'It is a bit complicated, officer. I might have been being silly. I told him that I think I am in love with Dennis and he left in the night.'

What a ridiculous thing to say. Dennis hasn't forgotten what happened. Never thought 'in love with' was loitering in the room. Never crossed his mind for a second. He and she fucked while their real partners were incapable. At it like dogs in the road. He's not proud of the recollection. Hopes this stupid girl isn't going to blab about that to Sergeant Ash.

When the policeman questions her, Hendrika's story gets dafter. 'I didn't tell Dennis. He had Annabel. I could not guess that this thing was going to happen.'

She was good in bed; a truth he will not savour, wishes he'd never learnt it. She's turning herself into a murder suspect with this foolish excuse for Schylar's cowardice. He can see that and he is grieving. To the Ship, Annabel. He thinks he lost Mary long ago. Maybe she was ready for a proper relationship when he thought she was not. Hendrika means nothing to him. It was just sex, and without love that might be nothing at all. Schylar is the low life. He has done Burning Rock's work: brought the poison to the house.

'Have you told your Auntie?' asks Sergeant Ash.

'I will,' he says. His declared intention is no more truthful than Hendrika's assertion about Schylar's time of departure. Said it only to paper over a poor relationship, not burying evidence of a crime. Both have declared no knowledge of where Annabel acquired her drugs. Said they did not know the type of chemical ingested. He wonders if Hendrika lied about that one too. Perhaps she takes the same tablets as Schylar. Leaves them alone on nights when she mysteriously falls in love.

Dennis has seen his Auntie Jean and Uncle Stanley only twice since Antonella Vitale—in the guise of Annabel—has been his lover. The first time they came was after someone in the village telephoned them. Filled them in on his scandalous living arrangement. He has worried that it was Emma Bredbury, never raised it with her. Not proven, nor could he think of anyone else who might have made the call. His Auntie Jean repeated, 'I don't think you should be living like this,' so many times he offered to make a tape recording of it. Said he could put it on loop, save her the bother of speaking. He never raised his voice—never raises his voice—but it was a vicious argument they were having. In between the spoken lines. A disapproval of his life style akin to excommunication. Auntie Jean was seething, wanted Annabel gone. Seemed to think it was for her to decide what goes on at number three Croft Road, when it was for everyone except her and Uncle Stanley. No uptight stiffs in the flophouse. They expected him to have sold the house by this time, moved to Taunton. Given them a portion of the money for a bigger house, his own small annex. Uncle Stanley and Auntie Jean never had his best interests at heart.

Or maybe they did.

Supper Shared

They hated everything about his hippy lifestyle. 'What if one of them murders you!' Auntie Jean had said of his houseguests.

He thinks it would have made no difference. Not to the wider cosmos.

Their second visit to his house was last Christmas. A present and a card. Everything much more civil. Spoke politely with Annabel while they were here. Nothing said at all, at the bottom of it.

He'll not be phoning them. They can gloat about another dead Themagin in their own time. And Annabel was not a Themagin. Antonella left that world long ago, and now Annabel has taken her leave from this one. Dennis finds the tears spilling down his cheeks once more. The Dutch girl consoles him. The closest embrace. He would rather it was Susan Ash, cannot say it. No wish to sound so idiotic. Choosing a policewoman.

Then Susan talks very levelly to Dennis. He has stopped crying although there is a volatility within him; holding it together while believing he cannot. 'You don't know her family?' she asks.

'She never talked about them.'

The police sergeant raises an eyebrow.

'Never. Never ever.'

'Parents?'

'They might be alive. She never said they weren't. Her mum and dad divorced when she was young.'

'Children?'

Dennis shakes his head. 'She was thirty-seven, Susan. Died at thirty-seven. I know she's older than...'

'Same age as me,' says Sergeant Ash. The most personal disclosure she has ever granted him and yet he has believed her a support. More so than the many neighbours who will daily greet him, enquire after his health. The anti-flophouse petitions giving away their true feelings. Surviving in this life isn't easy. Some days it isn't even desirable. That seems to have been Annabel's conclusion. He doesn't want to hear the toxicology report. He got sick of them when he attended the coroners court in nineteen-seventy.

'I've asked the station to contact the American Embassy, Dennis. We have the passport number, an address that is only four years old, it shouldn't be difficult. I think someone may want her back.'

Dennis looks aghast. 'We all want her back but she's dead, Susan.'

'They may wish to bury her back where her family live.' And she places a hand upon his forearm as Dennis looks, once more, like the

223

bewildered child of years' past.

* * *

Hendrika insists on being there for him. Supporting her lover—though he thinks himself no such thing—when the police surgeon is preparing the body for its removal from the house. Wishes there was not so much as a grain of truth in her assertion.

'Where is she being taken?' asks Dennis.

'Post-mortem,' grunts a policeman who wears plastic gloves. A policeman so senior he has no need of a uniform.

Susan Ash has left and Dennis misses her. The reassuring presence which has seen him through similar and he is still standing. There is another lady in the house now, just arrived. She might be police, might be hospital or council. 'Have you spoken to a Mrs Marino?' she asks. He shakes his head and before he can query who she is, the lady asks, 'Did your lady-friend speak of a Mrs Marino?'

'Annabel? No. Never mentioned...'

'Never mentioned her own mother?'

'She's Vitale. I'm sure of...' Dennis's words taper away. He is sure of nothing.

He never learns the job role of the lady who asked him the question. She explains that Antonella Vitale's mother has been located, spoken to. She lives in Providence, Rhode Island. There is a lot to do before the authorities can release her body but this other lady, Mrs Marino, is next of kin. In due course, Antonella will be going home.

Hendrika talks to him quietly, says, 'It is for the best,' and 'You have me now.'

Today is a senseless day. Dennis has no idea how to demand that Hendrika leaves. It is his singular wish and the policemen and women in the house, plus his new-found helplessness, inhibit him from letting her know.

* * *

All afternoon Dennis feels numb, keeps himself busy for fear of falling off the edge. A telephone call to Mary. Thankfully he gets through before the police have arrived at her house. He does not say anything to her about Schylar beyond him being asleep along with Annabel when he and Hendrika went to bed. He doesn't mention which bed, nor any of the gymnastics which happened up in his room. Cheating

Supper Shared

on Annabel while she expired. Not Hendrika's falling-in-love bullshit either. He feels an iron coat of remorse upon him and the Dutch girl's flattery is a slap. Stings where he is most sensitive.

The few stark facts he manages to impart—leaving Annabel in the lounge chair, never checking after his initial return from walking the sister's home—must shock Mary. She says she should never have brought Monica and he agrees completely.

'I'm so sorry,' says Dennis.

'I'm so sorry,' says Mary.

Hendrika brings him a mug of tea while he is on the telephone. He takes it while fearing Mary will hear or sense the presence. He wishes her to think that he is on his own, wants exactly that state for himself. Knows not how to insist. He would like Hendrika back in jeans. The orange shorts which she changed back into upon the last policeman leaving Croft Road, repulse him now. It is November. How legs so plain and pale bewitched him last night is a mystery. No greater purchase than the morning dream. What he did last night he shall never do again. Not with this girl. Not with any.

* * *

She won't go. He doesn't ask her, just treats her coldly. Expects her to pick up his rejection. When she puts a hand upon his back, he steps away.

'Are you going to find Schylar?' he asks while the girl is preparing supper.

'Fuck him,' says Hendrika, suddenly sharp as she has not been all day.

'Do you think it was his fault?'

'Oh God, I hope not, Dennis. Schylar doesn't share his stash really. Tries anything and everything but he is a chemist. He tells me he knows what he is doing. I am guessing that Annabel stole them.'

'Stole?'

'I mean shared. I wouldn't mind her taking anything from him. But his drugs are the biggest blow in the head.'

Then, when they are sitting side by side at the small table in the kitchen, eating the pasta dish which the girl who loves cooking has rustled up, he says again. 'Will you go to find Schylar?'

'I don't want to leave you in this state, Dennis. He knows where I am.'

This might get messy. The neighbours in this small town have seen another body removed from his house. A different girl living here won't be gossip, it will be headline. He wishes he had a broom; needs to sweep her out. He has already seen too much of Hendrika from Holland. Will regret to his dying day the way in which they cavorted through the last night of Annabel's life.

* * *

The phone rings and Dennis finds himself talking to an animated Stephen Bredbury. He tries to stop him; expects to receive a rollicking for having the two sisters in his flophouse when a stranger had brought round the most dangerous of drugs. He hopes he can explain how unpredictably the events unfolded. If he could have foreseen any of it, he would have changed the lot.

'I'll be with you for the December party,' says Stephen. He goes on, even shouts, 'Party!' down the phone. Might have been drinking, students can be so full of themselves. It dawns upon Dennis that Mary has not been in touch with Stephen today. Last night's events on Croft Road are outside his span of knowledge, the call a coincidence. 'I've got fieldwork to do from now until mid-January. You can come with me along the coast. I've to collect loads of different sea weeds. Keep them lab-ready.'

'Stephen,' says Dennis, struggling to choose his words, 'no party this month. Annabel...' He swallows too hard and tears come. Roll down his cheeks as the lump in his throat obstructs him from speaking.

'She's not left you, has she Dennis?'

He tries to compose himself, cannot get any words out.

'I know you'll be feeling down about it but it's probably for the best. She was a bit old for you if you think about it. Other girls...'

'She's died, Stephen.'

As he tells his friend from school days all that has transpired, making the drug-taking sound a later event than the supper at which his sisters were present, Hendrika stands beside him. She tries to look into his face—he will not meet her eye—touches his long hair, moving it behind his ear. It will not hold in place, not without a headband. It is not as if he has never tried.

Even after Dennis has told his traumatic tale, Stephen signs off saying, 'Let me know if you change your mind about the party.' A farmyard animal might have greater sensitivity.

* * *

Supper Shared

Being a free and easy hippy is hard work on more days than it isn't. It's a random thought, and one that has lodged itself firmly in his head throughout this night.

Dennis dug a pair of pyjamas out of a drawer he seldom roots in, wore them for fear that the Dutch girl would want to keep him company in the night. He dug a second pair out which he insisted she wear when his hunch proved correct. She has not reiterated her love for him. Explained that her declaration was all she could come up with—a little ruse—to justify the sudden departure of Schylar. The drug mule, and she skirts across this critical point.

'It is not what we did last night that caused your girlfriend's death,' she tells Dennis.

It didn't help. And for him it was memorable for all the wrong reasons. She allowed him pleasures that he does not wish to associate with the loss of Annabel. Coaxing life back into his spent cock with her mouth. Thoughts which are hard to remove however little they belong. He should have sat with his girlfriend, protected her through the trip she could not contain. He cannot sleep tonight and he feels no comfort from the girl who is sitting up with him. Not upright but her wide-awake head is lying sideways on the pillow facing him. Hand again stroking his hair.

'Hendrika,' he says, 'this is too much. I lost my girlfriend today. Cheated on her with you and I really wish I hadn't. Can you see that? I'd like you to leave in the morning.'

Her face hardens. 'I lied for you, Dennis. Did not tell the police your girlfriend was a thief.'

This is crazy. She lied for Schylar. Dennis has no wish to cause him trouble, knows he had no role in Annabel's death beyond poorly hidden drugs. Is this the freedom of hippieism? Do what you like until it kills you. It preys heavily on Dennis's mind that the police should have spoken with Schylar. The Dutch girl kept knowledge of where the drugs came from secret. It is what hippies do. It's not the illegality of the drugs which concern Dennis. It is what they have done to Annabel. Nor is it Dennis's way to appeal to wider authority for judgement on private matters. Not his and not Annabel's. Authority stinks. Would put Herbie in the jungle with a gun if it got the chance. And still Dennis wonders what he has been doing since the Themagin suicides. Running a flophouse that had none of the madman's tapes playing, just a little undercurrent tugging away somewhere beneath the carpet.

The Flophouse Years

From the next day until far into the new year, Dennis remains alone in number three Croft Road. Hendrika finally accepting her support was a burden he could not bear. Whether she went and found Schylar, or simply fell in love with the next available hippy, Dennis has no wish to learn.

Chapter Six

Ravenscourt Park

Part One
1.

On the thirty-first of August, nineteen-seventy-four, Dennis throws his first party in nine months. Mary does not think the monthly happening is back on, it is not even the first of the month. Tonight's event is her going away party. A don't-forget-us party, he calls it. She is off to be a proper physics student. Imperial College, London. She worries about Dennis, a nebulous worry without centre. His hair is only just growing back after last December's savage cut. He looked good with it short but it isn't him.

Thompson is here, back in the open-plan lounge of Croft Road. Mary collared him before the party got in full swing. He swore on his mother's grave that a little hash is the only substance he has brought. His mother is not dead, Mary is sure of that. She works behind the bar in the George Hotel, Lyme Regis. Mary saw her there, talking to him, their facial similarity is uncanny. That was just a week ago. The whole Bredbury family were in the pub—three siblings and her put-upon mother—eating a meal to celebrate her school results. Her success, the securing of that coveted university place. Dennis accompanied them, Dennis almost family. He and she agreed the barmaid must have been his mother. And Bobby was there too—the lad who is going out with Monica—but the pair of them are still kids. Don't go on proper dates, not staying out late in the evening dates. And Dennis is not Mary's boyfriend. Never has been. Their relationship can never be that straightforward. He is simply the nearest thing she has.

Her brother, Stephen, has turned out downright weird. A different third-year student than he ever was in years one and two. And a world away from the inhibited school boy of old, nothing like he used to be when last he lived in Charmouth. He's a pot smoker now, full blown. Smokes the stuff night and day in his bedroom on Morgan Crescent;

their mum doesn't seem to have figured it out. It messed up his degree to Mary's thinking; third class is not class at all. Mary calls him a loser when he's out of earshot, says it to his face when he's stoned.

Monica is far too young to be at the party so she cannot come. Mrs Bredbury said so, and after last November it seems only right to respect her wish. But it is also Mary's leaving party—Monica may miss her more than any other—so respect it they will not. Their mother believes that Monica is sleeping over at a friend's house in Broadwindsor. And Mary is determined that she should not be disabused of the notion. Must remain unaware that a friend of Mary's has driven Monica and the said friend to the party and will take them all the way back to Broadwindsor at eleven o'clock. The friend's mother specified the time and she doesn't know Monica should not even be here. Deception is a complicated business. Bobby will be at the party; Mary has asked Dennis to keep an eye out. 'Necking is allowed but no hands under clothes,' she told him. From free love to the police of public morals, it is quite the transformation.

When one of Mary's friends sticks Laughing Llamas on the stereo, she glances at Dennis. He is not beside her, sits on the floor across the room talking with others. He long ago told her how he came to despise Jimmy Crook; she recalls feeling flattered by the interest the rock star took in her. Mary had drunk four tins of cider before that party started, glugged lots of wine while she was there. Might have done anything with anyone, days that are behind her. The music sounds great and there is zero probability that a member of the band will show up. Annabel was the connected hippy and there have been no flyers for this party. The average hair-length of the boys must be six inches shorter than it was last November. Only Thompson still tries.

Dennis is not a boyfriend but he and Mary have a most special relationship. She loves him but never speaks the words out loud. That aside, honesty is its bedrock; they share an intimacy unencumbered by any of the physical demands which couples are apt to make upon each other. Mary last tried it on with Dennis way back before she'd even started Sixth Form—maybe he really was too much the gentleman, wouldn't take advantage of a drunken minor—and he has since told her that he's through with girls. That's a funny thing for a twenty-one-year-old lad to declare, Dennis has been through a lot. It was around Easter that he confessed to Mary all that took place the night Annabel died. How much he had let her down. The coroner's report confirmed the death was her own reckless stupidity, an outrageous volume of amphetamine flooding her every organ. A heart that couldn't cope. Dennis confessed to her a deed connected only by coincidence, an infidelity with the too-willing Hendrika. It should shock Mary but she is an analytical girl. She threw herself at Dennis two years ago, at three or four other Charmouth boys when she was still doubtful if boys truly found her desirable. That is no longer a question. Head Girl in her final year at Allington Grammar, even she liked the photograph of herself and Pete Green, Head Boy, which was prominently displayed in the main corridor throughout her final schoolyear. Enough people have told her that she's good-looking for her to start believing it. Recognise the lucky ticket fate has handed her. She's been keeping a level head this past year, relishes the prospect ahead. Immersion in science. She wants friends along with the intellectual fulfilment—any girl would—and Dennis might be the best of them. He calls himself the worst, quite contrary to her opinion. Dennis Harris has lived through a hundred times more shit than he deserves, it would mess with anybody's way of thinking.

Jason Hardcastle is here. He was in the year above her at school and they went out for a few weeks. The biggest dick in Charmouth, literally and figuratively. He seems to be without a girl at this party, an unusual state for Jason. He keeps telling Mary how brilliant it is that she's going to London. 'Making it big,' the term he uses. Jason works as a bingo caller in West Bay. He also bemoans her departure. 'Charmouth will be changed forever.' She will stop and talk to him when sincerity means nothing.

'Seen my sister?' she asks Dennis.

'Tin of cider in her hand,' he says. 'I told her it was her only one.'

Mary grins. 'You'll make a great father one day.' It is not how youngsters are meant to speak to each other. And it would require a breach of the celibacy he has declared. 'Was she with Bobby?'

'He's kicking a football in the garden.' She gives him an anxious look. The back garden at number three is not large. Since Annabel's passing, weeds have overtaken the small vegetable patch. There is an area of paving, she and Dennis have taken dining chairs out there to talk or read in the sunshine. Playing football in so restricted a space sounds a foolish idea to her. 'There are a handful out there. They'll come in when they lose the ball.'

'He should be with Monica.'

'Or maybe not, Mary. She's too young for boys.'

Mary rests a hand on his shoulder. 'A great father, like I said. Enjoy the party, Dennis. I'm going to.'

* * *

She guesses that Dennis has put on this record. Templeton Ca., his favourite band now he's turned a little less hippy. Odes to modern life without any of the Llamas' drug references. A good Californian vibe to it. Mary is dancing, twirling so her dress rises up her legs. Tanned at this time of year. She is centre stage. Mary beckons for Monica to join in the dance; the little sister is sitting cross-legged on the floor, embraced by Bobby. Far better they are down here than up in the boxroom.

Thompson, who was in range of the beckoned finger although not its intended recipient, rises and joins Mary in moving to the music. Quite unusual for him, the man formerly known as Major. Mary and Dennis have discussed all the boys and girls they know from Charmouth, Lyme, Bridport. This one is an enigma. In his mid-twenties now, his long hair seen on roofs all over West Dorset, the starring role in every re-thatch. A true craftsman, according to Dennis. For about two months he saw a girl called Georgie. Georgie-gone-to-Uni. No sight of a girlfriend before or since.

'Do you think he's the other way?' she once asked Dennis.

'Could be, not that he's ever tried it on with me.'

'Well, Dennis, I learned long ago that trying it on with you is time wasted.'

Dennis mostly smiles when she says stuff like that. Little digs at what went on between them those two years back. Went and never came back. They are different people, perhaps as changed from their younger selves as Thompson is from the self he chooses not to reveal. He dances very well, a bit of a hip roll. She raises her hands, shimmies herself beside him and the man reciprocates. She cannot recall watching Thompson dance before—he must have done it: so many parties—he has none of the self-conscious rigidity that epitomises most boys on the floor. Jason is dancing at the other side of the room and he's utterly hopeless. Rhythmless. Moves like a marionette. She realises it is her own sister dancing with Jason. No longer in the arms of Bobby. Her boyfriend—if she is old enough for one—is not in the room. Mary pulls in her lip, doesn't want Monica dancing with big-dick Jason. That was never in the plan.

'Not happy dancing with me?' says Thompson. He must have seen her facial expression drop. To say these words, he has pulled her into the briefest hug. The sound of Not Simple, the rocking Templeton Ca. number—ode to an unnamed barmaid—fills the room.

Mary puts her own hand around the back of Thompson's head. 'Sorry...' They are both swaying with the music as they talk into each other's ears. '...you dance brilliantly. My sister is dancing with Jay-Jay. I don't like it.'

> *Cigarette butts, empty packets of nuts*
> *So many things that have been discarded*
> *Imagine they lead me to a hidden treasure*
> *Imagine they lead me to the promised land*

Major doesn't respond to her question; he leans his head away from her and, along with half the room, joins in the chorus.

> *It's not as simple as this – and – it's not as simple as that*
> *Not as simple as that – no, no – and it's not as simple as this*

Even Mary mouths the words while looking intently at her sister. Then Major analyses the issues. 'She's a smart kid. Dancing won't get her pregnant.'

She grimaces. Thompson has unearthed her own buried thoughts. Mary spent a total of six weeks fearing she was pregnant with Jason Hardcastle's child only for that other visitor to arrive. The most welcome cramps of her young life. Why she went near him is embarrassing to recall. Wasn't the only one which is no excuse; a dim-witted Don Juan who went through a posse of sixth form girls in quick succession. Thompson takes a hold of her hand, twizzles her round. The sound is not rockabilly but the beat allows them the conceit. Mary likes to dance and this is her party. In a matter of seconds, Jason and Monica are dancing alongside them, trying to copy their moves. Monica can, Jason can't; it is always the girls who do the eye-catching turns. Make or break the spectacle.

The singer boasts nonsensically to the celebrated barmaid. Again, most of the room join in the singing, not a chorus but a repeated line following the same melodic phrasing.

> *I know every man jack in the bible*
> *I do, I know every man jack in the bible*

Mary loves this song, silly words of hapless flirtation. Monica must have asked Jason to dance—must have agreed to the manhandling he performs—the older boy spins her round. Her little sister weighs nothing, Jason's part is barely clever. Thompson lifts Mary, he has a graceful manner. A dancer and a craftsman. The two sisters are the stars of the show.

> ***I know her husband's far away with the army***
> ***That's right, her husband's gone abroad with the army***

The daft songs are the best songs. She sees Dennis mouthing the words. He could be belting them out, most people are. A lone contribution cannot be heard singly in the cacophony; the roof of number three Croft Road is coming off. Party nights have been the best of times. She got uppity at them once or twice, so confused was she by her own selfish feelings for poor Dennis. Terribly nice of him to throw her this party, she fears she is leaving him to the wolves.

* * *

A little later, Mary is on the futon between Thompson and Dennis. Thighs are touching but neither show any inclination that could trouble a girl. Monica, meanwhile, is necking with Jason.

'What the hell is she up to?' asks Mary.

'Jason's always like that,' says Thompson. His comment adds nothing to her pre-knowledge.

'Should I ask him to leave?' says Dennis.

'On what grounds?'

'Wearing a khaki shirt—military shit—that's enough for me.'

'Seriously, what does she think she's playing at. She came with Bobby.'

'Have you talked to her?'

'Will you?'

Dennis rises from the futon, walks two paces and places his hand on Jason Hardcastle's shoulder. 'I'm cutting in for a dance,' Mary hears him say, and she laughs. No one is dancing now. Everything happens sporadically at a Croft Road party. Monica lets him pull her up from the floor. Dennis starts to dance and she wraps her thin frame around this other boy. At least it is one whom Mary trusts, the man who will never take advantage. Monica is making an exhibition of herself. If she kisses Dennis—she is trying, he is dancing—it will be the third boy of the evening. Mary wishes she'd never contrived for her little sister to come.

'Are you sure she isn't stealing your boyfriend?' says Thompson.

'Dennis is my friend. We're not going out.'

'What? I thought you'd been going out since forever?'

'Forever?'

'Well...apart from his dalliance with the old lady.'

There were times when Mary had many unkind thoughts about her, the sadly deceased Antonella Vitale as she now understands Annabel's true name to have been. So many unkind thoughts in the first weeks in which she lived in the flophouse: Mary truly wished her dead. All that changed with time. Dennis needed someone she wasn't. Her own jealousy was childish. About a month after it had happened—the November supper that chills her still—a deeper realisation came to Mary. Annabel was a warm, compassionate, caring human being. An utterly fucked-up one too, Dennis made that clear. She did drugs for time out from thinking about this life; never got over the suicide of a husband she had left many months before the dreadful event occurred. Self-poisoned exactly like Dennis's own parents. Same date. Annabel's departure from the stage was a mistake. Unintended. The coroner said as much.

'She never got to be an old lady,' Mary tells Thompson. 'Never got there.'

He seems not to be meditating as she is. 'I only meant old for Dennis.'

'Well, he's a great friend, but Dennis and I were never lovers.' She feels a need to clarify this. Temper the town's rumour mill.

'Never? I bet you were.'

She turns back to look at the dance floor. Dennis is rocking her sister in his arms, talking to her in a low voice. No idea what he is saying, putting her straight about Jason, most likely. Then the little one wriggles away, leaves the dance floor for the kitchen. Perhaps Jason and Bobby are having a fight in there. Mary would rather that than watching either of them slobbering into her kid sister's mouth. Fifteen, that's all Monica is. Her mother has a point, the flophouse is not suitable for one so young.

Dennis comes back to the futon, slides himself beside her once more. Many times, in the past half year, the pair of them have contemplated the world from this vantage point. Today the world has entered the room to be with them. Thompson has gone in search of another beer. She hopes he isn't getting his bong out. Dennis said there were to be no drugs before eleven; before the little sister goes

The Flophouse Years

back to her slumber party. 'What's with Monica?' she asks.

'Bust up with Bobby, apparently.'

'Cry about him. Don't start snogging Hardcastle.'

'My message in full. I think she's way too angry to cry. Monica's like that.'

'You've got her right. What was their break up over?'

'She wouldn't tell me. Too embarrassed, I think.'

She picks herself off the sofa, walks through to the kitchen. There are quite a few party-goers in there, only one of whom has his hand cupped around her sister's breast. Mary pinches Jason's ear between finger and thumb.

'Fuck off,' he tells her, his mouth no longer clamping Monica's.

'She's got to go now,' says Mary. There are ten minutes before the allotted time but she will not be letting this randy boy grope her sister for the duration. 'Come,' Mary says to Monica.

The littles sister follows Mary into the garden. No one else out there at this time.

'You're like Mum, won't let me do a fucking thing!'

'What happened with Bobby, Mon?'

'Nothing.'

'If that was true you wouldn't be snogging Jason. What happened? Did you quarrel?'

Monica turns away from Mary and projects an eruption of vomit onto the weeds beside the fence. She goes down onto her haunches and coughs, spits. The proud young girl seems suddenly weakened. Puts a knee on the grass before her and leans forward.

'Mon, what's the matter? Drunk a lot...' Mary stops talking, kneels beside her sister with an arm around her shoulder.

'I can't see!' shrieks the younger girl.

Mary helps her to sit down on the lawn; Thompson has come to the back door and Mary asks him to fetch Dennis. 'Look at me,' she says to Monica. 'Look into my face. What do you see?'

'You're there but you look all wrong.'

Dennis is beside them, only for Monica to turn and puke on his shoes. 'Hey,' he says, 'what have you been doing? What have you drunk?'

'Jason made me.'

'Okay, but what was it?'

'Never do what Jason says. Never!'

Dennis and Mary show their concern with contrasting emphases.

'I think it was a drug. He said I should drink it quickly.'

Thompson steps back into the kitchen. With previously unseen authority, he pulls Jason out into the garden. 'What have you given this child?' Another hippie policeman in these changing times.

'Only Bacardi. We all drank it at her age.'

'How much, Jason?' asks Dennis.

'She went daft on it.'

Monica is throwing up again. Gulping in air between up-chucks. Another almighty heave: breakfast, dinner and tea.

* * *

A couple of potheads are smoking in the lounge, Stephen is one of them. He only came when the pubs closed. No longer close to Dennis, not since his sister has taken up the best-friend role. Always civil but they've had little in common for years. Dennis is washing a few glasses, clearing up. Mary is on the phone in the hallway.

'I didn't mean to wake you.' She thinks she hasn't; her mother says she cannot sleep when her children are out, expected back. 'I'll help tidy up here and then sleep over,' she says.

Her mother seems put out by this. 'Won't Dennis walk you home. He always walks you home.'

It's an absurd request, Charmouth as safe as a cabbage patch, no need of a chaperone. 'I'm tired, I'd rather just crash here.'

'Crash?'

'Sleep.'

'Are you sleeping with Dennis, Mary?'

Suspicious mothers are unbearable. Her assertion untrue and yet the whole of Charmouth seems to think it. 'I am doing no such thing.'

Mary doesn't tell her mother that Monica is not in Broadwindsor, she remains at the flophouse in which she shouldn't have been in the first place. Sleeping off a bottle of Bacardi in Dennis's bed. Exactly where he and she will sleep is to be determined. It will not be together, will not involve sexual intercourse which was the core of her mother's interrogation. If that were to happen, it would have done so long ago.

'You say Stephen is there?'

'Yes, Mum. He's here.'

'Why doesn't Stephen walk you home?'

Because I feel duty bound to look after your headstrong youngest daughter, she does not say. 'You know what he's like.' She really must. Her mother once took more pride in her eldest than in either of the girls, it's no longer the lay of the land. A pothead with a crummy degree, looking for paid employment with an over-fussy attitude. 'I'm not a deckchair attendant,' he told her when she pointed to an advertisement on the sea front. And she agrees with him: Stephen wouldn't be up to the job.

Once she has appeased her mother, Mary seeks out Dennis. It is only twelve-thirty but the days of hippy revelry are over. She helps him tidy away glasses, thanks him for throwing her a lovely party. 'You've only to get rid of the Bredburys and you'll have some peace,' she says.

Dennis turns to her, holds her in the tightest embrace she can recall. 'You can take the other two with you to London, Mary. You're the one I'm going to miss.' She feels his lips upon her forehead where he places another of the chaste kisses which have epitomised the months since he lost Annabel.

They venture into the lounge, Stephen and Thompson say they will sleep there later. When the dope runs out, Mary guesses. The pair have no need of sleeping bags, the night is not cold. Upstairs there are a couple of Bridporters sleeping in the spare room. Doing a bit more than sleeping if the rustling and grunting noises they make mean anything. Mary enters Dennis's bedroom with him. They have both been checking on Monica since they put her into his bed. Jason left once they had berated him sufficiently. The girl sleeps heavily, noisily. Booze has befuddled her. The vomiting was over before she came in from the garden.

'You sleep with your sister,' whispers Dennis. Plenty of room, the double.

'And you?'

He gestures the bit of floor beside the bed. She pulls her dress quickly over her head and slips between the sheets. Dennis has turned his back, taken down his jeans.

'Come into the bed,' she whispers, 'it'll be comfier.'

Mary lies in the middle, a drunken sister and the boyfriend she never had on either side. She senses him looking at her face periodically, glancing across at Monica. His flesh against her stirs a small feeling inside. Not a feeling she could act upon with drunken Monica equally close. Nor is it one she has given up on entirely, that seems exclusively Dennis's choice. Mary enjoyed the physical pleasures she took before settling into this platonic post-Annabel relationship with Dennis that is both easier to navigate and simultaneously unmoored of meaning. Feels a little ashamed only of one or two choices she made. The no-good boys. The activity itself was quite something. She never lost the longing after Annabel's passing, imagined that she and Dennis would, after the right number of months, consummate the love that never left. Even wondered if she would dare move into the flophouse. Probably not, her mother still exerts an influence over her, although it is diminishing as she grows in certainty, maturity. She never asked him directly, never offered herself. Feared to do so might insult him. The private boy, living in the house from which he has watched on as the police removed the corpses of both parents and his only proper girlfriend. 'Too fucked-up to fuck,' he self-diagnoses. Tonight, she can hear him sleeping, the faintest buzz at the ignition of each intake of breath. Mary turns herself towards him, places a hand as gently as she can upon his growing hair. He makes a noise of acceptance, that's what she thinks it is. Nuzzles his ear with her nose, lightly kisses the cheek turned towards her and tries to sleep. Sleep in the arms of Dennis.

2.

London is another world. She must use the underground to travel from her halls of residence to the lecture halls. Or walk, she finds that the more unnerving: shouty people on the streets, haranguing each other for reasons she can never fathom. Mary thinks the escalator at Hammersmith Station holds the population of Charmouth upon it at any given moment, does so all rush-hour long. Not the same people, she isn't stupid. Nobody from Charmouth is here except her. The same amount: the maths works out. It is a long staircase; most steps have a pair upon them. A number of people equalling the entire population of her home town swallowed into the ground and a proximate number regurgitated back up from it every minute of the hour. London is a monster, Charmouth insignificant. Eaten up and then spewed back out again.

The other students are nice, funny, one or two are pretentious: we all grow up at different speeds. She is close to Linda, her biologist room-mate. Tanya, the only other girl on her physics course, she also counts as a friend.

There were a lot of freshers' week events. Many of the lads from her course did a Monica: drank too much and chucked up royally. Every day of the week on a couple of counts. She thinks that is what sixth form was for. Trust her precocious sister to get going before she's even started fifth.

The lectures are a revelation. She loves studying science, the detail and the precision. Tanya is her ally in its pursuit. She hasn't got the measure of the boys: half go red at the sight of her and the other half have asked her out for a drink, a date, one even said 'a shag'. She has taken up none of them, chose to decline primarily because she is here for three years. No wish to burn through the boys at pace, nor to resurrect the reputation she was briefly getting in Charmouth. Annabel rescued her from all that, a selfless, sacrificial deed, one that still fills Mary with confusion and regret. She saw her dilated pupils, a scientific observation which Mary put to no use whatsoever.

She and Tanya were initially together in Simon Godfrey's tutor group. The head of department—the big bowtie-wearing man that he is—was briefly her tutor. He smells of gravy, morning and afternoon. Evening too, one might surmise, but she has had no reason to meet him at that time. In her second week here at Imperial College, he asked her if she minded moving to Mr Stephenson's group. Two of the cohort have pulled out before their feet are under the table, both happened to be under his tutelage. She agreed while worrying that he might be a difficult man, his demands the reason they left the course. Pure speculation, she didn't speak to either who left and had not met her tutor-to-be at that point, his lectures occurring later in the term.

Tanya called her lucky, said that Paul Stephenson is a dish. Silly word and still Mary's found she agrees with the judgement. The youngest lecturer by a decade, mid-thirties is her guess. Forty tops. He wears jeans to work, has an intensity in his voice when discussing a scientific concept, and a lightness when touching upon anything else.

University life is everything she hoped it would be.

* * *

'I'll be home for half-term,' she tells Dennis on the telephone.

He seems pleased about that, far less interested in her commentary about London, the sights. 'Once was enough,' he says. 'I saw the Llamas' concert up there.' She knows he will remain a small-town boy. He has told her many times that he has no intention of leaving Charmouth. His house and history. Staying put was his assertion when he returned from Taunton; Mary was a dizzy kid, knew his parents had died—the how of it, cyanide and the bizarre religion—couldn't sense the weight of it at that young age. Mary looked up to

Dennis back then, admiration which she never granted Stephen. Back when he first slept alone on Croft Road, her mother would invite him round to their bungalow for a hot meal at least once a week. Dennis at the table. Still a boy but with the trappings of manhood foisted upon him, choosing to live alone in Charmouth above living with family in Taunton. At that young age she thought the same: that she would always live where the incoming waves run up the beach. Sand between the toes. Now she cannot imagine living back. The depleted choices. She loves Dennis but perhaps he is the inversion of her childish analysis. A man stranded in a childhood he cannot leave. This is where it all happens. These Londoners—many of whom cannot have been Londoners until five, ten, fifteen years ago—are all moulding something new, fresh. Original.

She tries telling him about Speakers' Corner where she has heard passionate orators decry the many barriers to a better world. 'They can be funny; they can be profound.'

'They can be a pain in the arse. I had a fair-few big mouths at my parties. You must remember them?'

She thinks they were different. Hippies with gobs on. The stupid government's near-sighted failure to legalise drugs was the usual rant. Setting time aside at school to take them, an occasional deviation on the same theme. Some at Speaker's Corner get on to that stuff, many are far better, follow a more coherent thread. Buddhism, rationalism, communism, solipsism. 'Studying is right for me,' she tells him. 'Paul says I've an aptitude.'

He asks her to clarify who Paul is; she confirms that she refers to her tutor. 'First name terms,' he says.

'Don't be jealous.' Her blushing cheeks are unseen by him on the far end of the telephone.

'I can't be, can I? I'm in the same camp as your mum, won't rest until you find a lad more suitable than Dennis Harris.'

When he says such things, a sadness invades her throat. The backs of her eyes. And she will not argue, his reactions are unpredictable these days. 'Love you too much to want you,' he said last Easter. 'Can't be dragging you down with me, Mary. I really can't.' She has wondered if this was his mindset when she was sixteen. Just before Annabel, when she sneaked back to his party intent on being his girl. It threw her off balance, not getting her way. Since then, her life has run along an upward course; middle child of a single mother raised all the way up to Head Girl at Allington Grammar. To Imperial College, London.

The Flophouse Years

Poor Dennis marooned in Charmouth while she relishes being away from the place. Dwelling in bereavement. Honouring the parents who dishonoured him. Loving the late-lover who never made the connection she promised. Annabel sounded to have been troubled beyond words, unable to speak to Dennis about her own loss, and Mary knew nothing of her connection to the Themagins until after her death. Hated her without knowing her, and that is unquestionably the most stupid thing a person can do. She often thinks her own success is down to her hard-working mum—always encouraging, never restricting—then Mary forgets to phone her. And for days at a time, here in London, she barely thinks about him. About Dennis. There is so much to see and do, a lot of science she must grapple with. She feels guilty now and then about ignoring him but their friendship is not a marriage. Not close. He writes two letters for every one she sends. Linda, her room-mate, says all the students will lose touch with their friends from home. 'It's natural. We're here and they're there. They can't see what's important to us, we no longer feel moved by what consumes their provincial lives.' Mary thinks it a cruel truth.

3.

The Bredbury household is quieter than usual this Christmas. Her brother, Stephen, works in Bristol now, a laboratory assistant in a hospital up there. He has drawn the short straw for the holiday shifts, has the New Year off as recompense. The two sisters shared presents, exchanged with their mother also. Then the three ate a modest Christmas dinner, a similar one will take place when Stephen is here and Mary has departed. The first winter getaway of her young life.

'Is it okay if I pop out and see Dennis?' asks Mary. She saw him a couple of days ago. He has seemed terribly distracted all the while she's been back in Charmouth. Christmas alone must be grim; she knows he is keeping Auntie and Uncle at bay. Still lets floppers in, although the numbers have dwindled. Right down to naught if the absence of anecdotes about them is the measure.

Her mother nods, must know it is not much of a family Christmas this year. She seems reconciled to Mary's friendship with the unluckiest boy in Charmouth. Tells her now, as she has done in telephone calls to London, that Dennis is in her prayers.

'Can I come too?' asks Monica.

Mary looks again to her mother who continues to nod.
'I suppose so,' says Mary.

* * *

When Dennis opens the door, he wears a look of total surprise. Not an ounce of pleasure. Shock: that is the look. Shocked to see her and she thought them the fastest of friends.

'Happy Christmas, Dennis,' shouts Monica.

'Hiya,' says Mary, leaning in to kiss him lightly on his unshaven cheek. Hoping to melt his inexplicable fear.

'Mary? Hi, Monica. There are a couple of people here.'

She saw a car by the front gate, parking is tight on Croft Road, Mary had not connected it to this household. 'Sorry,' she says, 'would you rather we leave.' He looks back at them without answering. A blankness to his face that confuses her. 'Wrong time. Sorry, Den. I should have phoned.'

'No...come in...I...' He scratches his nose, still wearing a look of discomposure, as if unsure what even he is doing on his own doorstep. It pops into Mary's mind that he doesn't recognise them, has not taken in that it is she and Monica who have come calling. Could he have taken a drug? Then she realises that isn't it. He addressed them by their names, simply didn't show the pleasure she expected her Christmas calling to bring.

'Visitors,' he shouts over his shoulder, into the open plan. 'Come in,' he repeats when he has turned back to the two girls.

Mary and Monica follow Dennis into the lounge. At the back a couple sit at the dining table.

'Hello,' says the man rising to his feet. His inflexion is odd, the hint of an American accent. Or possibly not, it's only there in the odd word. He must be Annabel's age. He has short hair, a hollowed-out look to his pock-marked face.

Dennis gestures that the sisters should join them as he slides himself in. Feet under the table.

When Mary does the same, the woman already seated says, 'Hey.' Their eyes meet and Mary feels surprise. This lady is beautiful. What she is doing with Crater Face is hard to guess. They are probably the same age as each other—mid-thirties or there abouts—she a world more attractive. Black hair, cut short. The curls might be natural, Mary cannot tell. They frame her elfin face but there are tell-tale lines of age near her eyes. Still her face has a perfect set. Green eyes, deep and serene, as if she is reposing in the certainty of a better future. Her skin is white, it is that time of year. White and unblemished.

'This is James and Hazel,' says Dennis.

The man leans across and shakes the hand of Mary, then that of Monica. 'James.'

Hazel gives her own hand a tiny arc. A cute wave at the girls. She says the word, 'Hey,' again. Her greeting sounds American; however, it is but a single word.

'And Mary and Monica,' says Dennis, completing the introductions. She has watched him closely. Nothing of drugs or alcohol in his movement, his diction. Yet he might be in a trance. A demeanour which troubles Mary; Dennis looks as forlorn as he did when he first lost Annabel. He has Christmas visitors who arrived before her, and she would have thought they were here to lift him from such despondency.

'Family?' James directs at Dennis.

'No.' Then Dennis looks quickly into Mary's face. 'They are like family to me. Known them forever. As long as I've lived in Charmouth. Better family than I ever had.'

Mary notices the lady look away. Perhaps it is the dismissive comment that has offended her. She may be unfamiliar with the Harris family story, but if she is in anyway linked to Annabel, it would be surprising for her not to know. 'Are you sure this is a good time?' asks Mary.

'These guys just dropped in.'

'Are you staying in his flophouse?' asks Monica.

'What's a flophouse?' says Hazel. Mary detects no hint of American in her voice. Not for the phrase just spoken, sounds as English as the Bredbury girls now she's stopped saying hey.

Dennis explains that people sometimes stay. He is easy about company. Not that it happens often nowadays.

'Can't that be a bit dangerous, risky?' says Hazel.

Before an answer emerges, both Dennis and James laugh uproariously. It is as if Hazel has said the most stupid thing on Earth.

Monica taps Mary's arm, gives her a funny look. The pair have discussed the perilousness of the open house he keeps; Emma Bredbury has lectured Dennis about it countless times. The younger sister sides with Hazel. 'There could be a killer on the loose.'

Her phrase only prompts further laughter from the two men. 'There is,' says Dennis. He gestures an upturned palm towards Hazel.

Ravenscourt Park

She looks a little embarrassed while sitting more upright than previously. Neither man says anything further and then she lets a grin cross her face. Only sparingly, her composed look resumes it's place on her face as she starts to speak. 'What your friend refers to, girls, is that I am a jailbird. I've been out of prison barely two months. On the loose but—please believe me—I am not a killer.'

Mary feels distinctly uncomfortable; questions form in her mind which she does not dare to ask. There have been a few rum visitors to the flophouse over the years, only at the larger parties to her knowledge. Not sat across a dining table, not unless you count Schylar.

'Can I get you a drink?' asks Dennis.

'Yes,' says Monica.

'No,' says Mary.

'Why were you in prison?' Monica enquires of Hazel.

'Trumped-up charges.' She shrugs her shoulders, a dismissive wave of the hand.

Mary—a clever girl in normal times—asks her if she is a draft dodger. Dennis told her about Annabel's friend, Herbie. She makes a connection only to subsequently hear how foolish it is.

'I'm English, Mary. And a woman. We've never been drafted to my knowledge.'

'What was it then?' she asks, glancing repeatedly at struggling Dennis. A killer on the loose and he seems to have given her refuge in his house.

'They charged me over drugs. A drugs thing. It was all nonsense. I've served my time.' Then Hazel looks directly into Mary's eyes. 'This is your sister?' A nodded confirmation. 'She's young, I don't want to try and influence. It was something and nothing. Trumped-up charges but not for this table, okay?'

Mary notices Dennis looking distantly upon Hazel, a scowl of disdain which he lifts when she turns her face his way. The ugly man just grins. The talk frightens her while this man seems to find it light, humorous. She has no sense of who these guests are, how they fit into Dennis's life. 'It's none of our business,' she concedes.

'Look at us,' continues Hazel. 'Five folks without a proper Christmas to celebrate. I can't say I've ever been an enthusiast. Not for baby Jesus and what have you. Our precious Christian heritage. Maybe it all gives people something to anchor themselves to. A perspective.' Then she looks directly into Dennis's face. 'From what

I've read, the early Christians were crazier than we were.' Then this elegant and unpredictable lady pats his hand, pats him like she might a well-trained puppy. 'A whole lot of water under the bridge.'

Mary can make no sense of it. This couple must be Themagins. Crazier than we were, she said. Mary doubts any religion can be more insane than that one, knows she may be biased. It has scarred her friend's life irreparably. Dennis did a few drugs in the aftermath, Annabel killed herself with the damned things. Hazel got away with prison. Something to do with drugs. Pushing or smuggling, surely. This is the oddest Christmas gathering. Mary's first impression of Hazel was only that she looked beautiful. James looks like the druggie. Perhaps those are the lines fate has drawn upon their faces, or perhaps Hazel looked still finer before her prison interlude. It is disturbing to contemplate; she regrets bringing Monica here. Again. Feels more worried than she ever has about the company Dennis keeps. And she has worried about it many, many times.

He has risen to fix drinks in the kitchen. Orange squash.

James asks if the girls have always lived in Charmouth. Polite talk that means nothing. What the hell is Dennis doing entertaining a convicted drug pusher? He didn't even puff on Thompson's crap at her going away party. Mary stands from her seat, goes to assist Dennis in the kitchen. She glances over her shoulder at Monica, does it twice as she is crossing the room. The younger girl looks relaxed. Even asks Hazel about prison: did she try to dig a tunnel?

Dennis has come to the door of the lounge with a glass of orange in his hand. 'Who are they?' she whispers.

'Stay,' hisses Dennis.

'And Monica?' she replies.

He moves into the lounge, up to the table holding out two glasses of squash. 'You should leave, Monica,' he says more firmly than he has spoken all visit.

She looks cross. 'Why?'

Then his demeanour changes; Dennis turns from his troubled, introspective self into someone hot and angry. Berserk. Spills orange squash as he raises a demonstrative right hand. 'No! You leave!' he shouts at the two guests. The grown-ups. 'Get out of my house!'

'Hey, fella,' says James, 'this is just a social call.'

'Get out! Get the fuck out!' The boy is screaming. Yelling. 'Get out, I said!'

Monica starts to cry; she can never have seen Dennis like this. To

Mary's near-certain knowledge, no one in Charmouth has ever seen Dennis shout. He is the quietest boy. She feels shocked by his mood change, takes a hold of his arm. Trusts him implicitly, will support him without knowing what has prompted his anger.

Hazel is the calmest. 'It's been an emotional time for us all,' she tells Dennis. 'Memories can get a hold sometimes.'

'Fuck off! Fuck off back to Bristol!' He is not listening to her, or to James. Something has snapped. Maybe everything.

'Please?' Mary waves a hand, directing them to the door. Her own eyes stream tears, and even they make no tangible sense to her. The upset in Dennis is intense. 'Please do what he says.'

'Why don't we all sit down and talk over what it is exactly which is troubling you.' Hazel sounds like a counsellor.

'Go to your fucking car!'

It's unbearable to Mary, hearing Dennis swearing in anger. 'Go,' she says. 'Go or I'll call the police.' It's an idle threat; these guests have done nothing more than Hazel's admission of time served. Monica has taken herself away from the table to the futon, sits with her head in her hand. Wailing blue murder. The turn in Dennis from worry to rage is the hardest thing to watch.

James rises, puts a gentle hand on Dennis's shoulder. 'If it's really what you want, man, we can go.'

'Leave him alone!' shouts Mary. She even swipes a hand at him, as if to intervene—fight—stop him from manhandling Dennis. She doesn't land the blow, the flat of her hand gently pushing his arm off; James offering no resistance. It is Dennis who is out of control; both visitors remain calm, composed. Could be observing a toddler's meltdown. Mary looks directly into his eyes, the sweaty pulp of James' cheeks and brow. 'Please leave, please do as Dennis asks.' She speaks the words quietly, holds his eye. Will brook no contradiction. It might be the smallest thing she is doing for Dennis, might be the biggest. She cannot let him down.

Hazel rises. 'Some people,' she says.

Dennis glares at her, eyes narrowed. Points at the door as a rasp that is not even a word leaves his mouth. Reiterates the demand.

The unwelcome visitors go to the door, James leading by two paces. 'Nice meeting you, Mary, Monica,' calls Hazel as she exits the house.

Only the three of them remain. Dennis sinks onto the futon beside Monica. 'Sorry,' he says in her direction, before putting his head in his hands, shouting, 'Fuck!' more loudly still than all his earlier directives and expletives.

Mary runs a hand across the sobbing Monica before seating herself next to Dennis, wrapping him in a hug he barely accepts. 'Who were those people?'

'It's Burning Rock. Hazel is Burning Rock, the other one's Ganymede. She murdered my parents. Supplied them the cyanide. It's what got her into prison...'

'Call the police, Dennis,' says Mary. She remembers the name. The Themagin girl called Burning Rock; Dennis has described events which involved that woman more than once in the last year. Even confessed his own teenage crush, he was younger than Monica when first he met her.

'The police have been and gone. Two years in prison she got, and they never proved what I've said. Only that she brought some from the states, smuggled it into the country without a licence.'

'Why were they here?' asks Monica.

'Never quite got that out of them. I thought they'd come to finish me off.'

* * *

Dennis cannot talk about it. Monica's presence may be the reason, that or the memories the pair drew from him are simply intolerable. Could be both. Mary has heard it all before while the younger sister doesn't know the backstory. The bare outline, yes, she has no idea that Dennis's father once made love to Hazel while their respective partners looked on. Did something in the same ballpark with each other. Mary cannot forget it; Dennis's past frightens her. She wonders how he has remained so normal despite it all while simultaneously worrying that he has not. Too close to him to see how very strange he has become, that is how she regards herself. Dennis even let those terrors through his door. A coach trip away from rational behaviour.

'Will they come back?' says Monica.

'Mon,' says Mary, softly. 'Let's just sit.' They are all trembling; Mary might be the most composed and she feels struck by lightning. Dennis looks like he has been through a fight that has finished him. Left him for the crows. He hasn't spoken in an age. None of it was apparent to her when they first came through the door. She wonders how this visit ever came about; it is more than four years since a Themagin was last in Charmouth, she is sure of it. Daren't think what might have occurred had she and Monica not come calling.

When Dennis tells the pair that they should be getting back—enjoying Christmas, not his 'little moment of misery'—she detects his need to be alone. It is how he has lived since he was seventeen. She has learned over the months that neither the random hippies stopping over in the flophouse, nor the now-deceased lover with whom Dennis shared a connection which they left completely unexamined, could move the rock from the entrance of the cave.

'Are you sure you will be okay on your own?'

Dennis nods his head from the bowed position he sits in.

'Really?'

He keeps nodding, finally looks into her face. His lips upturn momentarily, the smile of the friend she cares for most in the world. He is still Dennis.

* * *

In the evening, Mary phones him. He sounds flat, confirms that he has been on his own all day. No return of James or Hazel.

'I really think you should phone the police, Dennis. If she's only recently come out of prison, she probably isn't allowed to come to your house.'

'We're all grownups, Mary. The police never charged Burning Rock with murder because she never killed a living soul. Asked people to do it to themselves. Toogood is the one who convinced each and every one of them they were so very special that they should go along with it. Their own Valhalla waiting for them.'

'And he had the decency to go the same way,' says Mary.

'Decency or cowardice. In its own way, it was interesting to see her, you know. Burning Rock. I felt nothing. Hated her in the past. Carried on hating her for years; today, nothing. I freaked out because having you and Monica in the same room as them was unbearable. They've got nothing to do with you. Nor Monica. The less your sister knows about people like them the better.'

'Oh, Dennis. Come round tomorrow. Monica's talked to mum, and she was cross we didn't telephone her but she cares about you. She said the thing about telling the police. She thinks it would be only right.'

'Please, Mary. No police. I think Sergeant Ash will stick me in the mental hospital if she needs to come here again. It's only ever madness at three Croft Road.'

* * *

The Flophouse Years

She spends the rest of the evening with her mum and Monica. After watching a couple of comedy shows on television, Emma Bredbury takes herself to bed. Mary scarcely took them in; thinking about Dennis while watching. The two sisters sit on the sofa.

Monica rises up, turns the set off. 'Rubbish and double rubbish,' she says. She sinks back down on the sofa, turns her face into Mary's chest and buries it there. 'He's our best friend and we don't know how to help him.'

Mary feels her shoulders heave, poor Monica crying again. It must have been a bewildering afternoon. 'I try, Mon. He'll be around tomorrow and I'll have it out with him then. Make him promise.'

Monica is hugging her tightly; Mary thinks only how trite her own words really are. Little sister is right, there may not even be a how. What happened to Dennis isn't in the books, no remedy known to man.

'Do you remember when he argued with Mum?' she asks.

Mary shakes her head, doesn't recall Dennis being argumentative at all.

'When Mum told him not to let strangers sleep over in his house. Back when he first started doing it.'

'That was years ago, Mon. You were tiny, I thought it went over your head.'

'You know nothing does that. Dennis said the most dreadful people on Earth went through his house at his parents' invitation. A wide-open door couldn't be any worse.'

'Did he say that?'

Monica is sitting up now, looking at her sister from beside her on the old sofa. 'You must remember. And Dennis doesn't know the difference, does he? It's all been too much...'

'You're right about that. I think he's strong inside but it's hard for him...'

'If you married him instead of going to stupid university, you could keep all those people out. He wouldn't let them in if you were there.'

Little sister shouts this at her. Not loudly but not listening to objections, nor taking in her impassive face. Mary has thought about it herself, done so several times when she was waiting for him to arise from his post-Annabel doldrums. Not the marrying exactly, or even her assertion about not going to Imperial. Mary has a life to live, she would have liked it to have been hitched to Dennis. Tears roll down her cheeks; so much that she once wanted has slipped from view.

4.

'Where are you?' Five o'clock on Boxing Day and Mary is phoning Dennis once more.

'Sorry, Mary. I didn't want to spoil your family time. I've done enough of that.'

'Dennis, you know it's not like that.'

'You would say that. You're very sweet, Mary, but you really don't need me now.'

'Dennis.' She is unsure what to say. That it isn't need, it is care. She feels conflicted, he is correct that she has a life beyond Charmouth. Cannot imagine not thinking about—feeling the purest love towards—this lost young man. 'Dennis, should I come to you? I'm away tomorrow, you know?'

'Away?'

'I told you. Skiing with the girls from university.'

'Skiing? You're going to Switzerland tomorrow?'

'Scotland. I told you. Tanya's family have a lodge.'

'I thought that was...' His voice tapers away.

'I'm sorry. Let me come round.'

'Not today, Mary...'

'You must, Den. I'll be straight to London when we come back from...'

'Skiing, studying. You're living the life, Mary. I'm really pleased...'

'So let me come and see you today.'

'I'm so sorry about yesterday. Say that to Monica too, from me. I'm just not in the mood for people yet. Not today.'

5.

The concourse at Waterloo Station is teeming with people, Saturday morning shoppers and visitors, although it is only early March. She told him she would wait outside the Wimpy Bar. From fifty yards away she can see it's him. His hair has grown back, looks like a hippy. She likes seeing him look as he used to. When he approaches, Mary gives an enthusiastic wave.

'Dennis, we need to catch the tube out to my place. You'll need to buy a ticket?'

They go to the booth together and she tells him which one to buy, then together the pair take the escalator into the bowels of the Earth.

'You're looking great, Mary.' Neither has seen the other since Christmas day. A few phone calls, letters. She smiles at his compliment. 'Will I meet this boyfriend?'

'I've cleared my weekend for you, Dennis. I'm not planning to see Paul.'

'I was hoping to confirm whether or not he's right for you.'

She gives him a playful tap on the back, dare not punch him as she would have done when she was a schoolgirl. 'I'll be the judge. You're not cross with me?' This troubles her, how her befriended state feels to Dennis Harris. Paul Stephenson invited her to a party that took place in his family home. A mother and even a divorced wife were present. She and a male student were the only attendees from her course. She has not worked out the reason for the other guy's invite. Her tutor has since taken her for two meals and a visit to the cinema. An old-fashioned wooing in comparison to her rash sixth-form antics. She feels only warmth towards Paul although being with him is not yet the easy company she enjoys with Dennis.

They have to stand up on the tube. In silence, it is the way Londoners travel, glancing hurriedly at fellow passengers and quickly back down at one's shoes. The train goes only a short distance before she tells him they must get off. Change tube line.

'That one just took us under the river,' she says.

Dennis looks bemused. Still giving her little smiles. They quickly catch the next train. Not as crowded but only a single free seat. Each try to persuade the other to sit.

'It's a bit of a walk, I'm afraid,' she says when they alight at Hammersmith. She takes his hand as they walk through tunnels but Dennis laughs, removes his from hers. 'I'm neither boyfriend nor kid brother.'

Escalators and stairs, fresh air greets them when they've a flight still to climb. After going through the turnstile, they finally emerge at street level. The air is very chilly, freezing or thereabouts. This is a colder snap than anything January or February brought them. As they walk past Victorian terraces, abundant in this part of west London—Dennis carrying a rucksack with a few belongings inside—she again attaches herself to his arm, holding his left in both of hers. Leaning in as she walks.

'If he sees you, he'll be jealous,' says Dennis.

Mary thinks it's stupid, Paul will take her as he finds her. She is so pleased her old friend has finally come to this new home from home. She even wonders if a trip or two to London might rattle Dennis out of his unjustified commitment to a life in Charmouth. A life centred too fully upon attending to the old folk at Plaza Court. That's her view, she knows he gets a lot from the role. 'Should he be jealous?'

'I love you, Mary. And that's why I'm not going to ruin your life. Stick with this Paul fella.'

She wishes she hadn't asked while knowing she half agrees. She lived a life of childish torment when he took up with Annabel. And now they have moved on in their lives, she suspects there can be no going back. She doesn't like his reasoning, his constant denigration of his own worth. Thinks it a consequence of all he has lived through. His wish to do right by her is a testament to something noble in him. He guffawed the only time she tried to explain it. 'You know you've to sleep on the floor. Can't have you climbing into bed with me while Linda's in the room.'

Dennis laughs, he's told her many times that he's finished with girls.

* * *

In the student halls, Mary takes him into the bedroom where he puts his bag down. A small twin room, space for a sleeping bag between the two single beds. Linda has had girlfriends stay several times already; Monica has visited twice, cosied up together in the single. Her roommate says that she is fine with a boy coming, having quickly established that she has no need to retreat from the room, give them the privacy a different male visitor might require. Linda also said, 'I hope Paul doesn't find out.' Mary shook her head, thought then that she should tell Paul all about Dennis but she has yet to do so. He and she are still to learn who the other is. Their interior lives.

They go along the corridor to the shared kitchen where Mary makes them each a plate of beans on toast. Dennis tucks in, talks with the other students who are also eating, cooking. The only boys here are boyfriends, it is a girls' hall. The lads talk hangovers and missed lectures. One asks Dennis what he studies and he tells them he's looking at doing night classes. 'A social worker friend of mine thinks I should get the same qualification she has. Got to get an A-level or two to be accepted on the course. I don't know if I'm clever enough but I'll give it a whirl.'

'Is that Jane?' asks Mary. 'The one I met at your parties.' He confirms it is, and she turns to her student friends. 'Dennis always used to throw the coolest parties. These two women were pretty much making out with each other on the sofa in the lounge. How about that? Two women. Wild times, weren't they, Dennis?'

He nods quietly.

She knows that there have been no such wild times in the last fifteen months or more, raising it suddenly feels silly of her. Reminding him of times he has left behind. 'I'm glad you're still friends with Jane. It's a good idea to do what she says.'

A male student giggles. 'Any lesbians to send to my parties, Dennis.'

He doesn't reply, stares into the student's face until the other boy looks away. Mary shouldn't have brought it up. All students show off, first years particularly. She expected to be different and it is disquieting to find it not so. Her boyfriend is a lecturer, that might require her to act the grown-up. She has yet to share with Dennis who Paul is. His age or status. She who previously told him everything, ranted once or twice about her own stupidity for going out—sharing a bed—with one or two regretted Charmouth boys. Four. Wouldn't have regretted physical intimacy with Dennis, it just never happened.

While they are eating, Linda, Mary's roommate, says, 'Look!' pointing demonstratively at the window. It is snowing. A powdery white has replaced the lunchtime sky. Large flakes slide down the sash windows like ice-skating spiders. All the students get excited by the sight. Go over to look out into the gloom. Comment on the sheer density of flakes in the air. 'A blizzard,' says one. It's moved the conversation away from lesbians.

* * *

They spent over an hour in the kitchen, all present highly impressed by the little which the former hippy revealed about himself. His parties. When one of the boys asked, 'You have a house of your own?' Mary tried to nod at the listening students with a serious face, indicate it was a line not to be pursued. 'My parents died,' he said as if telling them his house is semi-detached. 'I'm an orphan.' They had the sense to follow Mary's bidding whether they saw her expression or not. Now—snowfall a little less intense than it was—the pair from Charmouth have ventured out, walked to Ravenscourt Park. It is only a short trek from the student halls. The flakes never stop falling; a white cloth formed wherever grass lies.

'I suggested you didn't come until March to let the weather to warm up,' laughs Mary. 'Got that wrong, didn't I.' She wears a navy-blue bobble hat, a scarf to match it. Dennis is underdressed. A thick windcheater and woollen gloves are all he has brought with him to London. There are very few people out in the forbidding weather. As they go into the heart of the park, they step upon virginal snow. 'It's beautiful here,' she declares.

'Is it only the snow?' asks Dennis. 'I expected London to be dirty and smelly.'

'There is some of that but I love it, Den. Can't imagine living back in Charmouth.'

'No. You don't need it like me.'

As they wander further from the road, taking in the trees and hedges which have turned white, snow draped upon them, the volume of flakes in the air intensifies once more. Snow swirls around the couple, sitting on their collars, on Mary's woollen hat. At a bench, she bends and pushes the fresh snow off the seat, both her gloved hands form a single shovel. She stops at half a bench. 'Sit here, Den. We can wait until we're three inches buried, then walk around like snowmen.'

He drops onto the bench. 'Still wet,' he says, and she slides down into him, an arm across his shoulders. 'Charmouth isn't the same without you…'

'Dennis…last time I saw you…Christmas day…why did you even let those people in? That awful woman, the ugly man.'

'Hard to say, Mary…'

'Say it though, please? Just tell me.'

'Mary, it hasn't been easy…when Annabel died…' They are both looking out across the flat white lawn; early afternoon and the heavy sky has darkened London. Even the white of the snow looks austere, shadowy.

'I know it's been hard for you,' says Mary. 'Harder than I'd know how to bear. But letting those two in? Why…?'

'Mary, I knew who they were when I answered the door. I only saw them close to when I was a kid—time has chiselled a change or two in their appearances—and still I knew them straight away. Seven years since I first saw them; I've worked that out. The only time I saw James. Ganymede, that was his Themagin name. Hazel, I saw again. Was in the house three weeks before everything happened.'

'I know, Den. I remember everything you've said. Told me that the girl was beautiful. You said that before I ever saw her. And I can see it but, dear God, was she frightening.'

The Flophouse Years

'No, you've got it wrong. I told you that she brought my parents their vials of poison, another one in the delivery for me. The police found it, still sealed up when they took it away. I can't prove it was her but it must have been. I met Burning Rock two years before any of that. Nothing frightening about her at all, not scary until you attach what I learned later. She was a gentle devotee of the cause. Like Too the Ship, like my washout of a mother. Burning Rock only did what her faith demanded, whatever Toogood said she should do with my dad, with any Themagins. Her and that Ganymede went and performed rituals...'

Mary knows about the sex, the wife swapping. She feels embarrassed on her friend's behalf. 'He was ugly as hell, Dennis. Are they really a couple?'

'They were, Mary. I've been thinking about them since they've been and gone. Maybe he did time in prison in America. Didn't say at Christmas, not that I asked. Never had short hair in the sixties. That was the reason she came alone to deliver the poison, you see. He was in the US and she'd come back specially. Because of the comet, that's what told Toogood it was time. Maybe James did the same job as Hazel. Did it in America. The personal delivery service. Ganymede and Burning Rock.'

'And Den, why let them in? Why not refuse? When Monica and I came in, I thought they were floppers, or friends of Annabel's or something. I was terrified when you started shouting...'

'You gave me strength, Mary. I thought they'd come to finish the job. Before you came, I was trying to work out if they could have been involved with Annabel. It isn't possible, I've seen that since. Schylar was never a Themagin. Not a single one in Holland, you know.' Dennis blows the snow from his lips, claps his gloved hands together and the powder arcs away from them. Mary brushes the snow off his long hair and he giggles. 'It's gone down my neck,' he says, and she hugs him in apology. 'I think Toogood took almost all the Themagins. I reckon one or two went a little later. Not just Annabel. But it's knowing I could have gone with them, that just won't leave my thoughts. It's like missing the bus. Should you catch the next one? Make my own way. I thought my parents were lunatics believing they could catch a spaceship, and they said at the time that, ideally, they wanted me with them. It's a pull, Mary. If Burning Rock had offered me a drink of any old shite when she was stood there on the doorstep, I'd have taken it. I know I would.'

Ravenscourt Park

Mary finds tears escaping her eyes, her arm is around his shoulders. 'No, don't say that, Dennis. Don't ever think like that.'

'It was how I felt, Mary. And they only wanted to talk. I guess they were trying to make sense of it themselves. I shouted at them because I couldn't stand the situation—you and Monica getting dragged into my freaky life—not because they had done a thing to deserve it.'

'They deserved it, Den. For what they did years ago, if not that day.'

'Annabel came to me in the same spirit.' Dennis pauses, glances into Mary's face and she catches a look of concern upon him. 'She meant well, she really did. Solidarity between survivors...' Dennis erupts into tears after talking more levelly than she has ever heard him on this terrible subject. January the twentieth. Mary tries to comfort him while feeling as wretched as her friend now sounds. The snow upon them is cold and she hugs him ferociously. There are some things we should never have to face, and poor Dennis has seen them twice over. '...turned out not to be a survivor at all, but she tried, Mary. That poor girl couldn't quite face it all.'

'I'm sorry about her, Den. Sorry that you had to go through all that over her as well. But the other two, the living—Burning Rock—would you let them in again?'

'I doubt that they'll come back, I wasn't exactly hospitable. I'm not changed though, am I? The crap of years ago is never going to stop haunting me. The biggest part of what I think about before I go to sleep each night.'

Mary sees that the falling snow has covered the footsteps they made from gate to bench. They sit huddled together like hobos. They might have floated here, the evidence that they walked across the grass just fifteen minutes ago is no longer present. A blanket thrown across their steps while nothing seems able to erase those fateful days in January nineteen-seventy. Not for the boy in her arms. She thinks of Dennis back then: she was fourteen years old when he was orphaned. A schoolgirl serving him up a casserole in the bungalow on Morgan Crescent, neither knowing his parents were already dead, upstairs in the house he was to return to. It is only since Annabel died—their long, long talks—that she has truly dwelled upon his confused feelings. She used to think him sensible and his parents daft. Now it looks more like a lucky roll of the dice. How can any kid navigate safely away from their parents? She pushed against her mother's wishes with the crummy boyfriends of her lower sixth years, re-bonded nicely with her when she started to see sense in her mother's caution. For Dennis it has been a single severance.

She knows he was naïvely keen on the outlandish religion when his parents first took it up, when he was too young to argue. He had relished the special status it seemed to give him, even as they implored him to tell no one at school. Being a Themagin meant being chosen by God; a God named Aris Toogood. Dennis has talked her through each up and down of it. He rejected it as teenagers do when they become embarrassed with the thought of who they had been just one or two years previously. At sixteen, Mary broke her Danny Clare records—snapped them in half—the two singles she owned. Sentimental teenage love songs and she was shifting her allegiance to the Llamas. Briefly trying the free love Dennis scarcely got a shot at. Breaking vinyl seems excessive looking back. Dennis Harris lived while his parents died: chance timing. He was sailing through the maelstrom of hating them, when there are calmer waters before and after. Times when a child might do as a parent asks. What any of it feels like for the poor boy, she cannot guess. It all slips from the realm of the possible. It happened but it should not have. She can see no further than that.

'I sometimes think they really did it,' says Dennis. 'I imagine there is a spaceship heading off to some beautiful planet faraway. Toogood and Mum and Dad and all the rest of them are sharing one ethereal body, being whole in the new beginning. We who haven't timed our deaths so precisely could be missing out on the eternity that there really was a portal to. Mary, you're looking at me like I'm a total nutter, and you know as well as I do that the churches are full of people who think their prayer to Jesus is the same ticket. Heaven assured. It must be nice to have faith...'

'My mum thinks that, Den. She's never really made us go, not since we were very young. But it isn't crazy. I don't call myself a Christian but nor do I think my mum crazy. The Church of England doesn't ask you to take your own life.'

They look across the snow-covered park. White beneath the lifeless sky, dirty pale cloud, just the two of them hiding from the city. 'Jesus did it for them,' says Dennis, palms upturned, the comparison complete.

Mary wonders what has gotten into him. They never had this conversation before; the Themagins were the nutters, Dennis always left other religions alone. 'I don't know what Jesus was. If he died so that they don't have to, isn't that better than all the Toogood stuff that...'

'It's not better if it doesn't work. We'll none of us know until we board the spaceship, will we Mary?' He's leaning back on the bench, holding Mary's hand in both of his. The one that is not around his shoulders. 'More than two hundred, a lot more than that. Some of them just heard the tapes, some tried the we-are-one stuff. There may be a few who were left behind, the couple who came to my house didn't get all the deliveries done on time. I've read that. More than a few; it was a much bigger deal in America than over here. No idea who they all are but I think about them every day. Surviving Themagins...'

'Jesus, Dennis, that other stuff, the...' She lowers her voice although no one is close, not another soul in snowbound Ravenscourt Park. '...your dad and that woman having sex, your mum and that ugly man. Is that what's put you off?'

Dennis looks away into the trees. Gives no answer to her question. She wishes she hadn't said it, may have missed the mark completely. Or she may have cut into something he cannot allow himself to think about. When she was fourteen, when Dennis went to Taunton for weeks and weeks, she imagined Themagins to be like goblins—a story to frighten children with—and yet it's all true. They walked the Earth. Entered Dennis's home too many times; sex and poison. She shouldn't have raised it. No idea what he thinks and feels.

* * *

Back in the student halls, Dennis is shivering. She regrets keeping him out so long with only a thin coat upon him. The conversation felt important, good that he has got it off his chest. It's what she tells herself. She feels uneasy about the content. Weather aside, Mary feels chilled by his casual acceptance that those two Themagins might have come to kill him.

'You need a shower, Dennis. There's always hot water here, it might be the best thing about the halls.' He agrees, picks a change of clothes, towel and soap from his rucksack. Then, as she shows him the shower room, carrying similar in her own hands, Mary says, 'You go in. There are two cubicles in each shower room, so I'll wait outside. Make sure none of the girls go in and get a shock. Boys aren't meant to be on this corridor.'

'Had I best not...'

Mary laughs, 'You really aren't the first. Half the students have had boys stay over. You're the first gentleman.' Dennis turns away, enters the shower room. Mary regrets her joke: it is as if she is making fun of his celibate state. And his last girlfriend killed herself; she never thought herself an insensitive witch and today she keeps hearing it in her unanswered words. Last girlfriend: the late Antonella Vitale was Dennis's only girlfriend. Mary knows everything about him.

Her thoughts turn to Paul while she waits outside the shower room. She likes the way he treats her, makes her feel important. Raised up. She doesn't know him, not in any true sense. Can't guess what he would do if a killer on the loose came knocking on his tutor room door. Would he chat amiably about the impracticalities of space travel—the physicist with the answers—or head for the experience, regardless of the attached insanity. Call the police, perhaps. She doubts she could ever talk about such a thing with him, or that he could contemplate the experiences which Dennis has had. He would get stuck on the science. Comets do not obscure spaceships; what more need be said?

Two girls are coming towards the shower rooms; Mary knows them. All the girls in halls get along to some degree. 'Can you use one of those rooms, please? My friend is in that one.'

'Your friend?'

'A guy.'

'Get yourself in with him, Mary. Showering together is the best fun you can...'

'He's not my boyfriend.'

'...interesting. Then let me at him.'

Mary laughs along with the girls while standing firm, making it clear there is to be no joking with this particular friend. As she is blocking the door it pushes into her back, Dennis emerges, quickly showered and changed.

'He isn't your lecturer. Far too young.'

Mary laughs it off, tells Dennis he can wait in kitchen or bedroom, as she heads into the shower room he emerged from. Takes to the water. She feels strangely cold—loves seeing Dennis again while fearing losing him—needs these few minutes alone cleansed by warm water.

* * *

In the evening they go down to The Star and Garter with Linda and a boy named Richard. When the other couple are talking about a particular biology lecturer, Dennis asks Mary what the girl meant earlier.

'Which girl,' says Mary.

'At the shower. She expected me to be a lecturer.'

'Oh that. It was nothing.' Mary worries that she might be going red but Dennis asks no more questions.

They drink three more rounds, the girls on halves, the lads on pints. Richard tries to be the joker. 'Linda says you're sneaking this one into the dorm, Mary. I'd better not tell Stephenson, eh?'

'Shut up,' she says, and he laughs at her discomfort.

'Is Stephenson the same as Paul?' asks Dennis.

'Ha-ha. You know about him then?' says Richard, his voice a little slurred.

'Nothing to know,' he replies. 'I'm Mary's friend, nothing more.'

'You're cool with her shagging a lecturer then.'

'Richard!' Mary is livid.

'Speaking out of turn. Sorry if I'm too truthful.'

'You are not.' She turns to Dennis. 'I've not told you about him…' Then she leans in, has no wish to talk any longer with Richard Armstrong. '…we are not doing the thing he said. I'm not. Haven't.'

'He's a lecturer?'

She gestures that it is true. Nods with her eyes.

'A married lecturer?'

'No.'

As the Charmouth pair sit in silence, Richard looks from one to the other with a smug smile on his face. Enjoying the awkwardness he has prompted.

'Divorced,' she concedes.

'Christ, Mary. How old is this guy? This Paul.'

'Not old, Den. I think he's about thirty-five.'

'That's wrong, Mary. Sounds as if he's taking advantage. Much too old for you.'

Mary relaxes, even grins as she puts an arm around Dennis's neck. Kisses his cheek as she has done so many times back in their seaside town. She is dating an older man, not letting killers into her home. 'No secrets in Charmouth and I was daft enough to think myself living in London.'

'He's an old man, Mary…'

'Listen to you, Dennis. Listen.' She wants to laugh but his serious face prevents it. Too often are they out of step.

'What?'

She regrets not telling him all about Paul over the telephone back in January, the house party or the first date. He patted her hand in a couple of tutorials that gave her clues last term, to tell of them might have sounded silly. Like a schoolgirl crush. She doesn't think she has kept secrets from Dennis, not in the year after Annabel died. It was love-hate when he was living with her. Jealousy on her part that she wishes she had never felt. Doesn't like contemplating being so possessive of him as a result of her own mid-teen obsession. She thinks that coming to live in London will be the making of her. Would hate it to be the undoing of Dennis.

Part Two
6.

He lets her talk on the telephone for twenty minutes before relenting, agreeing to the outing. It is only the beach here at Charmouth, hardly worth the haggle. Dennis keeps reiterating that he is so pleased that she is happy. He reckons he means it. It is also the case that wishing this for her doesn't make him any keener to meet the man who makes Mary Bredbury happy. The physics lecturer. And the couple's stay at the George Hotel in Lyme doesn't improve the prospect one iota. It feels wrong.

'Why is he wasting his pounds on that place, Mary. I've got a perfectly good flophouse here.'

Mary told him that Paul booked the hotel room for a two week stay. They are spending a lot of time with her mother, a little with wider family, while they are down here. Sightseeing for a few of the days. 'My mother is completely charmed by him,' she laughed.

Dennis feels a tug of loss. Some weeks he thinks more about the Bredbury family than he does the Harris's. Peter and Sally Harris enter his mind but he pushes them out as quick as he can. Can't have them rattling around in there. He never felt on a wavelength with Mrs Bredbury, knows she has been good to him over the years. A caring soul from first to last. Mary, even Monica and Stephen, he can think about without complication. Well, Paul Stephenson is the complication. Dennis does not think himself good enough for Mary, and at the bottom of it, he might think her too good for all the men on this Earth.

'For the same reason we're not staying at my house, Dennis. I share a bedroom with Monica, and you have random hippies turning up at yours.'

'Hardly, Mary. Not any longer, not for the most part. There have been two here this summer, each for just a single night. It used to be forty.'

'Well, I'm glad they've stopped. You'd no idea who those people were.'

'Mary, Mary, they'd no idea who I was but they still came calling. It's stopping the parties that's turned the tap off. And I could throw one for you and Paul...'

'No, Dennis. I think Paul is more serious than that.'

He laughs, it is the rarest sound. 'You won't be marrying a hippy then?'

'Who said anything about marrying?'

'I did. Your family are holding the reception already. And your mother is so cool about the hotel, isn't she?' Her churchgoing mother sounds to have accepted their sleeping arrangements more readily than Dennis: the Christian less uptight than the hippy. The lapsed hippy. And Mary's mother was positively disapproving of his own older lover. Bent his ear more than once while Annabel lived, remembered her in prayer after prayer when she lived no more.

The phone is silent until Mary says, 'Not really, Den. Not comfortable about it. He's a university lecturer, she cleans other people's houses. Mum can't put her foot down with people like that.'

'Poor woman,' says Dennis. Mary seems keen to change the subject; he really shouldn't have raised it. What Mary does with Paul is none of his business. Should stop thinking about it. Giving up on girls is actually easier when this one isn't in town.

'You will come to the beach, won't you?' she repeats. Dennis doesn't answer. He has done so already, promised to be there. To finally meet the man who she has opened her heart to, parades before family as she never did when she dated Charmouth boys. 'He has asked me, Dennis. He's like that; he asked me before we...he proposed marriage and I laughed because I'm a teenager, can't be saying yes to that at my age. He didn't think...I don't like talking about this with you, Dennis. He had to show he was serious before we made love. And I always knew he was serious. You'll see what I mean when you meet him.'

'And he's not eyeing the admissions list. A new girl every September. It's how randy lecturers plan their next conquest, I am told.'

'Dennis! Don't judge him when you haven't even met him. He's nothing like you say.'

Dennis knows he shouldn't have said it. Couldn't help himself. He would be Mary Bredbury's lover—thinks about it more than a sworn celibate should—if he was not simultaneously quite wrong for her. It's a fortnight since the incident at work. Barely even an incident, a routine day with a little of the unusual thrown in. For three weeks, old Mr Tufnell had been bed-bound. The doctor told them on the second day that there was nothing more to do, not anything that could restore the health that had long been seeping from him. Three different members of his family sat with him for a few hours; in so protracted a dying they could not be there night and day. Then he slept for thirty-six hours; after all the coughing and wheezing of the preceding weeks, the small staff team hoped he would quietly slip away during this peaceful episode. After a day and a half adrift, Dennis called in to find him sitting on the side of the bed, attempting to put his socks on.

'Let me help you,' said Dennis, surprised to see him awake.

Mr Tufnell looked at him through filmy eyes, seemed not to believe what he was seeing. Must have heard all the earlier talk at his bedside. 'You're an angel,' he declared. 'Am I not to dress myself in heaven? You must be an angel.'

Dennis tried to tell him who he was: deputy warden of Plaza Court. Mr Tufnell couldn't grasp it at all, seemed to believe exactly what he, Lorraine and Yvonne had been expecting. That he had passed over to the other side. He insisted on feeling Dennis's face, running his hands across both cheeks, muttering, 'Oh my, the face of an angel,' upon touching it. Even asked if there were no curly haired angels here. Told him he that was how the angels had appeared in his children's bible, the nineteenth century.

When Dennis was back in the office, he told Yvonne—who had arrived for handover—what had just occurred. Yvonne who replaced Jill who replaced Fran who replaced Tracy. Working with Lorraine Chadwick remains an acquired taste. She laughed at the story and told him he could pass himself off as an angel anywhere. Then she went up the corridor to look in on him while Dennis started writing up the shift. She came running back to the office before he was onto his third entry. Poor Mr Tufnell lay dead on the floor of his flat, clothed for the first time in nearly a month. 'He needed that angel to help him over the line,' she said. Then Yvonne went bright red in the face. Realised to whom she was giving this back-handed compliment.

'Angel of death,' said Dennis, rounded off her analysis without a moment's thought. He has often felt it.

If Paul Stephenson is a tutor with a few faults, he'll still prove a better match for Mary Bredbury than this angel of death could ever offer. He shouldn't have made the admissions-list joke. 'If he makes you happy, I'm happy for you.' He means it whatever personal feelings it also arouses. He'll go to the beach—won't enjoy seeing her on teacher's arm—got to keep his chin up, Mary's been a great friend.

* * *

When he arrives at the kiosks, scanning the beach for Mary, Monica comes running towards him. She wears a red swimming costume. Looks happy and angry all at once. 'He could be her daddy, Dennis. That's what everybody will think.'

'Where are you guys sitting?'

'In front of the beach huts.' She points a flicked finger. 'There.' He sees a party of four, three sitting on raffia mats, her mother on a metal deckchair.

'Is Stephen not here?' asks Dennis.

'Coming later. Come and meet him.'

'How are you, Monica? I've not seen you...'

'I saw you last week in the Co-op. I'm always good, Dennis. Come and meet Paul Logarithm.'

'You look well, Monica. Grown up.'

'I am grown up. That doesn't mean I'm going to start kissing and slobbering over an old man. Mary can do it all she likes. You won't catch me rubbing noses with the nearly dead. Not kissing them.'

'Hey, don't be down on her...'

'I feel sorry for you, Dennis. I always thought you and Mary would get together.'

He shakes his head. 'I'm not for Mary. She's going places. You too, Monica. Look at you now.'

'Don't look! You have to put on your swimming trunks then it's fair to look at me.' The young girl is suddenly blushing at the scrutiny Dennis is giving her figure, her semi-clad self. She turns and he follows, pinching the back of her neck affectionately.

'Hi, Mary,' he says.

She leaps up from the sand, gives him a close embrace although she wears only a bikini and has a sturdily-built boyfriend sitting on the mat she has leapt from. 'I've missed you, Den.' She says it so quietly, so close to his ear, it feels to him like a plea to spring her from this gathering.

Then he sees the man has risen, standing beside her as Mary releases him from her python-like clasp. He wears a pair of navy-blue swimming trunks, curly black hairs prosper upon his chest, ivy their way across his shoulders, legs and arms. Something sprouting from every follicle. The girls' mother waves a hand from her deck chair; she wears a red swimsuit, similar to the one upon her youngest daughter. From further back on the rack.

'Dennis, isn't it?' says Paul Stephenson, pumping his hand. A firm grip which envelopes his knuckles.

'Yes, I'm an old friend of Mary's.'

'She's told me all about you.' Dennis quickly glances towards Mary. So much she might have said. 'No worries, Dennis, all your secrets are safe with me.'

He sees Mary grimace. At least that is what Dennis thinks she's done. Could be the sun in her face. An old school friend of Mary's called Babs is lying on an adjacent raffia mat; she wears as little as Mary. 'Hi, Dennis,' she calls. They know each other, Babs came to a few parties.

He sits himself on the edge of her mat, and Mary points at his jeans. 'Can't swim in them.'

'I'll change in a minute.'

'I'm going to dunk him today,' Monica tells the assembled group.

'Be nice to Dennis,' says her mother.

'Monica's great, Mrs B,' says Dennis. 'She treats me as savagely as she does everything else in this world.'

Monica is on her feet, a grin displaying parallel lines of brilliant white teeth. 'Ooh, Mr H. She stoops, to push him with both hands and Dennis falls backwards onto the sand. A foot on his chest, her tanned leg announces she has bagged a trophy. 'I'm only savage with you, Mr H, because you still have all your clothes on.'

'Leave him be,' says Mary.

'No way.'

Dennis raises himself up, grabs hold of Monica's ankle, pulls it back and forth. She falls on top of him, a happy shriek as she does lands.

'Your heads going under water for that!'

'I'm dunking you first, little puppy,' he laughs.

'No chance.' Monica pushes him back down once more. 'I'm making you eat this, Mr H. Your very favourite tea-time meal.' She has a fist full of sand hovering close to Dennis's mouth.

Mary and Babs, Mrs Bredbury too, are all laughing at Monica. At Dennis's embarrassment in the lee of her torment. The physics lecturer has his face in a book.

* * *

Dennis stands while the three girls are swimming, standing up to his neck in the seawater, looking back onto the beach. Paul Stephenson is still on his raffia mat, deep in conversation with Emma Bredbury who looks down on him from her deckchair. What they talk about Dennis cannot possibly discern from out here. In his head he does the calculation: Mary's boyfriend can be no more than eight or nine years younger than the woman with whom he talks on the beach. Much closer to her mother's age than he is to Mary's. Dennis guesses that there is a twenty-year age gap between Paul and Mary, she has not disclosed the figure. Not to him. And he remembers again how she laughed at him in London; he had the stupidity to raise the matter. He lived with Annabel for nearly sixteen months. Sleeping with his mother was the jibe of a few in the village. Mary included but she was young, confused, loved him more than he has ever been worth bothering about. He wants to give his blessing to her union with Paul Stephenson. Not sure what sort of a union it is. A summer or a lifetime? Sharing a hotel bedroom without falling out with her mother. Her hard-to-please churchgoing mother. Incredible that she should have warmed to the student-chasing slimeball. Monica's a decent distraction, keeps Dennis from dwelling on Mary's disappointing choice of boyfriend.

Little sister seems to have calmed down for the time being. The cool of the water might have helped and she's swimming back towards him right now. Mary doesn't seem herself to Dennis; looks as pretty as ever, just not as animated. He always thought her the pick of the girls in Charmouth—prettiest, cleverest—of the entire Dorset coast come to that. Today she's acting like she's thirty-bloody-boring. Far too similar to her ill-chosen boyfriend. The undergrad poker. His smarmy proposal of marriage in advance of what he was really after doesn't fool Dennis.

'Swim with me,' shouts Monica, and he flexes his feet, pushes up and starts to match her breast stroke. 'What do you think?'

'Of what?'

'Old Man River.'

The Flophouse Years

'He's a nice guy, Monica. Give your sister a break.'

She takes hold of his long-again hair, salt-watered and heavy. Then with a mighty heave, a grunt of air expelled from her lungs, breasts swelling forward more than Dennis imagined they could—Monica has a bustline now—she rises up out of the water only to push him down. His head under the water.

Dennis struggles, splashes. When his head is back breathing air, he coughs. Tries to laugh but it's a struggle. 'I've to do that to you now, Monica. Rules of the game.'

'Catch me first,' she yells as she swims out of his reach.

'All right over there?' shouts Mary. She bobs up and down in the waves a little further out. Her friend, Babs, does likewise a few feet to her side.

'I'm giving Monica what's coming,' he shouts. The little upstart shrieks when he catches her foot. As he swims, Dennis pulls Monica towards him. Ankle, knee, thigh. Then he has his arms around her waist. It could be a life-saving hold but for his wicked grin. 'You've to go under now titchy-tits.' A flat palm on her head as she screams. Monica is clever, under the water she pulls his arms and he too sinks down a little. Both come up together gasping for air. Monica spits water to her side, Dennis does the same. 'Sorry, little-un.'

'Got you worse.'

When they are coming out of the water, the four together, Monica continuing her relentless pestering of Dennis, she rugby tackles him in the shallows. 'Hey,' Dennis shouts, grabbing the waistband of his trunks fearing them accidently coming down with her attack.

'Enough,' says Mary, but nothing will stop Monica. When they are back on their feet, she slides her leg in between his as they walk on the sand. It might be judo; he certainly gets entangled. They tumble down together, sand sticking to their legs like pebble-dash. A coating on their still-wet skin.

'I need to get this sand off me,' says Dennis.

'Yeah, me too.'

Mary and Babs walk back to the towels and mats, mother and lecturer. Mary's boyfriend but Dennis is reluctant to let that designation take a hold in his mind. He and Monica splash water on themselves in order to wash off the sand. Then she starts to splash him, face, hair, everywhere.

'You make a shit day great, Monica. Do you know that?' As he is saying it, she jumps into him. Hugs family-friend Dennis on

Charmouth sands.

On the way back to the group, Monica keeps pawing his back, no longer fighting. As they join the rest of the party, he sees Stephen is here. An old friend but no longer a close one.

'Dennis is the only one still young enough for me to play with,' declares Monica.

Her mother raises an eyebrow as Dennis sits next to his old friend, the new arrival. 'Leave her alone, Dennis,' he says. 'She's still at school.'

* * *

The gathering has moved from the beach to Morgan Crescent. The back garden of the bungalow which Emma and Monica Bredbury share, Stephen will spend the night in, and Mary and Paul avoid through their hotel arrangement. All who were at the beach enjoy a barbecue, plus a few more family friends. Stephen is chief burger-flipper and Dennis assists. Margerine on buns. The garden is small and there are eleven assorted chairs out. Stephen whispers to Dennis that his mother invited Mr and Mrs Binding—their ageing neighbours—only because it is they who have loaned most of the outdoor seating. 'We've only three garden chairs of our own. Never needed a fourth because Monica doesn't sit still for two seconds.'

'The year-round rip-rap,' laughs Dennis.

Paul Stephenson comes between them, takes the prongs and the stainless-steel turner from Stephen's hands. 'Not too near the centre, they'll dry out.' He shuffles burgers up the cooking grate. 'You two go and mingle, I've got this.'

Stephen shrugs, seems to have no interest in the man who dates his sister. Takes a seat next to the elderly Bindings. Dennis continues to halve and put spread on the expectant buns. 'This family is a little different from your own,' he says to the lecturer. The hint of a question in his intonation.

'A little,' says Paul. 'Poorer is the one I think you're implying. My family live very comfortably, I'll be the first to admit it. My mother particularly. She's the only one left in the family home.' Dennis looks at him, has no idea about the man's family while this difference comes as no surprise. 'Oxshott, do you know it?'

Dennis does not, has never heard of the place.

'Born and brought up there; however, I've long moved on. Live in Epsom, myself.'

'You've been married,' says Dennis.

'Yes. Sadly, yes. That didn't work out. My ex-wife is no scientist and I think that became a gulf between us.'

'Mary said you've parted on good terms. Get along.'

'Thankfully. We have to, you see. We've little Sophie to bring up.'

Dennis is surprised to hear that a child is in the mix. 'Have Mary and Sophie met?'

'All in good time. I don't want to confuse her.'

'Mary is not easily confused, Paul. In fact, she'll be far more puzzled as to why you haven't told her before now. You've been going out for months.' Dennis feels incredulity at this new twist.

'Confuse Sophie. I don't wish to confuse my young child. Mary knows. Of course, she knows. No secrets between Mary and I. Little Sophie only starts school next month. And I'm quite certain Sophie will adore Mary as much as I, when the time is right to introduce them.'

Dennis stands open-mouthed, taking in the complexity of dating somebody who already has a family, a child with another.

'I understand you were close to Mary for a time, before she left for university. Please trust me to do the right thing by her. There is an age difference, one or two in the physics department have raised an eyebrow at it. Mary and I are entirely honest with each other. It is the only way our pairing up will work. Float on the water, I think you hippies say.'

Dennis lets this sink in. He jumped the gun with his accusatory tone. This feels like a lecture which Dennis hardly needs. Paul can't help himself one might assume. Dennis won't argue, has yet to find any warmth for the man he is not arguing with. He wonders if Mary is honest with Paul Stephenson. Can't see what common ground she could ever find with him. She may want children one day—Dennis is adamant he does not; another reason to remain celibate—and if she does or doesn't, she is way too young. Teenagers are children, Mary is a year away from shedding that designation. 'Mary is kind of like family to me.' As he says it, he is unsure if his words are a challenge or an olive branch.

'Yes. She told me a little about you. It must have been hard. And I remember the wider case. Twelve in this country, I believe.'

Shit. This is not a conversation Dennis wishes to have with Mary's boyfriend. Her stiff old-man boyfriend who he'd rather she didn't have. A physics student of her own age he could tolerate, he is sure he would feel differently. And twelve was not the number. It is the number reported on the first morning when his own parents still lay deceased in number three Croft Road, unknown even to young Dennis. Another couple in Hampshire were found two days later still.

'Did she tell you about my parties? I could have one tomorrow. For you. For you and Mary. I like throwing parties.'

'She did tell me about them. It's kind of you to offer, Dennis; however, I am not...' He emits a small laugh, as if for himself alone. '...the pot-smoking lecturer you might wish me to be. I know a few, it simply isn't me.'

Dennis never thought this well-built mannequin smoked pot. He was offering an evening of rock music without Emma Bredbury watching their every move. Not dope. He has given up the stuff.

* * *

When everybody has a burger in their hand, Dennis approaches Mary. 'Did Paul tell you I'm throwing you both a party?'

'Sweet of you Dennis, I just don't think Paul is quite the sort for...'

'He didn't say no. And it can be your family, plus the locals. Tomorrow, no time for the old die-hards to even hear about it.'

'Thompson always hears.'

'Not if we don't tell him.'

'By my family?' says Mary. 'Do you mean Mum as well.'

'I meant Monica now she's old enough. Not your mum, she might be even older than your boyfriend.'

Mary punches him on the shoulder. Playful. Puts the last piece of burger in her mouth and takes hold of his ears. 'You can be so annoying,' she says, shaking his head from side to side. Then she rubs her nose against his, the Eskimo-style greeting. 'Annoying,' she says in his ear.

'Honestly, Mary,' says her mother from a nearby chair, 'you can be as childish as Monica sometimes.'

Dennis doesn't mind. He has enjoyed having the two sisters grapple with him today.

7.

He thinks it was Monica who put the Laughing Llamas on the turntable. Likely she doesn't know what a bunch of shits they are. Monica never met Jimmy Crook and he is no longer welcome in the house. Dennis wouldn't let his mates in—if they turned up—either.

The Flophouse Years

Not that it is going to happen. Not since Carlsen, the Llamas' lead singer, left the world by a similar rout to Annabel. Took too much of some hallucinogenic drug or other for body and soul to simultaneously take on board. Dennis read the story in the paper, never saw the coroner's report. Felt little, his allegiance to the band long severed. He likes Monica's innocence about all that. She's wearing a pretty blue dress, floral. It suits her well. He can appreciate it while Crook would just be trying to take it off her. Get at the flesh.

'Go lightly on the cider,' he tells her and the young girl gives him a look of disdain. 'Your dress looks great. You've got good taste, Mon.'

'It's just a hand-me-down. I get all Mary's cast-offs.'

Mary and Paul are sitting on a futon. He holds a tin of beer, a cigarette. Pretending to be at ease, as Dennis sees it. He whispers in Monica's ear, 'What do you reckon to him now?'

'When we were window shopping in Lyme, he asked me if I needed anything. The toffee-nosed cheek of it! I'm not a charity case, never will be.'

'That's true, little chicken. You've a hell of a lot more gumption than Stephen. Mary too, I'm starting to think.'

'Aw, Dennis, it's nice of you to say that—probably—don't be mean about Mary. You should have gone out with her properly when she was still living here. I'd rather have you in the family than that walking quadratic equation.'

'Mary is terrific, Mon. And the boffins at every university in the land would see that. How could I ever compete? Good luck to her if he makes her happy. I want what's best for Mary. Nothing more.'

* * *

The doorbell rings and Monica hurries to the door. 'Come in, come in,' she says, a congenial host although Dennis is certain she doesn't know the new arrivals. Jane and Claire come into the room; the latter has not been in the flophouse since a couple of early parties. He mentioned this one to Jane while he was at work this morning, during a phone call about a new resident at Plaza Court. When Jane said, 'Yes, we would love to come,' he was surprised and delighted. Jane continues to take an interest in him, said she'll help him apply for the social work course when he's ready. 'You'll not get out of that place if you're not qualified. You have to think much wider than Plaza Court, Dennis.'

He will go back to night classes in September. He's decided it's the thing to do. Could get himself to university like Mary's done if he plays his hand right.

The two women have dressed casually. Claire in pink shorts and a white tennis shirt, Jane wears cut-off jeans, a light blue blouse with so many buttons undone, only the thinnest neck-scarf keeps her from being a scandal.

'Welcome,' he says, and each peck him lightly on the cheek. After introducing Monica, who beams back at them, he takes them to the couple for whom he is throwing the party. 'Do you remember Mary?' he asks.

'I couldn't forget her,' says Claire. 'She looked as gorgeous all those years ago as she does today.'

Mary blushes at the kind words and Jane laughs. 'She may not want your old lesbian compliments,' she scolds.

'Do you remember us?' says Claire to Mary.

'You're Jane,' she says. 'Dennis has told me lots about you. Talks about you all the time.' Dennis thinks this is an exaggeration. And Mary has muddled up her lesbians.

'I'm Claire, this is Jane.' She tugs her friend around the waist. 'Do you remember me from the party...' She looks up in thought to the ceiling. '...three summers ago, I think?'

Now Mary looks down, blushing still. 'I do remember you. Very daring. You spent the entire party wearing nothing much at all. Just a see-through waterproof. Gosh, you were daring.'

Claire erupts in laughter, Jane too. 'I'm afraid I didn't make the impression on you that you made on me, pretty girl. It was someone else walking around starkers, not I.'

'Heavens, I'm so sorry.'

'For what? I might pretend it was me next time. It must be quite the party piece. With that on the cv, I could find myself buried in invitations.'

Dennis whispers the order of events to Monica, as best he can recall. 'Mary must have drunk a few that night, Mon. Remembers all the facts and none of the faces.'

She nudges him in the shoulder, the quickest glance at Paul, next to Mary. Dennis sees that his eyes have narrowed, studying his girlfriend as if this conversation has been the greatest revelation. A kid misremembering a wild party: nothing wrong with it by Dennis's reckoning, being out of it was part of the fun.

* * *

The Flophouse Years

A little later—Mary and Monica both dancing mesmerically to The Browns latest record—Jane sits beside Paul on the futon, Dennis stands a little behind, eavesdropping.

'Mary has told me about you before,' he hears the lecturer say. It surprises him that she might have. Jane is his friend, not Mary's. 'We're both very broadminded,' he boasts. 'London ways. And my old mentor Jean Fletcher has been a life-long dyke. Not that Mary knows her; the old bird's long retired.' Jane struggles to get a word in, he goes on and on without so much as a pause for breath. 'You see, there's no prejudice in science. None whatsoever. Anyone who's capable will always get a fair hearing. I've long advocated for more girls on the courses. It's a shame not to tap their talents. I understand feminism, even if I don't look the part. And Jean Fletcher was way ahead of me; renowned physicist before I'd started prep school, I do believe. And she wasn't just a trailblazing woman, she was one of your own bent.'

Dennis senses that Jane is getting a little cross with him. The terms he uses sound derogatory although he claims to be open-minded. And she still keeps her sexuality under wraps at Dorset Social Services, Imperial College must be the more forgiving workplace.

* * *

He has only gone upstairs to use the toilet, when he emerges, Monica is waiting for him.

'Talk to me,' she demands.

'What's up, kipper?'

'You've had loads of these haven't you?' She opens Dennis's bedroom door and steps inside.

He follows, her lively company has become easier than Mary's now older sister is encumbered. And it is his room. 'I stopped...after everything that happened. The terrible stuff with Annabel; it could never be the same. We had some really great times before all that derailed me.'

'I didn't believe Mary when she said a girl was in the nude all through one of your parties...'

'Oh, that was one weird hippy girl, Monica. There were loads of weird ones actually. Always someone doing something mental. Happened every month. I don't know where all the hippies have gone.'

'Was she taking drugs? The one who got all naked: showed everyone the lot. Tits and blow-hole.'

'I don't think so. Not first off, anyhow. Wine or Bacardi, I expect.

And she liked getting her clothes off. Being freer and easier than the rest of us. It was her thing.'

'I couldn't do that, not in front of Mr Moneybags. I wouldn't mind if it was just you looking, Dennis.'

'Steady on,' he says, stepping into her to put a reassuring hand on her shoulder, not wanting to upset or encourage. Maybe the girl misinterprets, she grabs hold of his hand and pulls it down to her own breast, trying to spread his fingers upon her. 'Whoa, Mary,' says Dennis.

She swipes his cheek firmly with her hand. A stinging slap. 'It's Monica.'

'Sorry, Mon.'

She pushes him backwards on the bed; Dennis falls and she climbs on top of him, a leg each side of his prostrate torso. 'I'm Monica.'

'Sorry, sorry, sorry,' he implores. He tries to struggle upright, puts his arms around her, pulls her back close, holding her too tightly for Monica to move. Stops her from doing worse to him. 'Stay still, sweet girl. You've had more cider than I advised. I love you like a sister and you really need to find a better boy than me for all that. Specifically, a younger boy.'

He releases his grip a little and Monica pushes his hand onto her thigh, dress ridden up. 'A Dorset brother and sister, Dennis. We can make out if we want to. Our county, our rules.'

He laughs out loud. 'No, no, no.' She's quite a girl; his cheek still smarts and he suspects she was justified. 'No, no, no.'

From her position on top of him, Monica manages an inexpert kiss upon Dennis's lips. He closes his own. Feels her tongue but will not let it in. 'Mary said you were off girls but this is me your resisting Den. I don't get you.'

He rolls her aside, a firm hand preventing her from falling off the bed altogether. 'But resist you, I will.' He wraps his arms around her slender body and just as quickly releases them. 'I will.'

She looks at him through narrowed eyes. 'I don't get you at all. Why don't you punch out Moneybags, get Mary if you want her that badly. If you don't want me.'

'Of course, I want you, Monica, gorgeous girl. You ought to have spotted by now that I'm not boyfriend material. I don't want you to want me. I'll just keep saying it: you can do better. An awful of a lot better than me. You must. Got to have yourself a normal life, Monica.'

* * *

He and Mary have put their heads together but neither has the first idea how Thompson found out about the party. It is a select gathering, only twenty-five in the house. Fewer than half the number he drew in the old days. When he starts rolling his customary smokes, the glances around the room are extraordinary. Mary puffed on joints once or twice; he thinks she stopped as abruptly as he when Annabel died. His abstinence has extended to most types of fun until Monica started spicing things up these last couple of days. He is bemused by her, remembers not taking advantage of Mary when she was a similar age. Funny that he has to pull off the same stunt.

Claire tells Thompson she'd like to share the joint; Jane looks simultaneously shocked and amused. Monica is calmer now. Made up with Dennis and no one but the pair know they were rolling around on his bed, whatever the reasons for either's participation. She says a pull on the pot would be 'educational' and Stephen cannot possibly police her. Might have had a sneaky one of his own before Thompson even arrived.

Paul Stephenson walks up to Dennis. 'Mary said the police sometimes turn up at your parties,' he hisses.

'Relax.' Dennis feels like the adult in this exchange. 'No police at this tame affair. It must help lecturers relate to students, getting a little stoned now and again.' The man walks away as if the observation has gone unheard.

Just six sit cross-legged on the floor passing round the spliff. Dennis sits directly behind Monica, not joining in. 'Two puffs max. Absolutely no more,' he tells her. On the second she leans back into his waiting arms, turns her head and kisses him on the lips.

'Watch it,' Mary tells him. 'She's trouble.'

8.

'Pssst,' hisses Monica.

She stands inside her hotel room, he on the corridor; through the minimally opened door, he sees her. She wears a fine beige dress, cut perfectly for her slim figure. Shimmering beige, a new colour which God has granted the county of Surrey. Within this finery she looks truly amazing. Dennis has been thinking that since lunchtime, thinking Monica Bredbury looks edible-gorgeous. Thoughts he usually savours only in the confinement of three Croft Road. Nights alone in the former flophouse. It is barely evening and the notion—

the sight of her restless beauty—has taken up residence in his head. Monica is one on her own.

'They've all gone. You've to help me get out of this dress.'

'Monica, where's your mother?'

'All gone for cocktails. What is a fucking cocktail?'

'Can you manage it without me, please?'

'No. This thing is made to fit like a second skin. I think you're going to need a paring knife.'

Against his better judgement he follows the beautiful bridesmaid into her bedroom, will help with the disrobing as discreetly as he can, although carnal thoughts of Monica Bredbury are at every junction in his brain. Mary wed and this one not. And Monica still likes him for all the funny year they've had. He's pushed her away about four times. She's too young, he's too old. She's too clever, he's too stupid. It's a hard act: wants her like chips need vinegar.

Inside her room he tells her that she looked nicer than the bride, worries it is wrong on many levels but Monica dismisses it. 'I don't. Mary looked brilliant, amazing. You just hate the big stiff post-box she's gotten married to.'

'You're a very clever girl, you know that?' he says as he unzips the back of her dress. 'Brilliant looking and clever. Quite a combination, irresistible but for my sworn celibacy. I should go now.'

'No. Stay. I've got jeans for the reception. I want to be the cheapest dressed at the ball. The ugly sister.'

Dennis tries to look away as the young girl shimmies her way out of the dress. Leaves the million-pound creation crumpled on the hotel room floor and walks to her wardrobe wearing only underwear. White knickers, a low-cut bra that would attract any man's eye. Does for Dennis. Nothing ugly on an inch of this sister. Of her or Mary, but the latter is, as of earlier this afternoon, joined in matrimony to her boyfriend of eighteen months. A Bredbury no longer: she is Mary Stephenson.

'The chambermaids hung all my clothes up. Can you believe that? Taken them from my suitcase, everything put over a hanger. I never thought to bother.'

'Mine too. It's the gold-star service.'

For the second time in his life, Paul Stephenson is holding his wedding reception in the Eastern Hills Country Hotel. There are a select few staying the night. When Mary told Dennis that he was to be one of them, it took a retelling for him to believe it. Realised then that she really does have a lot of sway with her former tutor. He hasn't marked her work in the past year and will not in her final year at Imperial either. 'Marrying teacher gets you a change of tutor group,' Mary told Dennis. This celebration is costing a fortune, far more than Paul could siphon from an academic's salary. It is the consequence of money that has been stuck to the Stephenson clan for generations.

'He's family now,' he tells her as Monica pulls her jeans up over her white knickers. He remembers to look away too late, she has seen him looking at her where he should not. Looking at the tan of her legs and arms and stomach.

'For the time being,' she says.

'You think it won't last?'

'Mary isn't about money, Den. I've no idea what she's doing.'

'There was no money for her in Charmouth. She might be getting a taste for it these days.'

'Has she changed that much?'

'I hope not, Mon. I don't know her so well now. We hardly talk.'

'You and I do, Den. We talk all the time.'

'Yeah. And you've one more year and then you'll be following her, leaving Charmouth. It's a tin-pot town, can't contain the likes of you and Mary. Just right for me, and I'm pleased you'll get to university.'

'A girl's got to study but I don't think that makes me the same as Mary,' she says, ducking her head. A smile for Dennis through her falling hair.

'No. You do your own thing.'

Monica has a denim shirt in her hand, she slips her hands through the sleeves and then does up a couple of the metal buttons. Just a random pair out of about eight. The shimmering white of her bra is visible from above and below. 'Too much?' she says.

'You need to cover up a bit more, Mon. If only to keep my hands off you.'

'I'm not trying to keep your hands off me, Mr All-Talk. Are you staying in your suit?'

'I thought that was the done thing.'

'Not if you're going to be my date for the evening. Let's go to your room, find your cheapest, plainest clothing. You've got to sink down to Monica Bredbury's standard of scruffiness tonight, Dennis. Mary's been taken off display.'

'Dress like you? Everyone else will be in fine lace and sparkling tiaras.'

'Yeah. Mum's loving that shit.'

His room is only two doors along the corridor, Monica comes in with him and he cannot stop her. He followed her own disrobing with interest. Couldn't hide it. Dennis has not brought much to choose from. The girl digs jeans out of his holdall, a checked shirt. 'Cowboy clothes,' she says, 'these should offend the in-laws.'

'Look away,' says Dennis as he turns to change.

She turns her neck and he lowers his trousers but when he is standing on one leg to remove them completely, she rugby tackles him. Knocks him sprawling onto the bed. Brushes her hands inside his unbuttoned shirt. 'Your face!' she says. 'I'd hate this wedding if you weren't here, Den.'

He doesn't say it but the feeling is mutual. And he might need to start lifting weights. This kid would beat him in a fight.

* * *

Dennis and Monica stay close to each other through the reception. His eyes were upon her more than they were on Mary even back in church. At the meal too, where they sat at separate tables, briefly followed the plan. Dennis struggles to relax in the pomp of the country hotel. Monica ignores the grandeur, laughs about the stupidity of waiters serving with deference when they should be necking the drinks; says it's what she would do if she suffered the humiliation of so menial a job.

'I wish you'd been at a few more flophouse parties, Mon,' he tells her. 'No waiters or champagne.'

'Sounds tonnes better. And a naked hippy would brighten up this stiff affair.'

'No, Mon, don't do that.' Both laugh as she gestures unbuckling her belt. 'The hippy parties are over,' he says, a little relieved when he sees her tighten the belt back up. He leans in and pecks her cheek and Monica turns, briefly lets their lips share the kiss. He wonders if even that is wrong here: Paul and Mary's wedding reception has not a sliver of hippiedom about it. It's the antidote. Stephensons and hangers-on have come dressed in tuxedos and cummerbunds, long evening gowns. Mary's dress is exquisite and she looks as if she belongs in it. Lilac in colour, cut to amplify the swelling of her young breasts, drawn in at her narrow waist. Dennis can see that she is beautiful while feeling far more drawn to Monica in the jeans. The wild child. Excepting Mary, the guests from the Bredbury side are dressed more plainly, less obviously moneyed. Dirt poor in one or two cases. Only Monica and Dennis defy the dress code entirely. Scruff it out. Waiters criss-cross the floor so gracefully their steps meld into the appearance of a glide. Holding trays abundant with glasses of red and white wine, from which they encourage guests to help themselves.

'Rude not to,' says Dennis.

'Drink the buggers dry,' says Monica.

In the hotel bedroom, before he'd even got his trousers on, Monica extracted a promise that Dennis would dance exclusively with her. 'One with Mary,' her only concession. Now they are here, the music is shit. There is a band—live music—but they are no better than the dross which washes up on council bandstands across the West Country every Sunday afternoon. Mostly brass, a little percussion, a clarinet. No point in putting in requests here. Not for the Llamas or Templeton Ca. They play dance tunes from Mary's mother's era. Some friends of the groom dance the Charleston. It is ridiculous. Emma Bredbury, Mary and Monica's mother, whose era the music hails from, beams around the room, even shares a dance with Paul Stephenson. Monica nudges Dennis; 'The happy couple,' she says, unaware that Mary is standing behind her. Dennis grins from ear to ear as the bride gives her little sister a cuff on the side of the head. Monica never stops laughing.

He tries to dance with Mary to the rubbish music. Holds her as if they are waltzing although he cannot pull it off. Always a hippy. He tells her that he wants her to be happy. She will be a great wife; Stephenson is the luckiest man in the world. When he says, 'What do you make of Sophie,' he feels Mary tense up in his arms.

'She's a brat, not so hard to outsmart really.'

The reply worries him. It isn't in the parenting manual and he has come to think no one should be let loose on kids without training. Learning how not to fuck it up. He will do the social work course if and when he manages to attain the two 'A' levels needed. Jane Taylor extracted the promise from him and Monica has told him to stop prevaricating. But parenting is a hell of a responsibility, the more he looks back on his own childhood the more he sees it. It could be more demanding than being the social worker he is aspiring towards. Twenty-four hours of every day. His parents weren't up to the mark, shouldn't have been allowed to procreate, to have him. Chasing fucking spaceships.

When he is back with Monica, she dances like a hippy. No

dancehall nonsense from her. He pulls her into a hug that is not a dance move at all, felt moved to do it regardless. Holds her close and squeezes. She returns the affection and as he glances over her shoulder, he sees her mother staring at them, a disapproving look on her face. He is only six years older than this live wire. What has Paul got besides the money to pay for her own daughter's wedding, and that should feel bad not good. Or they should have held the reception in the flophouse. If he ever gets married, it will be good enough for him. He looks into Monica's eyes. She smiles back, an arm around the back of the head and a kiss upon the lips. Cares not a jot what her mother thinks. Dennis's date for the evening, she has made that more than clear.

* * *

He thinks they are all bursting from the earlier meal, and still waiters take trays of batch buns crammed with roast pork and apple sauce from person to person. The smell of the hog roast wafting in from the courtyard. Dennis is chatting with Babs. She has told him of her fear of the taxi fare she must foot at the end of the evening, unsure exactly how far it is from here to Leatherhead where she has booked herself into a small bed and breakfast.

'You'll be staying here!' she says, incredulous and envious of his forthcoming night in the resplendent hotel.

'I probably won't sleep. This is really not my thing, is it? They let people stay but it's not a proper flophouse.' As he is saying it his eyes are exclusively for Monica. She's on the dancefloor, breaking her vow to dance only with him, taking a short spin with the tiniest one in the room. Sophie who would be in bed by now, concession granted for the opportunity—which few small children get—to attend her parents' wedding. If a stepmother is truly a parent. He sees that Sophie and Monica talk more than they dance; her auntie tactile and all smiles with the child. Odd, thinks Dennis, he hasn't seen Mary exchange a word with the girl who is to be a fixture in her household. Monica taking a greater interest, forging a bond.

'Do you want to dance?' asks Babs.

'Do you mind if I don't?' Eyes still upon Monica, the girl in the jeans, hair undone now, all over the place and attracting his gaze to an extent which gives him to think he might be being rude to Babs. 'They've not been playing my kind of music at this do.'

She doesn't mind, gives his upper arm a squeeze. 'I saw you dancing a bit with Mary's little sister.'

Dennis smiles apologetically. 'She's a character.'

*　*　*

'What's she like?' Dennis asks Monica.

'Paul's mother? I've not talked to her since the meal. Posh. Normal underneath, I guess...'

'No. His little daughter.'

'Sophie's cute. Spoilt and cute. It's all about what's been done to them at that age. The hand on the tiller.'

'Do you think Mary will like her?'

'I should bloody hope so, Den.'

Emma Bredbury is coming past them. Monica makes a show of taking Dennis's face in her two hands, kissing him upon the lips. She has drunk quite a bit, not evident when they were talking about the youngster, but this is a bit unprecedented. Provocative. Dennis likes the feel of her tongue while fearing her mother's scorn.

'Don't make a spectacle of yourself, Monica.'

'Older?' laughs the daughter. 'Should I go older?' She gestures the well-dressed guests, some upon chairs, others stood by the walls and four or five on the dancefloor still making motions intended to complement the bland music which drones on and on. 'Find myself a professor?'

'It's a lovely reception, Monica. No need to bring the tone down.'

On her final word, Emma Bredbury hiccoughs. Dennis and Monica cannot help themselves from laughing. The involuntary squark that the pontificating one has made.

'Mum,' says Monica, finding a warmth in her tone that was not there before, 'this is Dennis we're talking about. The honorary Bredbury. We all love him and Mary's not allowed to kiss him anymore, so I have to.' She pecks his cheek this time, as if to prove a point.

'I'm just happy for Mary,' says Dennis. He has not spoken anything but politeness to Mrs Bredbury all day. And this is more of the same. Dross. He feels an absurd range of things towards her older daughter, resignation may be top of the pile. Not a jot of warmth towards the man whose family money is paying for this. He expected Annabel to move back to Rhode Island sooner or later, couldn't take the way her departure came about. But it was Mary-gone-to-London who changed the landscape. He hopes she will be happy, knows there will be no return to Charmouth for her. He would like Mary happy, could see why a clever girl might wish to study at an elite university. Feels no optimism about her chances of a happy marriage. It is beyond him; Dennis can't understand the match at all. It might be worse than had she taken up with him, and the chance of that is a ship long sailed. Emma seems overjoyed with the wedding, the man she has snagged, and it has made him reappraise her a little less favourably.

'Doesn't she look a peach,' she says, waving a hand in the direction of her eldest daughter, now ensconced in conversation with Babs.

He nods. Cannot fault the observation, turns his eyes straight back to the plainly attired Monica.

* * *

The bride and groom are on the floor for a slow dance. It is that time in the evening. Monica insists on taking Dennis up for a smooch and he cannot resist her. Thoughts of placing hands around her waist, holding her close, have overtaken him. Won.

An old man neither can name, whom they speculate to be an uncle of Paul Stephenson's or similar, dances with Monica's mother and the girl whispers, 'I hope she's finally getting off with someone.' Doesn't whisper it quietly enough and Dennis splutters laughter at the stares her coarse comment draws from those close by.

They have been glugging back the wine more than most. Dennis notices that his hands have strayed to the denim of Monica's bottom.

'Sorry,' he whispers into her ear, as he raises them up.

'Grope away,' she says, 'it's the best bit of the wedding.' Again, her volume knob is stuck up high; people are looking at them.

'Come on,' says Dennis, an arm around the girl's waist and walking her off the dancefloor before both fall over or make fools of themselves beyond anything Mary might forgive. He and his pseudo-date slide themselves down onto one of two sofas in a dark alcove off the main reception hall. Monica once more embraces him, kisses him with a little drunken passion. A cough comes from sofa number two.

'Hiya,' says Monica. 'Where do you fit in?' She addresses an older couple of whom the lady's cough was timed to curtail the necking. Dennis is certain Mary introduced them earlier, he never took in who was who on the Stephenson side. A sister of Paul's maybe. They are sitting quietly on the sofa, not kissing, fumbling or taking the liberties that Monica does and Dennis feels no wish to curtail.

'I could ask the same of you except you look just like her. It's easy to tell.'

'No, I don't,' says Monica, an enormous smile on her face. 'I'm the scruffy one in jeans, aren't I? Nothing like my big married sister.'

'I'm sorry,' says Dennis. 'This is Monica and I'm Dennis. I've forgotten your names. Awful of me.'

'Sarah,' she replies, 'and my husband Philip.'

'His sister, right?'

'Paul's sister. That is correct.'

'Oh,' says Monica. 'You were here for the last one, I guess. When Paul married wife number one.'

Dennis tries to glare at her, this could be a most inappropriate conversation. Might go anywhere with Monica as liquored up as she has been for hours.

'I was. We were.'

'Do you think this one will last any longer?' Monica cannot help bursting into giggles in the saying of it.

'I'd thank you not to take the matter lightly. None in the Stephenson family enjoyed the divorce, young Monica. I do hope he has made a wise choice with your sister...' Dennis feels the same as Monica, exercises a little more self-control. The girl laughs openly at her something-in-law's pontification. 'Thankfully Mary seems more mature than you, young lady.'

'We're sorry,' says Dennis. 'She doesn't mean anything by it. We're only laughing because we've drunk so much of the good wine.'

'Yes. Drunk far too much of it, that's plain to see.' The groom's sister is not in party mood. Not the mood required for a flophouse party at least.

'Back on the dance floor, Denny,' declares Monica. She stands and pulls him up from the sofa. He sees Philip, the husband, grin. Gives a quick wink to the pair of them, wife excluded from the conciliatory gesture.

* * *

It's getting late and the pair have knocked back more than anyone else at this high-class wedding reception. Enacted a quasi-hippy party concurrent with the posher wedding that neither think is a suitable send off for Mary.

'I'm drowning drunk, Den. Make sure I find the right room,' says Monica.

He does as she asks, and once they are on the bedroom corridor, still to fetch door keys from pockets, she turns on him, kisses him still more passionately than she did on the dancefloor. Pushes a hand inside his chequered shirt, button skittering off to the floor as she grapples. He cannot resist her. Knows he should. Cannot. A year of looking; he likes how much she likes him. The wine plays the smallest part in it. He loves her with a healthy dose of lust in the mix.

Along the corridor, she pulls him into her room. No opposition from Dennis Harris. She found the room easily enough too.

'God that was hard work,' she says. 'Can you improve this day, please?'

He leans in and kisses her, feels the wetness of her lips on his, their tongues playing tag. 'I want to Monica. There are limits though.'

'Not for me,' she says pushing her hands back inside his opened cowboy shirt, feeling his flesh.

Dennis is entranced by the movement within her eager face. Eyes of green which shine lovingly. She kisses him, open-mouthed, hands lightly feeling his neck, his waist. Removes the blouse she wears. Kisses him again. He has doubts about the wisdom of staying, can only watch as she lowers her jeans. 'Denny, Denny, I'm not doing this alone,' she says, tugging demonstratively upon his belt.

'You're the best, Monica. You know that, don't you? But I can't...you know?'

'Can't? Still working, I take it?' She runs a hand up the front of the jeans Dennis has yet to remove.

'...but, Monica. Is this your first time?'

She leans in and kisses him again. 'Make it a good one,' she whispers in his ear.

'I can't be getting you pregnant, Mon...'

'I've brought a packet of three, Denny. You being so dilatory and everything. I'm with you on the best-not-get-pregnant thing. I'm not a stupid girl, I'm really not. Thought you'd have figured that much out, Den.'

She is anything but stupid. Monica Bredbury is everything he cannot resist. It is not the wine but the girl. Wine is nothing at all and she is a vivacious ball of intoxicating mischief. That it should happen now—an end to Dennis's chaste vigil for Annabel who he never truly knew—and happen so blissfully on Mary's wedding night, he couldn't have anticipated. And it is a surprise a year in the making. Dennis and Monica, careful and loving with each other between the fine linen sheets of the Eastern Hills Country Hotel.

The Flophouse Years

Chapter Seven

Good To Be Here

1.

Dennis is at university himself now. Finally getting qualified. He started one year later than Monica but that is not especially salient. Their fling didn't last. Jump-started him out of a rut though. Jump, rut, there is something funny about those terms in this context, he thinks. He has jumped and rutted with a couple of girls since and doesn't feel bad about it. Felt pretty good at the time, not that either turned out to be soulmates. They are the hardest things to find, aren't they? Even souls are slippery. Maybe we do, maybe we don't. He thought he was Mary's soulmate. Nowadays he wonders if it was simply a moment in time. She couldn't have been nicer to him when Annabel died: genuine, supportive, everything he needed when he was at rock bottom. Saw him passed that point. That he isn't the point of her life, he learnt long ago. Dennis expected her to find a better partner than he could ever be, and so she has. Big house in Surrey. He sees the lay of the land pretty clearly these days. Or thinks he does which might be the same thing.

Was he ever Annabel's soulmate? They certainly had a great deal in common. Themagin survivors. Never dared talk about it, of course. Hell of a stumbling block that. Whatever they shared, it was sunken so deep within each of them that it felt to be only a private burden. On his course, Trevor Bray—who is a big cheese in social work education—spent about twenty minutes talking about the elephant under the carpet. That every family has one. Dennis thought it was silly and meaningless until he spotted that he and Annabel lived exactly that way. Great big elephant obstructing windows and doors, blotting out the sunlight, and neither thought to mention its presence, suggest what might be done to let the light back in. Fed it on silence for months on end.

On a social work course, it seems nothing is to be swept away. Everything dwelt upon and learnt from. They all think talking is a cure-all. Right the wrongs of the past by blabbering on about them. In tutor group last week, a guy called Ewan went on and on about his mother being in hospital for a month while he was a child. Like it ruined his childhood, gave him nightmares. Trevor Bray praised his insight and he should know. Dennis isn't very good at it—personal disclosure, finding words for our darker feelings—he's a big fan of bottling it up. Mostly thinks it the wiser way; however, he won't be writing his chosen panacea in an essay. He's picked up the received wisdom in this place. The University of Exeter, Department of Applied Social Sciences.

He has a flask of coffee which he is drinking from as he thinks. Refills the little lid-beaker. Barely half a cup at a time. He still drinks instant with chicory. It's what his parents drank, a habit unbroken. First Mary and then Monica each told him it tasted disgusting. Wouldn't touch it. 'It's cheaper,' he told them. Monica laughed most at that. Said something clever about shit always undercutting caviar. Dennis said he never eats either so there's nothing in that lesson for him. He has only sat apart from the other students this lunchtime because he is supposed to be preparing a presentation. Can't quite concentrate today. He expects to wing it in the afternoon. When he has to give his talk. Mini-lecture they call them. His mind turns to Jane Taylor who he is seeing this evening. His unofficial mentor, that's how he thinks of her. Better than the official ones he has had so far. The placement he did in a nursery was great, except that the woman who supervised him was a nutjob. Another Lorraine Chadwick, different size and shape, same old steam engine for a brain.

Jane is a senior social worker these days. On a few occasions, and quietly—without a hint of distrust—she has reminded him to tell no one that she is a lesbian. Enjoys the company of women. Tell no one in Dorset Social Services Department, that is. Anyone who came to his parties would know, not that he throws them anymore.

Jane is worried that some senior managers might hold it against her. He can't see why they would, she's bloody good at her job. And Dennis isn't at all sure if Jane has enjoyed the company of women in the significant way the word lesbian implies since she and Claire split up. None of his business, of course; he doesn't pry. Never heard her say a word about a girlfriend since Claire, that's all.

Good To Be Here

Dennis often wonders if it's Jane's influence in the department that got him seconded onto this course. The county is spending a pretty penny on him. He suspects that the primary reason is sympathy: the council bigwigs have known about his parents—their suicides—since the day it happened. Day after, actually, same as Dennis. It was the Director of Social Services who agreed to keep the job open for him through his long absence. Plaza Court. Those days are a blur. Dennis is not terribly keen on this special power he has: the ability to elicit favours from others because they know his life has been shitter than theirs. He raised the concern with Jane. Asked her if he would still be shopping for groceries, bathing the old men in the flats, no secondment onto this social work course at all, if his parents had removed themselves from this life in a less newsworthy manner. Crashed the car or caught double pneumonia. 'Nothing can happen if the stuff that goes before it hasn't finished first,' she said. He thought it was a serious philosophical point for about ten minutes. She can be annoying as hell with that intellectual humour. Maybe he'll get her jokes quicker when he's qualified.

Jane doesn't play at senior social worker with him. Lets her guard down, they are true friends. She is in charge of about seven social workers as a day job. 'A worry of social workers,' she calls them. An apt term, he worries quite a bit himself. Doesn't know if he's really up to the job he's training for. Laughing about it makes it all feel lighter, more normal. He couldn't imagine a better unofficial mentor. He thinks he loves Jane but he doesn't fancy her. That's quite a funny way around.

Jane and Claire split up back in the autumn. One way or another he helped Jane over the break-up. Pleased to give something back, she was in pieces at the time. Moved into his spare room—the one his parents used to occupy—for about three weeks. Just while she sorted herself somewhere else to live. The flat in West Bay. He told her to stay as long as she wanted, laughed at the thought of the neighbours gossiping about him and an older woman again. Jane cried when he said it, and that surprised him for a minute. 'I'm not so old, Den,' she moaned. Sounded a bit self-pitying but if he thinks about it, he was a hundred times worse when Annabel did what she did. Exited stage left. Dennis saw straightaway that it was the break-up making her feel insecure. He gets basic psychology, it's the deeper stuff he can't fathom. Rejects. He was apologetic to Jane, told her how good she looks. That got her laughing through tears. 'Yeah, yeah, smooth talk can't change a zebra's stripes.'

He meant it when he told Jane she could stay but living alone suits him best. Likes his meditative time. They got on well in those three weeks because Jane's a bit the same way. Dennis got along all right with Claire back when she and Jane were an item. Two pals in a house share as far as the wider world was concerned. Liked her when he met her which must have been five or six times; and then Jane's stories during those three weeks made her sound like hard work. Hysterical. And worst of all, she carried on with another woman behind Jane's back. Whatever support Dennis was to Jane, it is the tiniest recompense for all she has done for him. Helped him to see beyond Plaza Court. She planted a seed long ago. Sometimes they would go months without meeting, it was as if she watered that little seed whenever they chanced upon each other. Met at work or she and Claire dropping into one of his parties. After Mary went up to university, Jane called in once or twice. It was like she knew what he had lost. Teased him about Monica too. Called her 'the sixth former' but listened when he explained it. Monica was actually the grown-up in their brief relationship, Dennis could see that from start to finish. And Jane has a stash of funny social work stories. It might be those which persuaded him to do this. Move on from Plaza Court after nine years at the place. She'll listen if he wants to sound off about the essays he has to write. Dennis finds them a challenge. 'Better problems than navigating that old witch, Lorraine Chadwick, don't you think?' She has said that more than once. Nail on the head: hard to say why it took him so long to see it.

He puts the top back on his flask. It's time to go back inside. The presentation has to be ten minutes long, that's a lot of talking. His heart thumps with thinking about it. The whole student body will be in there. Social work students, not the ones doing maths or geography. They wouldn't get it. Happens this time each week: two different students have a go at talking through something or other in front of all the others. It makes them research whatever topic they are given but Dennis is rubbish at that. Finds his own thoughts get in the way of taking everything in. Standing up in front of so many people is nerve racking. Trying to make sure he talks sense when the faces of the people listening aren't easily scrutinised, that is some knack. Both streams will be in there: the clever students who already have degrees, and his lot who scrabbled around at night school to get on the course in the first place. About four lecturers in attendance too. His talk is to be about transference. It's not a topic he would have chosen. Given to him by Bray, the lecturer. Transference and counter-transference, the pitfalls of the counsellor: that's the long title. It's quite a slippery subject. He found a couple of textbooks that told him what it means but they were dense. Pretty hard to grasp. He isn't sure he has it straight in his own mind and now he has to let his mouth loose on it. He made a few rough notes, thought he understood what he'd read and later thought he didn't. Wing it. Most students do. Not the ones who already have degrees, just his crowd.

Dennis stands at the front of the room. Everybody else is behind the little wooden rails, their seats tiering up. It's like being on stage in a theatre. He always enjoys the feel of being in the main lecture hall. If he puts the task aside—his talk about transference—it's pretty hilarious. A kid playing at professor. Rows of students awaiting his wise words. The porridge between the ears could be the let-down. He knows he's no academic. Lucky to be at university at all, didn't get there through a route that the likes of Monica or Mary have trodden. His high-flying friends. Even Stephen is cleverer than him. Jane would tell him to stop overthinking it. She says he learnt stuff the rest of the world has yet to contemplate. He's not sure about that. If your parents kill themselves to fulfil the aim of their religious convictions, it makes you dwell on a few things that your average Joe might not pay a minute's thought to. Being one on your own isn't being clever, it's just the way it is. Jane doesn't go for men. Told him she's never spent the night, or even half an hour between the sheets, with one. He and she sat up and talked through the night a couple of times but no bed was involved and barely any physical contact. A platonic hug. It's women all the way for Jane. She chooses to keep it private—below the waterline—not that what she enjoys is illegal or wrong. Seems like very few of us wish to be stuck with a label saying 'different' pinned to our backs. Good things do not stem from it. Not in the social world, not by the looks of it. We like to pretend we are all the same although nobody else can be Dennis Harris, there is no other Jane Taylor. Do we fudge it? Act like we have more in common with each other than we truly do, just for safety's sake. He contemplates that for a moment. Is he transferring his own self-consciousness to Jane? Equating his Themagin parents with her minority sexual preference. Neither he nor she have a damned thing to be ashamed of and still his Auntie Jean's catchall phrase, 'It's a shame,' jumps into his mind. Fills the void. She says it when silence is a better fit. 'Shame you don't have a

The Flophouse Years

black tie, Dennis.' When he visited her and Uncle Stanley at Christmas—finally driving himself to Taunton after years and years of lifts—she was a pain in the arse while intending to be kind. 'You've done well, Dennis. A shame your parents aren't here to see it. You've done well, all things considered. A shame about them.' That stuff doesn't help at all. He's decided to miss them off the Christmas rounds next year. Family isn't everything.

It will be good to see Jane tonight. She told him recently that he is the only genuinely free and easy person she knows. Added, 'It's truer now than it was in your hippy days.' That gave him pause for thought. 'Anything goes at my parties,' was his old mantra. Now he is more circumspect. Gives drugs and even Pretty Major Thompson the widest of berths. Still tries hard never to be judgemental of others. Struggles with it when he thinks about the fucking morons who were once his parents. There is nothing he would change in Jane Taylor. She fears that more widespread knowledge of her lesbianism could hold back her career. He wanted to point out that his odd fate, orphaning by religious cult, seems to have been a leg up. Perhaps she has no need to keep any of it secret, although sympathy simply for being who you are is meaningless to the recipient. Dennis can't make head or tail of it. Life screws us up and still we get off the stool when the bell goes for round two. Three, four and five. Gets easier over time, the punches land less heavily.

Mad Lorraine Chadwick—who is still holding the fort at Plaza Court—doesn't have a clue about Jane. A year ago, she accused Dennis of having an affair with her. Bonkers. He and Jane laughed about it for weeks. He even raised it after her split with Claire. 'If you want to try a fella, just let me know.' She was funny; took him in her arms and gave him a kiss on the lips, then made a face like a slightly disgusted wine taster. 'No. Thanks for the offer, Den, but it's got to be a firm no.'

'Transference...' Dennis nods his head at the darkness in which he knows fifty or more faces watch and listen. Letting his introductory word hang in the air. '...it's a bit like feedback from an electric guitar. An odd noise that might get in the way of harmony between counsellor and client. We wish to hear our client's experience but our own is coming out of the speakers unintentionally. In all the best rock music...' He looks up from the notes he is not reading from. They were all drawn from textbooks, not his own thoughts on the matter. Not a word about rock music. '...the rough enhances the smooth.'

The students are paying attention. Young people like electric guitars. Dennis says a little that he has scripted. 'The client who describes, in session after session, the unsatisfactory relationship they endured with their father, their mother, some other significant person who let them down. They may unconsciously invest the counsellor with similar qualities to those they despised in the person they keep bringing to mind. And it is also true, that the counsellor can suffer a similar countertransference. The unconscious feelings that we harbour and which we prompt in each other are not just hard to know, they are nigh on impossible to know. Psychoanalysts—a profession to which I resolutely do not aspire—dedicate about half their week to receiving analysis. Seeking to ensure that they understand what their unconsciousness thinks. Don't you think it simply drives them mad? Analysing dreams makes palmistry sound smart...' This makes the room laugh. They know Trevor Bray, and a few other lecturers most likely, love all that drivel. No worries, Dennis has resolved to say what he thinks in preference to what others want to hear. Resolved to do so life-long. '...whatever you are feeling towards your client, let them know. Let them hear the feedback too. It is this undercurrent of fear— of do not disturb—that messes with the dynamic. Not the fact that we all prompt a reaction in each other. Trust them. They know you are not a machine. Wouldn't want you counselling them if you were.'

When he has finished his ten minutes, the room erupts in applause. Not that he is fooled by it. Dennis has applauded enough student presentations to know what the deal is. They are not simply polite with each other, they go the whole hog. Raise the roof for a mediocre talk in the hope of getting the same on their own day in the spotlight. He didn't mess up; it wasn't a total embarrassment. He worries that he forgot to say any of the stuff he read in the text-book. Teachers tend to rate that shit more highly than the personal ramblings Dennis goes in for. It could be a problem—this one goes toward the term mark—hopes he's scraped a pass.

A grey-haired tutor off the other course addresses the room. 'Does anybody have any questions for today's speaker?' He looks down at his notes before adding, 'For Dennis.'

Dammit, there's always this.

'Dennis,' says Trevor Bray, the psychology lecturer who set him the tricky topic in the first place, 'does it make a difference—in your view—if the counsellor has themselves suffered traumatic experiences, or not?'

He notices Greta—sitting in the front row—look around open

mouthed. In the first term, there was a session about mental health in which Dennis got upset, talked about his parents' suicides. Bray may know nothing about it, not connected him to the famous story. They say everything is confidential and Exeter University is not half as bad as Charmouth. It could be that the mental health tutor never told Bray about the hornets' nest on his shoulder. Dennis doesn't know either way. 'It probably makes a difference to how good a counsellor you are, just not in a simple fashion. As I see it, there aren't really any trauma-free people out there. It's only the measure on the Richter Scale that varies. If someone tells you their wife or their husband has been murdered, we would all think it must feel unbearable for them. Less so if it was only their cat killed in the road. They had to live through it, whatever it was. It genuinely upset them.' He stops at that. His mouth is having a bit of a day out on its own, any old codswallop might come sashaying out.

'But, Dennis,' Bray persists, 'wouldn't the more troubled counsellor feel encumbered by their past? It might prevent them from really tuning into what their client was saying.'

'If your wife or your husband was murdered that morning, I'd definitely cancel the counselling. But once you've cleared the decks, got over it, I don't see what difference it makes. We are who we are. Feeling ashamed about it doesn't help at all.'

* * *

'You gave a really good talk,' says Greta. She is a couple of years older than Dennis, worked in a kid's home before she came on the course. 'I could tell it was from the heart.' He likes her a lot but the tone of Greta's praise makes him uneasy. Preparation for a low mark. The phrase, from the heart, suggests that the brain didn't really pull its weight.

'I thought Bray was being an arse.'

'It's just his job, Dennis. He wants to put you on the spot, see if you're ideas stack up. We do it to the lecturers, time after time.'

'I wish we could have chosen our own topics for this one,' Dennis admits. 'I don't really get what transference is. Feelings are just a kind of splurge inside us, aren't they? Sorting out where they come from makes rocket science look easy.'

Greta laughs. 'If we don't understand our clients' feelings, how can we help them?'

Dennis takes a moment to answer. She makes sense and it might be why he's not sure if he will make a decent social worker. Often thinks he won't. 'Aren't we really just shepherding them to a point where it feels different. We need to hear when they tell us to stop. The idea that we are telling them how to feel about whatever crap they've gone through...' He doesn't articulate his own thought. It all sounds pretty oppressive to him, understanding the emotions of another. It's why he and Annabel never talked about it. All that Themagin stuff, too heavy by a large comet's weight. He did a bit of talking with Mary Bredbury; she asked how he was doing. Wanted him to say more even if he said he felt lousy. For a year or so she was brilliant, before going over to the dark side. Marriage: Mary Stephenson. And her secret gift was just listening. Not even telling him whether his mixed-up thoughts were right or wrong. He might have been feeling what anyone would who'd been through the same or he could have been a phone call away from wearing a straight-jacket. Mary paid him quiet attention, if she thought he was cuckoo, she never let on.

* * *

He gets on great with Greta but it begins and ends in Exeter. Within the walls of the university. She has never been to Charmouth, certainly not to Croft Road. He isn't sure exactly where she lives. A village with Bishop in its name. He asked about four times in their first couple of weeks on the course and he doesn't like to go over it again. Greta has a husband up there in Churlish Bishop, or Cherry-faced Bishop, whatever the name of her village is. When she talks about him, he sounds all right, although Greta not having a husband at all would suit Dennis better. He's a trainee solicitor which means he's clever. Dennis has no wish to meet the husband although doing so might knock a few of the thoughts he has about Greta out of his head. And his pants.

In the first week of university, they all participated in a lot of icebreakers. The heavy-duty, reveal-your-true-self stuff. Dennis was very self-conscious amongst near strangers—never mentioned the Themagins—but when a couple of guys started talking pot and LSD, he spotted that he was among the broad-minded. Would not be judged by the standards of his Auntie Jean. When he told a small group about his flophouse, the various oddballs who had stayed the night, they laughed at his anecdotes. All except Greta. That lunch hour she asked him to go with her to an off-site café. It felt like the prelude to a date. He had no inkling that she was wedded to a solicitor,

The Flophouse Years

they had learnt nothing of each other's backgrounds that early in the term.

In the café bar she was all questions. Tactile as well, put a hand upon his. On his cheek at one point, carefully eyeing him. Taking his measure.

'You are *the* Dennis Harris, aren't you?' she asked, before he had chance to ask her on the date that was on his mind.

He couldn't answer that one so easily. Guessed it was a yes—there isn't a Dennis Harris in Laughing Llamas or Templeton Ca.—never thought of himself as famous or even worth worrying about. It did bring back to him how, over eight years earlier, his name and story made local papers far beyond West Dorset. The entire South West was keen to claim a connection with the Themagin suicides. And it was only him and Dying Star and his mum, To the Ship, who linked that chain. Papers will always exploit a story that fascinates the public, Dennis figured that out at seventeen. Greta Walsh was the first person to raise it directly to him in a long time. In years. It was a unique tale, and many people might remember the story but not that detail. The name of the survivor. Dennis appreciated the privacy that she gave him to confirm her hunch. She was not for pointing a finger in class, it could have been the only reason she asked him to the café. She was concerned, wanted to hear how he had got on after all the hullabaloo had faded.

'I always worried that it would be impossible to live with,' she said, 'but you've done well.' That was a nice thing to say although he always doubts if he actually has. And her follow-up questions and comments suggested she shared them, shared his doubts. 'Was your flophouse wise at all, Dennis? Interesting characters dropped in and quite a few crazies by the sound of it.'

'The thing is,' Dennis told her, emboldened by her evident pre-knowledge, 'my parents did all that wife-swapping crap—screwing on the living room floor—as preparation for life on the spacecraft in the great hereafter. All the crazies that came after were pretty small beer.'

Greta took his hand in hers. 'Dennis, Dennis, I see that. But you come across as such a sensitive soul. And you're only really describing being unable to differentiate between people. See who's okay and who's trouble. It must have made you so vulnerable.'

He glanced her up and down, feeling grateful that she had singled him out. Her worries he could explain away. Greta has an energy and strength about her. Broad of shoulder, they are thin, bony. Her hair clings all around her skull, not curly, many wayward kinks framing her face. A dark complexion, not a borrowed tan: her own grainy and life-drawn skin. Dennis wanted to touch it, kiss it. Felt a little nervous to try. A new course—the unlikely university student that he was—far from certain he fitted in.

'It isn't really like that,' he said. 'I don't see everyone as the same. Some real pains in the arse turned up at the flophouse now and then. The issue for me is seeing that my judgement might be screwy too. I might be being unfair. If I don't like someone, I can still be civil.' Greta was observing him closely. He had no idea what she made of him. Dennis wanted to show her his easy-going side. Free and easy is the opposite of vulnerable. 'And you, my friend,' he said, pulling the hands with which she held his to his chest, 'would be welcome any day of the week.' Releasing her hands, he leaned in and kissed her lips. Hand around the back of the head and it became prolonged. He sensed only reciprocation. Then, when he uncoupled himself from her, smiled into the face he had grown to like, he saw she was not smiling back.

'Oh, Dennis,' she said, 'you might be a mixed-up kid. I'm married, not really available for your hippy snogging.'

'Oh, God. Sorry,' he said. Wondered what the consequence might be. Husbands can be quite pernickety about that stuff. Not the now-dead Themagins for whom sharing partners was positively virtuous, a precursor to the creation of paradise. Those without contrary instruction from Aris Toogood don't tend to approve. 'Really sorry.'

'It's all right, Dennis. I brought you out here because I've been reading about cults for years. They're interesting and always very sinister. Didn't want to grill you in front of others. Wrong signals. I get it, and hey, I'm seriously married but you meant well. Didn't know I was. You're a lovely guy. Don't worry yourself about it.'

That early awkwardness has never stopped the pair getting along, a pairing within the walls of the university. Never outside them. And Dennis seldom manages a day in Exeter without bringing to mind that kiss.

2.

Driving home, he thinks over the day he has just had. Trevor Bray was on the corridor as Dennis was leaving the Applied Social Sciences block. 'Good show today, Dennis,' his parting shot. It doesn't mean much either way. This is a tough course for Dennis. Great feedback from the first term placement, the one with the rubbish supervisor. The nursery manager tried to offer him a job. His hopeless mentor's job, no less. And the place couldn't have been more different to Plaza Court. All the clients were council house kids. With their council house tots. The parents were the kids. Quite literally. None of them older than Monica Bredbury, and she had the presence of mind to fetch along a packet of condoms. He loved playing with the little ones, showing parents how to engage them, not to act tough or indifferent with one-year-olds and two-year-olds. He can feel a desolate pessimism about their probable futures. Many parents made overnight improvements in their interactions with their tiny children. Few could sustain it over the length of a weekend away from the place.

He engages with everything on the course, expresses his opinions. Dennis is enthusiastic about university. Didn't believe they would have him when Jane first suggested it. Not the first ten times. And he gets along with everyone. Students, nursery staff and clients. The lecturers aren't too bad. It's more than a notch up from Plaza Court. A different world. At university, the essays are the bugger. He kept going to night classes, had to take three goes to get satisfactory A-levels. Psychology is gobbledegook. Mary and Monica both agree with him about that and they passed it first time. In fact, both sisters are several mortar boards smarter than he is. Jane tells him to absorb the concepts, not to fight them. He tries but the trouble is the very phrase sounds like something Aris Toogood would say. Absorb, believe, accept. Dennis won't have Freud or Marx or Trevor Bray telling him what's what. It's his bottom line.

The county pays him more for training to be a social worker than they did when he was deputy warden at the flats. It is absurd. Officially, the county only ever second unqualified social workers onto the course, therefore they have elevated him to that paygrade since September. Since he stopped working and started studying. He owes them big time, mustn't fail. He couldn't afford to run a car until last summer. Until the pay rise. A decent job will be his at the end of it. Generic fieldworker or maybe something with teenagers. Anything but mental health: that stuff scares him. Mustn't fail the course, not after the leg up everyone has offered. It is a weight on his shoulders.

As he approaches Charmouth it is becoming pitch dark. There was a big moon earlier in the journey which has become obscured in the drizzle of the late-January day. The weather is far bleaker here on the

Good To Be Here

coast than it was up in Exeter. The chip shop light is already on. Shining bright on the foggy high street. Inviting. He parks just beyond it, turns the collar of his windcheater up before leaving the car. It can't really fend off the blustery rain. He goes inside and orders his usual. A large cod, soaks it in so much vinegar it comes through the newspaper.

As he drives into Croft Road, he sees a figure through the misty rain. Standing on his doorstep. No telling from the hooded coat who has come calling. Small of stature; probably a she. He pulls in the gate and picks his hot package off the passenger seat. The vinegar has seeped onto the seat's fabric but his car smelt a bit rank anyway.

Once out of the car, he looks at the girl huddled under his porch. She turns towards him. 'Hey,' he says. She stares straight back into his face. Says nothing. The rain has plastered stray hairs to her forehead despite the hood that nominally covers it. He doesn't recognise her out here in the rain, no idea why she has come to visit. 'My house,' he tells her. 'Are you sure you have the right place? It's only me living here.'

He takes out his key. The girl is a child, a schoolgirl in her early teens by the look of her. Now he sees her from close to, he thinks her face familiar but cannot recall where from. She looks too young to have ever been at one of his parties. Five years too young, so long is it since those free-and-easy happenings.

'Can I come in?' she asks, 'I need to see.'

He hears from her voice that she is American. It's unexpected, odd. They get them in Charmouth occasionally during tourist season but not at this time of year. And yet she—a delicate looking child—wishes to enter the home of a male she does not know. It's a bit topsy-turvy. Not the first time Dennis has found his life veering this way.

'You haven't come to sleep, have you? I don't really do the flophouse these days.'

'My mom lived here,' she says. 'It's how I know the address.'

'Look,' he says, 'you're soaking wet. Come in if you want but I understand if you prefer not to. Only me here right now. I don't know about your mother. It must have been years ago.' As he says it, something feels quite wrong. This house has been in the Harris family for fifty years. His Granny never ran a flophouse. 'Are you sure she lived at number three?'

The girl walks in right behind him. She's like a stray cat, no hesitation in coming out of the rain. 'Who else did you say lives here?'

she asks. The child looks lost but speaks up for herself. Dennis feels uneasy—not that she is a threat—it is weird, not scary.

'Only me.'

'How long have you lived here?'

'Forever.'

'Then you must know my mom.'

'Is she here?' he asks. 'Has she brought you to Charmouth?'

The girl starts to cry; she is still standing just inside the doorway and bawling like a baby. Dennis has already gone to the gas fire. Stooped to light it. He stands as soon as the match has taken, goes back to her. A wet coat encases her, she is black haired, two plaits frame her cheeks. Tears stain her now-sullen face.

'Hey, sorry. I don't know the story. I'm Dennis. What's your name? Take your coat off and sit where it's warm. I'll get us two plates. Everybody likes chips.'

The girl pushes her face into her hands, crying as she speaks. 'You're Dennis? I'm Lilliana. You must know me?'

Dennis shakes his head. 'I'm sorry, have we met before?'

'My mom. You must know me if you're Dennis.' She shouts these words. Jerky shouting, head up and back down, seeing him but no longer holding his eye. 'You remember my mom. You do, you do, you must.' She is not loud, even the shouting is part of a dreadful upset. Dennis wonders what he has done, can't recall any mother staying in the flophouse. It was singletons and a few teenage couples availing themselves of the spare bedroom.

'She came to one of my parties?'

'She lived here. I wrote to her. She wrote me back. This is number three Croft Road.'

'She lived here...' Dennis suddenly feels a cold shiver down his spine. A recognition of who he has seen in her youthful features. '...Lilliana...I don't know you. I think I should. I am sorry...'

'She lived here. She lived with you. She must have told you about me...' The girl's face collapses. '...what did she say that you don't want to know me?'

'Lilliana, I'm so sorry. Lilliana Vitale, right?' The girl looks directly at him for the first time in a minute. Brief eye contact, a nod of the head. 'Your mum lived with me...look...she was as mixed up as I used to be. She never told me she had a daughter. Never told me much except the link...' Dennis has stood beside her, carefully and politely taken her coat from her hands and put it on the back of a dining chair, turned it to the gas fire. The girl wears a pair of black jeans, a white polo-neck sweater. She's as skinny as a rake. 'Lilliana, sit yourself down, please. I'm so sorry she never told me. I...'

'She wanted out of everything. America. Me. Left us high and dry.'

'Us, Lilliana? Do you have brothers and sisters?'

The girl is sitting, stooped over, shaking her head. The two braids of her plaits dance spastically with the jerk of her shoulders. 'You don't know? She never told you about MJ?'

'No. I'm sorry, Lilliana. She told me only a little. Her husband. Never said so much as his name though...' He is stuck. Can't think why Annabel never mentioned this girl. 'Who's MJ?'

Liliana shakes visibly as a great surge of tears come to her. 'Marco Junior,' she gets out through the involuntary wail. 'She never even told you about MJ?'

'We're going to talk,' he tells her. A little more calmly all of a sudden. A deep breath taken. Trying to do as he has learnt on the course. 'We're going to talk, Lilliana. I want to hear everything about you. About Anna... Antonella's family. First, please, who do you live with now?'

'Granddaddy. Grandmommy died, Dennis. There's only Granddaddy left now?'

'And Marco Junior?' he asks, and as the girl looks up at him with eyes as wet as the Charmouth evening, Dennis finds himself crying with her. Understands the fate of Marco Junior. A brother this poor child lost nine years ago.

* * *

They sit on the futon in front of the gas fire, a bag of chips away on the kitchen table. She is crying, Dennis feeling at sea, hoping that he can bring this waif some comfort. 'I'm glad you found me, Lilliana,' he says softly. 'Is your Granddaddy with you in Charmouth?'

Lilliana shakes her head.

'How have you come to the flophouse?'

'School trip,' she says from her bowed head. It's a cracking answer, brings a little smile to his face.

'Lilliana, have you eaten.' She doesn't answer that, squints at him as if he is talking nonsense but Dennis has remembered his Maslow. 'Two plates. I'll split those fish and chips. Talk to me, tell me about them. Your Dad too, Antonella never said so much as his name. I don't think she ever got over running away. God knows why but it screwed us all up back then. And Lilliana, honestly...' He looks directly into her filmy brown eyes. '...you are the person in this world I most want to get to know. The one.'

* * *

He suspects he is destined to be a second-rate social worker. Lily, as she has asked him to call her, cries incessantly. He has joined in more than once. She is angry with Annabel—Antonella, Mom to Lilliana— as he is not. But Dennis can see now that he never knew her. Fifteen months of confused cohabitation. Never knew who she was, what made her tick. Not why she left two children when she walked away from her marriage, or that she'd even had them to walk away from. Must have known only one was left alive after the horrors of the twentieth of January. Must have. Names were published; Dennis bought a copy of The Correspondent just to see it, to have confirmed in print that his parents were officially lost to cometary madness, put his finger on the names—alone in his Uncle Stan's darkroom—for fully thirty minutes, as if making a final connection with Peter and Sally Harris. Threw the paper away within days, considered his need to see it just another part of the lunacy. He cannot recall another name in that long, long list.

Lilliana Vitale is fifteen years old. It is more than she looks but that might simply be the distraught state she has got herself into. Her honesty floods the room. Every utterance a torture. All the girls in her school year—fifty-six children in total—have a bed for the night in a youth hostel in London. Fifty-five remain up there, taking up the places their families have paid for. She ran away. Did it just to have this conversation with Dennis. Her upset that he has no prior knowledge of her, she now blames entirely on her mother. Angrily narrows her watering brown eyes each time she says the name. The word mom. Hopeless social worker or not, when he learnt that her grandmother died in June, Dennis figured it was the key. One or two lessons must have got through. Young Lily has lost the person who has mothered her from the age of six until the present. Now she is seeking out information about her birth mother although she knows full well that her quest can deliver little. A small insight into Antonella's final months. She has long understood that she has no mother; attended a funeral as Dennis did not, Antonella Vitale interred in Providence, Rhode Island.

'So, Marco was your dad's name and your brothers?'

'Both gone, Dennis. They both went.'

He nods. Shares with her that most singular fact of his own life, losing two close relatives, almost nine years ago to the day. Poor Lilliana lost three although the route by which her mother departed might be the most inexplicable. Thrice lost. Took her leave of the family, then the country. This life.

'She never talked about him, about your dad. Said she left a year before…or in the year before.'

'It was weeks before, Dennis, only weeks. She was one of them, you know?' He nods. Likes hearing Lilliana speaking, talking about all that Annabel wouldn't. 'My mother was the same for a long time. Same as Daddy. A real screwball. That's what Themagins were: screwballs. He called her Dark Heart.'

'Your daddy called her Dark Heart?'

'No. Aris Toogood made it up. Her Themagin name.'

'Did they meet, Lily? Toogood and your mum.'

'I'm not sure, Dennis. My daddy did. A few times. Talked a lot about it.'

Dennis ponders yet another name for Annabel. He thinks he shared his—the given name Ancient—with Annabel, but the conversation has slipped from view. He thinks he did but could be mistaken. May have said only To the Ship. The most stupid name. Dark Heart is not a stupid name, not even a fair one. The weight in the words burdensome.

'I can't think why she never told me about you. Missing you too much, I suppose. I wish she'd told me, Lily. I was interested, only we were both a bit wrapped up in ourselves. Trying to forget the other stuff.' It is beyond fathomable. Insane. He and Annabel never even scraped a surface. As if the damage of that day—January twentieth, nineteen-seventy—had rendered her mute. A son taken. A daughter left to Themagin chance. 'Have I told you she used another name?'

'What do you mean?'

'I didn't call her Antonella. I called her Annabel.'

'But why? What was wrong with her proper name?'

'Nothing, Lily. I just didn't know it. Annabel is how she called herself.'

'That's not true, Dennis. You're making it up. I heard you say Antonella before I ever said it. I called her mom. A shit mom she turned out.'

'Don't say that, Lily. She let you down but I think she was a good

The Flophouse Years

person.' He's been telling himself that for as long as she has been gone. Even as he says it, he expects he would think the same as Lilliana if he were in her shoes. He blames his own parents—specifically, his dad: Peter the dying star gets it hook, line and sinker—for all the teenage shit that he's still struggling to put behind him. 'I learnt her name from a letter that arrived here; it came just a few months before she died.'

'My letter! I got the address. Grandmommy got it, she tracked her down. Mom wrote back that she couldn't come home yet. Then she died from stupid drugs. Did you do them, Dennis?'

'It was a funny time, Lily. I don't touch them now...'

'And she was a mother and she did it. Got stupid out of her head with drugs and pills and being a hippy...' She puts a hand on the plate, into the ketchup. No control or direction, just pushing away what is close. Lilliana crying inconsolably once more.

'You're here, Lily. Your mum and me were both survivors of that mess, like you are, Lily. All got through the twentieth. Maybe her experience and mine were too different. No similarity in our tales, never managed to think ourselves into the other one's shoes. I was a child at the time. Not tiny, like you. But seventeen is still a kid. I was a kid, for sure. Small town upbringing, parents in cuckoo land.'

Liliana lets out a spluttered laugh. Repeats the phrase cuckoo land, but there is more anger than pleasure in it. Laughing down her nose. 'I'm fifteen and I'll never do drugs,' she says. She's lifted her hand from the plate, looking at the ketchup on its heel as she speaks. An indignant tone. 'I'll never do drugs, Dennis. That's cuckoo land too.'

'Very sensible, Lily. I'm just saying that both my parents went on the twentieth. I didn't know, I went out to work that morning, when I came home, they were gone. Gone to the stupid spaceship, I thought...' Lilliana has stopped crying. Her slight body still makes involuntary heaves, breathing in all she has lost. Her head stays upright, eyes fixed upon Dennis, the former boyfriend of her late and inadequate mother. '...not actually to it. I thought they were pretending in some way. I'd given up on all their Themagin nonsense ages before.' He looks at her trembling shoulders—fifteen years old, about the same age as young Monica when she watched this girl's mother in her last throes of life—he decides to talk candidly. 'I was your age, Lily, when I came across what they did. The wife swapping sex parties—you know about that stuff, I'm sure you do—and then they wouldn't let a teenage boy join in. I was through with that nutty bunch after that. No one wants to see their parents humping...' He stops talking, passes the handkerchief in his pocket to the laughing and crying girl.

'I never knew any of that. Only learnt about it last year in the school library. They had to take me home; I was so upset by all I'd read. It was too wacky to believe. Horrid that no one told me before, prepared me for what I'd learn about my mom and dad. I wondered if it was that which drove my mom away—I don't think so because she became a hippy anyway—I expect it was me. She didn't take us with her. What happened with your mum? They weren't on any spaceship really.'

'No, they weren't and I didn't believe they were. I just never thought there was this...Lily, do you know that when I found the bodies, a day late, too bloody stupid to check in their room...' He realises his own hands are shaking, he allows himself a small shiver which quickly takes over his whole body. Dennis can go for months at a time without entering this sealed chamber of memories. Must share it all now—he will, he wants to—never imagined meeting another of his improbable type: a child of Themagins. '...when I found them—dead, nude—I thought it a terrible con trick, no one goes to space that way. I had to get the police and everything.' He puts the plate of uneaten chips from his lap down onto the carpet. A couple spill, his hand is shaking so much. 'There was a vial for me. The policewoman found it. Or one of them. Not with my name, just a spare vial of poison...'

'Me too,' Liliana jumps in, bitterly. 'I know there was. MJ was nine, he had one.' As she speaks, the gulp of her crying is a basin unblocked. The sound of pain and its release. She leans in to Dennis and wraps her fingers around the sleeve of his sweater. Ketchups him and he feels grateful for the sharing. 'I reckon my daddy tricked MJ into drinking it. I should have been there. I was at Grandmommy's because I had a bad cold. She had us after school and didn't drop me at Daddy's—at White Dwarf's, that was what MJ and I called him—only because I was too poorly to go to school next day. Grandmommy always looked after us if we weren't well. Daddy working...'

Liliana stops talking, looks at the man before her; tears are streaming down his face. Dennis mouths, 'Oh God, Lily,' as the order of events register with him. The luck and misfortune of the respective Vitale children.

'He phoned me, Dennis. I'd not gone back home when Grandmommy took MJ back. Stayed behind with Granddaddy. Daddy phoned me that evening. He was different, telling me he had to go away. Didn't even say space. I didn't think he was going anywhere, didn't take it in. It's like he was to do it in the future. Way down the road. He never said death. Never said he was taking Marco. Taking MJ.'

'Oh, Lily. That must have…what did…' He has long exhausted what social work skills he has. Wants to know who this boy was. Annabel's son. Taken by Toogood. How can he ask it of the poor boy's sister? With what words do you burrow into a child's pain.

Lilliana leans back on the futon now, spindly legs tucked beneath her. She seems to trust him. Talks and cries. 'He didn't take MJ. He murdered him. That's what my dad did. Toogood was in on it but my dad could have done a hundred other things. For a long time, Dennis, I thought my mom was clever. Getting out. Now I think she was terrible. Why didn't she take me? Why didn't she take me and MJ away from our crazy dad?'

Dennis leans across and hugs the sobbing girl. His own face still awash with tears. MJ is only a name to him but Lilliana's words bring the boy into the room. Annabel's son. Too young to know why he had to call his daddy by the stupid name, White Dwarf. He lives no more; it is unbearable.

The doorbell rings. Dennis rises. 'Back in a moment,' he tells her. His young visitor seems to have relaxed into his company. They have too much in common, it is uncanny and challenging. Upsetting. He feels immensely thankful that she came to find him. This startling and resourceful child.

When he opens the door, Jane Taylor is on the step, rain on her coat and hood. She steps inside, barely invited. Dennis has forgotten what he had planned for this evening, forgotten much of the last nine years although it inches back into consciousness with the shocked look Jane gives his tear-stained face. 'I've a visitor,' he manages.

Jane comes into the lounge and stares at the young girl. It is obvious that she too has been crying.

'Is this your girlfriend?' asks Lilliana.

'Just a friend,' Jane replies, glancing back at Dennis.

'You go for the older ones, don't you?'

'Lily, this is Jane. She's a good friend. Jane…' He scratches the side of his forehead, '…I didn't know of her until this evening. Waiting on the doorstep when I got home. Lilliana is Annabel's daughter.' Then he looks directly at Lilliana. 'Antonella's daughter. A child of Themagins.'

Good To Be Here

Jane leans into Dennis, whispers very quietly in his ear. 'Are you sure?'

He realises that Jane, who met Annabel on only four or five occasions—a few parties—will be as surprised as he is to learn that she was ever a mother. 'You bet,' he says gesturing the girl, his own reddened eyes. 'We have a hallmark, Jane. Themagin kids. No one's going to fake that.'

Lilliana looks crossly at the incomer. 'Can I just talk to you, Dennis? Who is she?'

'Lily, Jane here met your mother a few times. She was a real nice person, you know, however muddled up she was about all that went before.' He hears the Americanism in his own speech. It should be no surprise that this visitor is getting to him. 'Jane, Lilliana here...' He pauses, thinks better of what he was about to say. 'Lily, do you mind if I tell her...you know?'

'I want to talk to you, Dennis. I don't know her.'

'How old are you?' asks Jane, coming close now, placing a reassuring hand on Lilliana's forearm.

'Don't touch me,' says the girl. As she says it, she reaches out and takes one of Dennis's hands in her own. 'Did you really know my mom?'

Jane looks flustered, eyes on the two hands clasping each other. The young girl's and her friend's. 'Not close, like Dennis here, but I liked her. She was one of the good guys. Sorry if...' Even this confident senior social worker quickly runs out of words. She came around to see Dennis. Can't have planned for the counselling of waifs and strays.

'Dennis says she can never have forgotten me; I don't know whether to believe that. She didn't tell any of you guys that I was back there. She knew my Daddy had gone.' Then she looks down her lightly freckled nose. 'Checked out.' Dennis senses that she is acting with detachment exclusively because of Jane's presence, the true stranger. She and he are children of Themagins—unknown to each other before today—thoughts about their like will have twisted through each other's sleepless nights. She only mentioned her dad to Jane. And what of Annabel? She might have thought about MJ every night she was lying next to him on the narrow bed. Thinking and thinking of her dead son—never saying—or the daughter she had so let down. That's what it looks like now. How could she live in the light of knowing one made it and one didn't? And Annabel didn't live, not as she should have. Not as the mother she was. Evaded the issues of her life until the shadows she lived in swallowed her completely.

'Lilliana,' says Jane, 'Annabel talked with me about growing vegetables and the Vietnam war. She never talked about the Themagins. Not with me. Dennis told me about that connection after she passed away. After she sadly passed away. How old did you say you were?'

'I didn't say.'

Jane cocks her head. 'Hmmm?'

'What? How old?'

'Please?'

'I'm fifteen.'

'Really?' queries Jane.

'Sure.'

Jane looks to Dennis for clarification. 'Not sure what difference it makes,' he says. 'If Lilliana says she's fifteen, then she is.' He turns back to the young American. 'I'm so blown away that you came to find me. It's a wonderful thing. If I'd known you were out there, Lily, you would have heard from me already. Truly. Only reason you didn't was Annabel, your mom, never said...'

Jane cuts across him. 'But where should you be?' she asks. 'Who are you here with?'

'She's run away from a school trip,' says grinning Dennis. 'Came to see the flophouse where her mom used to live. I can see that it was the more important to her. I get it Jane. It makes total sense.'

'Have you phoned this in?' says Jane to Dennis.

'How do you mean? Phoned who?'

'Where is the school party, Lilliana?'

'London,' she says, shrugging, pushing out her bottom lip.

'Whereabouts in London?'

'The Youth Hostel.'

'Do you know the name?'

'It's the big one. My dorms on the fourth floor.'

'What's the matter?' asks Dennis.

'I think quite a few London policemen might be actively looking for your friend right now.'

He glances at Lilliana; she doesn't alter her disinterested look. 'I guess they might be,' concedes Dennis.

'What's the name of your school,' asks Jane.

'The Moses Brown School.'

'And that's in Providence, right?' says Dennis.

Good To Be Here

Lily nods from her seat on the futon. Legs still tucked beneath her.

When Jane goes to the telephone in the corner of the room, starts the phone call by requesting the police and stating her position, senior social worker, the girl mouths, 'Sorry,' to Dennis.

'For what?' he says. 'I get Jane's point—didn't think about it myself and I'm supposed to be some kind of trainee social worker—I couldn't be more pleased to see you, Lily. You finding me like this, it's the best thing. Really, it is.'

The girl reaches out, holds his large hand, just one within her two smaller ones. 'Good to be here,' she says quietly. 'I've so much to tell. But only to you, Dennis; not to her.' She squeezes her eyes together, the last dregs of tears leaking out as she smiles.

As they sit in near silence, they hear Jane tell someone that Lilliana Vitale is safe and well at a house in Charmouth. She goes quiet, just saying 'Yes,' in reply to some questions, 'I'm not sure,' and 'I don't know,' in reply to others. 'Yes, definitely inform her grandfather. Inform him that she is completely unharmed. Right as rain.' There is a pause and she adds. 'With friends.'

When Jane comes off the telephone, faces them again, Dennis looks at her intently. 'Did you have to?' he says. 'Lily has come here to find out about her mother. You should see that.'

'I do, Dennis, I'm just clearing the decks. Let me tell you what will happen: the police will come round in a little while, convince themselves you are all right, Lilliana, and Dennis not some kind of hostage-taker. I can get night duty to sign something off if I'm lucky. The out-of-hours social worker. The police will be pleased if they can pass this one along. They work well together, I hear.' She turns to her friend. 'Don't be cross with me, Dennis. The police have this address down for all the wrong reasons. I doubt if they were ever very thrilled with your flophouse.'

Jane goes back to the telephone, makes another phone call and Dennis realises how right she is. The deaths, the drugs. He doesn't think of it that way, it is simply the house he lives in. Always has. What has gone on here has been a nightmare—not necessarily the parties, many of them were terrific—the other stuff. People dying before their time. Before she passed away, he and Annabel—in their own ways—enjoyed each other's company; later, he and Mary did so although he looks back and knows he was depressed, flattened out. She was just a visitor, never lived here. Lodged in his head whether she was in the house or not. He never gave her back all the solace he took. Good

The Flophouse Years

times with Monica. Another visitor, never the same connection but she lifted him so high when Dennis was finally getting over the loss poor Lilliana is still struggling with. The loss of Antonella Vitale. Monica helped him more than she ever knew. Jane sees what the police must see, and Dennis alone lived every minute. The private hours, months and years.

'Dennis,' says Lilliana, 'when my mother wrote to me, she said she missed me but didn't know if I could fit in with life in England.'

He takes her hand in his once more. 'You, me, your mom back then, we might not always feel like we fit in with life in England, America, any place at all, but we have to. You coming and finding me like this—it's wonderful, Lily—gives me a greater sense of belonging than I've had in years. In my life. Don't listen to them saying you shouldn't have come. The police and your school, even Jane—who is a terrific friend to me—how can they see what's important for you and me?' The young girl squeezes his hand. Squeezes it so tightly it hurts. Dennis loves that feeling. 'They cannot, Lily. They can't see it but I can. I do; I would've come knocking on the classroom door at the Moses Brown School if I'd only known Lilliana Vitale was studying there. If I'd known who you were. I can't make up for what your mom did, Lily. Can't guess what was in her mind all that time. But you and I...' He takes a long breath, seems a little lost for words. '...we're still here.'

Her brown eyes look into his blue ones; the smallest of smiles.

Jane has come off the phone, must feel like an intruder. 'Can I fix you two a drink?' she asks. They neither answer before she leaves for the kitchen, they hear her filling the kettle.

Dennis and Lilliana talk quietly. He asks her about Rhode Island, her home. Just a grandfather living there now. She tells him that her school is a Quaker school. 'I'm a Quaker,' Lily declares.

He can hardly make head or tail of it. Annabel was a Roman Catholic, not a practising one but raised that way. That is what he always believed; he's starting to think he never knew her at all. The very name Annabel was a fabrication.

'Your mum and dad were Quakers too?'

She tells him her dad was Catholic before he became a lunatic. A Themagin. 'He would never have coped with the silences that Quakers draw strength from.' Dennis nods at that, appreciates how thoughtful this little lost orphan is showing herself to be. Then Lily shakes her head. 'He loved Toogood more than he loved Mommy.' With these two observations, and for the first time this evening, she sounds older than her fifteen years.

'Oh hell, all that,' says Dennis. 'My dad too. I can hear his words in my head—the Toogood tapes—find myself mouthing them occasionally and I want to spit and spit until they've left me completely.'

Lilliana leans into Dennis on the futon. He tells her a little about the flophouse, that both he and her mother enjoyed the company of strangers. Hosting anyone needing a bed for the night. 'It wasn't just having sex with everybody? Free love?' she asks, more knowing in her tone than he has thus far thought her.

'Not Annabel or I,' says Dennis, correcting it to Antonella when she gives him a funny look. 'There was a bit of that about. Not your mom. Not me.'

When Jane returns with cups of tea—a drink which Lilliana turns her nose up at—she lets them in on the plan. 'Dennis, Lilliana will need to return to her school party, but it's too late to be going back there tonight. The night duty social worker is vouching for me.' She turns to the young girl. 'You can stay in my flat tonight, Lilliana. I think it will beat returning to London at this time of night. I'll drive you to Dorchester tomorrow, to the train station. We'll meet one of your teachers there.'

'Can't I stay here?' she says to Dennis. 'In the flophouse?'

Jane shakes her head. 'No one would allow that, Lilliana. Although no one could treat you better than this man. It's just the way it is. When the police have been here, I'll wait up as long as you like. You guys talk without me.'

Jane returns to the kitchen. Lilliana and Dennis sit in silence for a moment. Contemplating that this is to be only a stolen hour or two.

'They might be a while coming,' he says and Lilliana looks blankly back. 'The police. It's not a flashing-lights job, I don't think so.'

'It's stupid, Dennis. I came here to meet you. I should be allowed that. You too. After all we've been through.'

'You're a child, Lily. Still younger than I was in January, nineteen-seventy. They messed up with the likes of us back then, don't want to be doing it twice. Need to see you're all right. Shall I tell you about your mum?'

The girl takes a deep breath, leans back on the futon. 'Yes, please.' A pained look overtakes her face as she speaks.

'Do you know that she went out to San Francisco? A bit of hippy stuff, I don't know...'

The Flophouse Years

Lilliana nods her head. Tells him that her grandmother found quite a bit out through old friends of Antonella's. Found out after she'd left the country.

'August the first, nineteen-seventy-two she turned up at my party. My fourth. I hadn't been doing them very long.' Dennis struggles with the tale. A live-in lover with two children and she never shared that most salient fact. One child. One gone on a spaceship to nowhere at all. That now appears to be where Annabel was living too—nowhere at all—and Dennis had thought it was with him. He doesn't tell the child about finding her mother in his bed. He always thought her seduction of him pretty cool but Monica is the only person he ever told it to. Someone who had been as forthright with him as Annabel was that night. 'We fell in love,' he tells her daughter. As he speaks the phrase, he finds he cannot think of it as love even as the word is ringing around the lounge. Number three Croft Road has known a little love. His granny loved his father in the long-gone days when Peter Harris was the son of the house. The comfort of Mary, that of the more zestful Monica, both felt like a true, if transient, love in Dennis's mind. He and Annabel only accommodated each other, participated in quite a lot of distracting sex. Nothing more. The connection of their most private body parts; shared steerage of a successful flophouse. She did wonders with the garden. He worries that he let her down, let down a grieving mother. Annabel's age confused him. He bristled when sixteen-year-old Mary accused him of shagging his mother. Doing it with a substitute mum. But he was short of mothering in those days. Had been short of it for years and years. To the Ship was a hopeless case. He wonders if it is the same for Lily. Let down before the big let-down. Maybe? Dennis wasn't there to know. Annabel was just like Lilliana: a lost child struggling to live in a world from which other loved ones had departed without her. Dennis was no use to her whatsoever. He likes watching Lily hanging onto his words as he talks about the parties, the polytunnel farm. He wants to connect with this girl but cannot tell her how desolate he feels knowing he was not even a sounding board for her poor mother. Has loved her memory more than he managed her person. The lust of it shames him; he thought making love was all there was to it. Monica Bredbury said it was normal. We're all a bit animal, shouldn't overthink it. He can explain none of these ideas to Lilliana. Cannot work them out for himself. His social work course reminds him of the questions at every turn. Not come across an answer yet.

Good To Be Here

Before he is very far into the telling—Lilliana asking awkward questions about drugs, how often her mother took them—the doorbell rings once more.

'Got it,' shouts Jane who has stayed in the kitchen. Dennis has no idea if she's been listening in or reading a book. Sorting out his higgledy-piggledy cupboards.

He feels no surprise at all when Inspector Ash enters the lounge. She introduces herself to Lilliana, thanks Jane for filling in the duty social worker, who has determined he needn't visit because she is in the house already. Her uniform is such a dark blue it's black. A skirt the same impenetrable colour as the stockings or tights that cover her calves, her shins. A shiny blue-bottle policewoman. Dennis is glad it's her: the one with a bit of sense.

'This is an odd one,' she says. A police inspector now, risen up the ranks. Her face is calmer than he has ever seen it on her visits to this ominous address. 'When duty desk told me there was something at Croft Road, I knew it wouldn't be straightforward. I actually thought you'd abducted a child from London for about five seconds. Then it came back to me, what a nice kid you are.'

Dennis looks embarrassed. She has known him since the very hour he found his parents dead in their bed. Susan Ash has been good to him and he must have been hard work. Three dead bodies in the house; the air rifle was a piece of piss. 'Do you understand who Lilliana is, Susan?'

'I do,' she says, nodding. 'I think Jane here filled in Steve, the night duty social worker. I get it.' Then she looks at the girl. 'Lilliana, may I speak to you privately for a moment.'

Lily looks at Dennis who nods and only then does the girl agree. Lilliana and Inspector Ash go into the kitchen together.

'How do you feel?' says Jane to Dennis.

'Honestly? It's incredible, Jane. I'm in shock. I can't be at university tomorrow, not until I've come to terms with all this. It feels like I've given birth.'

Jane can only laugh, pulls him into a quick and gentle hug. 'This is some day, eh? Annabel never mentioned...'

'Not a whisper.' He holds her in the hug. Says quietly, 'I feel I neglected her—Annabel—didn't give her a quarter of the comfort she needed...'

'Don't start blaming yourself. Neither of you knew how to cope with what no one on Earth has had to face before. Don't be blaming

The Flophouse Years

yourself, Den. Look at how you're brightening that girl's day.'

Dennis looks directly at Jane, releasing the warm hold. 'She had a brother, Jane. Lily had a brother, a couple of years older. Not told me the half of it. A brother called MJ who went on the twentieth. Died.' His voice is quaking, a kind of pain, and even Jane's face reveals a wave of shock. 'It's a lot that Lily has to unload here. Share with me. I'm on her wavelength, we're on each other's. Like you said, we've been through what no one else ever has. She needs to do this.'

'Dennis, be very, very careful. This might upset you terribly. Just hearing about all that went on. I'm not really sure that you should be doing this.'

'Jane, I want to hear it. All of it. It kills me that I've known nothing of Lily until now. Kills me dead.'

She places both hands upon his shoulders, holds him so that they look into each other's eyes. 'You're right of course, Den. I know nothing of what you feel; you are who Lily sought. Clever kid. Your both right, Den. I was wrong.'

'Wrong to call the police?'

She lets a small laugh escape. 'Not that; I don't want you arrested for anything under the sun, Den. And the world doesn't understand you yet. I'm struggling and I've known you for years. I get why talking to her is important. A must for you both. I get that. I was wrong to think it might be too much for you to handle. This is your life, Den, and you are very good at it. However shitty it must feel now and then.'

Susan Ash comes back into the room with the teenager. She tells Jane that the runaway may spend the night at her flat in West Bay. She takes the address down, a contact phone number. This plan—and Jane is a senior social worker—beats using a bed in a children's home. The Inspector explains to Dennis that her visit here, her need to see and speak with Lilliana Vitale, is a check on the girl's well-being, a minor inexplicably missing from a London youth hostel. From her school party. 'A necessary bit of box ticking, nothing more.'

He offers her a drink, a cup of tea, but Susan Ash says she needs to get back to the station. 'Dennis,' she says, as she is preparing to leave. 'I always liked you but my calls to this address have mostly been utterly harrowing. One way or another. I actually think this is a nice visit. I've always wondered why in hell you stayed in this house after all that has gone before. I was wrong and you have been quite right to stay; Lily couldn't have found you anywhere else. Not every police inspector would tell you that but it's true. You knew better than me.

Good luck to you, my friend.' And then she glances at the child whose welfare she is vouching for. 'This kind lady will take care of you...' She gestures towards Jane. '...well done, Lily. I'm pleased you have found what you came for. Found Dennis.'

Jane sees Inspector Ash out to her car, then comes back into the room and tells Dennis and Lily that the rain has abated. 'I'm going to take a walk around Charmouth,' she says. 'You guys make sure you're still here when I return.'

* * *

The two plates of barely eaten fish and chips are still sitting on the carpet. Cold. The girl's is awash with tomato sauce. She bathed her chips in it but couldn't bring herself to eat them. Dennis pushed them aside with his foot when he swung the armchair round, wanted to face his friend on the futon, be close enough to hold a hand in his. One or two chips found the carpet, over the edge of the plate with his inelegant push. This cold food has been looking at them through social worker and police inspector visits. No time for tidying up, they will attend only the emotional mess. Nothing else matters.

'Your mother...I've said that I knew her as Annabel. The only name she gave me. There was your letter, and I sneaked a look at her passport, saw her real name, and then never mentioned it to her. We were like that. Close in the here and now but Annabel scarcely talked about the past.' The kid's tears have stayed, she is looking at him with curiosity, smiles a little. A weird smile, braces. Dennis loves watching her facial responses. He feels richer for knowing that this child is alive in the world. That Annabel is a little less gone. 'She told me that your father was in the movement, that she was in it until she left him. That she did that—moved out—a little while before they all went...did what they did. Went nowhere at all. She never told me his name. His real name or the Themagin nonsense. Never told me hers either. The Dark Heart rubbish. My parents—Dying Star and To the Ship, if you can credit that—called me Ancient. What kind of a name is that? It can be very hard to believe a single second of everything that happened, looking back. Hard to believe but it did.'

The girl nods her head studiously. 'Daddy made us call him White Dwarf. It was such a stupid name, Dennis. My daddy was built like a football player, not a dwarf anything.' She laughs as she says it, then coughs out a laugh with a vein of salt running through it. More tears come and she hangs her head, mouths the word, 'Sorry.'

The Flophouse Years

Dennis waits. When she has composed herself, he continues. 'I can only guess what was behind your mother's silence about you. Her daughter.' He swallows before adding, 'About MJ.' Lilliana nods her head, listening to the last person to see her mother alive. 'She had everything to be proud of, I can see that. She couldn't bear losing you. That must have been the story. Like she could not be Antonella ever again. Left the movement, left your dad. The poisonings must have rocked her to the core. I don't expect she saw it coming any more than I did.'

'I was six years old, Dennis. Would the hippy communes have been such a dreadful place to take me? Was yours?'

'Lily, I never had kids staying. No rules about it, nothing like that. But it never happened. I don't know what it was with your mum. If she'd said the word, you could have come in a flash. I couldn't...'

'When she left...' Lilliana stretches out her arms, spindly, slender fingers, as if she is reaching for something but then only turns them in the air to her left side. 'Me and MJ were like the grownups in the house. MJ was. He looked out for me. Told me to call Daddy by his stupid name but we never said it to each other. We had names too, I never ever say them, Den. Names that were much too stupid and crazy. Not me. Didn't say them back then although Daddy used them all the time. MJ was the best, Den.' She talks clearly, keeping her own shallow breath down. Whispering the words. 'Mommy leaving without him made no sense to me. MJ was her world. She was okay with me, I guess, but I don't know anything anymore. Those Toogood tapes, Daddy played them day and night. I don't remember a word. Thought they were stupid even then. A proper religion believes in God. Themagins believed in whatever droned out of their tape machines. I don't believe MJ knew what was done to him or why. He would have socked Daddy one if he'd known what he was going to do. He probably did it very sneakily, put the poison in MJ's soda pop or into his orange juice. That's what I think he did. The murderer. I don't remember Daddy talking about a spaceship but he might have. Might not. He may have figured that MJ was too clever to think any of it true. Daddy believed rubbish. He couldn't say the words to me on the telephone. "Going away." That was all he said. Took MJ. He was a child, Dennis. I don't mean like you keep calling me a child. I mean a real one. Nine years old. He saw through everything my Daddy couldn't. He was...Oh, Dennis...my daddy was a murderer. Killed the best brother there ever was.'

She leans forward, across the narrow divide of futon and chair. Wraps an arm around his neck. Dennis hugs the distraught girl. He lived through it too but can barely imagine what the poor girl feels. She loved MJ—plain to see—loves him now like nine years have never passed.

'Lily, I recall your mother talking about that time—the Themagins—only once in all our time together. She told me a bit more about her own childhood, only ever mentioned the marriage very briefly. Said nothing more than that your dad had gone the way of mine. Of both my parents. This was a conversation within a day or so of her moving in. But she said the oddest thing, Lily. She said, "I couldn't live up to the expectations of Number One." Most of her talk wasn't like that. We both agreed everything about them was nuts. At least, I think we did. I called him an evil bastard or something—Aris Toogood—and she never argued about it. I don't know why she never told me about you and MJ, but I remember that phrase. "I couldn't live up to the expectations." She was thinking about you, not the old charlatan, I'm sure of it. Couldn't see it at the time. No clue. I think...' Dennis realises that there is sweat on his brow. The gas fire has scarcely done its job, the girl looks shivery, settled in his home but not truly warm, and yet this conversation has found a furnace inside him. '...it's a guess, Lily. She felt guilty. Or maybe she thought she was the problem—that's what I used to think—left your dad to the Themagins because she thought they were wonderful and she was the problem. Maybe she thought they were okay for you and MJ too. When she first went, she couldn't have known how it was going to end. None of us figured that. Twentieth of January turned the tables for the whole world. I remember the police lady—Susan Ash, who you just met—when she came to this house, after I'd found my parents' bodies. When I called it in. "We hadn't assessed them as dangerous." That was her take on the Themagins. Something like that. I was staggered and not that they had missed it; the idea that they were, it seemed impossible. Themagins didn't intrude on the wider world. Lived a fantasy really. Lived it, died it. Dangerous as hell but it took me months, maybe years, to think of it that way. Even Aris Toogood, on those tapes, was forever softly spoken. Your mum didn't know what she was doing. It never looked like leaving anyone to killers. Never looked that way at all. Looked and sounded like lambs, the lot of them. Killers they turned out; hindsight can see what we never. I think that's what she couldn't live with. Left you with them initially because she thought she wasn't good enough and the Themagins were, couldn't come back for you because she had let you down far worse than can be imagined, than a normal life ever leads a person to contemplate. Let MJ go where no one should have to.' The girl squeezes his hand and Dennis says, 'Just a guess.'

'You were clever, knew better than to believe what my Daddy couldn't see through.'

'Lucky, Lily. I was lucky. I was a naïve fool at that time. Gullible enough for anything. It was adolescent rebellion which kept me off the stupid ship, kept me from joining in with whatever my parents had lined up for me. If they'd been against it, I would have been for it. I wasn't clever, just found myself on the side that lived. You were a tot; do you think your memory of back then is reliable?'

'I was six years old, Dennis, and I'll never forget MJ. Never ever.'

'No. You won't, Lily. I get that.' As he says it, he leans in and gives the girl the gentlest hug around the shoulders. Knows how much she must fear forgetting. The innocent boy, a world different from her father. From his own dumb parents.

'The phone call...' Lily talks over her hugging soulmate; Dennis releases her, leans back into his chair. '...I told you. Remember? The last one I had when Daddy said he was going away, I asked him, "Like Mommy?" and he said, "Not like Mommy. I would never desert you, Lilliana." I didn't know the word he used. I thought desert meant ice cream. Then he said, "I'm not leaving you; I'm finding us somewhere better to live." He never told me that he hated Mommy but I knew he did. And after she left, although me and MJ saw Grandmommy nearly every day, stayed over quite often, she had no more idea where my Mommy was than Daddy did. No idea at all. The thing that I couldn't get over, Dennis—when I had a counsellor who came to Grandmommy's house to explain about Dad, and about MJ, that my father had taken his own life—for about a week, maybe a month, I thought it was not death at all. He couldn't have taken MJ, they just couldn't leave me, it was all going to work out. I thought for a while that my mom would come back for me. That she would know where they really were. My Grandmommy, Granddaddy too, talked it over with me a bit. I didn't believe anything they said. I think they readied themselves each time they tried to talk. I thought they were making it up because they didn't cry or anything, and it was their grandson they were talking about. I've realised since that they were just holding it together. Barely doing that, really. I think it might have been months before I began to think I'd never see MJ...' She is crying—shoulders heaving—face criss-crossed with tearstains old and new. 'What does it say about us?' she asks. 'Parents who never wanted to see us grow. Want out more than they want to be who they are. Both of yours and both of mine, Dennis.'

'Lily, I can't explain it either. You deserved more. I can't explain Annabel, your mum...'

'For a long time—for years—I thought Daddy was wrong to leave me with Grandmommy. If he'd come and collected me, taken me with MJ, I wouldn't feel what I do. I still think it some days, in truth. But you, Dennis, you knew my mom...'

'Lily, I know what you're saying. It troubled me for an age. Like I shouldn't really be here. But think about it. Toogood's teaching...' Dennis speaks as softly as the lightest rain. '...it is bullshit, no point pretending there was ever any merit in it. We're not in the wrong place, Lily. You finding me is the best. The most fantastic thing. Our parents took the wrong turn, not you and I. Annabel...sorry, Antonella—your mom—she came close. I think I let her down. She found me and I thought she had come to help. She needed the help. Not that I didn't want to give it, just that I wasn't really offering much. Couldn't understand what hadn't been said. I think...' Dennis again touches this young girl's hand, clasps it firmly, searches her tear-dirtied face. '...I spent years after all that happened—your mum passing away—thinking I was the bad news. I thought that if I got too close to anyone it would bring them down. Like there was a curse on me. I didn't believe it like a religion, didn't believe in curses. It just seemed like there was more crap stuck to me than to anybody else. My friends...' Jane, Monica and Mary come into his mind. '...they always said I was fine, when I felt the opposite. They were right but they couldn't see my view. It's like we are forever feeling sorry for ourselves, wearing this heavy, unmovable overcoat that weighs us down. Toogood was evil, it doesn't matter what motivated him. No one should even want that kind of power over others. And they all seemed stupid. My parents, your dad—I don't mean to be rude about him—they kind of offered themselves. Failed to question what was always knock-out crazy. It made us susceptible though.'

'How do you mean?'

'Lily, a couple of years ago, maybe four, the woman who gave my parents the poison came to see me. Her and a guy. I knew who they were. I'd been in my teens first time around. I saw all the Themagins that came to our house...' Dennis pauses, this troubled child has already told him she knows the whole story. The religion was a sex cult. Sex and death, Eros and Thanatos. They went the full Freud, Dennis paid close attention to that lecture up in Exeter. '...I had seen more of them than I wanted to a year or more before the comet came. When they came back—both still stubbornly here, the woman had done time in prison for something linked, and I never really understood the detail—I let them in. My friend—I had a good friend back then who helped me a lot—she said they might have killed me, might still be doing the work of the cult. I had thought it already and it never stopped me from letting them in. It seemed like a way to get closer to the parents I'd lost. Letting go is so hard, Lily. It can be fucking agony. But it's the one certainty, the thing we must do. We've got to let go. Our parents certainly have.'

Young Lilliana nods her head at his words. For the first time this evening, she looks becalmed. He still doesn't understand it in full. Dennis has no idea why Annabel didn't tell him she had a daughter. If she'd sorted out her paperwork, her visa and everything, she could have sent for her. He wouldn't have minded having a sort of a stepdaughter. This one would have been just about perfect. And parents don't do drugs, not ones who love their children. Annabel was always a pretend hippy. If she did free love, it was before she came to Charmouth. She should have just stuck to being Mom, then she would still be here. And Dennis would have got his shit together for a little girl like Lily must have been back then.

Antonella, she could have stuck to that name. It's a decent one. He was stupid about it when he was younger. When he didn't like it. He thought she was ditching the ugly name but that makes no sense looking back. When you run it around your head long enough it becomes the person who owns it. There must be many beautiful Antonellas in this world. One less because of the overdose he still feels guilty for not spotting in real time. Calling in a doctor. She was the mother of a child who needed her, a widow, and she'd already lost a son. Dennis guesses that one was the febrile fact in the mix. The never telling. Suffering alone. What a weight poor Annabel carried. He never knew until today quite how useless a partner he had been for a woman who must have been desperate for more.

'What did she tell you, Dennis? About home; I know she didn't tell you about me?'

Her question kicks him out of his self-blame. 'She told me a little.

Born in a thunderstorm…no, not that. A hurricane…' Lilliana nods her head vigorously. Must know the story better than he does. From her grandmother, perhaps, from the one who gave birth in that storm-damaged hospital. 'It doesn't add up, Lily. What Antonella told me doesn't add up. She said her daddy was no good.' He is looking intently into her eyes as he speaks. Worries it will cross a line. 'Was she making it up? A violent man. Left your grandmother to go and join the Boston police. It can't be right. You live with him…'

Lilliana waves a dismissive hand. 'My granddaddy isn't Mommy's daddy. I know all that.'

It is Dennis's turn to narrow his eyes. A wish to learn more about Annabel's past. Who's who. She seems to have acquired a stepfather. 'She never said,' is all Dennis offers.

'She should have, Dennis. Granddaddy wasn't her dad; he was better than that. I don't know the exact date; I think more than twenty years ago when he and Grandmommy got together. Married, actually. Did what you and Mommy never did.'

'They got along? Your mum and your new granddad.'

'Sure. I was pretty young but they seemed to. He was the Quaker. Is the Quaker. Mommy never joined, I think it was only because…'

'Hey, Lily, backtrack a moment, please. Your Grandmommy wasn't a Quaker?'

'She is. Was. I don't know the way to say it. Became one when she met Granddaddy. That's what she did. Grandmommy and Mommy were both Catholic to begin with. My daddy too.'

'And Annabel never…your mommy never joined the Quakers.'

'I don't know why she didn't, Dennis. She tried everything else.'

Now Dennis hangs his head. Laughs at her comment with a strain to it. 'I wish my parents had joined the Quakers.'

'You didn't say everything Mommy told you?' Lily observes.

'It wasn't much that she did say. Not really. Left out all that matters most.' He looks squarely in her eyes. 'Never so much as told me your father's name. I think I've said that. Didn't say what their marriage was like. I knew she'd left it. Thought it was because he was hard to take, that might have been me filling in the gaps. I guess I knew he was no hippy, that Annabel never went near them until she left the Themagins.'

'I can't picture it,' says Lilliana. 'My mom was never a hippy while she lived with us. Can't see it at all.'

'And always a hippy with me. Annabel: Charmouth's quiet

The Flophouse Years

American hippy. Half the town scandalised that I was living with an older woman, the other half happy I was no longer living alone. Never told me that she was a mum to anyone, Lily. Never told me about you, never told me about MJ. Looking back, I've not the first idea what was going on inside her head.'

'She got away from the crazy Themagins, didn't she? Left Providence for San Francisco. Then came here. You know what I think?' He hears the lump in her throat, as the young girl prepares to say something heartfelt. Dennis gestures that he wishes to hear it. A flat palm on her forearm. 'I might do the same. I might live on either coast. Or come and live in England. Marco Junior can do none of these things. He guided me through those times. I feel like he's still guiding me and he was only nine when he died. When he left this life. He'll always be a clever older brother to me. He can't try England or New York City. When Daddy used to play those tapes, people around the house sometimes, me and MJ would be upstairs. Meant to be sleeping, MJ would tell me stories. Said he was going to learn to drive the car. Take me with him to find Mom. I believed him. My big brother: who better to look out for me. I wanted it to be true, to do all he said we would do. Then he never got to drive. If he found Mom, it's only been in heaven that they've met up again, and I don't really see it. Can't imagine God letting druggies in, letting them spoil heaven. Themagins either. It took me a year to believe it had happened—Daddy and MJ—believe they were really dead. Not because I thought they were someplace else. It was because I didn't want MJ to be anywhere but here. Wanted to turn back time. If I see MJ in heaven, I'll thank him a million times. Not so the other two...'

'You miss him every day, Lily. I hear that.'

Lilliana takes a hold of his hand. Sits as tears again roll down her cheeks. Smiles at him, brown eyes shining through the film upon them. He expects she is contemplating her brother. After a time, he asks a question or two. The girl shares memories, talks of the boy who cannot be replaced. When she asks him why Jane hasn't returned to the house, Dennis looks at his watch. Ten-thirty.

'Do you think she's forgotten about me?' says Lilliana.

'I think she's giving us time for ourselves,' he says. 'Knows this is no ordinary reunion. Don't be hard on Jane, Lily. She's helped me and I've been a hopeless case for years at a time.'

* * *

Good To Be Here

Dennis sits in the easy chair; his guest stretched out upon the futon. Lying down, twisting her body to look directly at him time and again. They exchange their stories, second time around, some greater detail, some lighter touches, listening hard to each other. Mutually rapt.

'Sometimes, Dennis, I think I've forgotten my dad. The tone of his voice, what he looks like. I've got a photograph but it's hard to trust. He doesn't look like a man who would do what he did.'

Dennis nods, and when Lilliana waits, doesn't continue speaking herself, he confirms something he has told Mary Bredbury, and Jane who is still walking around Charmouth in the drizzle. Told exactly nobody else. 'In the scary weeks when I was first back here—living alone, not yet eighteen—I destroyed every photograph there ever was of my parents. Unless Auntie Jean has a couple left. Out there...' He points in the direction of the front door, the high street. '...I was doing everything to look sane. Working my job in the old folks' flats. Everything. And in the middle of the night, it was driving me crazy. I felt like I had to forget them, what they looked like. Everything. And we can't, Lily. We can mislay a little detail here or there. Confuse one person with another in imagining how they entered a room or spoke when they felt flustered. That they are our parents and opted to leave us as they did, there's no forgetting, no erasing. Can't tear it up and stick it in the dustbin. It stays with you, I'm afraid. And deep down, I've no wish to be anyone else. My parents messed up on an epic scale but I'll stick with being me. And I'm liking that you are you. Loving it, Lily. Does that make sense?'

'Dennis?' she says in the slowest drawl he has heard. A worry in her voice and a trust in the raising of whatever worries her this much. 'I think Mommy, Antonella, might have really gone with them. Kind of scared to do what they did—the poison—but took herself from the face of America anyway. Couldn't take herself back. Had to be as far from family as she knew my daddy was.'

'Yeah. She was unreachable sometimes. Completely unreachable when she did the...' Dennis remembers what his tutor at Exeter is always saying, Jane's counsel too: name it. Name the issue. Leave no room for doubt over what you are raising. '...you know...did the drugs. Got completely out of her mind on them sometimes. Took way too much. And she left the movement before the absurdity of the plan was known at all. I'm not sure if she was leaving the Themagins or just her husband. You and MJ, Lily, that makes no sense to me. She must have had a lot of regrets. I think...' Dennis pauses, isn't sure how to make this point when they have found a little serenity in this tumultuous evening. '...I wonder if she thought she'd lost you all before the letter. If she didn't know who'd survived and who hadn't.'

Perhaps it was unwise to say it. Lilliana cries again. Not loud, not distraught. Just a leaking face. Kids of Themagins sometimes do that.

'My daddy wasn't an easy man,' she says. 'And Mom probably guessed he'd...you know...' She rises from her prone posture on the futon, steps to Dennis's chair and falls into him as she talks. '...never compromise. Take us.' She is hugging him like a limpet. 'Marco Junior,' she splutters. 'He's the one I really miss. Only us left, Den. No one else I've ever heard of survived. Not even Mommy.'

* * *

They share words, thoughts, stories, share them incessantly. Jane returns at eleven-thirty but has no wish to arrest the heartfelt talk. Will not intrude with her own irrelevant observations. She takes a book of Dennis's upstairs, just to pass the time. Tells them to talk all night if they like. 'It's only work tomorrow; nothing remotely as important as you guys.' Dennis is grateful to her. An uncomplicated friendship.

He and Lilliana are the survivors of Comet Toogood, Comet Tago-Sato-Kosaka. Of a madness that wrought utter decimation upon their families, their childhoods. An insanity they have neither fallen prey to, however close to the precipice they might now and then have wandered.

At one o'clock, Dennis ups the stairs and taps on the spare room door. Jane answers.

'We're beat. My new best friend is falling asleep.'

'Time to take her to mine, I'm afraid,' she says, but Dennis tells Jane she is too tired to drive.

'I can pull this mattress down the stairs, if you like. You and Lily crash in the lounge like old times. I'll be upstairs.'

Jane offers no argument. She understands the child's welfare, best interests. Will not let Lilliana down. A night in the flophouse sounds the most fitting end to a day she will remember lifelong.

They have exhausted themselves one way or another—talk and thought—all three enjoy deep sleep until daylight enters their respective rooms. Then Jane is to take the young girl to Dorchester where they will wait for a member of staff from the Moses Brown School to arrive by train, to return Lilliana to London.

Good To Be Here

'Will you write to me?' Lilliana asks her deceased mother's former lover as they are on the road outside the gate, hovering by the car door she must enter.

'We're soulmates, Lily. I'll write—I guess you need to be back with your granddaddy after this school trip is over—but I'll do more than write. I'm going to see you again. And again. And just knowing you are out there, makes this world a better one for me.'

Before Lilliana ducks into the Vauxhall Viva, Dennis takes her in his arms, hugs her tightly and she returns it. A little weeping, fraught movement of her shoulders, as she does so. This long-lasting embrace will not bring back his father and mother—Dying Star and To the Ship are spent—nor Antonella who would be Annabel, nor Marco Vitale, the name of Lily's father as he has learnt. Poor, precious MJ, of whom Lily spoke so often. He hugs her like it might. Holds onto the one who lives. This is the surprise: that another soul is out there in this world who knows the real Dennis Harris more fully than he ever imagined being known. Someone who gets him. It is a world of possibilities.

Printed in Great Britain
by Amazon